abc

"When I wrote my son_ all African-Americans, by lifting us from the t_ _ _ _ _ _ _ _ _, _ _ _ _ _ robbed of our heritage. The song — like this book — cries out, 'It's time to know the truth, our time has come, rejoice, a NEW AGENDA's due!'

John Ballard's series of novels, **SOUL to SOUL**, reunites us with the richness and diversity of our African heritage, and instills pride within us of our ancestors.

For me, life is all about growth. To grow, to realize one's dreams, and to believe in oneself requires strength. This strength, in part, comes from a deeper understanding of who we are.

SOUL to SOUL serves as a cornerstone upon which our youth will grow strong. I invite you, both black and white, to open your soul to the message of hope and pride that this book celebrates. Peace."

Janet Jackson

"**SOUL to SOUL BRINGS AFRICA ALIVE!**... *from the richness of big city life in Lagos, to the harshness of life lived in a desert refugee camp.*

The music of Africa, the closeness of the African family, the beauty of living your life as an art, are shown in terms young people can relate to. Most importantly, **SOUL to SOUL** goes to the very heart of what it is to be a human being – to honestly share yourself with another"

Shari Belafonte
Spokesperson, World Neighbors

"**SOUL to SOUL CREATES A BRIDGE AND A BOND BETWEEN THE YOUTH OF AFRICA AND THE YOUTH OF AMERICA!**... During my lifetime I have fought for a free society in which all persons can live together in dignity. But we cannot do this if we ourselves are divided, if we ourselves have hatred in our hearts, if we ourselves cannot talk to each other. **SOUL to SOUL** is a challenge to you, our youth, our pride. our future, to give the scourge of racial hatred its final blow!..."

Nelson Mandela

"ENLIGHTENING!... THOUGHT PROVOKING!... SOUL to SOUL BRINGS US FULL CIRCLE!...The series' power to visually thrust acceptance and encouragement into our innermost being and provide us with not just a ticket to Africa, but also a conduit to our conscience, is invaluable. For the young (and not so young) readers of Soul to Soul, Khartoum, Casablanca and Ouagadougou are no longer just dots denoting exotic places on a map of Africa. In Soul to Soul, they come alive— with smiling and tearful faces, souks and medinas, refugee camps and rock concerts, and stories about our brothers and sisters. Intimate stories about our blood kin.

Communication. If understanding unlocks the deadbolt, then communication is the key to the alarm system. Without the ability to communicate, whether in French, English, Pular, Swahili, or with the eyes, there will be no friendship. Soul to Soul is an investment in lifelong friendship — a comfortable friendship with self, with others, and with the world."

Jesse Jackson
President and Founder, NATIONAL RAINBOW COALITION

"A COMPELLING WORK OF ARTISTRY!...Rarely have the bonds that link African-Americans to the motherland of Africa been so brilliantly and sensitively explored. Soul to Soul is a precious treasure that brings fresh understanding to our sense of oneness with Africa — a oneness that has endured, despite time and distance."

Dr. Benjamin L. Hooks
Executive Director, NAACP (National Association for the Advancement of Colored People)

"SKILLFULLY CRAFTED!...RICH WITH HISTORICAL SIGNIFICANCE!... African American young people are starved for books that portray themselves in a positive and realistic manner. They cherish heroes and heroines from the past, but they yearn for contemporary characters with whom they can identify.

If multiculturalism is to truly flourish in America's school systems, Soul to Soul is an essential tool."

William H. Gray, III
President, UNITED NEGRO COLLEGE FUND

"PARENTS CAN'T TEACH WHAT THEY DON'T KNOW. This country has spent so many years mounting distorted teachings, trying to distort all the facts; and as a result you have young people not knowing about where they came from – nothing about their heritage – and now it's finally coming out.

I think that's the main reason why we're still dealing with racism within this country – because of people not understanding each other and not being aware of each other's cultures – or their own!

This is why **Soul to Soul** is so important. **THESE YOUNG PEOPLE ARE TRYING TO FIND OUT ABOUT THEMSELVES — ABOUT THEIR ROOTS. THAT IS WHAT WE NEED — BECAUSE WE HAVE TOO MANY FINE THINGS ABOUT OURSELVES WE'VE FORGOTTEN."**

Malcolm-Jamal Warner
Co-star, *The Cosby Show*

"SOUL to SOUL BRIDGES THE GAP BETWEEN AFRICA AND BLACK AMERICA. Brock James (a young saxophone player who joins the Soul to Soul Tour) rediscovers his past and, along the way, discovers a pride that had been missing in his life. His is a story that stands for the ability of everyday people to be heroes."

Rev. Hosea Williams
Former Executive Director, *Southern Christian Leadership Conference (S.C.L.C.)*
Council Member, *City of Atlanta*

"AS A PEOPLE, WE ARE REALLY NOT THE DESCENDANTS OF SLAVES, WE ARE THE DESCENDANTS OF AFRICAN KINGS AND QUEENS WHO WERE MADE SLAVES. Slavery was not our beginning. And I think that's an important idea for young people today to have, because – if you grow up developing the kind of mentality that makes you feel that there is something inferior,that there is something wrong with us, that we are a problem – then you may have little chance of becoming fully aware of who you are. Who we are is not a problem. We, like everyone, have problems; but who we are is a people.

SOUL to SOUL OFFERS A REAL FAMILY REUNION. IT IS A CALL TO BRING OUR PEOPLE BACK TOGETHER, TO REALIZE THAT IN OUR HISTORY, EVEN DURING SLAVERY, IT WAS THE EXTENDED FAMILY (AN IDEA THAT BEGAN IN THE TRIBES OF AFRICA) THAT GAVE US NOURISHMENT AND OUR IDENTITY."

Dr. Dorothy Height
Executive Director, *National Council for Negro Women (N.C.N.W.)*
Executive Director, *Black Family Reunion*

" *FROM JAMAICA TO HARLEM, FROM LAGOS TO NAIROBI, SOUL TO SOUL BREAKS DOWN THE WALLS OF PREJUDICE THAT DIVIDE US* and opens our hearts to what unites us as people.
These two teenagers, in their attempt to reunite two Ethiopian refugees, a young man and his wife seperated during the famine, put their own lives at risk — and teach us a lot about what it truly means to be a human being."

Sheryl Lee Ralph
Co-Star, *The Distinguished Gentleman, It's A Living*

" *A STORY OF LOVE...* in the spirit of Rastafari!"

Rita Marley

"SOUL to SOUL will awaken the youth of America and the Western world to our rich Ethiopian culture and help them understand our way of life. At last - young people will know we Africans do not live in trees!"

Roman Abebe Carroll
Educator, *from Ethiopia*

"COURAGEOUS... EXCITING!... A challenging novel about 'real life" in Africa today — and what young Africans go through."

Ahmed M. Hussein
Student, *from Somalia*

"BOLD!... UPLIFTING!... TRUTHFUL!... A challenge to the West to reconsider their priorities — to reach out beyond their borders and and embrace cultures other than their own."

Oliver Nokwe
Student, *from South Africa*

"BRILLIANT!... A GREAT JOB!... the paradoxes of rich-poor, intellectual-illiterate, industrial giant-backward villages come through on terms youth can relate to."

World Neighbors
Kenneth Tull, *Vice President*

"I was enormously touched by MacBurnie King. It is so fine when young idealism remains alive!"

Robert Coles
Professor, *Harvard University*,
Award-winning author, *Children of Crises*

"A PORTRAIT OF PERSONAL COURAGE and individual responsibility. I recommend that this novel be made available to young adults who will continue to be presented with the most critical challenges in the history of mankind."

Nancy J. Lavelle, Ph.D.
Publisher, *The Education Network News*

INTRODUCTION to SOUL to SOUL

by

Coretta Scott King

Young people possess within themselves the power to transform their lives and, in turn, the world community. It is up to us to provide them with the tools and opportunities to do so.

In recent years I have become more aware of the scope and depth of the crisis in illiteracy in the U.S. and around the world. There *is* cause for hope. Hundreds of community, national and international organizations have begun to challenge illiteracy. Yet, even for the millions of those of us who *can* read there remains another kind of "illiteracy" — a lack of understanding of each other, a lack of appreciation of the commonality of the human spirit. I find an alarming percentage of young people who suffer from misinformation about cultural, geographic and historical realities. And I fear this may prove to be a major obstacle in the years ahead to international understanding, cooperation, and even to prospects for world peace.

What is so desperately needed is an aggressive effort to reach out to our young people in creative ways that elicit their interest in diverse cultures and humanitarian concerns. The MacBurnie King Global Culture Series fills this need.

In *Soul to Soul*, John Ballard has written a compelling novel about building bridges of solidarity between the young people of the U.S. and Africa. It is a moving story of two American teenagers who become involved in the cause of African economic development while traveling with a group of black American musicians through a variety of African nations.

Soul to Soul demonstrates the power of compassion and commitment that each of us has to transcend political and cultural boundaries. In addition to the story, the richly-illustrated text includes invaluable information about African geography, history, family and tribal traditions and profiles of diverse African peoples, such as the Maasai, the Kikuyu, the Ibo and the Zulu, to name just a few.

Soul to Soul is about courage and caring and creating new bonds of interracial brother and sisterhood that can break down the barriers of ignorance, fear and bigotry that still divide humanity. This inspiring story of hope and goodwill should be read not only by young people but also by all those who would help build a more cooperative and caring world community.

Coretta Scott King

Executive Director,

The Martin Luther King Center for Social Change

MacBurnie King in...

SOUL ━━━━━━
to
━━━━━━ SOUL ™

— a daring adventure!

a novel by
John Ballard

first in the Soul to Soul series

**World Citizens
Book Publishing Company**

FIRST EDITION

Library of Congress Cataloging-in-Publication Data

Ballard, John Henry, 1945-
  Soul to soul: a daring adventure: a novel / by John
  Ballard: (with an introduction by Coretta Scott King). — 1st ed.
       p. cm. — (Soul to soul series: bk. 1)
    Includes bibliographical references.
    ISBN 0-932279-10-4
    1. Afro-American musicians — Travel — Africa — Fiction.
  2. Americans — Travel — Africa — Fiction. I. Title. II. Title: Soul to soul.
  III. Series: Ballard, John Henry, 1945- MacBurnie King soul to soul series: 1.
  PS3552.A465M34 1993   93-6649
  813'.54—dc20   LC 93-6649   CIP
                                 ISBN 0-932279-10-4

Printed in the United States of America

Publisher's Note

The MacBurnie King Adventure Series is committed to bringing the peoples of the world closer together so that world problems, such as prejudice and hunger, can be solved.

This novel is a work of fiction. Photographs have been provided to "bring home" to the reader the life-threatening conditions under which too many of Africa's peoples strive to survive and to "bring alive" for the reader the too often unseen richness and beauty of Africa's diverse peoples.

Of the over 25,000 photographs personally viewed by the author, those selected correspond as closely as possible to the regions and ethnic groups portrayed.

The models portraying the principle characters were also personally selected by the author in order to insure the greatest degree of faithfulness to his vision.

About the Author

John Ballard

In his freshman year at Harvard, Mr. Ballard interrupted his studies to help lay the groundwork for the civil rights march of Dr. Martin Luther King, Jr. in Selma, Alabama. There he experienced, firsthand, the violent imprisonment and racial hatred that characterized the country at this time. Returning to Harvard, he earned a *magna cum laude* for his senior thesis which focused on the identity choices of African-American teens living as a minority in a white culture.

Opening *The Harlem Community Service and Information Center*, he coordinated inner city groups to interact with the Mayor's office during the difficult summer of 1967. He also helped, along with many others, to launch Claude Brown's now classic novel *"MANCHILD IN THE PROMISED LAND."* Mr. Ballard has directed several films including the feature *"The Orphan"* (starring *Tony Award* winning actress Joanna Miles and *Grammy Award* winning singer Janis Ian)

a movie depicting the nightmarish world of an abused child that won *Box Office*'s highest rating.

While directing, Mr. Ballard oversaw the adaptation of many of his screenplays into successful novels, including *"HOOPS,"* adapted by the highly respected writer, Walter Dean Myers. *"HOOPS"* portrays the father-son relationship between a Black street basketball player and his coach. An ALA Best Book of the Year Award winner, HOOPS was followed by the *Parent's Choice Award* Winner, *"THE OUTSIDE SHOT."*

In 1985, the author was invited along with astronaut Stuart Russo and Governor Quie of Minnesota to observe the relief efforts in Sudan and the plight of the Ethiopian refugees. The heart of these observations, plus twenty years experience with third world issues, forms the basis for his most recent series of books, *"SOUL TO SOUL."*

FICTION

"Monsoon - a daring adventure"
- *First in the MacBurnie King adventure series*

"Brothers and Sisters"
- *Third in the MacBurnie King adventure series*
- *Second in the Soul to Soul Series*

* **"Hoops"** - *by Walter Dean Myers*
- *Winner of the ALA Best Book of the Year Award*

* **"The Outside Shot"** - *by Walter Dean Myers*
- *Winner of the Parent's Choice Award*

* **"The Orphan"** - *by Samantha Mellars*

(* indicates a book or novelization adapted by another author from an original screenplay or story written by John Ballard)

NON-FICTION

"Heroes, Villains and Fools"
A ground-breaking work dealing with the role models available to black teenagers growing up in a white culture (available through Harvard University, William James Library, 1967, 240 pages)

"The Soul to Soul Guide to African-American Consciousness"
The first comprehensive, easily read text to combine both African and African-American culture inside one cover and treat both cultures as one community.

"Roots, Reggae and Rastafari - a movement that has rocked the world!"

"The MacBurnie King Guide to End World Hunger"

Dedicated to...

>MARTIN LUTHER KING, whose encouragement when I
>was 18 gave my life a vision.

to my tutors...
>ERIK ERIKSON and ROBERT COLES, who helped give my
>vision a voice.

to my schoolmates...
>ABDUL-AZIZ "JIMMY" JIWA, "CHRIS" OHIRI and AFOLABI
>AJAYI, whose voices were stilled long before their time.

and to...
>the ARTISTS OF AFRICA, whose voices we in the West
>have just begun to hear.

Soul to Soul ™

soul (sol) n. **1.** the principle of life, feeling, and thought, in humans, regarded as a distinct spiritual entity separate from the body. **2.** a human being. **3.** noble warmth of spirit.

— Webster's Dictionary

soul (sol) n. Slang **1.** the awareness, pride and feeling among black Americans — adj. Slang **2.** characteristic of black Americans or their culture: soul food; soul music.

— Webster's Dictionary

"Life is a daring adventure — or nothing!"

"The Lord gave us black folks soul, so we could light up the world.
We are the guardians of soul! You can hear it when I blow my horn.
You can see it when I walk across this stage.

Soul music! Come join in the dance of life.
Soul food! Come taste the sweetness this whole earth can offer you.
Soul Brothers! Soul Sisters!... Black, White, Yellow, Red...
Now that I got it — I can give it to you.
Now that you got it — we can begin to *unite!*...
See things eye to eye...
Walk hand in hand...
Talk heart to heart...
And *love* each other — Soul to Soul!"

— **Brock James,** age 19
tenor sax, *The Quicksilver Band*
(on the Soul to Soul Tour, Nairobi, Kenya)

contents

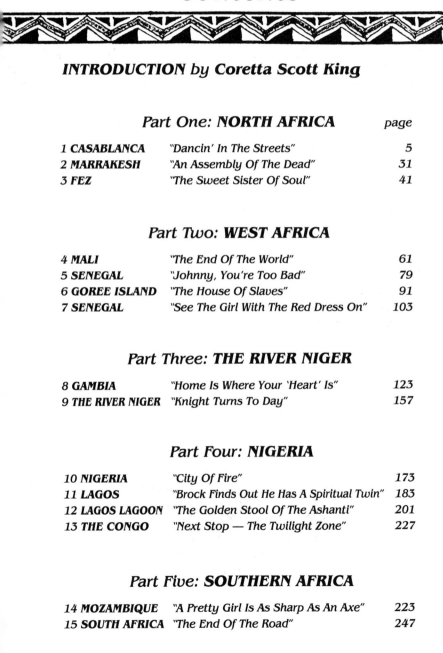

INTRODUCTION *by* **Coretta Scott King**

BOOK One: **Soul to Soul**

APPENDIX

coming attractions
acknowledgments
organizations

photo and art credits
from me to you
world citizens passport

The Soul to Soul guide to
African-American
Consciousness

NORTH AFRICA

"Dancin' In The Street"

Callin' out around the world
are you ready for a brand new beat?
Summer's here and the time is right
for dancing in the street.

They're dancing in Chicago
down in New Orleans
up in N. Y. City

All we need is music, sweet music
There'll be music everywhere
They'll be swinging, swaying, and records playing
Dancing in the street

This is an invitation across the nation
a chance for folks to meet
There'll be laughing, singing and music swinging
Dancing in the street

Philadelphia, PA
Baltimore and DC now
Can't forget the motor city...

It doesn't matter what you wear
just as long as you are there
So c'mon every guy, grab a girl
Everywhere, around the world.

words and music by:
William Stevenson, Marvin Gaye & Ivy Jo Hunter
as performed by **Martha and The Vandellas**

TANGIER, Friday, May 27th

I relate best to people who are kind of . . . *fractured*, in some way. Fractured souls, fractured hearts, shattered lives . . . people who are off-center, off-beat, *on the fringe* — or torn around the edges.

So I've got an unusual collection of buddies, "used teens." When we walk together, we're like a travelling freak show.

Why these people are all attracted to me, I don't know. For a seventeen-year-old girl there's nothing so exceptional about me, except maybe my nose, which is crooked. It starts off perfectly all right from between my two green eyes, but then when it comes halfway down — it heads off sideways, like maybe it was about to have a conversation with my right ear.

Plus I'm not about to become the person my mom wants me to be.

So my decision to split didn't come as a surprise to the four people in my life who know me real well.

What I want to know is — how do you piece back together the human soul once its been blown apart? It's like there was this big bang, this big explosion, and then we *shattered*. Pieces of us are drifting apart all over the universe . . . How can we collapse again into some giant big black hole?

War is like that; mom's divorce, too. Fractured lives strewn about, families split apart . . . people who've lost their home, their lives wasted, like the lives I've wasted.

I want to . . . make things whole again. I want to . . . not be scared anymore, by life. I want to seize life like a stick of dynamite and run with it screaming into the black night.

I don't know if I'm crazy sometimes thinking thoughts like this; but it was with this in mind that I made the decision to go to the job interview. I knew if I got it, my life would change.

At the interview they asked me, *"Why is this job important to you?"*

I laughed.

> *. . . recorded on the Gibraltar Ferry to North Africa*
> *TANGIER, Friday, May 27th.*

Kingdom of Morocco

PEOPLE
Population: 22.8 million. **Ethnic Groups:** 99.1% Arab-Berber. **Religions:** 99.97% Sunni Muslim, .03% Jewish and Christian (mostly foreign). **Languages:** Arabic (official), French, three Berber vernaculars. **Literacy:** 35%. Education (free through primary school) is the largest expense in the government's budget. In Fez, students from around the world study Islamic law and theology at *Quarawiyin University,* which is more than 1,000 years old. **Lifestyles:** Morocco has rapidly industrialized over the past 10 years (the population will soon be half urban). 42% of the work force remain traditional subsistence farmers. **Infant Mortality:** 98/1,000. **Life Expectancy:** 52 years.

GEOGRAPHY
Area: 409,000 sq.mi. (171,953 sq.mi.); the size of Oregon and Washington combined. **Capital City:** Rabat (pop. 900,000) **Other Major Cities:** *Casablanca* is the center of trade and the leading port; *Rabat* is the seat of government; *Tangier* is the gateway to Spain; "Arab" *Fez* is the cultural center; and "Berber" *Marrakech* is a major tourist attraction. **Terrain:** Only the narrow *Strait of Gibraltar* separates Morocco from Europe. Morocco's coast contains some of the world's most beautiful beaches. The land is divided into flat rich plains in the northwest and arid high plateaus in the east. The rugged *Atlas Mountains* have walled off this corner of Africa from invaders for centuries.

GOVERNMENT
Government: Constitutional monarchy. The King is chief of state. A prime minister, appointed by the King, is head of government. **Colonial Power:** France. **Independence:** March 2, 1956.

ECONOMY
Yearly GDP Per Person: $600. **Exports:** $2.2 billion (f.o.b.): Wine, olives, cereals, leather goods, phosphates, manufacturing. Morocco's richest natural resource is phosphate (3/4 of the world's known reserves). Its second biggest asset are its fisheries.

HISTORICAL NOTES
Morocco's strategic location has shaped its history. Foreigners have come in waves, some to trade or settle, others to invade. Arab forces swept over the land in the 7th Century A.D., mixing with the local Berbers and introducing Arab civilization and Islam. France's "sphere of influence" over Morocco began in the 1030's. The Treaty of Fez (1912) made Morocco a protectorate of France. But France's exile of the Sultan, Mohammed V, in 1953 sparked active opposition and the French government was overthrown.

TOURIST ATTRACTIONS
Ancient walled city of Fez, tanning vats, suq's (marketplaces), seaside and beaches of Casablanca, the markets of Marrakesh, Tangiers, Berber communities, the Atlas Mountains.

morocco

"Dancing In The Streets"

CASABLANCA, Sunday, May 29th

NEIL SILVER ripped off a chord that struck our set-up crew like a bolt of lightning — an ear-splitting scream to attention that would have done Jimi Hendrix proud. Ever since we landed in Tangier, Neil'd been psyched up for this concert; and the music that screamed from his candy red guitar was like nothing no one had ever heard this side of the Atlantic.

I was rolling this cart of Orange Crush soda pop over to him —when an arm reached down from the sky and ripped one off. Then it disappeared up over the edge of the stage balcony.

I watched a young black guy up there coolly pop it open in his teeth, then chug it down. Clutched tightly in his other fist, under an arm of rippling muscles, was a gleaming gold saxophone.

"Nice horn," I yelled up to the guy.

"You know how to play?" He leaned over, calling down to me.

9

"No."

"Then how come you're comin' on with all that nice horn bullshit!"

"All I said was—"

"Don't be layin' bullshit on me," the guy glared down and tossed the empty soda bottle back on my cart. "You know how to play this thing or not?"

"What are you — like, master of ceremonies?" I said sarcastically.

He leaned back, laughing. "Yeah, you got the master part right."

"So, what're you master of?"

"Whatever you got," he winked and blew off a string of sweet notes.

Now my job was "gofer," like in *"Hey MacB, gofer coffee,"* or *"gofer phone change"* . . . but I'd just about had it with this black Rambo in jeans. So I shoved off, rattling the cart past some little Arabian kids trying to sneak into the concert.

"Hey girl, come on back here," he shouted down, patting his lap.

"I ain't no *girl,"* I mimicked him.

"You ain't no woman neither — so what are you? Some little teeny bopper about to go off crazy if she sits on a man's lap?"

I just kept pushing my cart past the stage, doing my best to ignore his howling, over to where the *Soul to Soul* groups were making their final run through before our tour's opening night.

It had been grueling, these last two days, and my head was still rocking from the ferryboat ride from Gibraltar. Most of the other kids on the tech crew were beat too, walking zombies. But as opening hour closed in on us, you couldn't help but gct high. We were here, finally — in Africa.

"Hey Ne-ee-eil!" I screamed over the noise, holding up the sodas. "You got French money for these?"

Neil Silver was all crazed, running over a last minute routine his band *Quicksilver* had just worked out. So he didn't even see me. I just stood there, watching him prance around in those silver-toed boots he thinks are so great. They've got silver spurs made from real silver dollars. Probably the only two dollars he's got.

Neil's from Brooklyn and only made the tour because the head-liner sponsored him through a drug rehab. He's OK when he's not clowning around. Short and stocky, with really long greasy black hair he tucks up under an equally greasy Mets baseball cap.

I'm from New York which is how I got over here — I met him when *Quicksilver* played the Drum Club in Soho. It was Neil who got me the job doing interviews . . . but so far I'd been too scared to ask for one.

"You get one?" He finally grinned that sly lopsided grin of his, cocking his baseball cap back to wipe the sweat off his forehead.

"Got *two* —" I groaned, hoisting twin six packs of Orange Crush up onto the stage, "— minus one casualty."

"I meant an *interview*. Did you get one yet?"

I shook my head no.

"What about him?"

"Him who?"

"The guy you were just talkin' to." He pointed back over his shoulder up to the stage where black Rambo was setting down stands for the drum section.

"Him? . . ." I couldn't believe he was talking about the same guy; but Neil knew his stuff. "Who is he?"

"Brock James."

"That's Brock James? . . ." I said, more embarassed than amazed. "I thought he was like, you know, crew or something." I took a long look up at Neil's new sax player lifting a heavy speaker into place, his biceps bulging like Popeye's.

"So, will you see if you can set me up?"

"What do I get in return?" Neil nuzzled up to my neck. "A commission? I'd like to take something off the top."

"Yeah, I bet you would." I removed his hand from my neck where it had fluttered up like a rabid bat. "Neil, just get me the interview, OK?"

On the streets of Casa B

"You can get water from a tap — or from this one-man refreshment stand . . ."

Showtime! You couldn't pack any more bodies into Casablanca's sports stadium. Anybody with a camel, a pair of sandals, or a Mercedes was there. Overhead, two spotlights beamed down like giant eyes from the grandstands, picking out faces from the crowd. Faces of ancient women with tatoos on their lips. Faces painted with the latest day-glo fashion. City faces. Tribal faces . . . All screaming out things I couldn't understand in Arabic.

Next to me, a kid ripped off his *dishiki* and pulled on an oversized T-shirt from our concert. It bagged down around his tiny brown hips, the *Soul to Soul* logo scrawled in blood red across his chest. *Hey, you're squashing me,* I wanted to yell. We were packed in so close I could hardly breathe.

Above me, hot shot TV reporters were chatting away in the Press Box, clapping their buddies' backs. Everybody seemed to know everybody else. *This is as close as I'll ever get,* I thought. *Courage MacB;* someday you'll get to climb up inside with them, write your own bylines.

Q: *"Name? . . . "*
A: *"MacBurnie."*
Q: *"First name — or last?"*
A: *"The last is King, MacBurnie King."*

I leaned over her lucite desk, waiting to make certain the interviewer wrote it right — "Mac" not "Mc." But if this woman could get me into Africa, it wouldn't be too cool to correct her.

I was nervous enough just looking at the walls of her New York office. Every magazine cover was framed and staring down at me — Sting, Prince, and hopefuls like my buddy Neil Silver.

Q: *"Quite generous of him to get you the interview,"* she peered at me through wrinkled eyelids covered with purple glitter, trying too hard to look like the kids she wrote for. *"Just how do you know Neil?"*

A: *"I met him when he was recording 'Tarnished' live from the Drum Club in Soho. You know how he always tosses out those silver dollars after his show? I caught one and brought it back to his dressing room."*

Q: "Yes, uncanny who he throws his money to, isn't it? He always seems to get a return on his investment."

I wished I hadn't said that, about the dressing room. But it was too late; her purple nails were now clacking out more comments about me on the Interview Sheet.

Q: "Neil, of course, is a rehabilitated addict, you know. Do you have any addiction?"

A: "No. Yes. I mean he was. That's how we got to be friends, after he did the program. I'm not exactly pretty. I was never his, you know, lover or anything."

My mouth was going on and on like it does when I get real nervous. She stopped typing and kept staring at me. I couldn't tell if I was talking faster than she could type, or if I'd blown it.

"Neil was in pain. This guy he'd gone through the detox with . . . he'd just tried to kill himself, and he didn't know if he could make it alone. So we . . . just talked."

Q: "About . . . ?"

A: "I wanted to get away."

Q: "Why?"

A: "My home."

Q: "That's not a good enough reason to go to Africa, MacBurnie, is it?"

A: "I also applied to work with some student volunteers in Ethiopia. I've worked with hungry kids before."

Q: "You have your parent's consent?"

A: "I have my father's . . . "

Q: "You live, however, with your mother?"

A: "If you call what we do together living."

She asked me a lot of questions about my writing, leafing through the stack of samples I'd brought her, like what kind of reporting did I think I could do for them? What were my goals?

Q: "I see you have interviewed celebrities before."

A: "Yes," I lied, watching her purple nails pick through

15

each interview.

Q: "Quite impressive . . . " She pulled out the one Neil and I made up about Tina Turner's visit to my school. "Look, many of these do-gooder operations never really get off the ground. If you are selected, MacBurnie, I want you sending us articles on each group. Juicy tidbits. Their clothes. Their sex lives. Pieces I know our kids will buy — understand?"

A roar from the crowd jarred me from my thoughts. I craned my neck to see, shouting up to the guys in the Press Box, *"What's happening?"*

From out of the end-zone came a storm of thundering hooves. Two dozen horses galloped across the dusty field — straight at us!

Turbaned riders twirled their rifles like they were cheerleader batons, firing shots in the air! Volley after volley of crackling gunfire slashed through the night sky. Then, inches before I'm trampled, the sweat-soaked horses reared up above my camera, hooves pawing the air.

"What's going on?" I yelled again up to the guys in the Press Box.

"Fantasia! . . . Fantasia! . . . " an electrician hollered down over the gunfire, like somehow I was supposed to know. *"Berbers,* the horsemen are berbers. It's the traditional opening here in Morocco!"

Before the dust had a chance to clear, a giant spotlight shot through the stadium, piercing the dust cloud with an eerie halo of light. Inside it, shields of armor clashed and clanged . . . Here, riding in on an Arabian black stallion, came the mega superstar of soul himself — Marvin Knight. Behind him rode his back-up musicians, the *Knights of Passion,* waving banners high overhead as they circled the stadium . . . and the rock music for *Here Comes the Knight,* his signature song, began.

Marvin Knight was the hottest "new-old" thing back in the States. Old — because he'd been on top in the seventies. New — because his comeback album, *A Knight To Remember,* had just gone platinum. I hadn't seen him up close in person yet. But he looked just like he did on TV, riding his black stallion, Thunder, to the front of the stage.

"This is *not* Casablanca!" he bellowed into the mike, planting his lance into the ground. "This is not even Morocco! We are not Muslims here today, not Christians! We are not even *Africans!* . . . Today we are *world* citizens! When we *meet* each other — we walk side by side. When we *talk* to each other — we speak heart to heart, and when we love each other, *like we're gonna do tonight — we do it Soul to Soul!"*

The hottest rock group in Morocco played some real stops-out funk, six guys in jeans with heavy French accents — while girls belly-danced around them in red silk veils.

Performers had been arriving at all hours of the night. Third World groups with names I'd never heard before, Carribean Zidego and some Zuk singers in from the Canary Islands.

The American list was beginning to read like a "Who's Who" of Soul rock — The Starlighters, The Sable Sisters, 'Dixie' Monroe, Stevie Wonder's back-up group. Top billing was reserved for the woman Marvin Knight once married, the 'Sweet Sister of Soul' herself — Shana Lee. She's shorter than she looks on her videos, but twice as pretty.

What really broke open the show was some old reggae guy in from Jamaica, Ras Marcus.

He'd arrived two days ago, but nobody had seen him since. We'd heard all kinds of stories. How he'd been holed up in his hotel room with some bodyguards carrying guns. How death threats have followed him ever since Marley was shot. So I didn't know what to expect when this old guy stepped out on stage in military camouflage trousers with a raggedy T-shirt on — gold, red and green — *"Ethiopia Survival"* scrawled across his chest.

He must've been about six-foot-six. Fiery nostrils, a broken nose and a nest of dreadlocks shaking down over his shoulders to mid-back. A crew of wicked-looking street dudes followed him up. Black jeans, black T-shirts — no glitter outfits here, just straight stuff.

They started to kick up some kind of Afro-rhythm on drums and a guitar, and Ras Marcus' voice came in low and smooth. Not with a song — but with some hard-edged words that left no room for misunderstanding.

"*Dan-ger-ous,* reggae music is *dan-ger-ous* they will tell you, *sub-ver-sive.* People ask me *'I-Ras, is this true?'* I-and-I will tell you, *yes-ss-ss . . . "* he hissed into the microphone, his one gold tooth glinting menacingly.

"People ask I-Ras: 'Is reggae *ghetto music?'* I-Ras tell you *yess-ss-ss . . .* Reggae is *outlaw* music, it come from the *tribe.* Trance music, *hyp-no-tizin'!"*

He was the least slick of them all. Something about his raspy voice pierced through all the hype and hit home. Like he could reach right inside your chest and grab your heart. The audience was up on their feet, cheering each word of the prophet.

"I-and-I come back from my little island Jamaica . . . to give you a cultural shock wave. To carry back to you the message you gave I-Ras — *per-son-ally . . . "* The old master paused to wipe off the sweat dripping from his forehead with a red bandana.

"*Listen, Israelites!* I-Ras tell you, we black Africans *are* the lost tribes of Israel, sold into the bondage of a *tropical Babylon!* Come now . . ." He picked up his guitar and started to play. The audience began to sway to the sound of the real thing. This was reggae like I never heard before in the clubs back home. This was reggae live from the prophet himself.

"We must break down these *bound-a-ries* that divide our nations, an' topple these thick walls of *pre-ju-dice! . . ."*

> "*. . . Them belly full but we hungry*
> *A hungry mon is an angry mon*
> *A hungry mob is an angry mob*
> *A rain a fall but the dutty tough*
> *A pot a cook but the food no 'nough*
> *You're gonna dance to Jah music — dance*
> *We're gonna dance to Jah music — dance . . . "*

Sweat was pouring through the T-shirt that clung, soaked, to his chest, running off his trousers, forming puddles around his combat boots as he stomped from side to side. Around me, the whole crowd was now shucking their shoulders, clapping to the rolling beat. All knew the words by heart, and all shouted back their answer each time he called out:

". . . Forget your troubles — AND DANCE!
Forget your sorrows — AND DANCE!
Forget your sickness — AND DANCE!
Forget your weakness — AND DANCE! . . . "

Yes, there *was* a danger here, one I didn't yet understand — but there was a saving grace, too.

Ras Marcus had not only stolen the show, but also the hearts of these Moroccan kids who had trekked so far just to catch a piece of a life that lived, somewhere, outside of what they knew. Now they knew there were people from that somewhere who cared for them.

Ras Marcus made sure of that.

He made sure of it for all of us.

Fantasia!

*"Two dozen horses galloped across the
dusty field — straight at us!
Volley after volley of crackling
gunfire slashed the night sky . . ."*

"Neil's new sax player could
really blow — but what really
broke up the show was some old
reggae guy in from Jamaica — Ras Marcus."

I got it! My interview with Brock James. All I had to do was make it through the morning's filming of some motorcycle factory for Marvin's documentary video. He's trying to raise money by showing an upbeat Africa, "Africa on the move" kind of stuff. More than just starving faces.

First came an Italian *Ducati,* next a German dirt bike, each rolling off the end of the assembly line. Other reporters were asking questions, but I was too tired. I'd stayed awake all night in my cell room at the YWCA, recharging batteries, erasing tapes, and jotting down questions for my interview with Brock.

Finally we're bouncing along in the Video Van down to the docks. It was now noon, and I *still* hadn't gotten free to go interview him! Blinding white skyscrapers walled us in. Streets teeming with people blocked our way — young secretaries in smart French fashions; kids jumping in front of our van hawking newspapers; our radio blasting, *"L'amour, l'amour, dans Casablanca, il y a toujours l'amour . . . "*

It looked like a little chunk of Europe was cut off and dropped here on the north shore of Africa.

Two o'clock and Marvin's *still* filming this stuff . . . so Neil and I slipped out along the beach, jogging down to meet Brock.

"How many of those do you have to take?" I yelled, letting him catch up with me. He was all out of breath, huffing and puffing in his boots through the sand like he was about to have a heart attack.

"Seven a day — 'till I'm out of the detox six months." Neil washed down a handful of pills with a Coke. "Makes the craving go away."

Running the icy bottle across my cheek, he tried to snuggle close to me like a little boy.

"Neil . . . when you threw that silver dollar out there to the crowd — were you throwing it at me?"

"Sure . . . " he muttered, hugging me close. It made me feel better, but I knew he was lying. "Couldn't miss your freaky face out there, leanin' up on the stage."

"Me and my nose?"

"Yeah," he kissed me on it. "So MacB, what's the matter?"

On the pier in Casa B

"I don't know. This just does *not* look like Africa."

"What did you expect — Tarzan?" He started hopping on one foot, pulling one silver-toed boot off, while a girl in a string bikini wiggled by.

"I guess I just didn't think it would be so . . . modern."

Beach club after beach club strung along the sparkling sand, polka-dotted with rainbow-splashed umbrellas. I even spotted a windsurfer looping through the crashing breakers. Neil wasn't listening. He'd gone off hopping on one boot through the sand following the bikini.

We met at the bar of what was loosely called a hotel — a crumbling leftover from a Humphrey Bogart movie with fake autographed photos of Bogie and Bacall.

No Brock.

Twenty minutes go by . . . Neil orders a third round of this squiggly appetizer that's supposed to be fish and does his one boring magic trick, weaving a silver dollar through his fingers.

Brock James shows up half an hour late, with the blond Brit kid, Bad Boy, in tow. Brock was larger than I remembered . . . six-feet-four maybe. Same ripped-up jeans as the night before, same Rasta T-shirt, hand-signed by some of the stars, with the sleeves rolled back over quarterback shoulders. Wedged under one sleeve was a pack of cigarettes. Slung over the other was a beat-up metal case that I could only guess held his horn.

A ragged scar zig-zagged back from his right eye, disappearing into a thick crop of tightly curled black hair, rising straight up to a flat top that looked like it had been chopped off by a buzz saw. A single ring swung daintily from his left ear. On closer look, I saw it was a gold eighth note.

"Alright, so shoot. Fire away," Brock demanded, straddling a chair and facing its back toward me like a wall. Two beautiful almond eyes glared at me over his big fists folded on top.

Nervously I shuffled through my papers, trying to find a good question to start with. "Uh — what is it like, Mr. James, to be a black

American in Africa?"

Brock laughed, mimicking me, " 'What is it like to be a black American in Africa?' . . . Well, after I put the bone through my nose, I'll start gobbling up all you white tourists and let you know."

I guess that question didn't go over too big.

So, nodding toward his sax case, I tried something more personal. "Do you carry your horn wherever you go?"

"Do mothers leave their babies on the sidewalk?"

Strike two. One more and I was out. "What does it feel like playing in the shadow of the superstars?"

"What is this? What kind of questions you got here, girl?" Brock snatched the paper away from me. He started reading each question aloud, mimicking my voice, laughing to Bad Boy and everyone at the table.

I died.

"Did you ever consider a more mature approach?" Brock looked up from the list.

"Brock, you're all of two years older than me."

"Hey girl, I've lived nine lifetimes on the street and just come back from the grave. I've got more life wrapped up into *one month* than most white folks get in ten years." He leaned back, grinning over at Bad Boy; then zeroed in on me, "You ever interview a black man before?"

"No, but I'll let you know when I find one."

"You're looking at the mold."

"All I see is a little boy with a big mouth."

"Ooh-*whee!*" Neil wailed, clowning and slapping him.

" 'Boy,' huh? . . ." Brock shook it off. "Well, least I ain't no virgin."

"What makes you so sure I'm a virgin?" I said, trying to hold my own.

"That look in your eye."

"What look? . . . "

"That *squeezed up* thing you do every time I look hard at you, like this —" he leaned in and, stupid me, I flinched.

I wasn't about to tell him about my personal life, Patrick, that mess.

"Neil, you got a virgin to interview me?" Brock threw a wadded-up napkin at the Brooklyn kid. "What's this for, church magazine or somethin'?"

"Teen Time." Neil answered.

I wished Neil hadn't said that. I knew what was coming next.

"*Teen* Time?" Brock lept on it. "*Teen* Time?" He said it again, letting it slide gleefully along his teeth. "So, girl, you want me to say somethin' cute for the *teenie-weenies?*"

"Hey Brock, ease off," Neil dove in again.

He could tell I was about to cry, but I wasn't about to give Brock the satisfaction, so I grabbed up my cassette recorder and stomped off, pulling myself up as best I could until I got clear of the door.

"Screw you, Brock, OK? Just *screw off!*"

I could hear them still talking about me as I left. Brock was feeling like a creep in front of his friends, and Neil was telling him to go out and talk with me.

"I ain't talkin' to her. She's crazy." Brock was appealing to everybody. Nobody was agreeing. "She's *nuts,* man." Still no one was agreeing. "Well, why don't the rest of you clear out too!"

"Sounds like a good idea, man." Neil got up from the table and threw some coins down.

"My thoughts precisely," Bad Boy said, and split too.

marrakesh

2

"An Assembly of the Dead"

MARRAKESH, Tuesday, May 31st

I DON'T remember much about the bus ride to Marrakesh, except for two things — one, the bus was air-conditioned —and two, Shakespeare handed out the Press Kits.

Shakespeare's this African kid that's Lenny Stein's personal assistant. Real shy — even though he's a college kid. Cute too, in a quiet sort of way. He's got his hair cropped skin-close and wears these prehistoric heavy-framed glasses that hide eyes at once both wise and terrified.

We call him Shakespeare because every time he opens his mouth he sounds like King Lear. One of those flawless diction, British-educated accent types — and a walking encyclopedia on Africa.

"Mr. Stein requests each spokesman peruse this in it's entirety."

31

MEMO #72   SUBJECT: Daily Procedures   TERMINAL: All Tour Personnel

- *Do carry your passport at all times*
- *Do tip for all hotel services*
- *Do report any cuts or insect bites*
- *Do drink bottled water or soda pop*

- *Don't photograph any soldiers or military installations*
- *Don't change money on the black market*
- *Don't drink ice*
- *Don't eat any leafy vegetables or unwashed fruit*

Neil was reading it all aloud from the kit, "Says here we're not to take *any* girls to our rooms."

"Man, this is cruel." Brock smacked his head in disbelief. "What about that teeny-bopper on our tour?"

"MacB? . . . Off limits." Neil leaned over to Brock and whispered, "She's just a kid running from a bad situation. Apologize to her, man. She's sittin' right behind you."

"Apologize! Damn, she ought to *thank* me," Brock just chuckled. "This way she can pick a career she can be successful at."

"I understand, man . . ." Neil muttered in his imitation of cool, playing up to Brock. And Neil's supposed to be my friend.

I shrunk lower in my seat, pretending I couldn't hear them.

They were black and white, the Press Kits. With our *Soul to Soul* tour logo scrawled across Africa in blood red. But when Shakespeare got to my section of the bus, he ran out.

"So sorry," he apologized, embarrassed, doing this shy half-bowing thing he does everytime he sees me. "Only spokesmen get them."

I told him to tell Lenny Stein that I was a spokesperson too.

Lenny is tiny and white — a PR guy from Madison Avenue who promoted a host of black artists when they were unknown, going back to early blues greats like Bo Diddly and Dinah Washington. When Marvin came to him with the idea of a *Soul to Soul* benefit tour uniting American and African artists on the same stage, it was Lenny who made it happen — hitting up hamburger chains, cola sponsors, anybody and everybody who owed him a favor.

He's the most *precise* guy I've ever met. A five-foot-four bundle of nerve endings who packs a portable P.C. with him even into the john. I get real nervous when I'm around him. Like he's never got time to talk, always buried in his computer, pounding out another of his famous "memos".

MEMO #134   SUBJECT: PR Materials   TERMINAL: Gofers

WE HAVE A LIMITED SUPPLY OF PUBLIC RELATIONS MATERIAL. THE MONEY WE RAISE IS BEING SPENT WHERE IT IS NEEDED MOST. WE SUGGEST YOU BORROW A COPY OR SHARE ONE.

I tried to focus my eyes on the computer print-out and figure if I was really angry or not. But I could hardly keep my eyes open.

Make them go away, I whispered more to myself than at Brock and Neil who were still laughing it up.

Outside my bus window, white-robed men were whipping by — turning the reflection of my face into a dizzying blur. Voices shouted through the glass. Snatches of words long forgotten . . .

"GET OUT OF HERE! I never want to see you again. Do you hear me? . . . Get out of here now or I'll call the police!"

Screams and the screeching of our bus crashed into each other as we clattered across the Moroccan countryside. My stomach was churning. My thighs stuck to the plastic seat in a feverish sweat.

I felt sick — so sick. But if I told anybody, they'd probably send me back home. So I just sat there clutching my stomach, trying to sleep. My head, bursting with voices, kept bumping on the glass window where I let it rest. Getting hot, then cold, then hot again from the busted air-blower gusting down on me . . .

"Steve —   GET OUT OF MY ROOM!" I see her shove my father away. "What did you come back here for anyway?"

"To make it up to you . . . apologize."

"You have got to be joking. You think that you can just come crawling back here and I'm going to forgive *you . . . GET OUT!" She*

screams and throws something at him.

I've never seen Mom angry like this, just going off crazy. I run into my room and push my dresser over to block the door.

"You're not throwing me out," my father's begging.

"Bastard!" She screams and I hear something break. "DON'T YOU TURN YOUR BACK ON ME."

Nine. I'm nine — hiding crouched inside my toy closet, my knees drawn up around my ears to shut out their fighting. Right outside my door, I can hear him breathing . . . his sad voice all thick with pain.

"Burnie, let me in . . . Open this door right now." His fist is shaking my door, until I want to scream.

"Go away, Steve! You can't see her."

"I want to see my daughter. Let me see my daughter . . ." he keeps crying. "I want to say goodbye. I have a right."

"What right? . . . You have no rights here."

Doors slam. Screaming out in the hallway. I can hear my dog barking crazily, chasing after them.

Then . . . quiet.

I crouch in my closet in the dark for a while, listening . . . looking up at all the stuff he made for me. Dolls he carved. Elves perched up on my bookshelf, their marble eyes glinting down at me.

Even the silence in here is stuffed. Filled with nasty names you are called again and again. Sharp words that cut like a knife. "STUPID girl. You're just like your father. LAZY! STUPID! You LIAR! . . . I never want to see you again." Words honed over a lifetime and held at the ready. Like a blade still dripping with blood . . .

I push back the dresser, unlock the door . . . and poke my head out. The living room is a mess. A mirror is cracked into glass splinters where one of them threw an ashtray. From the dining room, a record of Johnny Mathis still plays . . . but no one is there to hear it.

I follow the crying sound down the hallway into her bathroom. She's sitting squashed on the tile floor, one hand draped over the yellowed toilet, the other pulling at the flusher handle. Heaving into the bowl, shaking hysterically.

"Mom? . . . " I take a step in, scared. "You gonna be alright?"

Mascara runs crazily in a zig-zag line down her cheek. A smear of blood red lips snarl up at me, like some wounded animal that's crawled in here to die. "Get away from me . . . JUST GET AWAY FROM ME!"

I reach down to help her up — and she smacks me in the face.

I run crying back into my room, my ears ringing, and look in the mirror. My cheek's burning red where she hit me. My nose, bleeding.

"Make her go away . . . make her go away," I cry, seeing my reflection. Sad bloodshot eyes puffed with tears. My crooked nose now superimposed over the black Moroccan night.

Outside my bus window, mosques and mountains flash by. A lone boy riding a donkey seems to pass right through my frightened face —without us ever meeting! I'm trying to connect the past to what I'm seeing reflected in front of me. Draw a line between two lives two worlds apart. How I got to be here . . . and where I'm going.

After that night, my mother wouldn't let me get near her. It was like every time she saw me, I reminded her of "him."

In whose name do we turn our backs on each other? For what god do we walk away? . . . I never saw my father for two whole years after that. He was gone forever, our family never to be whole again . . .

I must've dozed off again because when I woke up, I saw *snow* — in Africa! Right out my bus window. Icy blue mountains. Cradled at their feet, the city of Marrakesh glowed in the early morning sun like a nugget of gold.

✢ ✢ ✢

Not enough room — that's what they told me. So while Marvin and his crew headed up the mountain to film the Berber tribes, I had to sit it out at the local square, *Jemall el Fna.* It literally means "Assembly of the Dead."

"The Rolling Stones came here and Jimi Hendrix," Shakespeare explained, leading me stiffly through the crowds in the one blue suit he owned.

The square was a thirty ring circus. Acrobats, snake charmers, fortune tellers, clowns . . . all did their thing. By my feet, a guy was mixing remedies *guaranteed* to stop menstrual cramps — made of pulverized snake bone.

Shakespeare and I sat in the shade of a little stall, gnawing away at a skewer of shish-kebab he'd bought for me. I didn't have any money to spend, so he split it in two pieces and quickly slid back along the bench, a polite foot away from me. He just sat there chewing awkwardly and nervously polishing his heavy framed glasses, too shy to say anything to me.

"You've been here before?" Finally I asked him, to break the ice.

"Many times, when we were students . . . " he flashed a half smile, not daring to look up, "to study the Mosques."

"You're Muslim?"

"Mm-mm . . . " he nodded, dabbing the grease off his lips carefully with the napkin. "North of the desert here — that's where most Muslims live. South of the Sahara is Christian."

"You got a girlfriend, Shakespeare?" As soon as I asked, I wished I hadn't. Because his head kind of jerked up suddenly, pulling off a whole chunk of the lamb which then dangled from his lower lip until he had to push it in with his finger.

"No, yes! Oh . . . *several.*" He changed his mind, covering it over quick with a lie. Neil already told me he hadn't. "And you? You are going with that saxophone player, yes? I see the two of you together."

"Shakespeare, I'm not here for romance."

"What are you here for?"

"Going to be working the rest of the summer in Ethiopia. At a refugee camp."

He nodded his head, thinking this over to himself, then looked at me with new-found appreciation. "The one we are raising money for?"

Our eyes met for a second. Quickly he brushed some crumbs off his blue suit, then dabbed his forehead with the napkin, sweltering in the heat.

"Shakespeare, don't you want to loosen your tie?"

"Yes . . . but I'm working. I need this job. I must make many contacts." He turned to me, "Do you think I am doing well?"

"Very well. Everybody likes you a lot."

"Do you think I ought to be more *political* when I speak?"

"Say what you think. Shana and Marvin can handle it. That's what they're here for."

"What are you here for? I mean *before* you go to the refugee camp — what are you doing on the tour?"

I'd asked myself this question; I'd been here almost a week and only gotten *one* interview done.

"I'm a reporter."

"Good, I will help you with your articles!" He flashed a big smile then covered his mouth quickly with his napkin, embarrassed. "I hope someday to go into politics, myself. It is quite difficult for me. People don't want to know the real Africa. Just the Africa of movies, of their dreams. Rudyard Kipling and Isak Dinesen. Elephants and lions. You Americans think all of Africa is hunger, Apartheid, and a safari." He glanced over, studying me. "But this is not the Africa of the *Africans.*"

"That's what I want in my articles, Shakespeare — the way *you* see it.That's *exactly* what I want."

"MacBurnie!" I froze up at the sound of my name. It was Lenny coming up behind me as we climbed back onto the bus. He was all angry they didn't make it to the Atlas mountains. Blizzards. No one was in much of a good mood.

"What's with you two?" Lenny barked.

"What two?" I say.

"You and Brock?"

I didn't know what he was getting at. I hadn't even *talked* to Brock since the time he totally demolished me in front of everyone.

"Look MacBurnie — you want to stay on this tour, right?"

"Right."

"You want to be a pro reporter, right? Get passes backstage, right?"

"Right."

"So do me a favor, OK? . . . *Leave Brock alone.*"

I sat down angrily in a seat way in the back. Neil saw me, so he slid in alongside.

"Why is he always coming down on me?" I groaned, nearly about to burst into tears. "Why doesn't he speak to Brock?"

"Brock already said somethin' to him."

"About what?"

"About 'why do you have a white girl here doing interviews?' " Neil saw I was hurt, but he just went on. "You don't understand Brock. He's just come off a very delicate time."

"Brock? . . . give me a break. *Why* do you look up to him?"

"Look, you don't know *nothin'* about his life, what he's been through."

"Let me guess . . ." I asked sarcastically, "he had a socially deprived childhood?"

"When Brock and I went through the drug rehab, he OD'd, practically."

"On what — testosterone?"

"The guy's brother was killed, alright? He's got no real family."

"Neil, you bow down to everything that's black, just because it's black."

"Hey, black musicians are cool."

"That's stupid." I buried myself in a magazine I'd picked up at the market.

Neil just kept going on and on — how Brock's got the "best horn around," a real "master blaster." He's got the rap, the mouth. Yeah, I think . . . *all* mouth.

"Where're we going — no, never mind. Don't tell me." I scrunched down into the seat, pulling my straw hat down over my eyes. "Wake me when we get there."

Gateway to the Kasbah

fez

3   ``The Sweet Sister of Soul"

FEZ, Thursday, June 2nd

EVER BEEN deep in mid-dream, when someone comes in and tries to wake you? You're still dreaming the dream you're dreaming, but whatever is happening kind of gets included into it. That's what it was like when I fell asleep rattling along on the bus ride to Fez . . .

. . . my door is shaking, rattling. Someone's trying to break into my room.

"I want you to go to your toy closet — right now Bea. And throw all this junk out."

"He made those for ME."

"I can't stand looking at them. Besides, you're too old now for dolls."

My mother, she stands there making me throw out everything he'd given me. The candy rainbow. The little elf doll set he carved for me. One I hide from her — Humpty Dumpty. He painted it for me on

41

an eggshell, pasting on a little green bowler hat and a toothpick cane.

Now when I come home from school I don't recognize my own room. She's thrown out everything . . . till there's not a trace of him left. No toys. No photos. My father's face, erased. His eyes and lips twisted into the faces of other men. Men who hand me Tootsie Pops and grin down at me, asking me to call them 'Daddy.'

"Steve! Steve!" My tiny fist bangs on the giant metal door to his art studio. Down comes my father rattling in the bird cage elevator. Dirty blonde hair flying out like he just stuck his finger in an electric socket.

"This is not a hide-out, MacB. I work here."

"She's trying to kill me."

"Your mother's not trying to kill you."

"Then how come I feel like I — I can't breathe?"

"Don't you see who your mother is?" He hands me a statue — half lizard, half woman — with dreadlock hair dangling down like snakes. Then I'm crying.

"Why can't I live here with you?"

"You've got to live at home."

"I HAVE NO HOME!"

The lizard lady lays a clawed hand on my shoulder — and starts shaking me! I try to pull away, but she keeps grabbing me.

"TIRED? . . . " the lady's terrible laugh echoes through my mind. I roll over and shove the arm off me.

"Go away!" I scream. I thought it was my mother, then I saw she'd become an angel in a white scarf, her black braids dangling down over me.

"You alright?" Shana Lee whispered, gently caressing her soft hand on my cheek.

"Sure . . . " I woke up uncertainly. "Where are we?"

"God knows . . . " murmured Shana, as our bus rattled on through the night. It was pitch black outside the window, save for a sliver of moon that cast an eerie white light over the mountains. "You want some gum?"

"Sure . . . " I nodded. I couldn't believe this was happening. Here I was four thousand miles from home, eyes looking like squashed Japanese beetles, and America's top singer, the 'Sweet Sister of Soul' herself, is offering me a stick of Juicy Fruit. Carefully, she unpeeled the silver foil, grinned, and plopped the gum into my opened mouth.

"If you need me, I'm right back here," Shana pointed two rows behind me, then got up to go.

"Hey!" I said, holding onto her wrist. "Can I interview you?"

"Sure, honey . . . tomorrow morning." She smiled, pulling the scarf back down over her braids. "Meet me in my room at seven A.M."

Now, dead as I was, there was no way I was going to miss that interview — even if I had to sleepwalk there. Check in at the hotel was at two A.M. I set my old Betty Boop clock with the two bell clangers to six A.M., dug out a pair of clean jeans, and laid my Sony recorder under my cot.

At five A.M. I woke to the sound of someone crying — right outside my window. Digging myself out of the rocks they call 'pillows' here, I climbed out to my balcony.

Miles of zig-zag alleys crushed in on themselves. A brisk wind blew up from the streets, whipping my hair back like I was flying high over some medieval city.

Again I heard the voice . . . and saw a lone man bellowing from a tower across from me, shattering the still night. He kept it up over and over, crying out in this mournful voice, *"Allahu akbar-rr-rr . . ."*

From out of nowhere, the streets below me now began to fill with row after row of people. I held onto the balcony railing in awe, witness to a miraculous gathering. What was it about Shakespeare's faith that brought so many together?

"Allahu akbar-rr-rr . . . " cried the voice again.

Thousands knelt as one, then seemed to freeze, leaning forward to touch their foreheads to the ground in morning prayer.

This must be the wrong room, I thought, standing outside the door. Inside I could hear a child's voice laughing and two people arguing in Arabic. The door opened, and this little elf person appeared. She stood no higher than the doorknob, all of her ten years packed into Ras Marcus look-alike army trousers and a Rastafari T-shirt with a raised fist emblazoned on her little chest.

Cautiously, she stuck her hand through a crack in the door. "Hi, I'm Raine."

"Yeah? . . . well, I forgot my umbrella." I shook her tiny hand. "So do I get to come in or what?"

"Rain-*e*," she emphasized, opening the door another crack. "My mother's still asleep."

Behind the little girl, I saw Shana striding out of the bedroom half naked, pulling on skin-tight leather pants.

"Oh . . . I forgot." She looked up, surprised at seeing me. "Look, *you* talk while *I* get ready."

She waved over her shoulder and disappeared back into her bathroom. I felt like an idiot with this little girl standing there staring at me while I shouted over the TV to a person I couldn't even see. And all the while Mickey Mouse is cursing out Pluto in Arabic.

"How're the concerts here in Africa different from those back home?" I yelled at the wall and started fumbling with my tape recorder.

"You notice the men here mostly stay together in the concerts. *Groups* of men. Have you seen that?" the disembodied voice called out. It was a sweet voice, affectionate. "Back home you just get *couples,* boy-girl. But here, when they crowd around you to get an autograph, it's just men."

"Maybe they're just shy, the women here?" I ventured. "What do you think of them?"

"The African woman? . . . She's just beginning to experience her freedom to choose, to make her own life. Women do eighty percent of the work in the villages. Its a difficult question —" her head popped out of the bathroom door for a split second. I'm standing now with her little girl climbing on my back.

"Why are you *standing* out there? Why don't you come *in here* where we can talk?"

X "Sure," I shrugged and followed her into the bathroom, carefully eyeing the sink, the tub . . .

She always made me sit on the edge of her bathtub while she bathed. My mother . . . Soaking her tired body in bubble bath. Pampering herself with perfumes, their flowery scent mixing with the sharp odor of alcohol . . .

She'd hold me captive in there. Make me listen to all her stories. Sometimes she'd get so drunk I'd have to carry her out. Crying, cursing her troubles out to her nine year-old daughter who was too dumb not to listen to her.

When I got old enough, I'd sneak in and borrow her make-up for a date. One night . . . she caught me. Flinging open the shower door she found me crouched inside, hiding.

"You — you're just like your father." She kept yelling, rubbing my lips and eyes until they got so sore. "You get that make-up off your face! You slut! Stupid, STUPID GIRL!"

Little Raine came in and sat on the tub, checking me out like a mini-version of myself. So I sat down next to her, and we both watched Shana put on her make-up. Wild colors circled her sink like they were scraped off some artist's palette. Powders and eyeshadows with names like *Burnt Ebony, Afro Ochre . . .*

I dug out my list of questions. "Now that you've been to Africa, do you think your music will change?"

"My whole life is changed!" said Shana, brushing some *Nile Blue* over her right eye. "There's no going back now. I can't rest after what I've seen here."

Swiveling her chair around to me, she whispered secretively, "I wish we didn't always have to be so *cooped up,* you know? . . . That we could go out and really be with the people."

It was like she was reading my mind. Ever since we got here it felt like we were in prison.

"I'm sorry honey, but we've got to go." Shana suddenly threw her make-up into her bag. "I got a call this morning. I've got more interviews. I'm sick of it. This schedule Lenny's got me on, it's *crazy."*

I saw her eyes become vulnerable, then excited. She gave Raine a little hug and looked up at me conspiratorily.

45

"Hey girlfriend, you want to take the day off with me?"

I couldn't believe the question. *Me* being invited to spend the afternoon with Shana Lee.

"Uh . . . sure," I stammered awkwardly.

"You got nothing else to do?"

"I'm supposed to let Lenny know my schedule."

"I'll handle Lenny, *you* handle Raine." She held out her hand, "Deal?"

"Deal," I grinned back, shaking it.

Shana started to get up, then stopped herself. That same conspiratorial twinkle filled her eyes.

"Wait! . . . " she threw up both hands, excited, and quickly put some ruby-red lipstick on. Then she tied up a scarf to cover her hair and lowered her shades.

"How do I look?" she giggled, then frowned. "No way of disguising it, huh?"

Even with the African clothes, the sunglasses and scarf, there was no hiding the one and only Shana Lee. She's so soft, gentle. I think it must come from the way she grew up. Shana's road to the top wasn't easy. After she and Marvin split up, nobody thought she could make it on her own.

"OK, come on," she winked, putting on the finishing touches. "Let's play hooky!"

Waves of people already filled the narrow cobblestone street — a mad tumble of donkey carts, vendors, bicycles and animals. Tugging Raine firmly behind me, I hurried after Shana as she turned into a dark alleyway . . . and stumbled into a scene straight out of the Middle Ages.

"Don't look now, but we're being followed," I said to Shana.

"Probably that press guy from Rolling Stone. He got backstage last night and wouldn't let anybody alone."

Sure enough, as we turned the corner, the man followed after us. He was a young, lanky guy in a short sleeve white shirt, jeans and sandals.

"My joyous greetings, ladies!" he called out, coming up right behind us. "You are looking for a tour, yes?"

"No," Shana said, hurrying us away.

"A tour guide, yes?"

"No!" Shana spun around. *"What* do you want?"

"The privilege of guiding you ladies about our city — yes?"

"No, *no . . . "* Shana continued down the street. But he just kept after us, coming alongside like we were old friends. Just as I was about to say *bug off,* I saw he was Shakespeare. Out of his one blue suit, none of us recognized him.

"In Fez, it is very easy to lose your way." He looked at me hopefully.

I looked back at Shana, who, sizing up the twisting tortuous streets, nodded, "How much you want to be our guide?"

"No money, please — this is my home!"

Wide-eyed, we followed Shakespeare into his ancient walled city. Down labyrinth streets, under crumbling archways, twisting dizzyingly through crowded alleyways . . .

Fez, he showed us, was really *three* cities — the old, the new, and the very new. When the French got control over Morocco in 1912, they built a mini-Paris for themselves southwest of the Old Fez — broad boulevards, public gardens, fashion stores and stuff like that.

Anybody who could afford it had moved out of the old town long ago. But still this Old City, barely a mile square, was bursting at its seams. He led us into a *suk,* or market, jammed full with people shouting and haggling prices.

You couldn't escape it; the air was a Moroccan stew, brewing with meats sizzling over fires and the rotted smell of animal hide laid out to dry across the rooftops.

"What stinks?" I yelled over to him, barely sidestepping a clattering donkey cart.

"The tanning vats." He pointed at some half-naked men wading

The Tanning Vats

in hot tubs of blood red dye. Some drowned the sheepskins while others cut the leather up into wallets.

Shakespeare knew everybody. Half the plaza were his blood relatives and each one promised us a *"very special good deal."* Vanishing inside a tent, his shy voice rose from inside, arguing in Arabic.

"For you, and for you . . . and for you." He emerged triumphant as Houdini, handing us each a pair of rainbow-colored slippers. Their pointed toes curled up on end. *"Babouche,* real traditional."

It was just tourist stuff.

"Shakespeare, you told me you'd show me how people here really live. So . . . how about it?"

The boy lowered his head, fiddling with his glasses. After much thought he hooked them back over his ears . . . and nodded.

The Suk

". . . you couldn't escape it, the air was a Moroccan stew, brewing with meats sizzling over fires and the rotted smell of animal hide."

From the outside it looked like nothing. But once inside we found walls and ceilings of stone all inlaid with sparkling mosaics spun into elaborate geometrical designs.

"My apartment is only on the fourth story," he kept apologizing, striding up endless steep stairs. Ten families now live in Shakespeare's building, long ago a mansion or *dar,* home of a really rich man.

"Ladies, turn your eyes, it is not proper to look on one's neighbors without permission . . ."

As he hurried us by, I snuck a peek. Below me, half a dozen families were washing their clothes in the fountain. Torn boxes, broken baby bottles and garbage were scattered about on what was once a beautiful tile floor.

"Squatters," he said sadly and rushed us on.

"Can't you evict them?"

"They are so poor . . . and there are so many here. These families, they come into almost every building. Even put up small shacks in the streets."

"Isn't it against the law?" little Raine asked, upset.

Shakespeare was silent — you could see he was plainly embarrassed by the poverty of his home.

"Doesn't it bother you?"

"They have nowhere to go, young lady. We must care for each other, *yes?"*

The door, splintered and needing repair, cracked open. In the far corner, resting on a brown sheepskin rug flat from years of use, was an old man. One bony hand held up his creased face, while the other cradled a yellow clay pipe. Silvery smoke spiralled up from its bowl and hung in the air — as if to wait for his words before going anywhere.

"La bas! La bas!" he gestured with his pipe, glad to see us.

"My grandfather," Shakespeare whispered, ushering us in. "He cannot move his knees from having worked so long in the tanning vats."

Facing the tired-out man sat an equally tired-out black and white TV, positively prehistoric. Test patterns danced on its screen.

"He cannot move to switch channels," Shakespeare apologized, turning it off. "Next year I will get him remote."

A woman appeared as if from nowhere and set down a brass tray and teapot, pouring us a round of scalding mint tea in tiny delicate cups. When she clucked out her greeting, I noticed a web of tatoos over her whole chin.

We must eat. His mother was insisting. "It would be a great insult not to accept her offer," whispered Shakespeare.

Not allowing us to help, she prepared the meal herself while we sat in the living room — me sipping at the sickly sweet tea, Shakespeare doing his best not to look embarrassed when his grandfather spat out a gob of tobacco and stuck it on the wall.

"My grandson, has he been good?"

"Oh," Shana nodded, "Very good."

"He needs this money for school. I made him memorize the Koran," he smiled proudly, tapping an old book worn from use which lay on the table. "But we are *haratin* Berbers, you understand? Dark-skinned. These *shluh* Berbers at school look down on him as inferior. My family has only been allowed the worst jobs. Well-digging. Tanning vats. This is why it is so important for my grandson to make something of himself."

Back out from the kitchen came Shakespeare's mom, carrying a tray covered with a pointed brass cone. When she lifted it off we found ourselves eating a regular feast . . . baked chicken *tarjine,* mounds of mutton *cous cous* mixed with sugared yellow raisins, and lots of veggies.

As we ate, one by one, others from Shakespeare's huge family began to show up — all curious to see these American sisters who had travelled so far to visit their home.

Old snapshots were taken out, family heirlooms passed over for our approval. And all the while, Shakespeare's mother kept pouring us more and more of this sickeningly sweet, green tea.

Then, like overstuffed Sultans, we eased down deep into the couch, beaming at our new friends. Dead tired, Raine crawled across to the ratty sheepskin rug and before I could stop her, cuddled up against the old man, fearlessly eyeing him as he puffed his pipe.

"La bas! La bas!" he welcomed her, his gruff voice chasing pipe

smoke out the window. Then, with one boney wrinkled hand, he began to caress little Raine's black hair. Amazingly, her eyes drooped closed!

With one simple gesture this ancient Berber had reached past our foreign looks and taken us into his family. Pointing from himself to her, he whispered slyly, "Young girl . . . old father."

I carried Raine, half asleep in my arms, winding our way back through the streets to our hotel. She gave me a goodnight kiss and a cartoon of Goofy she'd been drawing, then Shana tucked her into bed. Watching the two of them together, I wondered what it would be like to have a mother like that — a mother who took care of you.

"Thanks for helping me with Raine," she smiled; her whole face glowed from her day of freedom. She glided softly out onto the balcony and we sat out there together, watching the old city slowly sink into a dark, deep blue pool of shadows. For a long time I said nothing, not wanting to break the magic spell that had grown between us.

"MacB? . . . " She finally turned to me, "Back on the bus when I woke you . . . what was getting you down?"

I shrugged it off. "I'm just finding it . . . hard."

"What?"

"To fit in here . . ."

She put down her make-up.

"People hold back," Shana looked at me uneasily to see if she should go on, ". . . especially with white folks. They want to check you out. They're waiting to see if you really care about us — or if you're just here for some weird guilt trip . . ."

Then she took me by the hand, and I got real embarrassed. "What is it honey — a guy?"

"Brock James," I muttered almost like a curse. I could tell she didn't know who he was. "He plays the horn with Quicksilver, Neil Silver's band."

"Oh . . . He's new, right?"

"He just tries to be so macho, you know?"

"Sometimes, men don't have any other choice," she shook her head remembering someone, Raine's father I wondered. "When you grow up in a society that's got you locked out from birth, with no job and no chance of getting any — macho may be the only way left to be a man."

Macho was one thing, I wanted to tell her, mucho-macho another. Shana meant well, but she didn't know him.

"Sounds like he just hasn't figured out how to talk to you yet," she said softly, touching my arm. "You know, you two got a lot of differences."

"Yeah, he's different alright . . . " I just said and let it go at that.

The blazing African sun slid over the hilltops, pulling with it the carpet of gold light that had covered old Fez. Long blue-fingered shadows wove their way through the streets — until even the towering minarets above the mosques were seized by the dark hand of night.

Back home it would be morning, and my mom would be getting my little brother off to day camp. Here in Fez it was twilight. Back home Patrick, my old boyfriend, would be checking out what drive-in to take Jeanne to. Here in Fez it was still the Middle Ages.

I looked over at Shana, amazed at how she could so easily slide between the two worlds.

Tomorrow we'd be in Timbuktu.

PART TWO

WEST AFRICA

"Second Chance at Life"

Sayin' no goodbye, I just close the door
Don't take a look back over my shoulder
"Baby," she cries, "you can't leave home.
You got to wait till you grow older."

Drownin' in the dreams of my mother
Starvin' for some praise from my father
Can't somebody hear the fear that own's me
Can't hide this fear no more; it's about to kill me.

I wasted all my years
Wasted all those tears
Nothin' I could do was right
Nothin' we could do but fight

Too many words gone down
Too many miles come between us
Too many dreams gone wrong
Too many promises broke to free us

I'm not the kid in that wallet picture you show.
Maybe I never was or will be
your second chance at life.
I need a chance to escape from all you know,
Some chance to free my heart—
Some time to pull out the knife.

So I'm sayin' no goodbye, just closin' the door
Not takin' a look back over my shoulder
Gotta keep movin' on, find out what's in store
Tryin' hard to keep my heart from gettin' colder.

words and music by: Neil Silver and Bad Boy Jones
as recorded by the **Quicksilver Band**
on the album "Tarnished Silver"

ALGERIA

MAURITANIA

sahara
desert

Republic of Mali

Timbuktu · niger
niger
river delta · Gao

Mopti
Djenne
Segou
NIGER
BURKINA
Bamako
SENEGAL
niger r.
senegal r.
GUINEA
niger r.
BENIN
IVORY COAST
GHANA
TOGO
NIGERIA

PEOPLE

Population: 7.5 million. **Ethnic Groups:** Mande (Bambara, Malinke) 50%, Peul 17%, Voltaic 12%, Songhai 6%, Tuareg and Moor 5%. Population is homogeneous, except for desert nomads like the *Tuaregs* and *Moors* who are related to North African Berbers. **Lifestyle:** Most people in Mali live in small villages and earn a living by farming, fishing, herding, crafts, and trade. Only 16% live in towns of more than 5,000. **Religions:** Islam 90%, indigenous 9%, Christian 1%. **Languages:** French (official) and Bambara (80% of the population). **Literacy:** 10%. **Infant Mortality:** 152/1,000. **Life Expectancy:** 45 yrs.

GEOGRAPHY

Area: 1,204,278 sq.km. — the size of Texas and California. **Capital City:** Bamako. **Other Major Cities:** Segou (75,000), Mopti (64,000), Kayes (45,000), Gao (37,000). **Terrain:** Savanna and desert. Land-locked Mali is surrounded by former French territories. The richest farms lie *below* the River Niger. The West African savanna region is a "transition zone" between the coastal rain forest and the desert. The northern third of the country, north of Timbuktu, lies within the Sahara Desert and is sparsely settled. *The River Niger:* Downstream from Mopti, this famous river flows into a vast delta system of channels and inland lakes — then turns again into a single river near Timbuktu. In good years, this delta is flooded.

GOVERNMENT

Government: Republic. The President is Chief of State, *Minister of Defense,* and Secretary General of Mali's only political party. Traditionally, the desert Tuareg peoples have opposed the authority of the central government. In Mali, as in most of Africa, the vital issues of the 1990's are eco-nomic, not political. The government has shifted from an ideological commitment to socialism to a more flexible pragmatism. **Colonial Power:** France. **ndependence:** Sept. 22, 1960.

ECONOMY

Yearly GDP Per Person: $190 (among the world's 10 poorest nations). The recurring *Sahelian drought* has crippled economic development by a devastating cycle of famine. Large herds of goat, sheep, and cattle were one of Mali's greatest resources (normally 1/4 of exports). However, the droughts of 1973-4 and 1983-5, have wasted these herds. Rice is grown along the banks of the River Niger, and the Niger provides fish not only for Mali but also for her neighbors. In the past Mali was self-sufficient in grains. But rainfall over the last 20 years has become infrequent and erratic. **Exports:** Cotton and cattle, fish, groundnuts.

HISTORICAL NOTES

Mali is the last of a series of wealthy ancient West African empires (Ghana, Malinke, and Songhai) that controlled the gold and salt trade routes between the civilizations of West Africa, along the Sahara desert, to civilizations by the Mediterranean Sea. The last great kingdom was destroyed by a Moroccan invasion in 1591. French military penetration began around 1880. The brave resistance to French domination was not ended until the Malinke warrior, Samory Toure, was defeated in 1898 after 7 years of bloody war.

TOURIST ATTRACTIONS

Some of West Africa's most scenic country, the mosque of Djenne, the ancient city of Timbuktu, the river Niger, cliff dwelling Dogon people.

mali

4

"The End of the World"

TIMBUKTU, Saturday, June 4th

"I HEAR you been suckin' up to Shana Lee," Brock eased into my room like he owned it. Still wearing that Rasta T-shirt he conned the stars into signing, he lowered his sax off his shoulder and shut the door.

I reopened it. "Why do you have to turn everything good that happens to me into something bad? Or do you just go through life poking holes in everyone's balloon?"

"Hey, girl . . ." he grinned, "you gotta do what you gotta do to get over." Then, noticing Raine playing jacks on the floor, he shot me a knowing look. "Get the interview at any price, huh?"

"I've babysat before. I like it." I dug out some coins and put them in Raine's little hand, "Go get me some Pepsi — diet, OK?"

As soon as Raine left, Brock flopped down on my cot. "So, what do you think of her?"

"Raine? . . . or Shana?"

Brock just did that drumming-with-his-fingers thing he does. It's like his hands have a mind of their own, always fidgeting, peeling off matchbook covers, tapping pencils, tugging at his earring evasively — it's supposed to make you think his mind isn't racing in overdrive.

Then he started to leaf through my diary.

"Hey!" I snatched it out of his hand. "I asked you what do you think of her?"

"Some people dig her."

"Well, Brock, what about you?"

"I don't know. She's trying to be like Tina Turner — so cool, you know? But she don't shimmy those shoulders like Tina."

"You don't sing with your shoulders."

"Girl, *anything* I put my lips around — sings." He eased one arm around me, kissing my neck.

"Yeah, well, you just keep those lips on that sweet face of yours where they belong." I ducked out from under his arm, but he just grabbed me again.

"Brock — *get out of my room!*" This time I shoved him away, hard.

Brock backed off all wounded, like a puppy who'd just been whupped. His head hung down, avoiding my eyes. "Look, girl, I just came by to . . . you know, like — "

"Apologize?"

"Somethin' like that," he muttered, shifting his eyes to my sneakers again. I was beginning to wonder if I should wear the same pair everyday, just so he could recognize me.

"Well . . . ?"

"Well, what?"

"Do it!" I said impatiently.

"I just did it."

"*That* was it? That was an apology?"

"What do you want me to do — kiss your feet? . . ." he grabbed up his horn, furious, and headed out the door. "Aw, you're too stuck up, girl."

"Brock! . . ."

He spun around at me, "Now what?"

"I've been around enough addicts!"

I watched as his eyes filled with pain. "Brock . . . hey, I'm sorry." I tugged playfully at his *Soul to Soul* sweatshirt. "It was nice of you, your apology. It's just that my mother —"

"Screw your mother," he grabbed me and bent my arm back behind me so I couldn't move. Then he kissed me so hard he cut my lip.

"Get off me!" I hit him. *"Get out of my room!"*

"Where were you born — under an altar?" he shoved me aside and stormed out the door. Then, in a flash, he was back, flinging his sheet music down angrily on my cot, throwing his arms in the air. *"Alright! Alright, Goldilocks!* What can I do for you?"

I wiped the blood from my lip, eyeing him like he was a crazy man, "Get out of here! Do you hear me!" But he wouldn't move. And I started to get frightened. *"GET OUT!"* I screamed, but I knew no one was around to hear me. "You want to *do* something? OK . . . you can get me an interview."

"Done." Brock picked up the sheets of music scattered all over the floor. "With who?"

"Ras Marcus."

"Ras Marcus don't give interviews — everyone knows that."

"I thought you and him were so tight."

Brock went back into his tugging-at-his-earring thing, ducking his head, looking away, "Yeah, uh . . . yeah well, we are. But he just don't give no interviews."

Then when he saw I wasn't buying that, he grabbed up his saxophone and stormed out again, "MacB — you just don't know what you're askin' for."

When I went to close my door, I found a tiny body crouched in the hallway leaning against the wall. She looked like a mini-me, with her knees wrapped up around her ears to keep the fighting out.

"Do you love him?" she asked, looking up at me.

"Like Al Capone loved Eliot Ness. Come on," I grabbed her little hand, helping her up. "Let's get out of here."

The Motorcycle Kid

Names. Whoever invented the idea of first names ought to get an award for condemning people to a lifetime of misery and shame. Why can't we pick our own? Raine hated hers, and I hated mine. So we made a deal.

Rene (Ruh-*NAY*), her real name, was definitely out. As was *Ray* or *Ree* or anything that had nothing to do with the weather. So *Rainey* or *Rain* were cool. Why the weather, was a question I thought I had no business asking a ten year old.

Anyway, while Shana rehearsed for her concert, I decided to make that day in Timbuktu a 'Raine afternoon.' And what Raine most wanted to do was to ride a camel.

"It's *him!*" Raine squealed, pulling me past a mangy old camel baking in the marketplace.

"Him, who?"

"*Him!* My *dream* boy, remember?" She kept tugging at me desperately. But I didn't know what she was talking about.

"*MacBee-ee* . . . remember you were telling me what your dream was?"

"That was no dream — that was nightmare on Elm Street."

"And I said mine was a boy? A boy I could take care of?"

I looked over at this scrawny kid, maybe fifteen, leaning back on his motorscooter. A cigarette dangled from his lips. Definitely too old for her.

"That's *him.*"

"Raine, that's *not* him."

"Girlfriend, it is. Go talk to him."

"*I'm* not going to talk to him. He's *your* dream boy. You go."

"*Ple-ee-ase* MacB. I'm too nervous."

I crossed over to The Motorscooter Kid while Raine eased around the camel, her tiny hands tucked coolly in her jean's back pockets like she was really not interested.

"This your bike?"

"Yes," the kid spoke in broken English, puffing cooly on his cigarette.

"This your camel?"

"Yes, I am also the father of the camel."

After arguing a price, I got her hoisted up onto its saddle in front of me. At once, the camel rolled forward on its knees and I felt this mountain under me rise up, swaying sickeningly high over the earth.

Perched on top, Raine was in seventh heaven, showering questions on her dream boy while he led us through this city of mud walls. Women gossiped, floating by us down a timeless maze of sandy streets. Donkey carts churned up a yellow haze that hung over the flat, low, mud homes like a sun-drenched cloud. Timbuktu . . . the Golden City.

It was another world, a lost world. Real desert. Everything was the same mud-gold color — the streets, the walled-in houses with their shuttered windows, even the goats and camels . . . We were at the end of the Earth, the very last desert crossroads that tied the Arab north with tribal people on the coast.

"Mansa Musa," the Motorcycle Kid whispered up to me like it was a secret password.

I looked at him like he was crazy.

"Mansa Musa," he whispered it again, pointing ahead to where Shana was being videotaped alongside a statue of a king. Her voice came drifting across the dusty streets to us, telling of a time when so much gold passed through this legendary kingdom — they traded it for salt.

"You traded gold for *salt?"* Raine flirted with the Motorcycle Kid.

Shuffling after the video crew, the boy led us through the ruins of his city. What was once a palace now housed a laundry shop selling cheap factory-made clothing. Where once a university stood now was a clearing for an outdoor market swarming with black-veiled Tuareg women picking over fruits, vegetables, and pots.

Behind the market was an awesome spectacle. A sea of camels stretched out across the desert to the horizon. Men and women were pulling up their tents, packing up their homes into rolled up blankets. There must have been thousands.

"What you are witnessing now is our death. The end of these desert nomads and their old way of living." Shana signaled the video camera to follow her. "With no more trade, so many families now crowd into the city in search of food."

". . . black-veiled Tuareg women picked over baskets full of fresh fruits and vegetables."

"Women gossiped, floating by us like ghosts down a timeless maze of sandy streets.

Timbuktu . . .
the Golden City

I peered out through the dusty haze, watching the exodus of this boy's proud people. A salt caravan of over a thousand camels was preparing to leave. Maybe one of the last. Children ran about, helping their mothers and fathers lash down their belongings onto their camel's backs, shouting instructions from under hooded robes in the windswept sands.

"Aren't you going to take any photos?" Raine looked up at me.

I shook my head no. I felt too sad, watching these huge families leave, and too small in the face of forces I couldn't see or change, forces that could obliterate an entire people. The more I found out about Africa, the less I knew . . . about the rise and fall of empires, about the splitting apart of humanity.

What is Islam? What is it like to be Muslim? Africa was still a giant jig-saw puzzle, its pieces carved into patterns that defied me to fit them together.

"It's getting dark. Hey! *Hey!*" I called over to Raine, trying to pry her loose from the kid who was now offering her a cigarette. Time to get back to the hotel we were loosely calling civilization. Clutching the Polaroids I took tightly in her fist, she ran ahead to show her mom.

Kitabu Diary

So glad to get back to my room. I hate the way I stand out here. Sitting on top of that camel with my yellow hair sticking out. Everyone staring at me.

We sleep four to a room. Two of the girls I've roomed with before. Both African. Aiche — a student from the University who's an expert on desertification, and Sale — who doesn't speak a word of English. Both are Berber, and both are only here for the North African leg of our tour.

So far all I've seen of Aiche is her two large dark eyes, peering out from behind her black veil.

Now I watch silently from my cot as she removes it, uncovering high cheekbones and brilliant eyes that flash from smooth dark skin. Hanging down over her forehead are clusters of silver coins, tied by bright colored thread to the hood she hides under.

These women literally wear their wealth on their bodies, sewn right into their clothes! . . . Each of her arms is weighted down with big silver bracelets, one at the wrist, four others higher up near the elbow. Silver rings circle each finger . . . and strung around her neck hangs a necklace heavy with huge nuggets of amber.

"You look so glum," Aiche turned to me suddenly.

"I just seem to . . . stick out, you know?" I tried to laugh it off, pulling at my stringy excuse for hair.

The truth was I felt like a freak. Everywhere I went people stared at it. I'd tried to cover it with my hats, but I've got an oddball collection, left over from my equally oddball collection of hit-and-run boyfriends.

"You just need to . . ." Aiche started to twist it in back while Sale giggled. Then both girls started fussing over me. "It is so *thin!*" she laughed.

Taking each lock in two fingers, Aiche twisted them around a wire, then weaved the wire back into my hair until a row was created along the side of my head — clear back to the nape of my neck.

"Aiche, let me see!"

"Wait!" Carefully, she outlined each of my eyes with dark *kohl,* then added four dots above my crooked nose. "You must have more confidence in yourself; you are a pretty girl."

She lent me one of her hoods and I held up the mirror, "How come your hood is pointed and mine is round?"

"A round hood means you are available for men, but only to *look* at you. A pointed hood means —" she stopped, and the two girls started giggling again.

"It means you are, how do your say — a *widow,* like me," Aiche confided gleefully. "And open to *all* proposals. No formalities, no waiting — instant marriage!"

Sale lent me one of her shawls; its soft cotton fell loose and cool over my shoulders. And the three of us stepped out together, ready to cruise the African night.

At night in this desert city, the narrow streets are lit only by an occasional electric lamp and a sky full of bright stars.

"It is perfectly safe to walk the streets." Aiche claimed, tugging at my arm. "Islamic law is very strict, you see? So there is little crime."

As we walked along, I could hear the bleating of goats behind closed walls. From inside the flat mud brick homes came transistor radios playing tinny Arabic tunes. Ahead of us, an ancient mosque rose out of the night, its dome sparkling with mosaics and gold.

"What happened, Aiche? I mean, to all the gold?"

"Without our gold there would be no Europe. It was *Africa* that financed your empires," she said, adjusting my shawl. "But when our trade routes died out . . . so did our great city."

A cry shattered the night.

"Up there!" She pointed high above the mosque.

Leaning out from a spiralling tower was a turbaned man dressed in white, crying out, *"Allahu akbar-rr-rr!"*

Again, from out of nowhere, I saw the dusty streets begin to fill with people. Some little Muslim kids scurried up front, carrying their wood prayer boards of Arabic writing tucked tightly under their arms.

"The call to prayer is one everywhere, just as Allah is one." Aiche hurried me over to the steps of the mosque. *"Laa Ilaha Illa Ilaah* . . . there is no God, but God."

I took a position near the stone steps and watched her as she took her sandals off and hurried over to join a row of supplicants. Sandals and shoes were spread out around me, neatly arranged on the steps in pairs. Rich and poor bowed together, side by side. I saw Shakespeare in a row of men up ahead fall on his knees and touch his

75

forehead to the ground. Row after row rose up again like a wave, then fell forward. As they raised their faces . . . I saw that the men's eyes were filled with tears.

"Five times a day?" I asked as Aiche returned.

She lowered her veil so I could see her. "We are not so different. We believe in the same holy men as you, all the great prophets, Abraham, Moses, Jesus . . ." She hurried us along to the big striped tent. "But you see, Africa is still two worlds. One that lives under the Crescent Moon and Star, and another that lives under the Cross."

Out at the street festival, a band of men squatted on colorful rugs, twirling and drumming their giant tambourines. Circled around them, women in bright embroidered robes kept time by clapping their hands, while two guys I couldn't see were dancing.

Aiche pulled at my sleeve. "The one on the left? . . ." cupping her hand over her mouth, she giggled. "He is cute."

I looked again and saw it was Neil murdering *Blue Suede Shoes* on his guitar. He barely recognized me.

"Hey Silver, where's your 'Master Blaster'?"

"Gone, long gone. He and Ras took a train up ahead to our next gig." Neil eased over in his silver spurs, rotating his Mets baseball cap so its brim covered his greasy ponytail in back. "Did he apologize?"

"Is rape an apology?"

"Aren't we being a little touchy? He told me nothin' happened."

"If he already told you his idea of *'nothing happening,'* why are you asking me?"

He threw up both his hand in mock surrender, *"Sorr-eee! . . ."*

"The one on the left? . . ."
Aiche cupped her hand over her mouth
and giggled. "He's cute."

Republic of Senegal

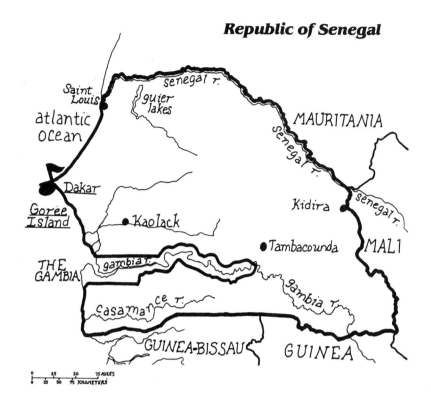

PEOPLE

Population: 6.4 million. **Ethnic Groups:** Wolof 36%, Fulani 17.5%, Serer 16.5%, Toucouleur 9%, Diola 9%, Mandingo 6.5%, other African 4.5%, other 1%. **Religions:** Muslim 75%, traditional 20%, Christian 5%. **Languages:** French (official), Most speak Wolof, Pulaar, Diola, Mandingo or a tribal language. **Literacy:** 5%-10%. **Infant Mortality:** 158/1,000. **Life Expectancy:** 44 years. Malaria is endemic in Senegal, and hepatitis is prevalent.

GEOGRAPHY

Area: 196,840 sq.km. (76,000 sq.mi.); the size of South Dakota. **Capital City:** Dakar. **Other Major Cities:** Saint-Louis. **Terrain:** Low, rolling, plains with savanna vegetation; drained by four major rivers — the Senegal, Saloum, Casamance, and Gambia.

GOVERNMENT

Government: Republic. The President is elected by universal adult suffrage to a 5-year term. President Senghor retired on January 1, 1981, and was replaced by his prime minister of 10 years, Abdou Diouf. **Colonial Power:** France. **Independence:** April 4, 1960.

ECONOMY

Yearly GDP Per Person: $400. After the great Sahelian drought of 1968-73, Senegal's debt position became disastrous. By 1981, 27% of all export earnings were being used to pay off these debts. Senegal took courageous steps to reform, but 1981 brought the worst crop year since independence. *Peanuts* (Senegal's principal crop), account for half of the labor force. This traditional reliance on one export "cash crop" (began under Colonial rule), has made Senegal hostage to the fickle climactic changes of the Sahel area. Fishing is a possible solution, but much of the catch is still brought in by fisherman using small motorized canoes. **Exports:** Peanuts and peanut products, phosphate rock, canned fish.

TOURIST ATTRACTIONS

Goree Island, cities of Dakar and St. Louis, fishing villages, game parks, excellent swimming, boating, fishing (for mackerel, barracuda, bluefish, bass, red mullet, and sea trout), sailing, skindiving, and spearfishing.

senegal

5

"Buffalo Soldier, Dreadlock Rasta"

DAKAR, *Monday, June 6th*

WHY THEY chose me to pick up Brock at the train station must have been Lenny's perverse idea of a joke. Two new headliners had arrived by plane early that morning — the British group *Lords of Discipline* and the lead singer of the French group *Jamais Bleu* — causing a major catastrophe at the airport checking in their gear.

So, with everybody at the airport, he had me switch from *baby-sitter* for Shana to *utility man* now for Neil. I sat grumpily with my arms folded as our cab rattled out to the train station, doing my best to let him know I was not pleased.

You couldn't miss spotting Brock's blood red rapper's cap and mirrored sunglasses, even in the mass of people that poured out of every train door. There was a quality about him that just attracted crowds. Kids kept jumping all over him, like he was really somebody, and the self-proclaimed "Master Blaster" beamed with pride as he

The Master Blaster Returns

autographed each of their T-shirts.

"*Three days,* man, it took us from Mali." He grabbed up Neil in a hammerlock, socking him playfully. "Next time book me a sleeper."

"How was it?" I asked politely.

Brock dumped his backpack onto Neil's shoulders. "A bummer, man. They took our passports before we got to the border. Then we had to get off the train an' get them back from the police. Man, I was shakin'."

"Why?" I asked. "You got something to hide?"

Instead of an answer, Brock was gone again, ducking and weaving back through the crowds like a prizefighter. "Forgot somethin'. Be right back!"

Neil, scared Brock might be trying to score some drugs, motioned for me to follow him.

"You serious?"

Neil flipped one of his silver dollars in the air. "Tails, I don't go. Heads, you do go."

"The problem with you, Neil, is that you're always clowning

around, and no one knows when to believe you or not." I snatched the coin out of the air and pocketed it. "Thanks for the tip."

I started off after Brock who, tired as he was, climbed all the way back up the train station stairs. The street kids with the T-shirts had scattered, leaving one little kid with hair shaved down skin close looking real disappointed.

Hiding behind a gum machine, I watched as Brock walked over to the boy. He knelt down and pulled the kid's raggedy T-shirt off, struggling with it up over his skinny arms, exposing a belly of bony brown ribs. Then he pulled his own T-shirt off and helped the boy into it, giving him a big hug and a kiss on the cheek.

"What happened to your T-shirt?" I asked coolly when he got back downstairs.

"Got too damn hot."

"Uh-huh," I nodded, watching the little boy scramble excitedly down the stairs after Brock. "That was nice of you."

"Let's just say I dig kids." He strode past me angrily. "He reminded me of someone, OK?"

"Who?"

"Some kid I once knew . . ."

"Your brother?"

Brock froze up suddenly, like I'd just cut open some old wound.

"Neil told me about your brother."

"Yeah, so what did Neil say?"

"Just that you loved him a lot . . ."

Brock wouldn't say anything more until we got clear of the police. Then he dug into his flight jacket, pulled out something he smuggled in all folded up in newspaper, and handed it to me. I unwrapped it skeptically. Inside was a bracelet just like the one Aiche wore, linked together with beautiful, shiny, silver coins.

"What is this — a bribe?"

"Advance payment." Brock hooked his arm around me as we walked to the cab stand.

"For what?"

"For what you're gonna give me when I tell you what else I got you."

I couldn't tell if Brock was being straight with me, cool or kind. Then he leaned over and whispered in my ear. "I got you the interview."

"With Ras!" I applauded. "When?"

He shrugged, looking away evasively. "When I say . . .You just be ready with your questions."

When I got back to my room, I unwrapped the bracelet again from the rolled up newsprint. Its silver coins dangled down, jangling, flashing like tiny musical chimes. . . flashing back . . . to me packing up my dad's stuff; his *"scraps,"* leftovers from the one back room my mother allowed him to use for his hobby . . .

Scraps . . . Pieces of people left behind. Half finished. A man half chiseled from rock. Models two feet long for grand ideas that never got off the ground.

"Dad, if you were God, we'd still be on day one of the Creation." I wrap the statue up carefully in newspaper. "What's this one?"

"That one's for you," he grins, stowing it away inside my book-bag. Then he sits me down and gets that serious look he puts on. I'm trying to hear the words, but his face is getting all blurry.

"Burnie, that I don't see you . . . doesn't mean I don't love you. Hey, hey Goldilocks," he wipes my eyes gently with his paint rag, and I sneeze.

I'm waiting for him to say something — anything. Late nights, I replay the whole scene over and over, looking at the picture I got of him in my wallet. But all I can remember is him putting my hand to his face . . . I can still feel that grizzled cheek of his on my palm, sticky and sweet from aftershave. Then his lips, moist on my forehead.

"I love you, emerald eyes — don't you ever forget that."

Then . . . he turned his back on me. Like Patrick, when I tried to get too close to him. Like God, when I prayed for him to save my friend.

"OK little darlin', you're on." A voice startled me, Brock's.

Before he had a chance to get too far into my room, I grabbed up a handful of blank cassettes and followed him out.

"Look, *you* don't say nothin'. OK . . . ?" he ordered, as we strode briskly down the hallway to Ras' room.

"Who's doing the interview — *me* or *you?*"

"*I'll* ask the questions first, alright?" Brock shot a warning glance at me. "Then, once we get rollin', you follow."

The big bodyguard who'd been stationed outside Ras' room since we checked in was gone. Brock knocked twice on the door. Dead silence. *I* knocked twice on the door. Dead silence. We looked at each other, not knowing what to do.

"Hey, open up man." Brock started banging on the door. It swayed open, creaking . . . Did he leave it unlocked? I followed Brock inside, frightened at what we might find.

The room looked like it had been ransacked. Drawers were pulled out and half emptied. Leftover sandwiches and magazines were strewn about. Across the couch, under a pile of blankets and clothes something lay in a huddled lump. A body.

"Ras . . . ?" Brock whispered hoarsely, moving towards the couch. As he reached out his hand to shake the unmoving figure — two bloodshot eyes gazed up at us over the covers.

"That blood clot, he shoot me in the ribs." Ras groaned, clutching his side.

"What're you talkin' about?" Brock eased him up, frightened.

"It's this dream I got. Come from long time ago in Kingston, when they gunned down Marley." The old man sat up on one elbow and squinted around the room for the first time. "Damn fool Cleavon leave the door unlocked?"

"Some bodyguard you got," Brock chuckled, seeing he was OK. "Hey, it's after one o'clock, man, in the afternoon. Tour bus be leavin' in an hour."

"No problem, no problem. I get I-spirit up an' go." The old man reached over and slipped a cassette into his box. Out poured some weird church music, a little tinkling piano, almost like Sunday School.

"Mornin' prayer," Ras mumbled, pulling on some lime green

socks, "Very *im-port-ant.*" Then he unfolded a rubberbanded enve-lope and laced together a new spliff.

Ras didn't so much roll it, as he packed it — heaping leaves, seeds, flowers and buds into a humongous paper hoagie. He struck the match, and a miniature bonfire erupted in front of his nose.

"Get *back* . . . Get back Yah Rastafari!" he laughed, startling himself awake for a second by the blaze. Ras had to be the most stoned-out rapper in the world. He could out-rap the best, and would lay a morning sermon on you for the least reason.

"Yaaz monnn . . . in the beginning there is the Imperial-I, Haille Sellaisse-I. Then come the I-and-I which we call *all* Rasta brethren —" he chuckled, pointing the spliff directly at me. "Includin' *you!*"

I giggled; this big-hearted man could steal your heart with his smile.

"How does it feel being a black Jamaican here in Africa?" As soon as I said it, I could see Brock's eyes roll up in his head. But this time my question got an answer.

"Feel almost like home," Ras chuckled. His bloodshot eyes glazed over, and his head began swaying to some inner beat only he could hear. "All black people dream of the day they go back home. It's the prophecy come round. Marcus Garvey, he tell us — *the time be comin' for all black folk to go back to A-fric-a.*"

"Why *almost* home? What's home?"

He leaned forward, chewing thoughtfully on the spliff, ". . . Ethiopia."

Then he looked over at Brock who was now nervously leafing through sheets of music scoring. "Youngblood, this girl she don't know much 'bout reggae."

For a second I thought I blew the interview. But he just put his hand right on my shoulder, fixing me in his squinted yellowed eyes like he really wanted me to know.

"Young lady from big city, we Rastafari say *Ethiopia* is our home. Haille Sellaisse our God. I-Ras lives only to *kiss* the soil of my homeland!"

I quickly set out my cassette recorder, "So how did reggae get started? Like, where did it come from?"

A scowl darkened Ras Marcus' face. He rose up crossly, towering above me. "Who is this girl? Why you askin' so many questions?"

"For — for the interview?" I stammered, scared.

"I-Ras gives *no* interview," he thundered, wheeling around to unleash his full fury at Brock.

"Hey," Brock backed off, "I didn't know she would be askin' so many questions."

"Boy, you *lie!*" Ras came down on Brock — hard. He was all over him. "You don't tell me about no interview. You tell me you just *deliverin' new scorin'* for my set."

Brock fell into his tugging-at-his-earring thing, shifting his head sideways and not saying anything. Ras was breathing smoke into his face.

"What did you tell this little girl?"

"Nothin' man," Brock lied again. "I just figured that we'd talk a bit, an', uh . . . the girl would get to ask a question or two . . . an' nobody would know the difference."

"Brock you *talk* Rasta, but you ain't got Rasta in your heart." He pushed Brock up against the dresser. "Maybe you bullshit young white girls, but you no bullshit Rasta brethren. I-Ras see *everyt'ing."*

"So what you gonna do, man?" Brock shoved Ras off.

"You think you *mean,* boy . . . ?" Ras' eyelids narrowed into two yellowed slits, sharp as razor blades. "But your meanness ain't through and through. It ain't in the *bones* . . . Not yet." He shook Brock, then released him disgustedly. "Not the meanness that you can fall back on, the meanness you need to make t'ings right."

Brock slumped down onto the cot, glaring angrily up at the old man. "I paid my dues, man."

"Just because you some big hero from out o' the streets — don't mean you no hero in my eyes."

"I *told* you man, I've turned Rasta."

"Brock, no way you can just *turn* Rasta. You must *do* the t'ing that Rasta do first. A Rasta-mon have love for *each* person —" he nodded over toward me "— *that* girl got Rasta heart, *right, Rasta-girl?* . . ."

He rested one huge hand gently on my shoulder and grinned that big grin of his down at me, his gold tooth glinting. Then he helped pull Brock up.

"Bring peace. Be lovin' mon. Rasta music bring the spirit of God. Brock, you must become *prophet*. You bring the spirit of Satan and you will become Satan. You dig?"

"I dig." Brock scowled.

"You dig, but you don't like, right?"

"Yeah, man, you're right again." Brock shook his head, finally joining in the old man's laughter.

Ras Marcus stretched his long arms up to the ceiling. His dreadlocks, shaking loose, cascaded down his back like a hundred twisting pythons. "Oh today I-and-I feel so *glorious!* Music be the *healing of the nation*. It be that way from creation!"

I had never seen anyone or anything like him.

After that, I can't explain it, but that whole fight with Brock just broke up everything Ras Marcus was holding back. He really wants Brock's generation to be true to their reggae roots.

He gave me my first exclusive interview!

And told us everything . . . about the early days in the fifties when reggae first started. It was called *mento* back then and was so dirty that the church kept the best *mento* records off the streets.

"I remember them times as a child, listening up late nights to my transistor radio when your music come cruisin' cross the water from New Orleans. Nights when you could reach right up and touch the stars . . . " he closed his eyes tight, drawing in a full minute's worth off the spliff as if he could put himself back there — back into a time when the choices of the streets were clear and a new beat called reggae was being born.

"The sweet sounds of Otis Redding, Sam Cooke, Fats Domino, Ben E. King came blowin' across the cool waters to us kids in Jamaica. Come Saturday night, everybody be dancin' out in the market . . ."

That's when the sound systems of legend were born, he told us. The baddest speakers he could borrow were stacked up in his truck with a dozen turntables and a pile of hot platters fresh in from Miami.

"Yes-ss, Jackie Ryan, he was the best. This mon, he built himself a two-track studio in Kingston — *Black Jack's* on Bay Street, I was a country boy fresh off the bus from Alligator Pond, scrapin' by in the streets with Jimmy Cliff an' those other nasty rude boys . . . "

Ras Marcus had chewed the spliff into a sooty, soggy, yellowed mess — and he now handed it over to me . . . I knew I couldn't refuse it and still get the interview.

"You ever hear of Chris Blackwell?" Ras nodded, watching me trying to get a good fingerhold on the wet butt.

"No." I said cool as I could, faking in a quick puff, not letting it touch my lips. Then I broke out coughing. I must have turned beet red, 'cause even Brock was cracking up.

"White Jamaican boy, right?" Brock chimed in, trying to regain some of his lost prestige. Produced that *ska* tune 'My Boy Lollipop'."

I quickly passed what was left of the soggy spliff over to Brock, whose condition for staying on the tour was that he 'stay clean.' He waved his hand no — sticking *me* with it. "Ras, what does it mean, reggae?"

"Reggae? . . . " Ras paused to dip a corncob pipe into a plastic baggie of Moroccan 'kif' that he produced miraculously from his camouflage trousers. "Reggae mean born from the people. Right out of the ghetto, you know? *Regular* people who ain't got nothin' and don't know nothing' but pain. Write that down girl — 'regular', that's reggae. Mon, its ragged."

"Rude Boys, right?" Brock chuckled.

"Yess-ss, Brock, I was once one of them Rude Boys," Ras puffed on his pipe, mischieviously. "You could say we 'redefined' the meanin' of street life."

The old man bent over stiffly and pulled some faded yellow papers from his beat up canvas bag. Brock and I, we both sat there looking at each other, wondering what was coming next. Then Ras Marcus began to toss them, one after another, toward us.

"Scrapbook!" Brock picked through the yellowed newspaper clippings. I knelt on the floor next to him as he unfolded an old creased photograph. There they were — Ras Marcus, Bob Marley and Peter Tosh in their Black Power berets. Another photo was with a young Paul Simon. Still another alongside a kid named Johnny Nash.

"Yeah, *scraps* . . . " Ras muttered, drifting off for a moment behind a tired haze of smoke, "That's my life you got there in your hands. Just *scraps* . . . pieces o' things."

"Damn, you lookin' nasty here, " Brock shook his head.

"Yeah, everybody tryin' to be the baddest lookin' Rude Boy on the block!" he cackled gleefully, chomping the pipe from one side of his bearded lips to the other, clacking it in his teeth. "Purse snatchin'. Playin' with dem German ratchit knives. Hoppin' the trolly."

Ras came alive again, his shoulders rocking as his voice fell into its old rhythms. He started to sing. Actually it's more of a rasping sound that he makes, starting low and hollow in his guts, then rattling up through his ribs. "Yas-ss, only *two* roads out of shantytown for a Rudie like me — a hit record, or bein' hit by a cop's bullet!"

"Brock, help me with dis t'ing," the old man got down on his knees, tugging at something. Out from under Ras' cot, we pulled three drums made from rum kegs. Each had membranes of goatskin.

"Oh man, MacB, lookit!" Brock's face lit up like a kid's at Christmas time. "This is the real thing, huh?"

"Brock, this is the *real* Rastafarian burra drum, used only in Trenchtown. Here, listen . . ." One hand let fly a rat-a-tat with the stick. The heel of his other hand hopped from one drum to another smooth as a butterfly.

It was magic watching the two of them together. Brock, who had no father, now like a little kid beside his big Daddy, soaking up all his years and challenging the old master. Ras, who had no kids, showing off his drumming, his dreadlocks swinging down rhythmically.

"Roots reggae is a heartbeat . . . you dig?" Ras winked. *"It swell up and hypnotize you."*

"Kinda like a two-four beat riff, right?" Brock picked up the sticks and laid it down as best he could.

"No, mon!" Ras snatched back the sticks. "You do it like this —"

"OK! OK!" Brock tried again to prove himself.

The old master just watched, shaking his head knowingly.

Something had happened between them. Ras had taken on this Rude Boy from Harlem like a son, a son that could blow a sax as sweet and as sad and as reckless as he was.

"Brock, I see the finest rock an' roll stars, best jazz drummers in the world, come down to our island — but they cannot master reggae time."

"Yeah, well . . . " Brock chuckled, flashing his trademark grin, ". . . you know they just ain't got the heart of Brock James!"

senegal

6

"*The House of Slaves*"

I AM I NOT A MAN AND A BROTHER?

GOREE ISLAND, Tuesday, June 7th

RAINE AND I were waiting for Brock under this street sign where we're supposed to meet, '*Bateaux d'Ile de Goree.*' Ras invited us to go with him on his day off to some island. *Why* an island, he wouldn't say.

"MacB, you're right." Raine sighed, gazing at the Polaroid I took of her Motorscooter Kid.

"Right about what?"

"That's *not* him. My dream boy doesn't smoke."

At three o'clock, Ras came huffing and puffing from across the street. Still no Brock. The ferry boat was about to leave — in *fifteen* minutes. So we started to hike all the way down the noisy pier, crowded with tourist ships in from France.

"So why'd you leave home and go to Kingston?" I asked him, stalling for time and wondering how Brock would find us.

"What's a mon to do with 'is life? . . . Cut sugar cane? Slave in a banana field? . . ." Ras chuckled, hurrying us through the crowd of tourists to buy us tickets. "So I go to West Kingston. Every*day* po-li-ti-cal violence. Harrass the poor people, the chil'ren. One night, I see them pull this woman straight out of her *own house*, an' search her, make her take off all her clothes front of everyone. I-Ras try to stop it, an' get my first night in jail . . ."

I waited out on the dock for Brock until the last minute, checking my watch, playing with the bracelet he gave me, its silver coins jangling down like chimes. Why am I looking out for this guy? He could be a really great musician, if he wasn't so busy strutting around with his biceps bulging out like Popeye.

Just as the boat blasted its final whistle, Brock showed up, shouldering his gleaming gold saxophone and casually munching on a bagful of kola nuts.

"Sorry I'm late, but . . ."

"You were supposed to meet me under the street sign."

"Sorry, I . . . forgot."

"How could you forget?"

"Look, I *forgot.* That's it, OK?" He shifted his sax defiantly, tucking it under his big arm for protection. Then climbed onto the ferry. It was a lumbering three-decker, freshly painted. Raine jumped on me, squealing excitedly as we jerked free from the land . . . and headed out to sea.

Chic beach umbrellas strung along the shore like multi-colored pearls. A lone windsurfer bobbed about, waving at us as we churned past. Groaning and creaking, our old boat turned to face the open ocean.

The wind hit us full force, splashing spray across the bow. We found Ras Marcus alone, leaning over the old wood railing, his dreadlocks whipping back in the wind like a shredded flag.

"It's like meetin' a livin' legend for me, man." Brock eased in on the rail, all starry-eyed to be alongside his hero. *"You* are a piece of history."

"That's right, mon," Ras chuckled sadly, his words almost lost in the crashing waves. "They carvin' my face right now up on Mount

Rushmore. Dreadlocks soon be hangin' down all over them South Dakota cowboys!"

Ever since we set foot on board, Ras had become strangely bitter, his face clouded over by some sorrow I couldn't understand. He just stayed there, leaning over the old wood rail, squinting out at the sea.

"Why we goin' to this island anyways?" asked Brock.

"Your people, my people, come from there . . ." his voice trailed off like he was far away someplace else, remembering some other time. We waited for him to say more . . . Finally he did.

"This Island we're goin' to, Goree Island, that's where they collected up all the slaves boun' for America. Kept 'em in prison right there 'til the whites got ready to ship 'em off as cargo . . ." Ras muttered in his raspy voice, ". . . it was the last land most folks would ever see."

As he spoke, the sleek modern skyline of Dakar slipped from view behind us. Ahead, I could see the dark shadow of the *Ile de Goree* rising out of the ocean.

Our boat swung around the island's ragged cliffs. Looming above us was an old fort slaving station. Its rusted canons, still pointing out to the pounding seas, glided silently over our heads as we slid underneath them.

"From here . . . we were put on slave ships. *Twenty million* Africans! The only forced migration in the history of the human race," he hissed, his gold tooth catching the glint of the sun. ". . . all sold into a lifetime of slavery — *Ibo* people from Niger. The mighty *Mandingo* people from the Ivory and Gold Coasts . . ."

Ras turned away from the railing to face us, pulling up his tall, lanky frame and breathing in the salt spray air. *"Three hundred years* the whites occupy my tiny Jamaica. Turn our beautiful island into a sugar factory. English landlords, gettin' rich off our backs. Makin' us sing in slave orchestras at *'Picaninnys Christmas'* . . . You asked me where reggae started . . .?" he looked down at me grimly. "Here, in the hearts of these frighten' slaves huddled in their prisons."

I grabbed onto the rail as our old boat wheezed and churned, backing in alongside a rickety dock. Raine jumped from the bow

*". . . the sleek modern skyline
of Dakar slipped from view
behind us. Ahead, I could
see the dark, rusted cannons
of the Isle de Goree
rising out of the ocean."*

onto the pier. Groups of tourists followed, hopping off excitedly into the heat, readying their cameras.

But I felt a chill come over me as I set foot on shore.

Goree Island looked like a skeleton. Its once brightly pastel-colored stone buildings were now crumbled and scattered apart like broken bones, bleached white by the blistering sun — as if somehow time or the pounding surf could cleanse them of the flesh tortured here.

It was weird, walking through these narrow, gritty sand streets, like I could see Brock and Ras stepping maybe in the same places their great-grandfathers once stepped. Soon we came to a stone house shaped like a boat. It was called the *Maison des Esclaves* — the House of Slaves.

I didn't know whether I should bring Raine in or not, but she wanted to see it, so I bought us tickets. I could feel her little hand clinging tightly to mine as we started down the old stone stairs, down to the dungeons.

We saw small cubicles cut out of stone, and found corroded fittings where the slaves were chained. There was a wood figure someone carved — a man hunched over in a ball with welts all over his body. This was not some wax museum — but the real place where it happened.

Wind rattled through the dank stone walls, blowing a steamy, stale scent through the rubble where blood once ran. I could almost still hear their cries.

It is a memory that will live in my dreams forever.

"They only took the youngest an' the strong," Brock whispered, easing in behind us. "Lots died bein' led in chains out from the forest down to the coast. A baby got too noisy, they'd just pick it up by its tiny feet an' bash its head in on a rock . . ."

Brock's voice cracked with emotion. We stood there silently, the three of us and one stranger — a young black man in a brown suit. He was looking at the same chains as I was. Could he tell that I was an American?

I felt very weird, scared mostly and ashamed. *But I'm only seventeen,* I kept telling myself. *I didn't do this.* But here I was, the only white person in the whole room — and had it not been for Raine squeezing my hand so tightly . . .

She didn't see the difference in me. To her I was like family. Not part of the people who had done this. Not the enemy.

A voice echoed through the corridors. Behind me, I heard the shuffling of feet. Hushed whispers. Half a dozen people filed into the room led by a powerfully built man in uniform.

". . . Some of us became collaborators, our own chiefs. Without them, the slave trade could never have existed. They were seduced by foreign trinkets, liquor . . ." The big man, a Wolof tour guide, showed us a glass case filled with brass buttons and trading stuff. "These chiefs, they became dependent for their power upon raiding other tribes. We waged war on our neighbors — even sold our own women as slaves."

A heavy-set lady with a Pan Am plastic bag clutched tightly under her arm peered into the dungeon next to me. "How many did they capture?"

"We can never know. Fifteen *million* Africans were carted away across the Atlantic Ocean — just in one hundred years. Whole peoples, whole tribes, lost powerful young men and women. The best, our pride, were sold away. Can you imagine? . . ." he turned to those of us who were not huddled by his side, ". . . what it must have been like for the people *left behind?*"

"Germs killed the rest," the heavy-set woman whispered under her breath to her friend.

The guide nodded yes, and she ducked her head away embarrassed, clutching her plastic flight bag. "Famine . . . disorientation . . . *whole societies* destroyed. No one left here to grow food. *This* is why we were left behind in the great industrialization race. Not because we were 'inferior' like they told us."

He strode across the room, sandals clacking on the stone floor, and pulled down some charts. "The Congo was devastated. The white people brought diseases. Smallpox and cholera jumped from tribe to tribe in epidemics. Inside the slave ships, disease ran out of control like a wildfire, killing *half* by the time they reached the New World."

"Can you imagine being led hundreds and hundreds of miles from your home, through forests, far from your family? . . . Seeing your wife and children killed, their bodies mutilated?"

He knelt down and opened an old crusted wood trunk — hoisting out armfuls of chains and rusted handcuffs, passing them around the circle for each of us to hold.

"The little finger-size cuffs were used for the wrists and ankles of children."

I saw Raine cringe when they passed through her hands. Solemnly, the guide crossed the room to stand in front of us. He held up a thick chain anchored to the wall.

"I need a volunteer . . ."

Everyone looked around at everyone else, but no one moved.

"One volunteer, just one . . .

Then I saw someone from in back bravely step forward. It was Brock. Raine and I watched silently as he climbed down into the dungeon.

"Down. Kneel down," the guide signalled.

Brock got on his knees, hugging his own body up into a ball, while the guide slowly wrapped the heavy chain around his ankles.

"It was stopped by this . . ." he held up a sharp, horrible spike to Brock's face. "It would be driven through the foot of any slave that tried to escape." Then the guide wrapped the rest of the chain around Brock's broad back, fastening the end to a neck collar.

"Why are they doing this?" little Raine whispered up at me, squeezing my hand, frightened. I was scared too, still the only white person in the room.

"To show people how mean we can be to each other. So that we won't hurt people anymore, or use them."

"Can we go now?" she tugged at me.

As she said it, I felt a cold chunk of crusted metal pass into my hand. It was a rusted iron ring. If you protested too much, your lips were pulled out and a nail was hammered through them. This ring was then *inserted* through the hole in your lips — and you could be pulled about like a dog. *Itenu* it was called, which means "shut your mouth."

"Yes . . ." I whispered to Raine, ". . . we can go."

I hadn't realized till then that Ras was missing. When I finally found him, he was standing in the far corner of the museum, alone. Staring darkly at a framed drawing on the wall, he didn't even hear me come up behind him. He was gone again, somewhere else . . . humming a slow song, low like a heartbeat . . .

"When I remember the crack of the whip — my blood runs cold. On the slave ship — they brutalized my very soul."

"Marley, right?"

He nodded silently, still staring at the drawing.

It was a slave ship etched in ink — showing all the places where the bodies were stowed. Hundreds and hundreds crammed into every nook and cranny of the boat. I tried to picture what it would be like, trapped inside with people dying all around me . . .

Suddenly, Ras turned and looked down at me. For a second it felt like I was staring straight into his soul. As if I could see in him all the pain and suffering he'd just taken from those people on that ship — and here was I, a "white girl," the "enemy" as Brock had told me.

But those yellowed eyes of his became soft and wet as he looked at me for a long, long while.

"Oh girl, so much sufferin' we have done, you an' I . . ." He sighed, turned . . . and just walked away.

Afterwards, we wandered silently down the sandy windswept streets, past the old slave quarters. The narrow paths were crowded with pastel houses, each peeling a different color of paint — peach, apricot, lime . . .

"It's Miller Time!" Brock proclaimed, tapping out a short string of notes from his saxophone. He made us stop at the *Chez Michou Cafe* behind the museum.

Ras was really down. I had never seen him this way. His dreadlocks fell forward, covering his face like a black shroud, as he hunched over his cup of tea in prayer.

"Dreamin'?" Brock ventured.

"A music man's gotta dream, boy." Ras muttered matter-of-factly. "It come with the territory."

Black Cargo — the Slave Ship

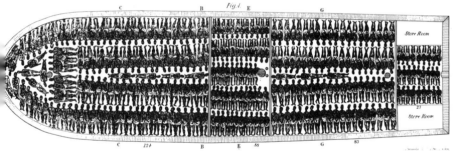

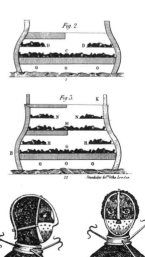

"Yeah, so what's your dream?"

"I told you," he looked at Brock, sizing him up. "You got to learn to *listen,* to hear what other people say. If you can't listen you'll never play reggae."

"To kiss the soil of Ethiopia, right?" I said.

Ras just nodded sadly. "What's your dream, *Mister* Brock?"

Brock looked around at each of us nervously, checking it out to see if it was really safe to say what was in his heart. Then he got all serious, his almond eyes filling with a dreamy look.

"I want to start my own group . . . call it the Rap an' Reggae Review, or maybe the Rap an' Reggae Rockers. I want to find a *sound,* a special sound. Somethin' all my own, that when people listen to it they'll be sayin' . . . 'Hey, that's Brock James — ain't *nobody* else can play that way.' "

"That's why you been talkin' to my drummer, Cleavon?" Ras winked knowingly. "You tryin' to *pirate* 'im away from my band?"

"Hey, we just been, you know, *rehearsin',* throwin' some things together. What's your dream MacB?"

I didn't know what to say to him. Or if I really wanted to get that close to a guy again.

"I know what mine is!" Raine leapt up excitedly, almost over-turning her bowl of sugared ice. "I want a *boy.*"

"Aren't you a little young?" Brock teased, poking her.

"Not a boy*friend* — a *boy*, stupid." She explained and squeezed my hand. "Like I told MacB. Some kid here I could find my own age, and we'd be *buddies* — for *life!*"

"What about your mom? Don't you want her and Marvin to get back together again?"

Raine shrugged it off painfully and disappeared back into her bowl of raspberry ice.

"So what is it for you, MacB — the 'Big M'. Marriage?"

He just doesn't know me at all. Not even my dreams. "I don't know . . ." I mumbled, "I just want to get on to the refugee camp, do some work there."

Brock gave me one of his looks, "You know, MacB, you're noble — terminally."

100

"What's that supposed to mean — *terminally* noble?"

"Terminally, like in *you're dead.* When you're noble, you're dead."

I didn't like what he was getting at — so I did what I always do when I get real irritated. I closed down.

"You love people when they're at a *safe distance.* The *'poor* people in Africa,' the *'poor* people in India' . . . Not *real* people. People close up to you."

"You mean like *you?"*

"Yeah, for one. You got all these big ideas 'bout *what I am* — and you don't even know Brock James. *You don't know me."*

I didn't want to hear it. He was getting too close to the truth. Much too close.

"What about friends?"

"I got friends," I said defensively.

"Ones who know you? Or just ones to hang with?"

"Look, I don't need you to tell me about friends, OK?" I got up from the table, taking Raine with me.

Friends. I had the dearest one you could ever have. He gave his life for me . . .

I shuddered, tying the scarf up over my hair. The wind was really blowing up now on the ferryboat ride back. It had been a long afternoon for us all. We'd collided with our pasts and our pain and, somehow, through it all, became a lot closer. I wanted to go to Ras and thank him for that look he gave me, how he took me deep into his feelings . . . But any words would have just made it smaller.

senegal

7

"See The Girl With The Red Dress On"

DAKAR, Tuesday, June 7th, 9:30 P.M.

WHEN WE got back to the hotel, Shakespeare was waiting for me in the lobby with some letters from the United States. The first was from my mom. It boiled down to two things: One — why don't you write? Two — how are you?

I AM WITH CHILD, I scrawled across the Polaroid of me and Raine on the camel and stuck it in an envelope. The other letter I was still too scared to open.

"Who's it from? Who's it from?" Raine's little hands tore at it.

"No one." I sank glumly against the lobby wall, reading it. It was from Teen Time; my article had been rejected . . .

NOT WHAT OUR READERS ARE INTERESTED IN. FOCUS MORE ON THE PERSONAL LIFESTYLES OF THE ROCK STARS. *THEIR* IMPRESSIONS OF AFRICA, *NOT YOUR OWN.*

Shakespeare and I had spent four whole hours writing out the story about his grandfather, only to have it penciled over with red marks.

"They'll publish the interview I did with Shana *if* I rewrite it." I said, showing Shakespeare the letter. "But stories about students like you, they call a 'waste of time.'"

"So . . . just give them what they want," shrugged Brock, kicking his combat boots up onto a chair.

"What they want are 'juicy tidbits' about Shana as a rock star —not about the work she's doing here."

"Girl, you're tryin' to 'save the world,' and you can't even get an article published," he snickered as I left.

Shakespeare snuck Lenny's portable computer into my room and we started to type the whole thing out again — corrections and all. Reaching over to turn on the printer, his hand accidentally touched mine.

"Sorry," he pulled away fast, embarrassed, and pretended to be fixing some wires in back. "You know, he likes you."

"Brock?" I laughed. "He's got some funny ways of showing it."

"He's always talking about you."

"Shakespeare, just because someone talks about you, doesn't mean he likes you." I flipped through my notes, thinking it over. "I don't sing. I'm not built like the girls he likes . . . *what* does he like about me?"

"What are you going to write?"

"Shakespeare, I asked you a question."

"And I asked you one — what are you going to write about?"

I looked up at this boy, thinking back on his crowded apartment and crippled grandfather. This time he didn't turn his eyes away, studying me carefully to see what I would do.

"I'm not going to stop writing about you, Shakespeare . . . or your family."

Shakespeare looked me over newly as I sat down again to type. "Tell them through *all* Africa, family is strong. You belong. In the tribe there are no widows, no orphans — everyone is looked after."

"What about all that stuff your grandfather told me about

104

other Berbers looking down on you?"

"America doesn't own the copyright on prejudice," he said, adjusting the keyboard for me. "You will find deep loyalty within one tribe, but deep rivalry from one tribe to another . . . It is not just because of a lack of rain some people are starving."

A bitterness crept into his voice and the smooth features of his dark face began to stiffen. "At the University, my schoolmates could be cruel. I may be darker, but I am smarter . . . you shall see."

He sat down, and we started a new article together and called it *Slavery's Child* after Ras's song. It was about what I saw here, what I saw on Goree Island . . . Everything came pouring out of my heart onto the page. About Neil's battle with crack and Brock's going to Africa to pull his life together. How frightened he looked when he knelt down in the dungeon . . . and let that guard wrap him in chains.

"There!" I tore off the printout with a satisfied grin. "Let them send *this one back*." Shakespeare got up to shut off Lenny's computer and I stopped him, "Shakespeare, *what* does Brock say about me?"

"He says you have *spunk*. You stand up to him. You don't put up with his guff."

"Spunk, huh? . . ."

I stuffed the article in an envelope along with a postcard I got at the slave station. "What if they stop sending me money? I'll have to go home."

"You want to be a reporter — not a liar, right?"

Brock was still in the lobby when we went down to mail it, drumming his fingers and shaking his head at me as if I was crazy. I handed him the article, and he read it over grudgingly. He wouldn't say it, but secretly I think he was proud.

"You're good with words alright. But words ain't people."

"Maybe you should stick your neck out too."

"Every time I do, you slap my face," he scowled. "Like I say, girl, you're terminally noble. You send them this, they're gonna send it right back to you — along with a little pink slip saying 'you're fired.' "

"That's better than lying."

"You got to start to look out for number one first." Hoisting his sax case onto his shoulder, Brock backed out the lobby door. "You start tellin' Americans the truth about what you see here in Africa — an' you'll either go home broke, or broken-hearted."

Kitabu Diary, 3 a.m.

Sitting in my bathroom, writing with the light bulb on.

Can't sleep. Seeing Ras' face crying and Brock in chains in the slave quarters. Listening to my roommate hum in her sleep, little weird hymn-things.

We sleep three to a room now that Aiche and Sale are gone. One singer from the group Tarot I hardly see because she's always rehearsing. And this other one I don't know. A new girl we just picked up here in Senegal. Veronique something; French, I think.

She sleeps with a plastic cross over her bed. Jesus with drops of blood painted on his wrists. Underneath she's got a red candle that's been burning all night, filling our room with the stink of musk.

Our talk so far has been confined to details: her job doing make-up on the tour, where to store stuff. She's so secretive about her life . . .

I got up to blow out her incense candle but didn't have the heart, watching her all balled up in her sleeping bag, a mysterious Mona Lisa lipstick smile painted on her pale face. Who was she?

Hidden tucked inside a fashion magazine, I found her sketch-book . . .

> IF YOU ASK ME WHAT I CAME TO DO IN THE WORLD
> AS AN ARTIST, I WILL ANSWER YOU: "I CAME TO
> LIVE OUT LOUD."   — *Emil Zola*

That's what it said on the cover. Inside I found a secret world to this frail girl I would never have guessed existed. Face after face

106

looked out at me from each page, each executed with bold simplicity — a few daring strokes of black ink, filled in with the radiant splashes of her watercolors.

Where all I'd seen was the *strangeness* of peoples' faces, nose rings, tattoos, she was seeing the *beauty* within them . . . the play of light on a thinly veiled face, the grace of a Berber's smile.

Maybe what Brock said about me making real friends was true . . . people right next to me that I don't know how to love.

Wednesday Morning, June 8th

Paris in Africa! That's what Dakar is. I'd invited the Singing Nun to go shopping with Shana and me, and she trotted along, lugging her wood paint box.

"I know a designer here. I have arranged everything. *Everything!*" Veronique hurried us up a tree-lined boulevard rimmed with sidewalk cafes. Young street artists chased after us, shouldering sentimental paintings of fishing boats.

"I have been doing the same thing," she pulled us away, embarrassed, "to support myself as an African student in Paris."

Veronique's mother, it turns out, is French Catholic. Her father is Muslim — a spiritual schizophrenia that's left her soul divided and her life, now, at a crossroads.

"So you're half African?" asked Raine. "Your skin is so light."

"I am Sengalese, born just a few kilometers from here. My mother came here from Paris, married a local jeweler. Then —" her voice broke off, ashamed. She wouldn't tell us much more about her past. Just that after her father ran out on them, her mother took her back to France.

Another fractured soul . . . so painfully shy.

"Voila!" she gave me a small smile, opening a mirrored door, "La boutique *Chic et Unique."*

She led us under a waterfall through rock cave walls dripping with vines of gold jewelry. Then we crossed over a footbridge past racks and racks of Parisian dresses.

Paris in Africa — Dakar!

*". . . outside the Mosque, we had to
wash our hands and feet."*

The girls get down

*Ramona, me, Veronique "the singing nun,"
Ayoko (on the oud) and Buchi Shavi*

". . . why can't I keep my mouth shut in photos?"

*"Veronique's mom is French Catholic;
her father, Muslim — a spiritual schizophrenia
that's left her soul divided and her life, now,
at a crossroads . . ."*

"Allo?. . . " the clothes designer sang out, recognizing Shana at once, even with her disguise. Madame Michelle insisted on closing her shop for the occasion. All her salesgirls gathered around the rock star, giggling shyly.

Veronique found a burgundy chiffon dress for Shana that clung tightly to her sleek legs. Then she wound a pink turban around Shana's forehead, offsetting her high cheekbones and burning gold skin.

"L'Afrique la chic!" she grinned gleefully. "Perfect for your Press Conference, yes?"

Now it was Shana's turn to work on Veronique. The girl was wearing a plain artist's rag that could generously be called a smock. A beige nothing of bleached-out color, with eeney-beeny pink flowers spotted all over it. She looked like a reject from a Laura Ashley catalog.

First Shana made her let her hair down. That, in itself, was a revelation. Long, luxurious black hair cascaded over my roommate's soft, pale shoulders. Mascara made her soulful brown eyes deepen into dark mysterious pools. But the red silk dress — that lit the fire!

"See the girl with the red dress on . . ." Shana giggled, lacing the strings up her back.

Veronique stood in front of the mirror like she was stark naked. Shoulders hunched forward to hide her breasts. Hands moved awkwardly back and front, trying to cover what was already covered.

"Relax honey," Shana smiled, enjoying her handiwork. "This is my treat."

Veronique couldn't wait to get out of that red dress. She tucked the gift away guiltily into her schoolbag, smiling gratefully —afraid, maybe, of what she saw in herself.

"You have a husband, yes?" Madame asked, eyeing Shana as she patiently autographed a magazine with her picture on the cover for a salesgirl.

"Sometimes . . ." was all Shana said, kind of sadly. "He . . . wanders."

"Quel dommage," the lady shook her head knowingly. "I cannot, even for a second, allow my husband's eyes to wander. We have

113

very — how shall I say *modern* women here in Dakar. *Tres independant.* Women doctors. Woman professors. How could I share my husband with another woman?"

Once we got outside, Shana squeezed Veronique's hand, thanking her and inviting her to continue on our tour as her personal stylist.

"Certainment, of course I love to come, but . . ." Veronique paused, flattered, yet still frightened. ". . . first I should consult my *marabout."*

"What kind of boot?" asked Raine.

"Marabout . . . how shall I say it? He is like a voice to God, a Holy man, *tu comprends?"* Veronique cocked her head down at Raine. "You see, I am raised Catholic not to believe in these things. But as a little girl here in Senegal, my father always took me to see him. It would be wise for you to get his blessings too, yes? For your tour? Bad luck to move about in my country without first receiving the blessing of your *marabout."*

Shana wasn't saying anything. Meanwhile Veronique was lugging her wood paint box up the street, loaded down with an armful of our dress boxes.

"Bon," she exclaimed with finality, striding out to hail a taxi. "Then it is decided. We go *tous ensemble,* all together, yes?"

What were we getting into? . . . A stern-looking official cleared us a way through the crowds waiting to get inside the emerald green mosque, then led us through two heavily guarded gates, down a whitewashed hallway . . . and stopped us outside a low, elaborately carved door. As I peeked in, I could just make out a dimly lit room crammed full of devotees kneeling on the wood floor.

"Shhh! . . . " my roommate put one finger to her lips. "You must take off all your footwear. Sneakers. Sandals. Sit *absolutely* still, yes? And when he receives you, do not make any . . . sudden move toward him."

I filed in after her, head lowered, and stuck close to Shana. There, inside a cubical behind bars of wood, sat a simple old man wrapped in a robe of indigo blue.

His eyes were sharp, watching each supplicant push their gifts in to him through the wood bars. One brought a favorite rooster. Another, a ceramic pot.

"Shakespeare told me, in Islam, no one stands between you and God."

"This is true," she stammered. "But here in this part of Africa we have holy men, secret brotherhoods."

Before I knew what was happening, Veronique was tapping my shoulder. *"He will receive you now."*

"Go on," Shana nodded to me.

My heart started to beat nervously. We moved up the line. Then, we were face to face.

I quickly pushed my hand through the bars, holding out the most precious stuff I had with me, the photos I'd taken. The *marabout* put them down without ever looking at one of them. Instead, he just held me in his sharp eyes, muttered a quick prayer and spit into the cupped hand of a disciple.

"So . . . ?" Shana whispered as soon as we were moved away.

Veronique, trying her best to look cheerful, couldn't hide the fact that something was bothering her. "You will have, how shall I say — *problems?"*

"What kind of problems?" Shana raised her sunglasses, alarmed.

Veronique frowned. "This he did not say. There are people who want to hurt you."

"Hurt *me* . . . or our Tour?"

She squeezed Shana's hand, clutching it worriedly to her heart. "I hope you will find what you are truly looking for, *mon amie."*

PRESS CONFERENCE, Hotel Senghor, Thursday, 6:00 A.M.

Shana Lee, wrapped in the burgundy chiffon dress we got her, stood nervously by the conference room door, ushering in the half dozen news reporters. Not as many as we'd hoped for, but Marvin Knight strode determinedly onto the stage, stripped bare of the usual flashy 'Knight Crusader' jewelry he wore in his act. Dabbing the

115

sweat off his brow, he fiddled with his notes on the podium.

"It's about time you boys showed up," he glared at the scattered group. "What you are about to see is reality . . . and reality isn't always pretty to see. So, if you're here just for pretty pictures of the stars — now is the time to leave the room."

A hush fell over everyone. I looked around and spotted Brock trying to hand out 8 x 10 glossies of the new group he was putting together. Behind me, two reporters from the British rock magazine *Downbeat* shifted in their metal chairs uncomfortably. But no one walked out.

Marvin nodded to Shakespeare in the back who shut down the lights. From the darkened stage, twin TV monitors now glowed like giant eyes, staring us down with their ruthless truth.

"This is it. The refugee camp we're raising money for in Sudan — *Kassala.*"

TV SCREENS

CLOSE UP: a boy's skeletal hand clutches at a dried out, shriveled breast. His mother's tired head raises barely one inch, but just high enough to glare defiantly at the CAMERA.

TRACKING SHOT (hand held): moving through rows and rows of WOMEN and CHILDREN squatting inside the makeshift tent of a ward. We burst outside into the blinding light of the REFUGEE CAMP. Stretching to the horizon, ramshackle SHELTERS lay scattered across the dusty desert.

PULL FOCUS TO: Shana alongside a young mother who still pokes at the lips of her dead little girl, trying to give her something to drink.

"This was taken on our first trip last October, when the famine was first filmed by Mohamed Amin for the BBC. Now it is June, *eight* months later, and still *no one in America knows what's going on.*"

One of the men from *Downbeat* now got up to leave, a little bald man with a gold earring, "You've been writing us press releases about this for months."

"And you haven't printed one of them in months."

"These people are *still* going to be starving — long after your road show is through."

"...thousands sat out on the hillside in the blistering sun, with nothing to shelter them but the one piece of clothing they wore to escape..."

Checking his anger, Marvin stepped down off the stage. "And you? . . . Do you know tens of thousands of Ethiopian refugees are pouring across the border — a *day!*" he glowered at the reporter. "We saw this famine coming for *three years.* I've written relief agencies in London, Paris, Washington, Moscow. *No one* is responding. No one wants to hear."

"What about the money you got from A.I.D.? *Two* million."

"Too little, too late. This famine has now spread south all along the Sahara and clear across Africa. *Ten* million people in twenty countries face starvation — right now, today, while you stand here arguing. Open your eyes. Look . . ." he signaled Shakespeare to start the video mixer . . . and a series of harrowing images flashed on the twin TV screens.

TV SCREEN, Stage Left	*TV SCREEN, Stage Right*
TRACKING SHOT (hand held): Shana stoops to help a WOMAN scrape at the dried out earth. A trickle of MUDDIED, BUG-INFESTED WATER oozes out. Careful not to spill a drop, the woman fills her rusted CAN.	CLOSE UP: a little GIRL, her belly blown full with hunger, squats by a mound of camel dung, her tiny fingers picking out UNDIGESTED SEEDS and shoving them into her parched lips.

"You really believe that music can save lives?" challenged the little man.

"No," Marvin hopped off the darkened stage to face him. "But these concerts, with your help, will grab us the headlines. It's the *video* that's going to show what's really going on — in Ethiopia, here in Senegal, and all across Africa."

"We're going to be filming farms our tour has subsidized. We're going to Nigeria where Shana, my ex-wife, will be holding an Art Show to raise money. And we're going down into South Africa, if we can." Marvin climbed excitedly back onto the blackened stage. His towering figure loomed over us as he strode back and forth, blocking the images which still flickered from the TV screens.

"We're going to *every major city in Africa* — communist, socialist, democratic — don't make no difference so long as they let us in.

We're going to talk to presidents about this famine. Prime ministers. Local businessmen. Anyone who will listen to what we got to say. And if we raise enough money, we're going to hold *a concert to end all concerts.* Broadcast it by satellite — *live,* around the whole world."

"Where will you start?"

"We start where it all began . . ." Marvin grinned mysteriously, finally waving at Shakespeare to turn on the lights, ". . . with our roots."

He strode off the stage and the press hustled after him through the lobby and out onto the street where our *Soul to Soul* tour bus was waiting. Plastered on its side in big block letters was our destination:

ROOTS VILLAGE
"home for blacks who can never know their home"

"We're going back to the actual village where Kinta Kunte was born," Marvin raised a triumphant fist in the air and climbed in. Shutters clicked as the few cameramen fired away. "Hop on the bus kids — we're goin' home."

Shana had given me a choice: fly on ahead with the crew to set up her Art Show in the city of Lagos — or go with her for this video trip through the drought-stricken desert. Stepping on that bus marked the end of my days in modern Africa. No matter what I saw or how I felt, there was no going back now.

"Alright boys . . . " Marvin shouted out the window, waving to the reporters we left behind, " . . . tell folks back in the States we're going home!"

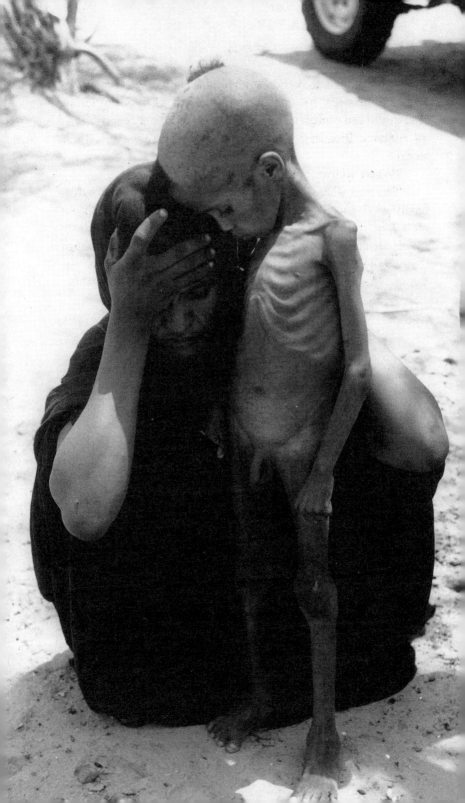

PART THREE

THE RIVER NIGER

"Tell me, why?"

Why, please tell me why?...
Must you sacrifice the innocent
While the guilty ones survive
Its a legacy of heartbreak
Running angry in the streets

Its brother against brother
One child after another
Look on the faces of their mothers
Hear them cry
And tell me, why?...

There's a sickness in our children
Why dream when you won't live long?
You can see it in their faces
You can hear it in their songs
Our countryside's a battlefield
Our children are at war

Its brother against brother
One child after another
Look on the faces of their mother's
Hear them cry...
Tell me why, Lord, tell me why...

words and music by: Steven Guyer

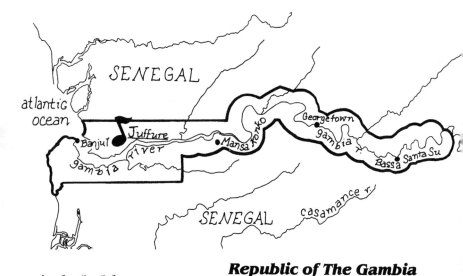

Republic of The Gambia

PEOPLE
Population: 740,000. **Ethnic Groups:** Mandinka (Mandingo) 36.1%, Fula 16.8%, Wolof 13.4%, Jola 9.2%, Serahuli 7.3%, other 1.4%, non-Gambian or not categorized 15.8%. About 85% of the people live in rural areas. **Religions:** Muslim 95%, remainder Christian and traditional beliefs. **Languages:** English (official), Mandinka, Wolof, Fula, other local languages. **Literacy:** 12%. **Infant Mortality:** 217/1,000. **Life Expectancy:** men 32 yrs., women 34 yrs.

GEOGRAPHY
Area: 11,295 sq.km. (4,361 sq.mi.); almost the size of Connecticut. **Capital City:** Banjul (pop. 40,000). *Terrain:* Oddly shaped by colonial rulers, the Gambia is a narrow strip of land only 11 to 32 kilometers wide. It stretches along the Gambia River, surrounded by the Republic of Senegal. Thick mangrove swamps border the lower half of the river, where vegetation rises to 30 meters (100 ft.). Sand hills and rolling savanna plateaus sit back from the river.

GOVERNMENT
Government: Republic. (One of the few African countries with a genuine multiparty system.) **Colonial Power:** England. **Independence:** February 18, 1965.

ECONOMY
Yearly GDP Per Person: $255. **Exports:** Peanut products (89%), palm kernels, fish, hides and skins. The Gambia's economy is almost entirely agricultural (75%) and dependent on groundnuts as its main source of money. Crop diversification is encouraged. Industry consists of peanut products, brewing beer and soft drinks.

HISTORICAL NOTES
This land was once part of the Empire of Ghana and the Kingdom of the Songhais. By the 16th century, Portuguese slave traders and gold seekers had settled along the lower river. Following their sea routes, England and France battled each other to control this area. France took control over Senegal, leaving the British to control the Gambia River throughout the 18th Century. In 1807, the British abolished slave trading throughout their Empire. They tried to end the slave traffic in The Gambia, but were unsuccessful.

TOURIST ATTRACTIONS
Game parks, lagoons, mangrove swamps, ancient "Stone Circle" of pillars (100 ft. high), peanut trading riverboats, Juffure "Roots" village.

gambia

8

"Home Is Where
Your Heart Is"

ON THE ROAD to ROOTS VILLAGE,
Thursday, June 9th

HOME . . . I don't even know what mine would look like or
what country to go back to. I'm part Irish, part Polish, with some
other blood mixed in there, too. The day me and my cousins ever get
together, we can replace the U.N.

Who are you, when there's no place you call home? Who knows
you?. . . You've got to have a home. Someplace you can say: *I am
that.* Hey, *these* are my people. I feel alright around them.

Rattling along on the Soul to Soul bus, I was scribbling this stuff
down in my *Kitabu* diary. . .

6:32 A.M., Road to Roots Village

Bus packed with relief workers and musicians.
Raine loading up on Famous Amos chocolate chip

cookies, pilfered from Lenny's secret stash. Lords of Discipline pick up our spirits. They start singing "Blowing In The Wind".

Everybody is now singing.

Marvin sits next to Shana who moves away from him. Raine tells me they had a fight and aren't talking to each other.

So Marvin starts swapping stories with the crew. Stuff about his grandparents, old tales from the South . . .

Everybody's remembering stuff about their roots. Benjamin, our cameraman, passes a wrist amulet he wears around for everyone to see. Shakespeare says it's definitely Nigerian — Ibo tribe.

Shakespeare was still real nervous when he spoke in front of us, standing stiff in that one blue suit of his, looking over at Lenny to see if he was doing OK. It must've been hard, being African and telling these American superstars what to do.

"Here we have a perfect example of 'colonial design'. . . " he began with his British accent. Hands shaking, he held up the giant map for Lenny. "When you whites carved up Africa for yourselves, you drew the boundaries of nations with no regard for the people living in them who you split up!"

Shakespeare fumbled awkwardly with the map, so I got up to help him. Gambia's definitely a wierd-looking nation. It eats a hole through Senegal's belly like a crooked tapeworm, two hundred miles long — but only twenty miles wide.

"Tribes who were enemies, now find themselves belonging to the *same nation*. A tribe living on the border of two nations is now supposed to be enemies with itself." Finally he got the map steady and wiped his forehead, relieved. *"This* is why we have civil wars. *This* is why nationalism is so hard. People have more loyalty to their own tribe across the border — than to a nation they didn't create!"

**On the road
to Roots
Village . . .**

"*. . . rumbling past forgotten villages . . .*

126

*. . . where what well-water still left
is much too dirty for drinking . . .''*

Kitabu Diary, 9:40 A.M.

*Crossing the Senegal River Valley to Roots Village . . .
Barren ground . . . twisted dead trees where once a green
forest stood.*

*Skulls with long grey horns poke out half-buried from
the dry dust. Carcasses of dead cattle are strewn about. A
group of children pick through their remains for any meat
that may be left.*

*We stare out our windows silently as our bus rumbles
past. It is my first look into the eyes of hunger.*

*Ahead, a group of women swarm around a government
truck, unloading bags of grain. They wave at us.*

*Here, 3,000 miles from Ethiopia, the drought has
touched the lives of these people, too . . .*

"These 'cash crop' programs you foreigners design for us," our
bus driver turned around, suddenly disgusted. "Why don't you talk to
us first?"

Shakespeare went to quiet him, but Lenny stopped him. "Let the
man speak."

"It's what I've been trying to tell you, Mr. Stein." Shakespeare
apologized. "Your project has harmed far more of us than it has
helped."

"That is *crazy!*" Lenny exploded, storming out from behind his
portable P.C. "How can you build a future without development?"

"You see here? . . ." the bus driver pointed out the window,
excited by his chance to be heard. "Look at these women. Most now
die by age *thirty-five.* Your Program Director hired only men to work
the peanut fields. So our women must walk *three hours* to raise rice
down in the lowlands where there is so much disease. Because of *your*
need for peanuts — *they no longer grow their own food!*"

10:20, recording live on the banks of the river

*The creature of squiggly slime lies lifeless in the mud-
hole at my feet. A thick tail curls back around stunted limbs,*

"We stare out our windows as our bus driver wheels past. It is our first look into the eyes of hunger . . ."

covered with a hideous grey mucus.

"It's been buried here for two years at least!" Lenny says excitedly, waving the camera crew over from the bus for a closer look. Carefully, a native holds out his goatskin bag and pours some more water into the hole, swishing it around.

At once The Creature comes back to life, begins to breathe . . . and flips over on its back!

"Few of God's creatures survive the drought here. But nature has devised a miraculous way for this lungfish." Lenny rotates the slimey fish in his hands as Big Benj zooms in for a close-up. "See, when the water dries up, it can no longer breathe through its gills — *so it switches over to its* lungs."

10:45 A.M., still recording

This is fifth *"take" of this promo spot Lenny's done. Napoleon couldn't demand more perfection. The poor little lungfish has been in and out of the waterhole half a dozen times. So Raine starts digging up a substitute — in case the worst happens.*

My job is to hold a Coppertone umbrella over the camera lens to keep the sun off. Suddenly Big Benj shoulders his videocam and starts slogging through the marsh, following after Lenny as he crosses to some small fishing huts.

Little kids come out to watch us. We must be a bizarre sight — stumbling off endlessly across the muddy sand, waving the giant Coppertone umbrella.

"For these people of the river delta, Nature devised no such miracles this past year. No way to survive from one harvest to the next. Here, Africa is holding her breath . . . waiting for the next rains to come."

"How're you and that boy doing?" Shana broke into my recording. I looked at her like she was crazy. "Brock . . . the one you were telling me about?"

"I haven't seen him since we had a fight."

"Men are funny, huh . . . Do I look alright?" She turned for me to fix her hair, like my clumsy fingers were really supposed to know how.

What was she up to? . . . Then I saw she was trying to catch Marvin's eye. He strode across the marsh, belly bulging up over his too tight jeans — still half man, half little kid. So I quickly started fumbling with her braids.

"Shana, I'm not an expert at this . . ."

"Just clip it."

I started to, but Shana kept turning her head to see where Marvin was going.

"It's my fault for driving him away. I don't want to chase after him, but I don't want to lose him again either."

"Shana, you don't have to explain it to me."

"Four years it took me to clear myself of Marvin. I was dragging him around with me like a dead body . . ."

Shana kept going on and on, not even noticing that Raine was now helping me with her hair. "Daddy gonna come live with us?"

"We'll see, honey, we'll see." She gave Raine a kiss and finished the braid herself. "Funny, huh? You spend so much time trying to get someone else to love you, when that's a job you've got to do for yourself. Well . . ." she cinched in her belt and let out a woeful sigh, ". . . here I go again. At least this time it's for a good cause."

Raine kept a lookout for her mother, watching as she strolled over in the general direction of her husband.

"You are the miracle," Marvin was smiling that big sincere look of his straight into the lens, and hopefully straight into the hearts of people back home. "What we need are Dollars for Development. *Storage silos* for when the harvest runs out . . . *clean water* to stop the spread of disease . . ."

I'd seen them do this kind of stuff before in the Press Conference. Corny, but it got the point across. What was new was that Lenny and Marvin were not only showing starving people, but the conditions that caused it.

"Dignity, that's what we must show people . . ." Lenny briefed

us, setting up a shot of the fisherman's family, a burly man bobbing about in the river while his family and a boat full of small, curious grandchildren watched from the shore. "These are *not* hopeless people looking for a hand-out, but hardworking men and women. *We* robbed them of their resources, built our civilization on their backs — and now we look the other way."

I'd never gotten a real look at Lenny in action before. He always preferred to hide in the background, letting his megastars grab the spotlight. But the conviction that came from the little guy, came from deep within his guts.

His "lungfish video" would be air-expressed back to the States, pieced together with soul music and flashy titles, then broadcast to pump up interest for 'The Big One,' our world-wide satellite concert in Kenya.

But what would happen to this fisherman's family here, I wondered? It was like we, too, had stolen a piece of them and shipped them away. What would *they* be given back?

"Excuse me," Marvin stopped me from climbing back into the bus. "You're the girl helpin' Ms. Lee out, right?"

No, I wanted to say, I'm a *reporter* — not a babysitter.

"I'm sorry, but I haven't had the chance to meet you before . . ." he extended his hand graciously and said his name like maybe I already didn't know it. *"Marvin, Marvin Knight."*

"MacBurnie . . ." I shook his big hand. This was stupid — why was he being so nice to me?

"Could you tell Ms. Lee that we're going to be flying to Lagos once we get to Gao. I've arranged for a small aircraft. And, uh . . . could you give her this?"

He slipped me a sealed envelope, but I could tell from the half-desperate look he gave me, it had to contain the most sorrowful love letter ever written. If men wore perfume, it would have been soaked in it.

I didn't give it to her until we got back into our seats. They now even *rode* separate — Marvin in the video van with the crew, Shana

133

Lee in the bus with the relief workers.

I tried not to watch as she nervously tore the envelope open. Whatever Marvin said must've hit home — because Shana's whole face sunk in sad-like and she bit her lip.

Then she crumpled it into a ball and threw it under her seat.

I wanted to say something, but didn't know what to say, so I kind of hid away behind a map, letting her alone.

"Where are we? *Where are we?*" Raine grabbed at it.

"We're in the middle of no place," I said, pointing at the thin blue line that hooked into the desert.

We were now *south* of the great Sahara Desert. But what I saw out my window was not on any map. The drought had lashed out all the way from Ethiopia across to Gambia — stretching its broad sandy belt right across the belly of the continent, buckling its people with famine.

NOON!

Outside my window I see a man desperate from the blistering heat, stagger under the weight of his pack. Two women break from the long line of refugees to help him up.

Old people, children have come down to the river as a last resort. But here, even the mighty Senegal river has dried out into a trickle as we roll along.

I catch my first glimpse of refugee camps — little clusters of huts springing up along the big bend of the riverbed.

Then all around us are cattle.

Some guys in blue robes with turbans wound round their heads wade through the huge herds, beating them with their sticks.

Fulani herdsmen.

"The horns are lyre-shaped,
beautiful magical beasts out of some fairy tale.
But, as we drive on, we find
other herdsmen are not so lucky..."

"A family of black-robed Tuaregs — one of the few nomadic tribes left — steps out of the blinding desert sands to tell us of the 'killer drought' that has destroyed their cattle . . ."

3:00 P.M. "A Sea of Bones"

Skulls, horns and ribs jut up from the sand . . . turning the desert into a boneyard.

Grown women come chasing after our van as we barrel on by. These great Tuareg herdsmen who once roamed the Sahara freely for centuries, now sit huddled up in the shade of a health care shack — their beloved cattle all gone.

"Stop here!" Marvin shouts suddenly to the driver. He wheels us bumping off the dusty road. In front of us is a wood shack: POSTE de SANTE

FEEDING STATION

At once, our bus is swarmed with women. One comes right up to my window, touching her fingers to her mouth and smacking her lips, like a mute signing "food, please."

It's a sound that frightens me, this smacking of fingers on parched lips . . . like blowing a last kiss goodbye.

We pass out all our sandwiches and cookies and whatever we've got for the rest of the day. Shana tells me not to touch any of the children's hands because of the cholera.

But I do.

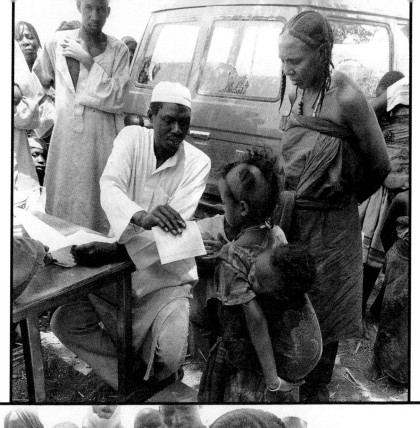

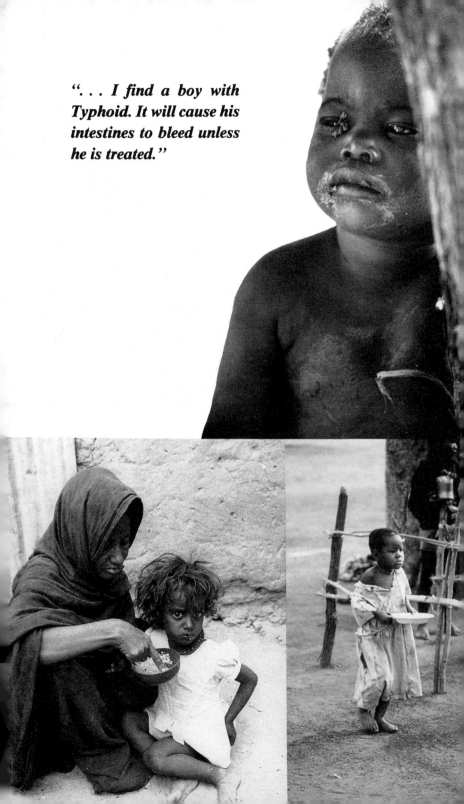

"... I find a boy with Typhoid. It will cause his intestines to bleed unless he is treated."

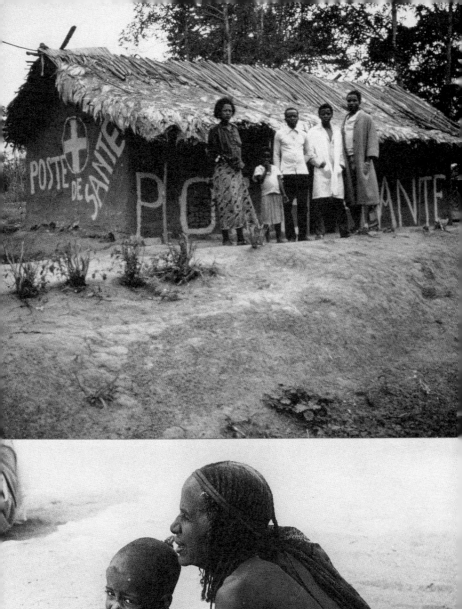

5:00 P.M., nearing Roots Village "... *our bus rumbles into a market town. Two Tuareg guys peddle me some bootlegged cassettes off a bicycle ..."*

*". . . each cassette is positively prehistoric —
so's the local movie."*

"Shakespeare's like a local hero here, cutting off fig
branches for the kids who follow us everywhere, and
helping the guys rope up crates of coconuts . . ."

"Uh . . . Ras, can I ask you something?" I caught up with him, hurriedly setting up my camera. It was so hot; between the insect and sun repellants, my skin felt sticky as flypaper.

"Ask away."

"How did they get that way?"

"Marvin an' Shana?" His face clouded over, watching the two of them head over to the fruit market, not even talking to each other. "When Marvin first took Shana into his act, he had the *name*. He move that girl from chorus to main lady — on stage an' off. But Shana still stood in Marvin's shadow."

Ras eased himself down, laying up against the shady side of the bus with a bottle of soda pop — waiting for Lenny to decide on the next shot. I sprayed my arms and face with more 6/12.

"But she could really sing, right?"

"Like Lady Day . . . Marvin spun out into the *stra-tos-phere*. *Six* gold albums together. Ten top singles on the soul charts in *three years!* The whole country was comin' down with soul fever: Selma, the March on Washington, Black is Beautiful, Black Panthers in the White House . . . " he chuckled to himself, taking a big swig off the sticky orange soda, then tied his locks back behind his neck to cool off. "Black music was turnin' into Knight music an' Marvin, he was seein' stars . . . One of 'em, he turn into his *new lady.*"

"That's what split up the act — a new girl?"

Ras nodded. "They never sang on the same stage since."

I saw a flash of pain pass through his bloodshot eyes while he watched Marvin. Ras, I knew, recorded three cuts on his comeback album and really loved the man.

"Look at him. Beautiful, huh? . . . " he shook a fat tear off his broken nose.

"How does a star like that . . . just die?"

"Whole country died, lost its soul. King killed . . . Kennedy gunned down. Soul music, it died out too. Now Marvin . . . he's got his last chance."

"And Shana? . . . ." I watched her hoist a ripe *guava* melon over her head, showing off her prize to the camera. "She was so young when they split up."

"Shana, she did that Christian number, disappear into the Church an' no one hear much from her for the longest time. You know, when she got the idea for this concert, Marvin was the first artist she called for help?"

"Cause he knows all the money guys?"

"Cause no matter what *anybody* say 'bout Marvin Knight — people respect him," Ras pronounced firmly. "He's a musical genius. Always was, always will be."

"So the Tour was really Shana's idea . . . ?"

"*Yess-ss. . .*" Ras nodded as they got in their separate vans. "It's her baby . . . but now it's his, too. Both of 'em, sink or swim."

6:00 P.M. . . . Roots Village — at last!

The cover of PEOPLE magazine hangs proudly framed over the door of the thatch hut. The photo is of an old Mandinka man's face beaming alongside the author, Alex Haley.

Ten years it took Haley to trace his roots back to this distant village where we now stand . . . a home for African-Americans who can't ever know their real home, whose real names were forever erased from the slave books . . .

But Kunte Kinte is now dead.

His wife, a bent over old lady, leads us out to the same mango tree where she and her husband once got married. Bare-foot kids follow us, pulling on my camera strap.

It's a dusty village . . . Rooftops of corrugated tin, thatch huts, baby goats . . . The old woman shows us the tree. It is bent, creased — looks as old as she does.

African men and American guys from our Tour stand around, staring awkwardly at each other. Big Benj, our cameraman, breaks the ice. He's now really hugging this African lady! Laughing and squeezing her in his big arms. Cameras roll . . . shutters click away. Now everyone wants their own 'Roots photo' alongside of her.

A Mandinka elder crosses over to Marvin and shakes his hand . . . then they, too, hug each other. Marvin is crying.

I feel my own heart crumbling, choking as I watch big tough Brock bend down and kiss the old woman — as if somehow through her, he could get back his own life.

147

Roots Village — at last!

"Cameras roll, shutters fire away as we all huddle around the widow of Kunte Kinte . . ."

*6:00 P.M.
The Music
strikes up! . . .*

"Drums! Flutes! Rattles! All mix together with our guitars — and the dancing starts . . ."

"*Marvin kicks it off, asking a giggling village girl. The elder struts his stuff alongside Shana. Soon everyone's caught up in it. Dancing, laughing . . .*"

*"Bad Boy
puts the
squeeze
on me . . ."*

9:00 P.M.

I look for Ras and find him alone, kneeling patiently by the campfire while some children climb on his back, tugging at his dreadlocks. He spreads out one big bear arm, so I squeeze in.

"Ras . . . ?" I don't really know how to ask him this, "How come you're so nice to me?

He pulls his toasting fork from the flames, thinking for a minute. Then reaches a long, bony finger out and taps me on my nose.

"My nose?"

"Takes courage to walk around like that, right?"

"You ought to know," I laugh, tapping that same half-broken bump up on his. "Welcome home, Ras."

"Home is where your heart is," he mutters sadly. "Ethiopia is a long, long way away. "

Midnight . . .

The campfire was still burning when Brock and Neil stepped out of the black night, looming over us. Ras spread out that grin of his and his gold tooth flashed like a firefly from the dark.

"Why'd you name yourself after Garvey, Ras, to scare people?"

"Little bit o'knowledge a dangerous t'ing," the old man edged closer to the fire, his dreadlocks dangling down dangerously low over the flames. "You know *why* Marcus Garvey was the most feared black mon in America?"

As he spoke, his creased face glowed orange in the black night and seemed to hover disembodied over the spitting flames, hypnotizing us. ". . . One Sunday in church, Marcus Garvey make his prophecy: *'Look to Africa, where a Black King shall be crowned. For the day of deliverance is here . . . ' "* Eyes squinting around at us, Ras made certain we were all listening. Then he raised three fingers, *"Three years later,* a black chief from Ethiopia crown himself Emperor. His new name? Haile Selassie. His old tribe name? . . . *Ras Tafari."*

"Haile Selassie, you see, *is* Ras Tafari. *Right-ful des-cend-dant* of King Solomon himself an' the Queen of Sheba . . ." he intoned, rocking back into one of those trances of his, ". . . King of Kings, Lord of Lords, the Conquering Lion of Judah . . ."

He dug out a small leather book from his camouflage trousers, licked his thumb, and started excitedly flipping through the old worn pages. "You see, New York lady, it is even written here in your Bible. Here — Revelations 5:2,5 . . ."

"Weep not: behold, the Lion of Judah . . . hath prevailed to open the Book, and to loose the Seven Spirits of God sent forth into all the earth."

The Lost Tribes of Isreal . . . did one of them take root in Ethiopia? Was Emperor Haile Selassie this Black King that was prophesied in the Bible? Brock was as stunned as me, sitting in sacred silence as Ras Marcus showed him the yellowed page.

Then, he clapped his Bible shut. Holding up two fingers, he swept his hand in a slow circle around the crowd.

"Only *two t'ings* hold us brethren together — black people can *only* be redeemed by going back to Ethiopia. And Ras Tafari is our living god. *Yes-ss-ss,"* he hissed in that raspy voice, then drifted off somewhere back inside himself. *"Marcus Garvey's words come to pass . . . Marcus Garvey's words come to pass . . ."*

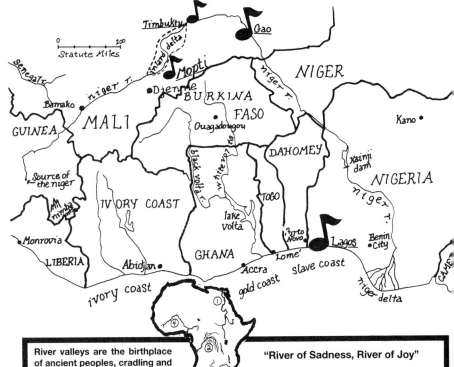

River valleys are the birthplace of ancient peoples, cradling and nurturing the Old World's greatest civilizations.

Africa has *four* major rivers:

1)**The Nile River** — at 4,160 miles (6,695 km), the world's longest river is actually *two* rivers (the *White Nile* and the *Blue Nile*). Down through the centuries the mighty Nile has been the only real link through the Sahara Desert to connect the peoples of the north of the peoples of the south. Near its banks, the earliest of African civilizations arose - *Nubia*, *Kush*, *Meroe* and *Egypt*.

2)**The Zaire (Congo)** — almost 3,000 miles (4,670 km) long, this mighty river drains the enormous spider-like river basin of central Africa. It was along this river that the *Bantu* migrated to take over most of southern Africa.

3)**The Zambezi** — at 1,700 miles (2,700 km), the Zambezi, flowing over towering cliffs to form Victoria Falls, gave birth to the mighty empire of *Great Zimbabwe*.

4)**The Niger — The Riddle of Two Rivers** — For many years European explorers believed the Niger River to be not *one* but *two* rivers, one flowing north, the other south. In truth, it originates 200 miles from the ocean then flows 2,600 miles (4,170 km) in a broad arc through some of the driest areas of West Africa. Without the River Niger, the ancient kingdoms of *Ghana*, *Mali* and *Songhai* could not have developed. Today it provides life blood to a host of countries cradled under its arm — Mali, Burkino Faso, Guinea, Sierra Leone, Liberia, Ivory Coast, Ghana, Togo, Benin, Niger, Nigeria.

"River of Sadness, River of Joy"

The Niger's "river god," portrayed by two serpents, symbolizes it"s dual nature - in times of flood it brings life to millions of West Africans; in times of drought it robs them of their lives.

In the spring, rain drenches the tropical highlands of Guinea, triggering a flood that begins to fill the delta five months later. By early fall, the River Niger has broadened into a 20-mile wide moving lake, spreading over the lowlands and creating an *inland delta* in the dry sahel desert of lower Mali. This labyrinth of lakes and lagoons, millet fields and paddies, stretches for 250 miles northeast to the legendary "end of the world" city of Timbuktu, providing a rich breeding ground for fish (it is potentially the world's most enormous inland fishery). When the river waters flood, the fish leave the river bed, scattering over the huge delta (the size of New Jersey). There they spawn and, as the water recedes, struggle back to the main channel. Along the way they are trapped by spears and nets.

In times of drought this system breaks down and hundreds of thousands die from starvation or hunger-related diseases. Pastures dry up, fish are few and the fields of grain by the riverside are bone dry.

FAMINE/REFUGEES

Today, orphans of the drought fill refugee camps on the banks of the Niger River. The *Tuareg*, once symbols of the proud nomadic life, have watched their cattle die. Forced to abandon their nomadic lives they gravitate towards the towns and the refugee camps, drinking waters from murky holes prone to disease. Protein deficiencies result in lasting brain damage.

the river niger

"Runnin' On Empty"

DJENNE, Sunday, June 12th

I TOOK a stroke into shore and a motorized longboat plowed past me, sending its wake of water over my face, nearly choking me. I was struggling to get out, but the river was now clogged with these long trading boats blocking my way.

Hey, can't anybody see me?

Scattered along the riverbank were some guys. I couldn't tell if they were a street gang or students from the Mosque where our bus just stopped to hold a songfest. They warned me not to swim, "river disease," but how else could you wash off this dust from Roots Village?

Most of us girls had checked into the youth *Campement* over a mile from the river. It cost us just six bucks a night. We had mosquito nets and hammocks — but no electricity, no water to wash with, and no buckets to get any.

157

That was an hour ago.

By now my body had turned into one giant goosebump. I couldn't decide which was worse — drowning — or getting out and facing these street toughs.

Finally I struggled out, hauling my shivering pale blue body up onto the muddy shore in front of all these black guys. I'm kind of gangly-looking for a seventeen-year-old. My hair gets all stringy when its wet, and the straps of the top of my bikini had cut matching red raw welts into both my shoulders.

They were drinking beer, goofing around on the sand with a big cassette deck blasting away, wheeling and dealing tapes. Some students I recognized from the Djenne Mosque had built a bonfire, so I stayed.

Brock turned up with that same guy from Ras' group, Cleavon the drummer, plus two girls that were backup singers. He was sweet-talking them into rehearsing for the Rap and Reggae Review he's trying to start. One skinny girl, Ramona, had wrapped on a skirt so tight she was in danger of catching on fire just from her knees rubbing together.

I don't know what started the fight, who said what to whom first, but in a flash Brock and Shakespeare were squared off against each other. Shakespeare's heavy rimmed glasses shook with sweat. His voice rose, defending these students like he was some big deal radical.

"This *is not your home!*" he shouted over at Brock.

"Look," Brock protested. "Africa's *every* black man's home."

Shakespeare took off his glasses and poked them into Brock's chest. "You come parading off these planes, hugging us like you're my 'long lost brother' that's come home. *I am not your brother.*"

"All blacks're brothers."

"You're an American." Shakespeare poked Brock in the chest again with his eyeglasses. I thought at any second Brock was going to pop him one. "You know what I see when you step off that plane? . . ."

"What, man?" said Brock, glowering.

"A wallet and a wristwatch," he sneered scornfully. "An American tourist. Here to spend a little money, get your picture taken with a naked native, buy up some jewelry, soothe your conscience a bit — then go home."

"Hey look . . ." Brock tried to laugh it off, but I could tell he was really hurt. Shakespeare could wrap words around Brock's head like it was a punching bag.

"You are a minority back home, Brock." I eased in to help him out. "I think that's what Shakespeare's saying. Growing up in a white culture, you kind of *think* different than Africans here do."

Brock, who had been watching me do my whole calm little peace talk, now smiled sarcastically, "And, *how* do I think different, MacB, pray tell?"

"Everything you say is about *black* folks, *white* folks, right? . . . In Africa there are no blacks, because everybody is."

Brock shook his head, embarrassed in front of the others. "Look, stay out of this, OK? You know nothin' about black folks."

"Why is everything always white folks and black folks with you?"

"Because everything *is* white folks and black folks. Hey, *look,* little darlin' — you know that the worst damage you white folks did was to my soul, not my body. And you're *still* doin' it! . . ." he glared at me, his eyes watering over painfully. "It's to my self respect. In the way you look at me in a coffee shop or on the subway train. You never look at *me* — you look at your own terror. I'm *not free now . . .*" he stuck his face in mine, "not until you an' I can look at each other — and have the wall between us disappear."

Everyone backed off uncomfortably, poking at the bonfire. Brock looked so lost I wanted to sit down with him. But Tight Skirt was all over him so he nestled down in her arms. The Djenne students passed out a basket of fresh fish and ears of corn . . . and we started charbroiling.

"This spot taken?" a voice asked from behind me. I felt someone drape a towel gently around my shoulders. Shakespeare. *Finally,* he'd started to loosen up! He even untied his tie.

"Why did you attack Brock like that?"

He looked at me funny, surprised that I'd even asked him.

Monday, June 13th

*"Outside the Djenne mosque, kids scurry about
with their Arabic prayer boards tucked protectively
under their arms . . ."*

"Crusted slabs of salt are piled along the river like sheets of lumber . . ."

Kitabu, 2:00 P.M.

Brock, Ras, and most of the crew had to take a train down to Nigera ahead of us. I'm waiting at the dock while Lenny tries to get our bus fixed. Nobody here can fix a carburetor.

Salt and more salt. Boatmen unload it in huge crusted slabs, stacking them up around me. Raine's shooting Polaroids, hopping in and out from one needle-thin boat to another.

164

Kitabu, 2:45 P.M.

Shana gets back from her expedition to the cliff dwellers. Now she's arguing with a man in a pointed Chinese hat. He's got an old mask she wants to sell at her Art Show. A real museum piece.

Raine and I give up waiting for her and go find our bus engine laying in pieces on the dock . . . We're all forced to get inside Marvin's van.

Now, Marvin's van had these plastic seats that stuck to your thighs — the kind that leaves butt-prints of sweat when you get up? So Raine and I grabbed the one metal bench between the sliding doors. But Shana got in one side, Marvin in the other . . . and *both* sat down on either end!

We were stuck, sandwiched in between them, Raine next to Shana . . . and me next to Marvin. Before we could do anything about it, the driver slammed the doors shut, and we were off, rattling along the dusty road.

Shana wasn't saying a word, pretending to ignore Marvin. She just started jotting down notes for her African Art Show speech. She's got college degrees in it.

Marvin buried himself nervously in a bag of Famous Amos he swiped from Lenny. Twenty minutes passed without a word between them. He'd eaten half the bag, cookie crumbs bouncing off his chin and getting stuck in my hair.

Raine and I just kept looking at each other like *who are these people?*

Finally Marvin mumbled something to me. It came out garbled through a mouthful of cookies, "Thanks for taking care of Raine."

"She's taking care of me."

"You and Shana getting along alright I see?"

"I guess so . . ." It was like he was talking to her through me.

"Heard you and Shana did some shopping?"

"Yeah . . . we did." I pointed at a cookie crumb stuck on his lips. "Could you, uh — not chew those while you're talking to me?"

"MacB, has anybody ever accused you of being *indirect?*"

"Look, if you want to talk to Shana, why don't I just get up and let you two sit together?"

I was trying to protect her, but he leaned right across me, "Shana, we've done a lot of talkin' getting this tour organized — but *we ain't really talked yet!"*

Shana put down her notes for the Art Show real slow, and turned to him with a sugary smile. "What did you want to talk about, Marvin?"

Marvin looked at me uneasily, not sure if he wanted to get into this in public. I rolled my eyes at Raine and we both squished down in the bench, pretending we weren't there.

"It's just good to see you, lady."

"It's good to see you too, Marvin," Shana smiled politely, then held up her art notes. "Now, do you mind if I finish this?"

"Lady, you can be hard when you want to."

"I had a good teacher."

They went back and forth like that arguing for half an hour. Shana finished her speech for the art show, and Marvin finished the bag of cookies — neither of them giving in an inch.

Tuesday, 6:00 A.M., Kaingi Dam

The plane Lenny promised us was a single prop Piper cub, outfitted with bush flight rigging. It sat out on the hundred yards of tarmac, chugging like a clotheswasher.

Shana shot Marvin one of her *are you crazy* looks, but climbed in anyway.

We putted over the delta swamplands, following the thin ribbon of river down to the coast and civilization. Below us, Raine spotted men scurrying frantically into the forest.

"They must think we're federal agents," our pilot chuckled, swooping down even lower to frighten them. "See those big palms over there? See that hideout? . . . *Moonshine.* They sell the liquor to the workers on the oil rigs."

Boomtown ports blackened the mouth of the river with Texas-sized rigs. *Shell, Chevron . . .* Below, you could spot the yellow hard hats of hundreds of workers hoisting cables up the oil wells.

Tidal swamps below us now oozed a brackish foam. Here the mighty River Niger met the sea . . . weaving through a maze of mangrove swamps, twisting through creeks of mud and sand, to empty into the Atlantic Ocean.

"You are flying over the largest population of people anywhere in Africa," Lenny called back to us. "The heart of Nigeria."

Marvin passed back one of Lenny's computer print-outs to Shana. On it was a list of questions reporters might ask at the Press Conference when we landed.

"You really think you can raise money with this Art Show of yours?"

"Yes, Marvin." Shana nodded coolly, studying the list.

"I hope so," he muttered, wandering back up the aisle. "Or you may just be looking at Marvin Knight's Last Crusade."

There was no room for foul-ups. If someone didn't get us another corporate sponsor soon, no way would we ever have enough money for our satellite broadcast.

This time I passed Shana a stick of gum. She buckled her seat-belt, nervously looking down at the airport — and I got all nervous too. Just who and what was waiting for us down there?

PART FOUR

NIGERIA

"Tomorrow People"

Tomorrow people
Where is your past?
Tomorrow people
How long can you last?

Today you say you're here
Tomorrow you say you're gone
If there's no love in your heart
There's no hope for you

Don't know your past
You won't know your future

music and lyrics by Ziggy Marley
*as recorded by **Ziggy Marley and the Melody Makers***

PEOPLE

Population: 100 million (the most populous country in all of Africa. 1 out of every 4 people south of the Sahara are Nigerian). **Ethnic Groups:** Over 250 tribal groups; the three largest are the *Hausa-Fulani,* the *Ibo,* and the *Yoruba.* The Hausa-Fulani (mostly Muslim) live in the north. The Yoruba are found in the southwest (half Christian, half Muslim). The Ibo (largely Catholic) are found in the southeast. **Religions:** Muslim, Christian, traditional. **Languages:** English (official), Hausa, Ibo, Yoruba, others. **Literacy:** 25%-35%. **Education:** Western education proceeded more rapidly in the south than in the north (with consequences that have been felt in Nigeria's political life ever since). Nigerians travel religiously to the United States, some 15,000-20,000 are currently studying in the United States. **Infant Mortality:** . **Life Expectancy:**

GEOGRAPHY

Area: 923,768 sq.km. (356,700 sq.mi.); the size of California, Nevada, and Arizona — combined! **Capital City:** Lagos (10 million). **Other Major Cities:** *Ibadan, Kano, Oyo, Kaduma, Jos.* **Terrain:** Four areas: ● a hot, humid coastal belt of mangrove swamp in the south; ● an inland tropical rain forest with oil palm bush; ● a dry central plateau of open woodlands and savanna grasslands ● a semidesert in the far north. **Climate:** Two seasons: dry and wet. The "dry season" brings the "Harmattan," a dense pall of Sahelian dust that drifts over the country. The "wet season" is dominated by tropical storms.

GOVERNMENT

Government: Military. **Colonial Power:** England. **Independence:** October 1, 1960.

ECONOMY

Yearly GDP Per Person: $225. **Exports:** petroleum (98%), cocoa, rubber. **Imports:** automotive kits, foodstuffs, machinery.

The oil boom of the 1970's created a dependency on oil (for more than 95% of export earnings) and a massive "village-to-city" migration devastated agriculture. Just 20 years ago, Nigeria was a major *exporter* of food. Now it *imports* more than $500 million worth of food yearly. In 1986, oil prices fell by $15 a barrel. Coupled with a sharp decline of overseas credit, Nigeria's boom times came to a standstill.

HISTORICAL NOTES

Over 2,000 years ago, people from a culture called Nok worked in iron and produced extraordinary terra cotta sculpture.

In the north, Hausa kingdoms and the Bornu Empire near Lake Chad became wealthy as the terminals for the trans-Saharan camel caravan routes. In the southwest, the Yoruba kingdom of Oyo (founded about 1400) rose to its height during the 17th to 19th Centuries. Its domain extended as far as modern Togo. As early as the 1400's, the kingdom of Benin built elaborate ceremonial courts to rival those of Europe. Its artisans worked in ivory, wood, bronze, and brass are prized throughout the world.

Early in the 19th Century, a Fulani leader, Usman Dan Fodio, launched a massive Islamic crusade that brought most of the Hausa states in the north under loose control of an empire centered in Sokoto.

TOURIST ATTRACTIONS

National museum in Lagos, Jnju and Highlife nightclubs, Durbar festivals, Ife, Nok and Yoruba art, Benin city, Lake Chad, museums in Jos, Emir's Palace.

nigeria

10

"City of Fire"

LAGOS, Tuesday, June 14th

*"**DO NOT** travel at night in Lagos."* Lenny's voice crackled over the loudspeaker. Why he uses a loudspeaker no one knows; we were all close enough to hear his voice. Maybe it's to make him seem bigger. "I repeat, do *not* travel at night in Lagos, not even in a cab."

"Why not?" someone called out, as we bumped screeching into the airport.

"Well, it's like New York — a lot of armed robbery, gangs roaming the street . . ."

Shana climbed out of the little plane first, Marvin next, posing as "The Happy Couple" and putting on their best smiles for the press. I followed after them, stepping into a blistering, tropical heat made worse by crowds of screaming fans. These people had been waiting, some camped out the whole night, for a glimpse of Marvin Knight's Crusade.

Security was a mess. Camera crews from the BBC dogged us the whole way, poking microphones into Shana's face. We went through the usual song and dance at customs, waiting forever while officials opened bags, searched through documents, and finally did what they knew they were going to do anyway — stamp our passports.

Lenny hustled me through the crowds, stuffing money into my pocket. "The cab drivers here are *pirates!* If he tries to overcharge you, *don't argue* — just get out, pay him what you said you would, and split." He glared at me steadily, "MacB, *is this clear?*"

"Yes sir, yes boss man," I saluted and scrambled through.

A lanky, giant of a man stood grinning, waiting to greet me on the other side of customs. Was I ever glad to see Ras. When I got through, he gave me a big bear hug. But where was Brock? I looked around half-hoping not to see him, and half-missing his wisecracks.

"Food poisonin' . . ." Ras frowned, tapping his tummy in answer, as if he could read my mind.

From paradise — straight into hell! . . . That's what the cab ride into downtown Lagos was like. At first glance everything looked beautiful — colonial homes lining neatly tailored suburban streets, rolling lawns with flowering trees, sandy beaches and lagoons.

"Look like Jamaica here!" Cleavon rolled down his window, letting in a gust of steaming hot tropical air.

But soon I felt a tickling in my throat. Something was burning. We came around a bend, and across the water from us lay a smoking hell-hole of a city.

Lagos lay sprawled like an octopus, reaching its decaying tentacles over the lush island, threatening to drag it back down into the lagoon. The roadside was littered with burnt-out crusts of cars every half mile, warning signposts of the devastation that lay ahead.

We crossed over Carter bridge — and entered the City of Fire. Smoking oil rigs . . . burning palm oil refineries . . . bonfires erupting from garbage cans in the crowded dark streets. The soot so thick you could taste it, burning your throat, seering your eyes . . .

"Fire an' burnin'. Flames burnin' everyt'ing down to the ground."

This is the smell of roots reggae." Ras Marcus broke out an envelope of brown ganja buds, enough for a week all rolled together in one fat spliff.

Our cab rattled into a waterfront slum. The road was crazy with men on scooters, donkey carts, and women bent over with back breaking loads. Bicycles were everywhere, carting huge tins of palm oil strapped onto handlebars so that the driver almost disappeared.

We came to a dead standstill.

"Rush hour?" I asked.

"Here in Lagos we call it the *'go-slow,'* " our cabbie sighed, "Nothing moves for two hours."

"Oh . . ." I muttered, taking in the slum. Everyone was fighting for every corner of the street to stake out as their own, selling hot fishcakes, shoes, T-shirts. Some lay slumped in doorways sharing a liquor bottle.

"They built this up by filling in the harbor," the cabbie said. "This was all water before."

Ras Marcus shook his head sadly, leaned forward, and passed the spliff up to the driver. "Our government do the *same t'ing.* They took all this garbage from Kingston an' dump it in the bay. That's what my home was built on, little lady," he tapped me on the shoulder, pointing out the window, "That's what us Rude Boys grew up on — *garbage. All* the shantytowns. Ghost Town, Trench Town, The Jungle. *Yas-ss,* we all grew up on a dump o' trash. Flies, misery an' death . . ."

I sat there silent in the cab for a while, thinking about what Ras had said about life springing up from garbage, when I saw a man peeing against a wall. The yellow line of his urine ran crazily out into the street where some kids played.

"Where'd all these people come from?" I asked, trying to make some sense out of it. "Why'd they come *here?*"

"Liquid gold! . . ." the cabbie drew himself a deep hit off the spliff, then tucked it out of sight under the front seat. *"Oil!* The oil boom here brought us *so-o-o* much money . . . but so much sorrow too. Not enough homes. Robbery. Pollution," he shook his head as we rattled over a pothole.

"Now we have no farmers left. They run to the cities looking to make fast money on the oil rigs. Before this oil, at least we made our *own food* and had enough for everyone."

A fly flew in the window, a big fat one. I squashed it against the leather seat. When I looked up, I saw an office building towering over the slums like a tombstone over a decaying corpse. We were crossing the bridge over to the "new city."

Out the rear window, I looked back at the burnt-out hills we'd just come over. Oil rigs rose like giant mosquitoes along the horizon, sucking out the very fluids the city was built on.

"What will you do, man, when the oil runs out?" Cleavon asked the driver.

"Nobody knows . . . Yes, Lagos you old whore," he chuckled. "You are selling yourself, piece by piece — just to stay alive."

By the time our driver pulled up to the National Theatre, Big Benj's crew was already hauling in truckloads of recording equipment. As we got out of the cab, Ras leaned over and grabbed my arm.

"Watch out for youngblood, OK? That 'food poisonin' I told you 'bout? . . ." he hissed. *"Phar-ma-ceuticals."*

Either Ras was crazy or Brock was lying, I couldn't tell right then which was true. The condition for Brock to be on our tour was that he stay clean — if he blew it before the big concert, why was that my business?

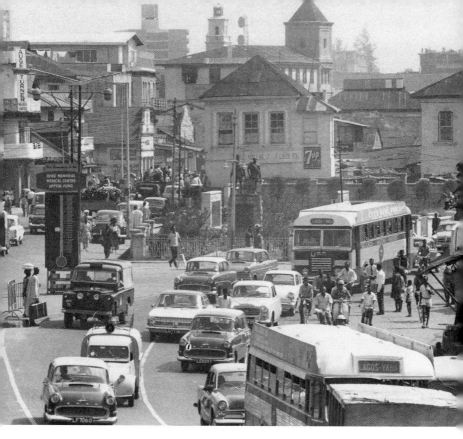

Downtown Lagos

"Our cab rattled into a water-front slum. The road-side was littered with burnt out crusts of cars . . ."

". . . that night Lagos came alive with 'juju' music and the best of Afro-pop!"

Fela
(Anikulapo-Kuti)

". . . he held forth with a 'mighty sermon' from his Shrine."

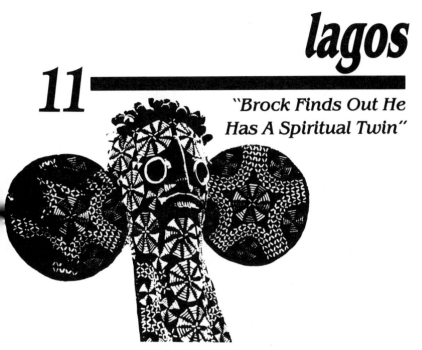

lagos

11

"Brock Finds Out He Has A Spiritual Twin"

NATIONAL THEATRE, Closed Rehearsal
Thursday Night, June 16th

BELLS TO boggle the mind! Clapper bells, calabash rattles, exotic bow lutes. Instruments of every size and shape stretched out across the stage from one end to the other. Even a slit drum cut from a solid tree trunk.

Tune-up time. In just twenty hours, Shana's African Art Show would begin. She was calling it *"African Unity Day,"* but we had no idea who would show up. Ministers of Culture from ten African nations, ambassadors from a host of European countries, even the bureau chief of the Russian press was being quickly called.

Over my head, Big Benj dangled off a scaffold, rigging tracks inside the posh multi-million dollar theater for the special camera he rented. Veronique was off with Shana in a dressing room somewhere, helping her with her make-up. Neil, I spotted down in the wings laughing it up with Sugar-N-Spice, an Afro-Anglo duo who'd just flown in from England. I, however, was stuck up in the balcony, folding *Soul to Soul* sweatshirts.

Looking down at them below, I felt like an outsider again. No matter how hard I tried to get close to people here, it was still no different. *Tourists vs. Africans. Africans vs. musicians. Musicians vs. reporters. Pro reporters vs. me.*

"You do this for a livin'?" a voice came up behind me.

I dropped the stack of sweatshirts defiantly on the display table. It was Brock. He looked strung out. "I heard you're back hooked on —"

"Hey, I ain't misbehavin'," he leaned over to kiss my lips. "I'm just savin' my love for you."

"Don't hold your breath."

He threw one combat boot up, half leaning on the bench, and started fiddling with his sax. A black *Sugar-N-Spice* T-shirt, newly signed by half the stars, clung to his chest skin-tight.

"You hitting up every group you see?" I said.

"Spice is gonna loan me his guitar player, we're rehearsin' her later tonight. Then I'm gonna hit Marvin up for a spot on the show tomorrow."

"Fat chance . . . all these tribal musicians came a long way to play, why would they want you?"

"Girls who hang with me soon find that out." A reed sat on his tongue as he grinned, sucking on it. Then he spat some saliva juice on it and jammed it into the sax. It was disgusting. His beautiful almond eyes were now jazzed, darting crazily from me down to his flying fingers, as he tapped out some shrill riffs on the sax.

"You're definitely on something." I scowled.

"What're you, CIA or somethin'?"

"Your *'little darlin'* — remember?"

"Yeah, well, little darlin's don't spy," he slid off the question again, hiding behind a pair of mirrored sunglasses he lowered over his bloodshot eyes.

Sweet sounds like the cries of birds drifted up to us from a group of musicians. Below, two men sat banging on some monster wood xylophone thing that ran half the length of the stage.

"Look Brock, you've got a good shot being on this tour. Why do you want to mess it up?"

"I ain't messin' nothin' up — *right Silver!*" Brock rolled up one sweatshirt and fired it football-style — straight into the arms of the Brooklyn kid as he charged up the stairs.

"TD, Brock-o!" Neil, out of breath, started in drumming on my table while Brock wailed away on his sax, clowning around.

"Do you mind? I can't hear." I shouted over the racket, glaring at them both.

"Ain't nothin' *to* hear," Brock said. "Unless you dig all that ding-dong rattle-rattle shit."

"I'm going down there." I dumped the pile of sweatshirts in his lap and strode on down to the stage.

Shakespeare was videotaping an Ashanti tribesman, gesturing to me gently that it was OK to come watch. He was a mischievous round-faced man with twinkling eyes.

"All these instruments you see? . . . Every one came from an animal in the forest. This *feli* —" he stooped over painfully, slowed by age, and proudly picked up a hollow wood box, "— it come from the *tuu-tuu* bird. When our women fish the river, they *love* the sound of these birds . . ."

"Weird," said Brock, coming up to us. He took the small wood box in his own hands, thumbing the notes awkwardly. It didn't sound as good. "How do you remember all this stuff? I don't see no music, no notes. You just memorize it?"

"No, we *speak* in music." The tribesman cupped a hand over his mouth, *"Clongco, pah pah . . ."*

As he spoke, an amazing thing started to happen. At first I just heard music notes. Then . . . I started to hear what he could hear. Voices, birds!

"When I listen to my music, I hear animals, the forest, people speaking . . ." Shana read to us from her art notes, rehearsing along-side the little tribesman. *"Our music is not like your music. Like our thinking is not like your thinking. The way we see the world is different than you do. So . . . we live in a different world."*

I was trying to follow what Shana was reading, but the more I thought about it, the harder it was to figure out. Then I felt Brock reach out and take my hand. For a second, he let down his guard and I saw his eyes fill with a desperate look, like he wanted to say something to me but just didn't know how.

"... *I know myself only when I am with someone else. In our music we cannot exist alone. Someone must speak . . . and someone else must listen.*"

He just kept holding onto my hand, squeezing it tight, as if he let go of it somehow he might be letting go of his life.

"You like it?" Brock played with the coins on the bracelet he'd given me.

I watched his fingers move dark against my pale wrist, "Yeah Brock . . . alot."

"Weird ain't it, all this fuss about skin."

We watched the two xylophone players pick up their sticks. Sweet notes toppled one after another. Rattles shook. Bells, tied to ankles, jangled.

The old man joined in on a bow lute and I saw that even his instrument was carved to look human. Its belly was built around the smooth stomach of a tribeswoman. Her arms, raised overhead, held up the strings.

This was no dead instrument to him — but a living spirit that allowed him to cross easily over from the human world into another world. One that lived somewhere beyond where Brock and I could now see.

"Hey brother, that rattle thing?" Brock nodded, admiring the gourd tied to the old man's waist, "I just got to use it in my rap group."

Right then, the old tribesman grabbed Brock by the arm, *"When you find your brother . . ."* he whispered, *". . . you will know him."*

Brock pulled away, frightened. I saw that same look of pain flash across his eyes — just like when I asked him about his real brother who died.

The Ashanti sat him down on the stage and told him it was one of their most ancient sacred myths — that every person in this world, all of us, began as *one . . . one tribe* that lived in the Sahara desert —*before* it was a desert.

Now Brock was really freaked, trying to figure what this guy was telling him. "You sayin' this desert *wasn't* a desert?"

"Before my great grandfather's time, before any of my people can remember, this desert was filled with great lakes, forests and animals. Slowly the land dried up . . . Some of us moved up North to the great sea — the European, the Indian, the Chinese. Others of us moved down South into the grasslands — we Ashanti, and the Zulu . . ." The tribesman reached out his bony hand to touch Brock once again, ". . . But still each of us is tied to the other."

"Tied together? How?"

"The Egyptians once had a word for it — *ka.* And here, separated from each other by thousands and thousands of miles, we Ashanti call it *kra!* Both mean the *same thing.*"

"What? What 'same thing'?"

"Spirit Twin . . . Each of us has a spirit twin."

"You mean somewhere in this world I still got a *twin . . .* sort of a soul to soul brother?"

"Exactly!" the old tribesman nodded. "That is what I've been trying to tell you."

Ka or *kra,* both the same belief, existing thousands of miles and thousands of years apart. *Coincidence? . . .* I wondered as Brock and I climbed back up to my sweatshirt stand. Or was this finally my proof that once we *did* all exist together, in one place, in one time . . . One family. One blood. One soul — before breaking apart and scattering ourselves all across the globe?

Brock helped me fold up the remaining sweatshirts. He seemed unnerved by the whole thing.

"What do you think of it, MacB? . . ." he finally said, almost embarrassed to ask my opinion about anything, " . . .'bout all this spiritual twin stuff."

"Don't look at me," I said. "I ain't your twin."

The "Talking Drum" of the Yoruba

one hand pulls a cord that squeezes strings that tighten the drumhead . . .

the other hand beats a curved drumstick in a rhythm and pitch that echoes the human voice . . .

". . . there are more twins in Nigeria than anywhere in the world. People here say it's 'due to the yams.' "

*Some
of the
guys
we
met*

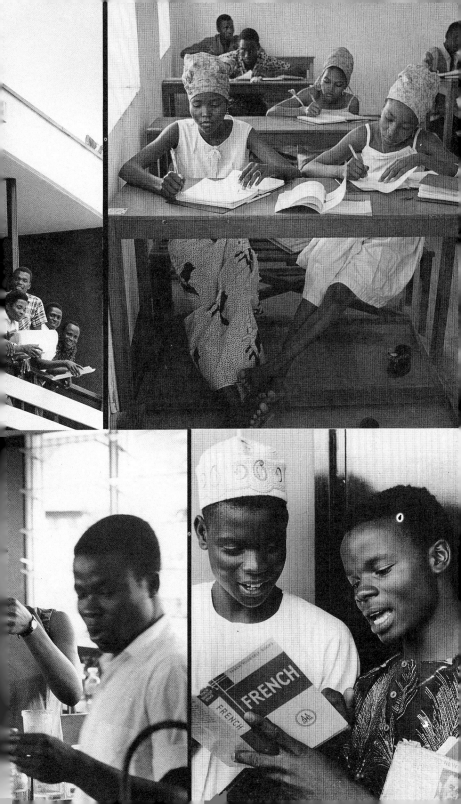

Brock and his ``girls . . .''

Friday, 8:00 P.M.

Brock James, I don't know why I'm drawn to you. Why I keep trying to put myself in places you might see me?

It was a closed rehearsal. I stood by the studio door for *two hours*. Then, when they got out, they just breezed by me.

"Neil, can you take this message into Brock?"

"He treats you like dirt and you're sending him a love note?"

"It's *not* a love note . . . I just want some help with my reggae article."

"I thought Shakespeare was helpin' you."

I tracked him all the way to some nightclub in the heart of downtown Lagos and hung around outside, watching until Brock and the others got in. They called it *'Gabi's Shrine'* . . . a club for Nigerian teens built by a revolutionary who single-handedly put African music on the world map.

"Dread watch yo' head," read the sign nailed over the low door. Under it stood a wiry dark man exchanging power handshakes with the singers as they passed through. Kids kept breaking in past the bouncers, demanding autographs. By the time I got myself inside I couldn't find Ras or Brock. Just Lenny, chatting it up at the bar with the guy we called Soda Man — a white Kola King billionaire who he was trying to get to sponsor our concert.

"Excuse me, Mr. Stein," I stammered. I always get so nervous around him. "You seen Brock or Ras? I've got to —"

Lenny raised one hand, stopping me. "I am not interested in *where* Ras is — or *what* Ras has to say."

Some deal was going on between the two of them and Lenny was in no mood to talk. Soda Man flicked his cigarette ash into a half-empty beer and kept talking about how he wants to cut down this jungle, and build some King Kola soda factories — right here along the river.

"He . . . threw up out back." Lenny turned to me reluctantly, "I finally get him to agree to some press interviews, and he gets sick."

"Sick? . . . from what?"

"You never know about these Rastafarians. They don't smoke. Don't drink. No drugs, no beer . . ." he mumbled into his bottle. "Must be all those I-Tal greens they eat."

The Press Conference! I smacked my head, remembering. Dumb, MacBurnie. Real dumb. I started jogging up the street when I heard a voice moaning from the alley. It was pitch black . . . but I took a step into the dark. A trash can crashed over. Someone near me stumbled.

"Come back here!" a voice cried out. "Where you goin'?"

"Home, mon. Where else you t'ink I'm goin'?" Ras stumbled out ahead of Brock, then flopped down, still hanging over the trash can, sick.

Throwing one of Ras' arms around his shoulder, Brock hoisted the big man up. I hooked myself under his other arm, and we all staggered off back toward the hotel.

Reporters were already clambering around the front desk, trying to get up to Ras' room. So Brock had to hustle him around back and up the stairs while I stalled them.

When I got upstairs to Ras' room, Brock had him over the sink, dunking his head carefully under the faucet so as not to hurt him. Cold water didn't do much good . . . Ras just shook out his locks and kept mumbling on and on about the record companies, about how they had tricked him out of his royalties.

"All them English companies — they *rob* me, mon. *Thieves!* They steal my music! They rob my soul!"

Brock got him cleaned up as best he could, fussing over the old man like he was the father he never had. We propped up his heavy legs on the couch and the proud Lion of Reggae stretched back, running his hand over the shaggy black mane that framed his face. His yellowed eyes narrowed, glinting warily at his first visitors.

They came in twos, the reporters, like couples visiting a priest for his blessings. And they worked in pairs — one asking the questions, the other recording every word for the press back home.

But some were clearly enemies.

After the usual *"Ras-isms"* — Ras on race, Ras on God, Ras on Africa — a short white guy, bald with one gold earring, started edging in for the kill.

"Other than in your island, Jamaica, and a few small clubs, you are really *not* so well known, true?"

"I don't play Las Vegas, if that's what you mean," Ras glared at the man coolly. "An' you won't be seein' me on Arsenio Hall."

The little man clicked his gold ballpoint pen annoyingly. "Can you tell our readers why?"

"Big Stars? All these fancy hotels? . . . They don't pay for a man with snake nests for hair, smokin' pot an' walkin' round the place. Scare all the tourists away!"

"So why haven't you changed your looks? Your hair?"

"These dreadlocks, they be my prison bars."

"Why the army clothes?" Little Man shot back, escalating the conversation.

"Because we are in a *war*. Our people fight *every day* . The soldier is my brother, so it is *his* clothes I wear." Ras was awake now, fixing Little Man in his razor-sharp yellowed eyes. "The young, they know I-Ras tell the truth. Babylon is built on the backs of slavery — the *brutality* of the white mon."

"So . . . you are advocating revolution?" Little Man paused provocatively. A crooked smile twisted up the corner of his thin lips. "Maybe an international boycott of certain products by all blacks?"

Just then, Brock stepped in protectively. "You all know Ras, but you *still* think he's gonna take a machete — and cut open your throat?"

Flustered, the little man clipped his gold ballpoint pen neatly back in his vest pocket, patting it securely. "So then just what *is* all this chanting and smoking about?"

Ras rose up off the couch to his full height, towering above the little man. "Rastas be the *heart* of Jamaica, We *are* the lost tribe of Israel, sold into the slavery of a Caribbean Babylon . . . An' when our chil'ren come back home, then the whole white Babylon will tumble down in blood . . ." He tossed him his little leather book. "Read your Bible, mon. It's all in there. Most honest book in the world."

Flashbulbs fired, blinding our eyes for some seconds. Ras Marcus, who never allowed his picture to be taken, just cocked his chin defiantly — and spread out that big grin of his, showing off his gold front tooth.

Then he rolled up a big, fat spliff for everyone.

"You newsboys always showin' us Jamaicans as little gingerbread dolls. Happy brown people splashin' about under a waterfall . . ." He grabbed the gold pen out of the nattily dressed reporter's vest pocket, "People are in pain there! *Write that —*" he stabbed the reporter's pad, " — write that we are in *prison* in Babylon. Black people, Rastafari brethren, *must go home.*"

A loose tape from a recorder flapped away. The reel, already run out, spun round empty. No one bothered to turn it off. Ras was still sermonizing, but all the newsboys were numbed out from the ganja. All but one . . . one Little Man . . . furiously scribbling away with his gold ballpoint pen.

Saturday, June 18th, 6:30 A.M.

How one person can choose, if they put their mind to it, to destroy the life's work of another person is something I'll never understand. I've done some pretty mean things — but the absolute desire of this little man to tear apart all we'd worked so hard for led me to doubt our Tour's chance to ever do any good.

The reporter had blown up what Ras had to say to banner headline proportions:

INTERNATIONAL BLACK MIGRATION PREACHED ON EVE OF AFRICAN UNITY DAY
In an exclusive interview with self-proclaimed "musical-terrorist"
Ras Marcus, this guru of guerilla warfare preached to this reporter
his sermon of hatred for whites . . .

As I read, I could feel my heart break. A sinking feeling of dispair swept over me as I watched the morning paper get passed from hand to hand around the theatre's coffee shop. The bubble had burst.

Shakespeare came down and slipped Ras a note, Ras Marcus was to meet Lenny for a *"breakfast conference"* — but we all knew what it was for.

They were going to cut him from the tour.

"Why are they doing this to him?" I said after Ras left, almost crying.

"Because what he is saying is the truth, man." Brock slammed his metal sax case down angrily on the breakfast table. "His music tells you what the real situation is. What's really going down in Jamaica, in Lagos, in the streets."

"Yeah, but you know entertainment and truth don't mix," growled Neil. He and Brock and half the Quicksilver Band were on opposite sides of the issue, arguing.

"Marvin *can't* cut Ras loose," Brock kept protesting, defending his hero. "He and Ras go way back. They're like brothers . . . Marvin owes Ras his life."

"What are you talkin' about?"

"Do you remember that comeback album Marvin cut? Ras told me he recorded half those tracks down in Kingston. Marvin was *dyin'* on the charts, man. Reggae gave him a new lease on life."

They could argue it forever and what difference would it make? This reporter already wrote his epitaph . . . and somewhere in this theatre Ras was having his last coffee with Marvin and Lenny.

"Sh-sh . . ." Brock whispered, holding his hand out and feeling his way through the dark.

"Brock, *what* are we doing here?"

He led me crashing through some drums and mic stands, then through another door and flipped on a light. Dials and switches covered a mix panel. A red light flashed on: RECORDING STUDIO B . . . We were in the control booth.

"I heard Ras tell Marvin he was going to play him his new song." Brock began flicking some switches.

"Are you *crazy?*" I started out the door, but he pulled me back. Just then — we heard voices. Brock switched off the light, and we both ducked down behind the mixing booth, watching through the fog our breath made on the glass panel.

It was Lenny and Marvin, followed by Ras . . . all furiously arguing.

"I don't need to hear the song," Marvin stormed in. *"They* need to hear an apology."

"I ain't makin' no apology," Ras hissed.

"Ras, *look at what you said!"* Furious, Lenny shook the newspaper in Ras' face. "My sponsors are going *nuts!"*

"What you on this tour for anyway, Lenny *Stein?"* Ras spun at the record promoter, challenging him. "This is *Africa,* mon — this is no place for no limousine liberal!"

"Ras, if you make any more speeches, if you even sing *'Rise Up Ethiopian,'* Soda Man walks. And he pulls the plug on our whole Satellite concert. You don't sing it — the concert goes on."

"Bomba clot!" Ras spat at them. "What kind o' concert you talkin' about? You dealin' with the Devil, mon. This Soda Mon got money in South Africa. Lenny, you sellin' this tour to Babylon — you sellin' my *soul* to Babylon!"

"I'm not selling anything, Ras."

"Look Ras —" Marvin jumped in between them, "— Leonard's caught between a rock and a hard place, *you understand?* He's carryin' Africa on his back and the USA and Russia on each shoulder."

"I can take care of myself, Marvin." Lenny stood his ground, "Look, I don't care *where* the money's coming from — South Africa or the moon. I do care where it's *going* — and the people's lives it will save."

"I don't like it, I just don't like it . . ." Ras slumped down on a stool, looking up at Marvin pleadingly. "This is Third World music. We ain't singin' no bedtime lullaby here."

"So — are you going to cut it or not?" Marvin demanded.

"If they want to kill me, only one t'ing I can do — defend the truth. You think I come here to be buried by the white mon all over again? I come for *you* — " Ras rose up, pointing bitterly at Marvin. *"You* the brother that got me here. Because I *respected* you."

We watched as the old Rasta drummer sunk down again on the stool, shaking his head. "I don't know mon, it ain't right. It just ain't right."

"Yeah? Well it's the only right we got right now." Marvin took hold of Ras' shoulders, glaring at him, eye to eye. "So you either take it or leave it."

For one long cold minute, Ras looked at Marvin . . . then almost broke out into his wide grin. "Behind all your prettiness, mon, you do got some smart head."

"I come from the same street you do, Ras." Marvin nodded, finally embracing him.

"Yeah, but I ain't sure yet which side o' the block you're walkin' on."

After they left, we got up again, peering into the dark recording room. Brock went to turn on the lights — and came face to face with Ras, still slumped sadly on the stool.

He was crying.

I'd never really seen a man like this, so broken. So I looked over at Brock to see if I should go or stay. Just then, the old man reached out both his hands — one to Brock, the other to me.

I held onto it tight, squeezing his big calloused hand, feeling all his love go out to us.

"They want to kill my music. Shut me up . . ." he shook his head at me.

"You going to do it?"

His yellowed eyes narrowed into two determined slits, "Little lady . . . can't be no compromise with the Devil."

lagos lagoon

12

"The Hand Of God"

AFRICAN UNITY DAY, Saturday, June 18th

SHAKE LOOSE! *Everything's going to work out right,* I kept telling myself, trying to put RECORDING STUDIO B and what I'd heard in there behind me.

Outside the theater, Lagos was alive with music everywhere I looked. Horns honking. Bicycles tooting in the *"go slow"* clog of cars. Even Shakespeare somehow got a beat going for himself — pulling up on a motorbike with a huge ghetto blaster strapped over the rear tire. Same old blue suit. Same old tie. But, over his nose, hung a new pair of black mirrored sunglasses just like Brock's.

"A good morning to you, girl," he smiled, puffing on each lens coolly and polishing them with his tie. Then he poked the sunglasses up against the bridge of his nose — as if there was some way I might not notice them.

"Shakespeare you really don't need these," I said gently as I could and lifted them off. "There . . . I like your eyes."

He kind of grumbled a bit, then took off with me on the scooter. Our job was to get our concert billboard painted over real quick — before the headline about Ras caused our newest sponsor to drop out. It had to have *"King Kola presents. . ."* painted on it. *By noon,* Lenny had warned us.

"Hey!" I shouted up to Shakespeare over the noise of the screeching traffic. "You got any idea how we're going to get this painted on a seventy-foot billboard in four hours?!"

Shakespeare dug into his suit pocket and passed me back a sheet of computer paper. Folded inside it was a business card . . .

OLATUNJI
SIGNS OF THE TIMES
Master Artiste — "Your problem is my specialty"

Finding out about Olatunji, and finding Olatunji, soon proved to be two very different things. After sleuthing through half a dozen beer halls, we followed a trail of his trademarked signs from shoe-shine shops into hair salons.

"Hey, why're you stopping here?"

Shakespeare pulled over to the curb and got off.

"Why are you chasing after a guy that has no regard for you?" he demanded, shutting off the engine.

"You mean Brock? . . . You just don't know him the way I do."

"Look, you don't have to run very far to find someone." He took off his sunglasses, forcing me to look him in the eye. "I am right here."

I couldn't tell if Shakespeare really wanted to be with me or if this was just his way of being nice. But no way was I going to hurt him. So I took his hand in mine, gently. "I'm here for you too, Shakespeare. It's just—" I stopped, searching for the right words. Why is it always the ones who like you, somehow you don't want —and the ones you want, somehow they don't like you? "— it's just that I don't feel the same way about you."

He thought about it for a moment, fiddling with his glasses. When he adjusted them again securely over his nose, I stuck out my hand.

"Friends?"

"To the end." He shook it, and his lips broke out from their usual studious look into a warm smile. "Come with me."

He tugged me over to a white wood cross stuck into the ground and told me to wait there for him. Then, without another word of explanation, he disappeared inside the church.

When these people pray — they pray! The walls shook with music. Sneaking a peak, I saw row after row of women singing. Each wore a spotless white dress with a sash belt of blue tied on the side. No lavish wealth here either, just a simple altar with tall candles every color of the rainbow.

Ringing a bell clanger, a woman strode up the aisle straight at me.

"Aladura Christians . . ." Shakespeare whispered, waving for me to follow her outside. "They believe in the healing power of song."

From under a pointed cap with ZION spelled out in blue stars, two bright brown eyes twinkled. She looked me up and down curiously, like I had just dropped in from another planet. Then, still ringing her clangor, led us around back of her church.

He was painting a brown Jesus onto the side wall when we found him. A wiry, fast-talking, little man with brushes and rags poking out of every pocket of his overalls.

After much dickering, half in Hausa, half in English, Shakespeare produced an envelope of money that stopped all discussion cold.

We hammered the paint can lids back on, carting the gear to his *"mammy wagon,"* a canvas covered pickup truck painted over with religious figures. I'd noticed others of these trucks before, cutting in and out of traffic wildly, unloading a dozen women at the marketplace all jammed circus-like inside. His had a sticker on the rear bumper: *"O Lord, My Shepherd — Please Guide Me Home."*

We roped the motorbike on back and scrambled in. The fact that his windshield was shattered into a spider's web of cracks, didn't seem to bother Olatunji. He just floored it, trying to beat it blindly out to the Art Show celebrations in time.

Ceremonies had begun . . . We, however, were still stuck on the bridge. Cars had backed up to watch the procession of longboats snaking down Five Cowrie Creek. Canoers glided underneath us. Inside, Royal Drummers from Ghana lifted their giant drum barrels high overhead in salute .

"Get us out of this mess, Shakespeare."

Olatunji swung his battered mammy wagon, with *me* in it, up onto the sidewalk! Hanging half out the opened door and peering around his shattered windshield, he steered us bumping up through the crowds with his one free hand.

LAGOS RACE TRACK, 2:00 P.M.

EKABO! (welcome) the giant billboard read, *to the SOUL To SOUL — African Unity Day Art Show and Concert.*

The racetrack was already filling up when we got there. Youngsters packed the stands, climbing up on the rooftops, perching like birds up on billboards — anything for a view.

Down on the field, six men on stilts were high-strutting about, faking falls over the crowds. Behind them, a circle of well-armed troops protected our stage.

"We got him, Mr. Stein." Shakespeare barked into his Walkie-Talkie, then paid some security men to help lower Olatunji like a human elevator down the side of the giant *Soul to Soul* billboard. When he began to paint the familiar King Kola face, the crowd started a chorus of hisses.

"Why're they boo-ing?"

"They used to finance bottling plants in South Africa," Shakespeare muttered, clearly worried.

Two enormous elephant tusks formed a parenthesis of ivory around the entry gate. Through them now, I could see a row of men striding onto the racetrack. Each lifted an eight-foot long trumpet, sounding the opening fanfare.

"The President rode in first, flanked by his two honor guards. One carried his gold Staff of Office, the other the Nigerian flag. After them came leaders from each of the tribes, Ibo, Hausa, Yoruba . . ."

". . . followed by a drum and flute corps in from Kano"

COME TASTE AFRICAN WONDER
THE ONLY MONEY BACK GUARANTEE
CHICKEN
IN THE WORLD IS SOLD HERE

CHICKEN SOUYA · TAX
JOLLOF RICE
VEGETARIAN DINNER
COMPLETE DINNER

". . . the chicken was spicy,
the music sizzling hot!"

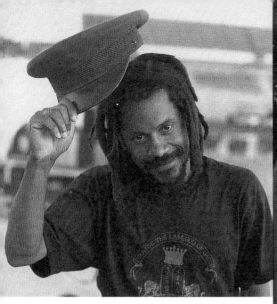

Finding the "right hat"

"...not so easy– but if you fold 'em right, they'll stick on "

"A Jumpin' Contagin

". . . they call it that because when you start to dance — everybody else has to."

Two new friends of mine. Two new friends of Raine's.

"Lenny wants us — now!" Shakespeare holstered his Walkie-Talkie and cleared a way down for me. Outside the dressing rooms, Ras was being grilled by reporters. Surrounding him, was a security guard and three soldiers with rifles.

"What are they doing to Ras?" I asked Shakespeare as he hustled me past.

"Don't worry about Ras, come on."

"Ras, RAS!" I tried to push my way through, but police had him surrounded. "He's not singing at all? Why? What did he say now?"

"It's nothing he said . . ." Shakespeare looked around carefully, making certain no one was listening. "Ras got a letter."

He showed me a copy. Crazy words you couldn't understand about white supremacy. My hands were shaking as I read it.

"This is a death threat." I looked back at Ras, so scared for his life.

Shakespeare nodded, "South Africa has a way of exporting violence . . . where you least expect it."

NATIONAL THEATRE, 4:30 P.M.

I now saw the real size of the protest. Lines of students circled the security entrance, carrying homemade placards scrawled with the slogan: *"KING KOLA OUT OF SOUTH AFRICA."*

"Be certain to tell Shana that Lenny said *two* sponsors have already dropped out," Shakespeare whispered in my ear, hurrying me up to the showroom. "If she doesn't secure one of these businessmen . . . there might not be a Tour."

Dancers, artists, craft makers, all filled the auditorium. Long boats stood up on end against the walls. Face masks stared out at the crowds, guardians of a glorious past.

Some woman at the Information Booth was doing her best to fight off the swarm of journalists.

"Bon, I am so glad you are here!" The woman said and dumped two hundred pounds of Press Kits into my arms.

I stood there in shock. There was Miss Innocence standing awkwardly by the booth in the tight-clinging scarlet red dress we got her. She'd let her hair down and braided it sexily with shells.

"Brock says I am a *'conne de negresse,'* you know? A 'black woman who doesn't know how to be a black woman,' " she giggled shyly and took my hand, leading me up the escalator. "Come; follow me."

Shana, radiant in a bold orange African *kanga* dress, stood out like a wildflower from the field of grey pinstriped suits surrounding her. All were starchy, stiff-collared businessmen Lenny and Soda Man assembled as a last ditch group of investors.

Six mega-moguls. I got introduced to each — if being introduced means handing someone a Press Kit and having them say thank you. One was the owner of a Greek shipping line. Another, a fast-food tycoon. And still another, a big white German beermaker named Wolfgang Mueller.

Red muttonchop whiskers circled a red face split in two by a bushy brow — giving Wolfgang the overall appearance of a skeptical Walrus. He seemed determined to give Shana a hard time, machine-gunning questions at her, doubtful that a "rock star" should be guiding *his* tour.

"Ms. Lee, what do you feel is the most important thing to know about primitive art!"

"That it's *not* primitive," Shana Lee answered nervously. She was as jittery as they were skeptical.

"But it does appear somewhat crude," The Walrus insisted, "Not refined. *Radical*, wouldn't you say?"

"Picasso didn't think so when he copied it." Shana was circling the delegation, letting them size her up. What was at stake was not our tour, but also her dream — a new center to develop African artists. *Everyone* was against it, she'd told me.

"Most people totally misunderstand African art. *Radical* means bold, new, a *departure* from the past . . ." she said, glancing nervously at her notes, ". . . but African art *is* the past."

"So you're saying then, that this piece is *not* radical?" The skeptical Walrus pointed at a stark, angular figure. "Therefore . . . it must be conservative, *yes?"*

"If by conservative you mean staying the same over a long period of time. Over centuries — then, yes, *very* conservative." Shana Lee stuck to her guns. She was nervous enough about Ras' death threat without having to take pot shots from this guy. You could hear the voices of the demonstrators outside coming through the window behind her.

"But some of these 'figures' are quite *distorted,* wouldn't you say? . . . *Grotesque?"* The Walrus now challenged.

"What is grotesque to one person is only what one is unfamiliar with . . ." She turned bravely to face the men. "Our art reflects the way we see our world, just as your art reflects the way you see yours. Here, look closely —"

Shana swished gracefully up to the white businessman and handed him a wood carving. "Notice how symmetrical it is. In harmony. This is how we see life. What do *you* see? . . ."

As its heavy weight sank into his hands, I could see him make a face. Two stick arms poked out from under a round wood head shaped like a flat disc.

"What is it?"

"You are holding an *akua'ba,* an Ashanti fertility doll."

The big man's face turned beet red in embarrassment. Quickly he passed it to another businessmen.

"You in the West, you put your *personality* up on a pedestal and call it art. You glorify the individual, the *artist.* Here we glorify the family, the tribe." Shana took the big man by the arm and walked him across the room. "I have a surprise for you, Wolfgang . . . may I call you Wolfgang?"

Unclasping a red velvet rope, Shana turned to give him a mysterious smile, then led us to an exhibit totally closed off to the public.

Seven massive green heads hung ghostlike in the dark, hovering in mid-air. When my eyes adjusted, I saw they stood on pedestals. Each was encased in glass, and each was bathed in a glowing white light.

"When you Germans arrived here and found these iron heads — you were *awed!* . . . You believed you had finally found *Atlantis,* the lost civilization."

"Impossible. Even in Germany, no one knew how to cast bronze metal." The Walrus pulled at his mustache, puzzled.

"It was made from a lost metod of wax casting . . . lost forever. Some miners dug under the village and found furnaces used for smelting iron . . . *Iron furnaces!* Five centuries before Christ was born."

But do you know where they come from?"

"Only from legends . . ." Shana shook her head regretfully. "Tribespeople here tell me they were the heads of their great *Oba* Kings. But when the British came through, they toppled their altars and auctioned the heads off in Europe. Whole villages killed themselves rather than being taken captive. The English found pieces of bodies cut up and scattered everywhere . . ."

I could hear what she was saying, but my eyes kept being drawn to one, great, green brass head. This definitely was once a King! His head wore a crown of gold. Two beautiful almond eyes gazed down at me. Across cheeks grooved with sweeping lines were facial scars — *identical* markings as I'd seen on Olatunji, the sign painter!

opposite: half figure of an ONI, (an OBA king,) cast in bronze by the people of IFE and placed on an altar.

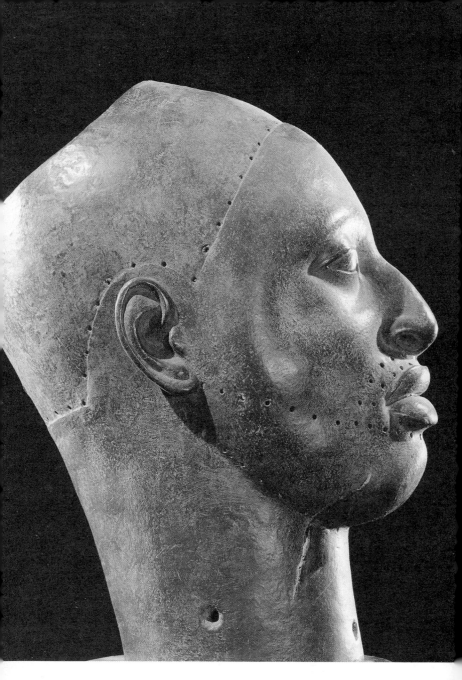

above: head of a ''court dignitary,'' cast in bronze by the people of Ife, using a wax method, now lost.

opposite above: lovers drinking cups, pottery from the Congo

opposite left: Two Janus — heads with double wing axe, a Yoruba wood carving from the Shango cult

opposite right: old man with pipe, cast bronze from Dahomey

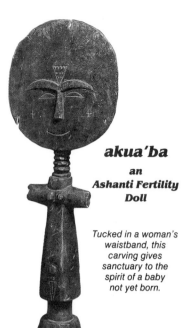

akua'ba
an
Ashanti Fertility
Doll

Tucked in a woman's waistband, this carving gives sanctuary to the spirit of a baby not yet born.

below: terra-cotta from the IBO people

"Miss Lee, what Lagos needs is *factories* — not art schools." The Walrus dabbed his bushy brow with his monogrammed hanky, removing the pearls of glistening sweat over his bushy brow "I just don't see the need to finance this art. It's too . . . *different.*"

"You *still* don't know what you are talking about!" Shana flew at him. "What is being financed *is* a whole different way of looking at the world. *Look at what you have lost* —" She ticked them off on her fingers furiously. "Family. Community. Caring for each other. We *have* to learn from Africa how to live together again."

Shana was hitting her stride now, heading downstairs to the auditorium, the men scrambling to keep up with her.

"This is not *art for art's sake.* Here art is *used.* Part of everyday life. Look —" she led us into a model village exquisitely laid out in miniature down to the last teeniest detail, steering us past beautifully carved bowls, ivory spoons, clay cooking pots . . .

"If *you* were Yoruba, Wolfgang, your family would make your own food, your own tools. *Every part* of your life would become an art. Your hair would be woven in intricate designs. Your cattle would be branded with bold designs . . . "

"How can you become self-reliant living like this?" The German threw up his hands.

Shana walked straight up to the tycoon and stood before him, face to face. "Wolfgang, you see only the skills you *want* us to have — not the skills we *already* have . . . In Africa, art *is* training. In Africa, art is this self-reliance you want. Come —" she flung open the security doors, leading us outside into the bright light.

We were escorted by armed guards through a roped-off walkway that threaded through hundreds of spectators. All were crammed inside a garden gathered around a towering wood scaffold.

The lines of protestors had thickened. I searched for Ras' face in the grandstands and saw businessmen, school children, dignitaries, Ministers of Culture . . . but no Ras.

"How much do you think they'll give?" I whispered to Shana.

"Keep your fingers crossed." Shana squeezed my hand, then was led up onto the scaffold.

"You scared?"

"No honey," she winked back at me. "Terrified."

Step by step, Shana Lee and the President climbed up the wood scaffolding. Beneath them, a bright red ceremonial drape fluttered impatiently in the breeze, concealing a gigantic statue that demanded to be unveiled.

I was so proud of her standing up there like a queen alongside the President. Cameras whirred. A hushed silence fell over the crowd as he began to speak into the microphone.

"The eyes of our fathers are on us today as we dedicate this great masterpiece to the new Nigeria and the old." The President's papers flapped in the breeze as he read from the podium.

"When we took our independence in October of 1960, our land was not *one* nation but *three.* Our first years were upset by corruption. Strikes. Looting . . . And violence. Ibos in Biafra were massacred by the hundreds of thousands. Civil war ripped us apart."

The President turned to Shana Lee gratefully, and handed her a plaque, "We were starving in the sixties and you, Shana Lee, you Americans, you organized concerts for the Biafra famine."

Tears were streaming from Shana's eyes down her cheeks, but she forced herself to not break down as she accepted the award for us.

"Today, Shana Lee, you Americans are here again . . . bringing with you this time young singers from all over the world. But it is not enough to just unite the new and the old. We must unite ourselves as people."

He looked out over the crowd that packed the garden, raising his right arm in a mighty sweep across them. "You have come from the countryside pouring into this city. *Hausa, Ibo, Yoruba,* and countless other tribes. Yes, we are many different peoples — but it is from our *differences* that we must now come together. From our rivalries, from the blood shed by our brothers and sisters — we must now unite. Moslem with Catholic, American with African . . . and Africa *with the world."* He waved his hand in farewell, then broke into a broad grin. *"I now give you Shana Lee!"*

Shana stepped up to the microphone, her sweet face barely clearing the podium. I could see her lips trembling as she began to speak.

"We are one world . . . one people. In this monument you are about to see, I hope you will find the common bond that holds us all together. Please . . ." she waved to the children below, " . . . please unveil this gift from our Tour."

A young boy, dressed in a school uniform stiff as a board, walked up to her shyly, but with great pride. Carefully, as he'd rehearsed before, he pulled back the covering.

It was a monument at once both powerful and divine. Three standing couples formed the base — each man and woman from one of the three main tribes. Above their heads, they held up an enormous globe bowl — carved with all the countries of the world.

Stretching on tip-toe, Shana passed the fiery torch up to the little boy. He proudly crawled out to the edge of the scaffold and, without flinching, lit the globe.

A flame leapt up. Cheers roared from the stiff businessmen.

"We have the children here to light the way," Shana leaned into the microphone, trying to be heard over the applause. Next to me, a group of kids was cheering wildly.

"Is he one of yours?" I asked a young girl in braids.

"He's from our school."

"Yoruba or Hausa?"

"He is *Nigerian,*" the little girl said with fierce pride, upset that I would even ask such a question.

People's Republic of the Congo

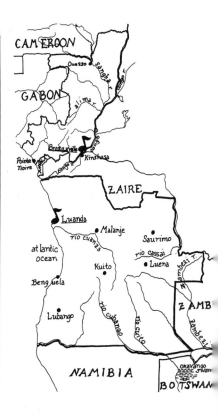

PEOPLE

Population: 1.8 million. Most 40% live in urban areas. 2 out of every 3 Congolese people live in either Brazzaville or Pointe Noire. **Ethnic Groups:** 15 main groups, 75 subgroups; largest groups are Bacongo, Bateke, M'Bochi, Sangha. **Religions:** Traditional beliefs 48%, Christian 47%, Muslim 2%. **Languages:** French (official), Lingala, Kikongo. **Literacy:** A high level of literacy —over 50% (by get was spent on education. **Infant Mortality:** 200/1,000. **Life Expectancy:** 61 ccounts 90%). 31% of its yrs.

GEOGRAPHY

Area: 342,000 sq.km. (132,000 sq.mi.); larger than New Mexico. **Capital City:** Brazzaville (pop. 300,000). **Other Major Cities:** Pointe Noire. **Terrain:** Coastal plains, fertile valleys in a central plateau. Much of the Congo is densely forested.

GOVERNMENT

Government: People's republic. **Colonial Power:** France. **Independence:** August 15, 1960.

ECONOMY

Yearly GDP Per Person: about $1,230. **Exports:** Off-shore petroleum (oil) is a major source of revenue, also tropical wood and sugar.

TOURIST ATTRACTIONS

Brazzaville, arts and crafts in Poto Poto, the Congo rapids, local music, Pointe Noire. **Warning:** Beware of police checkpoints in the countryside, carry ID at all times.

People's Republic of Angola

PEOPLE

Population: 8.5 million. **Ethnic Groups:** Ovimbundu 37%, Kimbundu 25%, Bakongo 15%, Lunda-Chokwe 8%, European 2%, other 13%. The *Ovimbundu* live in the center and southeast. The *Bakongo* live in the northwest (once they formed the Kingdom of the Kongo). The *Kimbandu* live in the area around Luanda. **Note:** Before the 1975 civil war, about 325,000 whites, mostly Portuguese citizens, lived in Angola. All but about 30,000 fled to Portugal. **Religions:** Roman Catholic, Protestant, traditional. The Portuguese brought the Catholic religion with them. The leaders of Angola's three liberation movements were educated at Protestant missions. **Languages:** Portuguese (official), traditional. **Literacy:** 30%. **Infant Mortality:** 148/1,000. **Life Expectancy:** 42 yrs.

GEOGRAPHY

Area: 1,246,700 sq.km. (481,351 sq.mi.); twice the size of Texas. **Capital City:** Luanda (1 million). **Other Major Cities:** Malanje, Nova, Lisboa, Luso. **Terrain:** Varied. A flat narrow strip of land stretches along Angola's coast, then rises abruptly to form a vast plateau and upland region holding one of Africa's great watershed areas. The South is semi-arid; here lies the Namib Desert.

GOVERNMENT

Government: Marxist people's republic, one-party rule. **Colonial Power:** Portuguese. **Independence:** November 11, 1975.

ECONOMY

Yearly GDP Per Person: **Exports:** Petroleum, gas, coffee, diamonds.

Angola, potentially one of the richest countries in sub-Saharan Africa, possesses petroleum (oil) rich farmland and rare minerals. Before independence, Angola exported oil, gas, coffee, diamonds, iron ore, sisal, fish and cement. But UNITA military operations kept the railroad effectively closed for years.

Chevron, Texaco and the Japanese company Mitsubishi have operations in Angola; most of Angola's oil trade is with the West.

TOURIST WARNING

At the time of the *Soul to Soul* flight stopover, the U.S. Department of State advised that travel to Angola was considered dangerous due to possible guerilla attacks. Fighting between government and UNITA forces had spread to most areas of the country. Travel to the capital city, Luanda, however was considered relatively safe.

the congo

13

"Next Stop — The
Twilight Zone"

Recorded at BRAZZA VILLE AIRPORT,
Monday June 20th, 7:30 A.M.

    Ras sits alone, still shaken from the letter. He sips a
soda, trying to cool his nerves.
    Outside my window I can see heavily armed troops in
green military fatigues stalking around our plane. Shoulder-
ing soviet rifles, sharing cigarettes, they wait until someone
decides what should be done with us.
    "There's no way they can hurt us in here, Ras," I
whisper over to him. "Is there?"
    Ras sips the last drop without answering.
    Hot. So hot inside I'd like to die. We've been sitting in
this plane over two and a half hours, arguing the cost of fuel,
waiting for clearance to go on into KwaNdebele — right into
the heart of South Africa.

Now Marvin's saying he may have to cancel the tour if we don't raise more money. He's got Shakespeare up there in the aisle in front of us, holding up a big board while he colors in the tally.

MOROCCO CONCERT	.4 MILLION
MARVIN'S VIDEO & TV SPOTS	1.2 MILLION
SHANA LEE'S ART SHOW	.4 MILLION
CONCESSION STANDS, T-SHIRTS	.1 MILLION
PRIVATE DONATIONS	1.2 MILLION
CORPORATE SPONSORS	3.6 MILLION

The Greek shipping guy did promise to buy the relief trucks needed for the refugee camp I'd be working in. With King Kola now matching us dollar for dollar, that translates into 14 million — still way short of our goal and not near enough for the world-wide satellite concert we're planning once we get to Kenya.

8:12 A.M.

A motorcycle with a sidecar careens up to our plane. Flapping over the handlebars is a red flag with a hammer and sickle.

"What are they?" I ask Neil.

"Cuban troops . . . maybe Soviet."

I watch Lenny climb into the sidecar and strap on a crash helmet. Tucked under his arm is his famous portable PC. If anyone can get us near South Africa — Lenny can.

11:42 A.M.

"Clearances! Clearances!" Lenny's shouting and jumping down the aisle, waving the papers over his head proudly. "We got 'em. We're going' into Angola!"

Everyone gets all excited.

LUANDA, Angola, 3:18 P.M.

Finally, an airport with a cafeteria.

Little did we know that "lounge" here means hot tin seats, a coin-operated coffee machine that spits back our coins, and light bulbs that could double as sun lamps. They buzz in the numbing heat and, for some unknown biological reason, attract every fly in a six mile radius.

3:51 P.M.

Everybody's sweaty, half dead. Rumors keep flying through the cafeteria . . . talk of changing our protest concert from the township to Swaziland, talk of rioting and shootings.

Finally L & M come in with the general plus a man from the outlawed African National Congress.

Lenny breaks the news, "We can't make it anywhere near South Africa. The ANC can't guarantee our safety."

Everyone groans. We have to fly nine more hours clear across the continent to land in Mozambique. From there he'll see what we can do.

Marvin's real disappointed. It's our first real defeat.

a woman freedom fighter in Mozambique's

FRELIMO army

PART FIVE

SOUTHERN AFRICA

"The Revolution Will Not Be Televised"

You will not be able to stay home, brother
You will not be able to plug in, turn on and cop out
You will not be able to lose yourself on skag
And skip out for beer during commercials
For the revolution will not be televised

The revolution will not be brought to you by Xerox
In four parts without commercial interruption
The revolution will not star Steve McQueen or Natalie Wood
The revolution will not give your mouth sex appeal
Or make you look five pounds thinner
The revolution will not be televised.

ABC will not be able to predict the winner at 8:30
There will be no more highlights on the 11 O'clock News
The theme song will not be written by Francis Scott Key
Nor sung by Glen Campbell, Tom Jones, Johnny Cash
or Englebert Humperdink
The revolution will not go better with Coke

The revolution will not be televised
The revolution will not be televised
The revolution will be no re-run, brother
The revolution will be...live!

words and music by Gill Scott-Heron
*as performed by **Gil Scott-Heron***

People's Republic of Mozambique

PEOPLE

Population: 13.4 million. **Ethnic Groups:** 10 major tribes. The Makura and Tsonga are the largest. 10,000 Europeans. **Religions:** 50% traditional African, 30% Muslim. 15% Christian. **Languages:** Portuguese (official). **Literacy:** 14% (Under colonial rule, education for blacks was strictly limited and 93% were kept illiterate. Since independence, the government has reduced illiteracy to 86%). **Infant Mortality:** 115/1,000. **Life Expectancy:** 47 yrs.

GEOGRAPHY

Area: 789,800 sq.km. (303,769 sq.mi.); twice the size of California. **Capital City:** Maputo (900,000). **Other Major Cities:** Biera. **Terrain:** Varies from lowlands (44% of the land) to high plateau. Mountains lie along the western frontier. Africa's 4th largest river, the Zambezi, divides the country in half.

GOVERNMENT

Government: Socialist one-party state. **Colonial Power:** Portugal. **Independence:** June 25, 1975.

ECONOMY

In 1975, the exodus of 200,000 Portuguese professionals disrupted the economy. Serious droughts forced Mozambique to import large amounts of food, much of it from the United States. Mozambique has great potential for a mineral industry. It mines coal and has unexploited deposits of iron and rare minerals. Mozambique also has hydroelectrical potential. But full exploitation of Mozambique's resources have been held back by insurgent attacks.
Yearly GDP Per Person: $220. **Exports:** cashews, shrimp, sugar, tea, cotton.

HISTORICAL NOTES

By the time Portuguese ships reached the shores of Mozambique in 1498, Arab traders had built up centuries old settlements and slave stations along the coast. Soon Portugal would battle the Arabs for control over these seaports. Trading posts and forts became the ports of call on this new sea route to the riches of the East.

When the days of ivory, gold and slave trading had passed, the Portuguese turned over the administration of their business to private companies controlled by the British who got rich by supplying cheap (often forced) African labor to the mines and plantations of their nearby colonies.

After World War II, many European nations granted independence to their colonies. Portugal, however, clung to the concept that Mozambique was an "overseas province" of the "mother country." Anti-Portuguese groups united to form the "Front for the Liberation of Mozambique" (FRELIMO). After 10 years of bloody warfare, Mozambique became independent.

Since 1980, an armed insurgency, the Mozambican National Resistance (RENAMO), has waged an increasingly violent bush war against the FRELIMO government — bombing government installations, economic centers, even civilians. There is increasing evidence that it is the Government of South Africa that is providing RENAMO with logistical support and training.

TOURIST ATTRACTIONS

3,000 miles of unbroken coastline. The old colonial town of Mocambique.

mozambique

14

"A Pretty Girl Is As Sharp As An Axe"

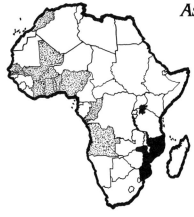

Kitabu Diary . . . MAPUTO, Monday, 8:30 P.M.

Neil sits next to me ramrod straight in shock. The tanks here are the MOVING kind . . . rumbling across the tarmac in line as we taxi along the runway.

"NO PHOTOS." Lenny cuts through the commotion, silencing us. He strides down the aisle, squinting into each of our faces, making certain no one's mistaken his message. "ABSOLUTELY no photos are to be taken here. Got that Neil? . . . Wake up when I'm talking to you. There's a military base here."

I step out into the hot, humid night. Armored jeeps buzz about. Troops march in columns along the edge of the runway. To them, we must look like somebody's drugged-out nightmare, filing off this plane . . . Tarot in their astrological capes, Sugar-N-Spice with their waist-long hair.

A red banner hangs down from the airport roof. When I get closer, I see on it a portrait of Lenin. Clicking his heels together, a general greets us. Stuck over his wife's right breast is a diamond hammer-and-sickle pin.

I shake hands with her and she smiles back at me, patting my hand warmly and posing for me. I take a shot of her alongside the general. And one of Shana Lee against the big portrait of Lenin.

Everyone's being real nice, but I keep thinking maybe they're just using us.

THE HOTEL TOURISMO, A Government-Run Hotel

Ever stay up all night and be so tired the next morning you can't decide which is best — to crash and miss the whole day — or try to stay awake so you don't screw up your schedule?

Veronique spent a week in the shower. By the time I got up to breakfast, all the scrambled eggs were gone and the coffee shop was empty — except for Spice.

Everybody had gone off early, he said. Tarot and the other groups by bus on the "Official Party Tour" . . . Ras, Lenny, and Marvin by plane to a tiny Kingdom, Swaziland, right on the border of South Africa.

"I thought we couldn't get into South Africa?"

"We can't, but some guy from the ANC is going to take them across by jeep at night, into a 'homeland.' Two demonstrators were shot there last week. Marvin wants to document the conditions South Africa's forcing these people to live in."

Kitabu Diary, 8:30 A.M.

. . . standing on red clay cliffs looking out over a surfer's paradise. One pure sand beach — 1,600 miles long. The tour guide Spice hired is going on and on about did I know Vasco da Gama's ship was anchored right below me, centuries ago.

All I can think of is the scrambled eggs I didn't have.

234

"*The tanks here are the moving kind, rumbling across the tarmac as we leave the airport . . .*"

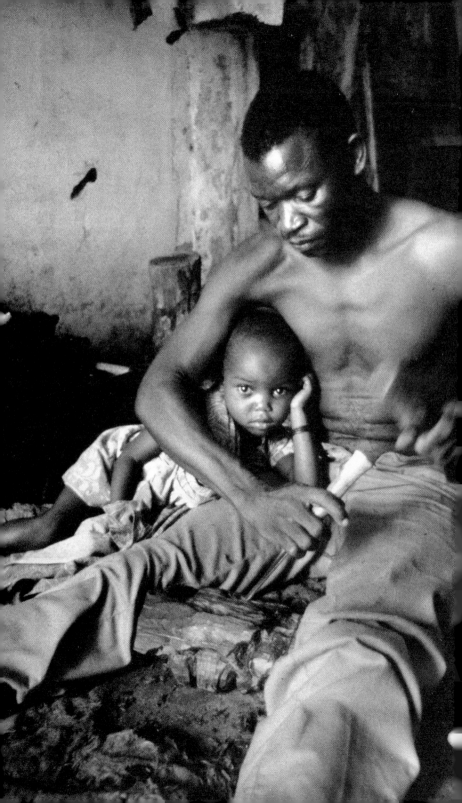

"Soldiers are everywhere. The Communist revolution is alive here . . . but still you find poor people sleeping where they can — inside the big wheels of an abandoned freight train — or propped up in an alleyway, like this father and son."

Kitabu Diary, Noon

Food at last . . . at a University coffee house on the Avenida Ho Chi Minh. I keep trying to let go of the way I see things. I want to tell the truth about Africa.

But whose truth am I telling? . . . A white girl's from New York City? Or Africa's like these students see it? How can I really be with people here?

Museum of The Revolution, Thursday June 23rd

Two days and still no word from Ras, Lenny, or Marvin.
Today our guide is a young woman from the Makua-Lomwe tribe, no more than eighteen but smart as a whip. Is she ever gorgeous. Her face is black, but she looks part Oriental — and her right nostril is pierced with a beautiful gold nose star.
She pulls a Hindu shawl around her sleek shoulders. On it I see the words: AHAD NI SHOKA.

"What's that say on her scarf?" I asked Shakespeare, closing up my diary.

"It's Bantu." The corners of his mouth curled up into a brilliant smile. "It means, *'A pretty girl is as sharp as an axe.'* "

"You like her? . . ." I teased, pushing him up toward her. "Shakespeare, if you like her, let her know."

Shakespeare moved up to the front of our tour group, glancing back at me for moral support until he finally worked up the nerve to speak to her. "Excuse me Miss, but . . . how do you feel now about the Portuguese?"

"Barbarians!" she snapped back over her shoulder. "Of all the colonialists, they were the worst. After slavery was outlawed, my father was still forced to work *six months* of every year in the mines of South Africa — without pay!"

"So, you're saying the English were *better*?" he challenged, removing his mirrored sunglasses so she could get a better look at him.

"I'm not saying they were good . . ." the young girl shrugged, now adjusting her own eyeglasses. "But better? Yes, *definitely*. With the Portuguese there was *no* training. At independence, we were all still illiterate. The officials who ran the country just left us with *nothing*. Only *forty* doctors, for our whole country! There was looting. No food. Everything just . . . fell apart."

Strung along the wall, one after another, were photos: collective farms, tractors, irrigation canals. "You see here? . . ." Her eyes sparkled excitedly. "First we liberated our banks, then our schools. No more will our children be raised with an elitist education!"

South Africa

"... millions of people were forced from their land, packed into trucks and made to live in areas too dry to grow food ..."

"... under white supremecy you could not marry freely, you could not choose your work, you could not travel, or vote, or even sit on a bench.

NET BLANKES
WHITES ONLY

*"In the big cities, police round up people who
are never heard from again . . ."*

*". . . while in the townships, like Soweto,
people live in conditions
you can't imagine . . ."*

". . . crowded into tin shacks like sardine cans stacked up on the hillside, sweltering in the sun, with no sanitation, no water . . ."

She showed me a photo of a student brigade — digging trenches on a hillside. "You do this for *one month* every year?" I asked her.

"Exactly!" the young girl took off her glasses, noting Shakespeare's crisp blue suit. "It is essential to destroy the idea that scholarly work and working with you hands are separate!"

"South Africa is doing their best to undermine our revolution. Daily we have been raided, and *bombed!"* she cried bitterly, showing us photos as proof. "They even bomb our *civilians.* Parachutes land outside the city. They blow up our bridges and dynamite our railways. *Even here in Maputo* they hide bombs!"

"But *not* in the museum, right?" I asked jokingly.

"Not yet . . ." the young girl answered me — but she wasn't joking at all. "Just last week, a girls' school right by the airport was blown up. Our health clinics, our country stores, *whole* villages they have destroyed. And you Americans wonder why we have chosen Communism?" She turned to me, "Should we forget that it was America that supported South Africa and *all* the colonial rulers here?"

"We can't rewrite our past. But —" I pushed Shakespeare up right alongside her, "— as this young man here keeps telling me, we can build a future with you."

Shakespeare reached his hand out, fumbling with the photos as he helped her stack them, "I would like to find out ways we could work together with you."

"I too!" she smiled, squeezing Shakespeare's hand. "We are Marxist, yes — but there are, as you shall see, *many* forms of Marxism. We are not *all so red,* like you see us. We need friends, too."

Shakespeare got a date. The young girl came back with us to our hotel. When we got inside, our crew was milling around the lobby, grumbling to each other.

Something bad had happened, but no one knew what it was. Marvin was back — but where was Lenny? We were told to meet at noon in the basement ballroom. It was called the Karl Marx.

PRIVATE MEETING
required attendance — all S to S personnel

The sign, hastily scrawled on a white piece of cardboard, hung from the brass doorknob to the Karl Marx Ballroom. Late again, I pried open the heavy doors and peered inside. Two television screens were set up on stage, facing the room full of metal chairs.

I scrunched into the last row past all these big crew guys and grabbed a seat Neil saved for me. Brock, I saw, was somewhere over on the right with Veronique. The room got silent, waiting as Marvin walked up to the podium.

"I asked you all to be here now —" Marvin began, but his voice broke off in pain. "I want you to hear this because we all started this together. And we all should know what's going on . . ." His tired eyes looked out over the audience real steady, taking in each one of us like we'd become family.

"Lenny Stein has been shot."

I heard someone across the room start to cry. I couldn't see who it was. People were on their feet, asking to know more. But Marvin was so shaken he couldn't talk. He was holding onto the podium to keep himself steady.

"Ras Marcus, he's been shot too . . ."

Through the crazy jumble of bodies and heads, Brock's reddened eyes locked onto mine. I watched as his lips began to tremble . . . then come apart. A cry of pain flew out, drowned out at once by other cries that shattered the room. Then he buried his head in the sleeve of his leather flight jacket.

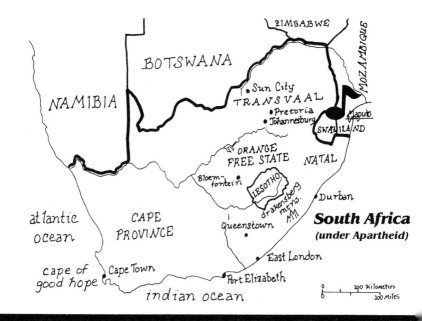

South Africa
(under Apartheid)

PEOPLE

Population: 31.1 million. **Ethnic Groups:** Black
— colored, Asian, African. White—English,
Afrikaaner.

BLACK AFRICANS (70% of the population)
are mostly descended from Sotho and Nguni
peoples who migrated southward centuries ago.
They are subdivided into 10 groups correspond-
ing to the 10 ethnically based "homelands"
(called national states by South Africa). The largest African ethnic groups are Zulu (6.0 million)
and Xhosa (5.8 million).

WHITES (10%) mostly descended from
Dutch (Afrikaaner is Dutch for "farmer"), English,
French,and German settlers.

COLOREDS are mostly descendants of
indigenous peoples and the earliest European
settlers. They live mostly in the Cape Province.

ASIANS are mostly descendants of the Indian
workers brought to South Africa in the mid-19th
century to work as indentured laborers on sugar
estates in Natal and constitute about 3% of the
population.

KHOI-SAN - the earliest people to live in the
area are a non-negroid, non-caucasian race that
has practically been exterminated over the cen-
turies. There are only 100,000 "Bushmen" and
"Hottentots" alive today.
Religions: Mostly Christian; some traditional
African, Hindu, Muslim, and Jewish. **Languages:**
English and Afrikaans (official), Zulu, Xhosa,
North and South Sotho, Tswana, Khoi ("Click"),
others. **Literacy:** Whites (98%); Coloreds (75%);
Asians (85%); African (50%). **Infant Mortality:**
per 1,000 live births. Whites (14.9); Blacks/
Coloreds (80.6); Asians (25.3); Africans
(% unknown). **Life expectancy:** White (70 yrs.);
Blacks/ Coloreds (59 yrs.); Asians (66 yrs.); Afri-
cans (55 yrs.).

GEOGRAPHY

Area: 1,233,404 sq.km (472,359 sq.mi.); about
twice the size of Texas. **Capital City:** Pretoria
(administrative), Cape Town (legislative), Bloem-
fontein (judicial). **Other Major Cities:** Johannesburg, Durban. **Terrain:** .Plateau, mountains,
coastal plains, scenic beaches. No major rivers
or lakes, so water conservation is necessary.

GOVERNMENT

Government: Executive—president, tricameral
Parliament with one chamber each for whites,
coloreds, and Indians, under a constitution.
Colonial Power: Dutch (1652 at the Cape), then
England (late 1700's). On May 31, 1910, Dutch
and British colonies became the Union of South
Africa ruled by England. **Independence:** May 31,
1961, this Union became the Republic of South
Africa, independent of the British Commonwealth.

ECONOMY

Most South Africans (black and white) lived
by herding or farming — until the discovery of
diamonds (1867) and gold (1886) ushered in
South Africa's industrial age. Now South Africa is
the world's leading producer of gold and gem
diamonds. Reserves of asbestos, manganese,
titanium and chrome are greater than half of the
world's known supplies. Reserves of gold total
almost half the entire world's supplies.
Yearly GDP Per Person: (Not available).
Exports: Gold, diamonds, corn, wool, sugar, fruit,
metals. Gold (bullion and coins) is more than half
of the total value of South African exports.

TOURIST ATTRACTIONS

Warning: Many toursits, entertainers and athletes are boycotting South Africa because of its
racist Apartheid policies.

south africa

15

"The End Of The Road"

KARL MARX BALLROOM, 12:40 P.M.

EVERYONE'S TALKING on top of everyone else . . . you could hardly hear what Marvin was saying. I'm trying to climb over a chair to Raine who was crying because of the noise.

"We were shooting some film in South Africa in a township homeland . . . when all this smoke started appearing. Trapped. We were trapped inside a woman's home. Everyone started ducking under tables. Ras, he tried to run out . . ."

Question followed on top of question; everyone was clamoring to get their's heard. One by one, Marvin answered them.

Q: "Where was Lenny hit?"

A: "The bullets hit through his lower spine and right thigh . . . He'll be alright."

Q: "And Ras Marcus?"

Marvin got real silent. We all waited for him to say something.

A: "He . . . was hit in the neck.

Q: "How bad?"

A: "We don't know yet. I'm trying to get our own doctor in there, a specialist."

Marvin nodded, and Shakespeare flicked on a slide projector. A series of photos flashed on the wall . . . a little boy's body lay crumpled face down in the dirt where he fell, blood oozing from the hole in his back where he was shot . . . another young man was left half slumped over the irrigation pump where he worked, his arm twisted horribly out of shape. There was a woman's body draped protectively over him, shot through the stomach . . .

Then came a photo of Ras' blood-spattered face, staring blankly up at us from the dirt where he lay. The mouth that once held so many smiles for me was now filled with crusted blood, his razor sharp eyes glazed over like a dead man's.

Q: "Was anyone else shot?"

A: "Thirty-seven people. . . . *Thirty-seven* were killed. The troops just waded in through the town streets, shootin' everything they saw."

Q: "Who did this?

A: "The government says it was guerrillas financed out of South Africa. They got a civil war here. Lenny may be out in a week or so. Ras, they say they've taken him away to some hospital in Johannesburg. There's no way you can get in to see him."

Marvin wrote the address of Amnesty International on the blackboard in big block letters so we could all write them to try to guarantee Ras' safety. Then, carefully, he placed the chalk back on the lip of the board.

"Look, what I'm tryin' to tell you is — the tour's cancelled. Lenny's been on the phone from the hospital calling everyone he knows back in the States — actors, business executives, people that *owe him their careers* . . . But the man's tapped out. You understand what I'm saying? We hit up everybody we knew, just to get us over here." He looked right out at each of us, "There *is* no more money."

Guys in the group started to shift around in their chairs uneasily. Nobody wanted to face what he had to say.

"Now . . . I'm not asking you to go on with me for free. Those of you who want to stay, can stay . . . the rest of you can go. I've made arrangements. We've got money enough to get the crew all back home. You've got to choose."

More questions . . .

Q: "Would staying mean we could still play the concert in Kenya?"

A: "Doubtful."

Q: "What about Ethiopia?"

A: "Forget it — unless Uncle Sam gives us a key to Fort Knox."

Q: "How much has been raised so far?"

A: "Twelve million dollars."

Q: "Where will it go?"

A: "The United Nations will divide it among the relief agencies."

Marvin ended the questions, set aside his notes, and stepped out in front of the podium to be closer to us.

"Nobody will think the worst of you for going home. We all know we've got our own lives to live, our families, our work. And I know each one of you personally, and how much you've given . . ." Marvin's voice broke. You could see he was fighting back the tears. "Ras, Lenny and me, we know why you came here. I know what's in the heart of each one of you. So you don't have to prove nothin' to me."

I looked over at Shana; she was crying, too. Everything got real quiet while we waited for Marvin to get his voice back.

"Lenny, he asked me to thank you. And Shana and I, we thank you, too. I gotta go . . ." The big man folded up his notes, raised a clenched fist and headed off the stage. "We'll be back next year."

"What if we stay?" someone called out.

Marvin thought about it for a minute, looking down at his glass of water like somehow within it might be the answer. Then he fiddled one last time with his *Soul to Soul* pen, clicking it in and out, "Nothin' much I can offer you. After I get Ras the medical help he needs, I may go on to Zimbabwe."

Afterwards, for those of us who hung around, Marvin got down to the bottom line.

It was even worse than he first let on. King Kola wouldn't foot the bill unless there was a concert, and Lenny and Marvin both had put up their savings to cover expenses for the play date that now would be cancelled.

It was a fold.

Marvin was going to Zimbabwe to shoot some kind of ending. The video, he hoped, would raise more money for the development projects. Some of the crew were invited to go on with him — but under new rules. You must pay your own way. No hangers on. And after Zimbabwe, he couldn't promise us anything.

My job covered air fare only. Hotels and meals I had to scrounge for myself. I was just calculating how I could do it when the ballroom doors burst open. In strode the same general we met at the airport, surrounded by armed soldiers and police with red berets. He was anxious to see what evidence Marvin had of South Africa's atrocities.

Marvin invited him to see the screening. It was the actual video footage he shot, uncut — including the part when the shootings happened . . .

T.V. SCREEN

CLOSE-UP — a black woman's face, raised high, defiant. Her neck, oddly elongated, is held up by a dozen COPPER RINGS stacked one atop the other, forming a cylinder up to her chin. ZOOM IN as she begins to speak in broken English: *"This home you see is not my home. We were put here against our will."*

CAMERA PANS across a dusty landscape . . . no trees, no sign of life . . . to find a dozen shacks made from corrugated tin sheets and packing crates. CHILDREN scamper around the dirt, kicking a lop-sided soccer ball.

CLOSE UP — *THE YOUNG WOMAN: "My name is Selephi Masilele. My husband, Mabhoko, and I, we have two boys; but we cannot see each other."*

VOICE OVER — *LENNY: "Selephi and her family must now live in an 'independent State' or 'homeland,' She cannot move. This homeland is called KwaNdebele in South Africa's Transvaal. Demonstrations have ripped the area apart. And the police have cracked down hard."*

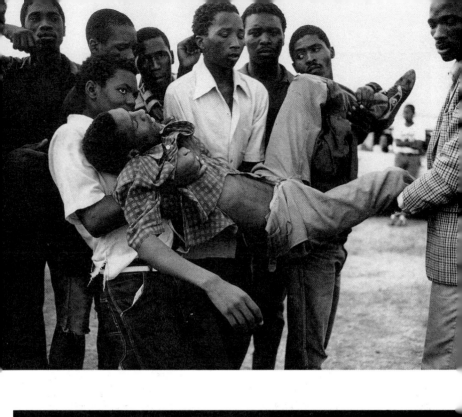

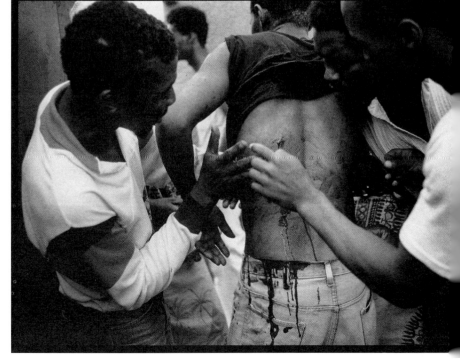

RACK FOCUS TO three WOMEN dressed in startling robes. They glide by a wall covered with bright geometric patterns — triangles and squares of bold reds, blacks, yellows — the unique Ndebele design. Their heads are held erect by RINGS OF COPPER. The CYLINDERS OF RINGS on their arms and legs force a slow-motion walk and perfect posture.

VOICE OVER — LENNY: "There are only women here in KwaNdebele. The men work in the coal mines by the cities and sleep barrack style, fifty in one dorm. Before, Selephi's husband could see his family once a month. Now Selephi's husband is not even home. They say to find work he must travel to Johannesburg."

CAMERA PANS with MARVIN, LENNY and RAS as they follow her inside a box-like structure of tin and pasteboard.

CUT TO:

INTERIOR, SELEPHI'S HOME — PAN ACROSS walls covered with NEWS-PAPER. At Ras' feet, one of her boys, no more than skin and bones, lays on the dirt floor. The other boy, Mabusa, carries in a jug of water. There are no electric lights. No plumbing.

CLOSE UP — THE YOUNG WOMAN (shaking her head no):
        "Isherefe, isherefe!"

CAMERA PANS to *RAS* (stepping in frame to explain): *"She says they got no thatch for a roof. All the grass here has dried out, you see? So she's gotta use this metal* (taps roof with his knuckles). *It's damn hot inside here, like livin' in an oven."*

RAS hands the MICROPHONE back to the young mother. The CAMERA goes crazy, SWINGING WILDLY across their faces, pointing up at a weird angle, then falling on its side on the ground. BARE FEET scramble through the dust. FACES are seen, out of focus, running by. SCREAMS are heard. The RAT-TAT-TAT of gunfire. SMOKE. More SCREAMS. The young woman's voice is crying: *"Mabusa, Mabusa!"*

SOMEONE PICKS UP THE CAMERA and is running with it. Now we're in the middle of people scattering under a table. Coughing. Smoke . . . A man carries the boy, Mabusa, across the CAMERA. It is RAS. We see a deep gash in his neck, a smear of blood against the newspapered wall . . .

Then we're OUTSIDE.

CUT TO:

RAS dragging the boy behind a bus. DIRTY STREETS swarming with women running and screaming. Behind them, we see an ARMORED JEEP. SOLDIERS are firing MACHINE GUNS into the tin shack homes. SIX BODIES lie slumped on the ground. One woman crouches to cover her child. It is Selephi. She is SHOT in the stomach. The SOLDIER walks up to her and shoots her again in the head. Then, her child is SHOT.

253

The SOLDIER swings his RIFLE BUTT at the CAMERA lens . . .
Then the SCREEN goes black.

We sat in stone silence. The lights came back on. Marvin was climbing back up to the podium.

"Let me know your answer by 6 P.M. tonight, so we know where we're at."

People were split up, milling around in small groups. It was like everyone was going back to what they knew best — their own little cliques. The French. The English . . . I spotted Brock hanging around Marvin, who was already answering as many questions as he could handle.

"Hey, Marv!" Brock was tugging at him, frantic and terrified. "You suppose that if I go on to this next gig with you, you could get me an' my boys a spot? We're ready — any time, any place, any —"

"Brock, get out of my face . . ." Marvin spun on him. "Every day you're whining to me about your act. *I ain't interested* in your act. You're never goin' to play on my stage 'til you start *listenin'* to what other people have to say."

"But look Marv, I've got Cleavon an' —"

"No *buts.* You understand?" Marvin glared at him, pointing a finger in his face.

Brock was crazed. He just couldn't handle it, that Ras, dear sweet Ras, who'd been like a big Daddy to us, was lying in a hospital somewhere with a bullet lodged in his neck.

*"In my music I want people to recognize themselves...
The truth isn't home grown, its a universal language.
Jah gave man his life forever.
In the end, all men will sing the same song..."*

— *Bob Marley*

coming attractions

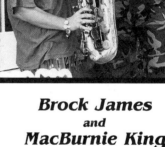

Brock James
and
MacBurnie King

return in

Brothers and Sisters

*"Real
love
knows
no
boundaries"*

— a daring adventure!

Book Two: "BROTHERS and SISTERS"
Introduction by **Nelson Mandela**

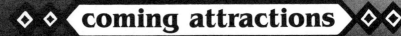

coming attractions

Brock James tells his own story...
Heart to Heart!

Book Three: "HEART to HEART"
Introduction by Janet Jackson

MISSING

NAME: Halima Desta, wife of Alem Desta;
AGE: 19; LAST SEEN: on foot crossing the
Sudan/Ethiopia border with 2 children;
DESTINATION: Kassala Refugee Camp,
IDENTIFICATION: a small "T-shaped" scar
on either cheek; IF FOUND: alive or
deceased notify Dr. El Badir, Red Cross
Center, Khartoum.

Having traded his identity
with Alem, Brock puts
his own life on the line
to reunite this young couple
separated by war and famine.
Join him — and a
host of new characters!

Josuf

a Dinka tribesman from the remotest regions of southern Sudan, "the Sudd," an unchartered maze of swamps the size of Maine. Educated in forestry in Cairo, now he is torn between his new teachings and the traditional ways of his ancestors.

Dr. El Badir

a Muslim woman in charge of the Kassala refugee center, responsible for the lives of over 100,000 refugees — men, women and children on the brink of starvation

Kaleb

an Arab trader who transports refugees and black market weapons across the treacherous Sudan / Ethiopian border.

*two teens from
two different worlds*   *– and the man who
brought them together*

MonsooN

**Each special edition includes
a unique sixty·eight page supplement**

A PORTRAIT OF INDIA

Meet her people
discover how 1 out of every 7 people in the world live

LIFESTYLES, CAST and RELIGION
60 PHOTOS by award winning photographers
ILLUSTRATIONS by Roseanne Litzinger
SONG LYRICS by John Lennon, The Eurythmics
John Denver and others
INDIRA GANDHI "Mother of modern India"
MAPS, a GLOSSARY of foods, clothes and customs
QUOTATIONS from Mahatma Gandhi

A daring adventure

across two continents

ACKNOWLEDGEMENTS

I thank the following people, and in the thanking of them, thank the many others not named here who contributed to making this book possible. Please accept my acknowledgement of them as my acknowledgement of you.

My thanks and deepest appreciation to...

my mother, Adele St. Balinth,—whose wit and storytelling, for better or for worse, rubbed off.

my father, John Ballard and my stepfather, Ty St. Balinth—who have always encouraged me to do the work I've chosen to do.

Jackie Ryan — for teaching my heart to sing.

Laurie Herrick and Dan Zukergood — my good friends, for believing in me and for literally putting several years of their lives on the line so that these books could be published.

Sidney Mackenzie — for the beauty and strength she found in Africa and passed on to me.

Rose Boyle — for being there for me 100% during my sister's dying.

Angel and Shelly, Debbie, Terry, Yvette, Jim, Stacey, and Alex — who've done everything else on these books that I haven't done, for making these books a reality when it looked least like they'd ever get done.

Lee Drozd, Grace Kono, Angela Lupisa, Carmen Torres and Jill Gwin — my typists, for putting up with my handwriting and, somehow, deciphering my words.

Anna Yanes — for doing most everything I didn't want to do in order to complete this book.

Dan Canell of Grassroots — an extraordinary man, for his tireless efforts to rid the Third World of poverty and for his encouragement of my work.

Gebre and Saba — for their insight into the Eritrean/Ethiopian war and for introducing me to the generous community of Eritrean people.

Also — to my friend from World Vision for sticking his neck out to arrange a flight for me into Ethiopia, to **Sharon** my comrade in arms, for our visits to the refugee camps, and to **John**, a remarkable Maasai scholar, for introducing me to his people.

Shelly Balloon, Judy Benjamin, Roman and Larry Carroll, Faith Catlin, Russ Collins, Viveka Davis, Leslie Diamond, Fernando Flores, Jane Gelfman, H.B. Gilmour, Jessica Gilmour, Jennifer Gooch, Kristin Hauptman, Jeannie Hawk, John Isaac, Werner Krutein, Tony Little, Walter Dean Myers, Catherine Parrish, Donna Parker, Sheryl Lee Ralph, Lori Rand, Tom Reilly, Charlotte Richardson, Judith Serll, Monica Sicile, Harriet Sternberg, Lynne Twist, Dennis Watlington, Michael Winn, Penny Wolin.

World Vision, UNICEF, the UN Photo Library, Grassroots, The Hunger Project, LAWHE, the Eritrean Relief Committee (ERC).

⚡⚡⚡⚡⚡⚡⚡⚡⚡ *from me to you* ⚡⚡⚡⚡⚡

I invite you...to participate *Soul to Soul*
to "be the bridge" between Africa and America!

Several years ago I decided to write a series of novels that I hoped would bring the world's young people closer together. I wanted to: (1) "bring alive" for you the richness and beauty of Africa's many peoples, and (2) "bring home" for you the crushing conditions under which too many of Africa's peoples strive to survive.

At the time I had no idea how I would do this. I had never written a novel. I wasn't an expert on Africa; nor had I been able to visit the continent. What I did have was outrage over the horrific plight of Africa's peoples trapped by famine and a fierce desire to do something about it — out of that desire I was invited to board a cargo plane destined for Sudan.

Soul to Soul was born out of what I saw visiting the "feeding station" in Kassala as the belt of famine tightened across the belly of Africa. Witnessing first hand the plight of the Ethiopian refugees, coming face to face with their suffering and our ability to do "only so much," we all, black and white, found ourselves overwhelmed by a flood of difficult questions.

What is it within us, that allows us to turn our backs on each other...that divides us as a human family? What is our role as witnesses to today's largest dislocation of peoples? (over the half the world's homeless refugees are in Africa).

Returning to the U.S., I was told by publishers that there wasn't an interest in novels dealing with Africa. Publishers of young adult fiction had shied away from dealing with "social issues". Teens were "not interested".

But the young people I knew *were* interested...in the hunger plaguing the world today...in the madness of nuclear extinction ...in the prejudices that divide nation from nation, young from old, black from white. Young people weren't lacking in the capacity to take on these challenges — what was lacking was challenging materials that *dealt* with the issues — instead of avoiding them. Speaking in colleges and high schools across the United States, I found most of us are appallingly ignorant of the nations of Africa and the true realities of what day-to-day life is like for the people who live there.

Misconceptions and misinformation are rampant.

We still speak of Africa like it was one country "...India, China, Africa..." rather than continent of over 50 countries, filled with peoples and cultures as diverse as Greeks a from Swedes. What do we know of the Ban sense of community and family missing from so much of our Western life today?

In the past, foreigners looked down on who are African as "primitive," even "savage people; and Africans have looked down on who are European as "evil," or "immoral." T truth is no culture makes sense to people fr another culture — until you are willing to loc beyond the external solutions and styles human beings have invented to find the common ground that gave rise to them.

We in the West sometimes can be very arrogant, believing that our recent technolo has given us the right to control the rest of world and that other, ancient civilizations should imitate us. We measure our new-found technologies against so-called "primitive" ones and fail to measure the everyday sense of well-being of our people If we did, we would find that our ability to lo or torture each other, regrettably, has not changed much.

We harbor in our hearts both the desir to care and the capacity to kill.

When cultures collide, too often fear o each other blinds us from friendship. We s our survival threatened by "outsiders," "aliens," "foreigners," and seek to destroy dehumanize what we don't understand. W choose: to *compete*, not to *cooperate*, to *segregate*, not to *integrate*, to *exploit*, not t *empower*.

The line between the rich and the poo the "haves" and the "have nots," the First World and the Third World, becomes an ev widening chasm few can cross. Buried by advancing civilization, overwhelmed by wha we call "progress," many loose their lives trying to cross over that line — that border lay down in blood to keep "us" from "them those boundaries of safety that measure th length and breadth of our souls.

It is too easy to turn your back on wha you don't understand. In this ever-closing world, this is a luxury we can no longer affc Whole cultures are being destroyed. Entire peoples in Africa — the *Nuba,* the *Dinka,* th *Tuareg* — are becoming extinct, their ways

living forever wiped off the face of this earth. What secrets, what healings, what wisdom will be buried along with the bodies of these people?

Will we allow our differences to destroy what we have in common?...Or will we allow what we have in common to overcome the destruction that can come from our differences?

I invite you to break through the "strangeness," the walls of cultural prejudice — and look beyond to discover what you have in common with other people. I invite you to think the thoughts other people think and see the world through their eyes.

At every moment you have the ability to care and nurture one another — or to destroy and dehumanize one another, to heal — or to harm, to give life — or to take life away.

The choice is yours...

What will you say to the next stranger you see? What actions will you take in your lifetime to either bring the world's peoples closer together or to tear people apart?

How do you want to be remembered by those you love?

In resolving to do these books, I found myself faced with even deeper questions — unexpected ones for which I still have no answer.

Can we really get inside someone else's skin and see life through their eyes? Can a "black" person ever discover what it is like to be "white"? Can a man ever understand what it is like to be a woman?...a child to be a senior citizen?...a Jew to be a Muslim?...

I don't know the answers. I don't know how deeply one can fathom the life of another.

What I do know is, that for me, this is the goal in life worth striving for. Whether we ultimately can or cannot know each other is not the question. The question is: *are you and I willing to make the attempt?* Are we willing to dedicate ourselves to putting aside our own point of view in order to appreciate another's ? Are we willing to take into our

hearts the concerns, dreams, and fears of another and begin to experience what they experience?

To me, this is the challenge: To expand our world view to include the world of another...To make what was once outside our reality — a reality...To embrace what once appeared to be "foreign" as if it were our own.

In this way, maybe we can bring the world's peoples back together — *hand in hand, heart to heart*, and *soul to soul*.

I have no problem with the notion "charity begins at home." My problem comes when it ends there. Like the song goes, "real love, knows no boundaries." We have healed some of the wounds in our own country - but a much larger accommodation and sensitivity still awaits us. If ever we are to end the problems of hunger, poverty, disease, and the threat of nuclear war that touches all of our lives, we must do it together.

We are all inter-related. To survive, we must become World Citizens.

But is it possible to live your life as a World Citizen? To always take actions consistent with your ideals?

I can testify, for me, it certainly is not. With every accomplishment there comes a failure. With every attempt to be consistent, I fall short.

So why have ideals?

My life is dead without them. I have found it is in the very attempt to fulfill your dreams that you will shape your life. So stop; pause for a moment to invent for yourself a purpose worthy of you — some vision which will get you up in the morning and sustain you through the dark times. Not an ideal that is impossibly high, that is destined to give you a sense of failure, but one that lies just beyond your reach, that will call on you to bring yourself to another level in order to fulfill it.

Most importantly, I have found that "you don't have to be a saint or a sinner to make a difference in this world."

▰▰▰▰▰▰▰ *I ask for your help* ▰▰▰▰▰▰▰

Are you willing to make this series on Africa known to schools, libraries and friends? I invite you to write me and let me know.

Also, I would love to know about you and what you are doing. It isn't often a writer has a chance to hear from his readers and I welcome your letters. I cannot tell you how much you have sustained me through the mind- numbing months of research, the ups and downs of writing and re-writing, the joys and disappointments of doing this work.

Thank you for your support John

ORGANIZATIONS

On September 11, 1988, more than 90,000 people gathered at the mall in Washington, D.C. to celebrate what has now become the most significant movement to reunite the black family since the 1960's. Across the mall's lawns, people visited exhibitions and workshops given under tents, consumed authentic African-American foods, and enjoyed music by some of the world's top performers. Today, millions of people have attended such events across the country in cities as varied as Los Angeles, Atlanta, and Philadelphia....

PLEASE NOTE: *The Soul to Soul series will feature the work of some of the outstanding organizations and dedicated individuals whose contribution to humanity is in alignment with the ideals of this series.*

Black Family Reunion

Purpose: To help families help themselves in the face of cutbacks in government support and increasingly dismal economic forecasts for African-Americans.

Founder: Dr. Dorothy Height, President, National Council of Negro Women (N.C.N.W.).
Founded: September 11, 1988 in Washington, D.C.

For decades policy makers have ignored the important connection that family structure has to social and economic progress (even though this relationship was spelled out by Senator Patrick Moynihan over 25 years ago). Little enough has been done to assist the economic progress of African-Americans; next to nothing has been done to assist the social cohesion of the African-American family.

In fact, the black family has been under siege, often described as a chaotic and crumbling institution on the verge of collapse. The media, especially, has portrayed the black family as unstable and lacking in family values. In media circles, the term "single parent" has become synonymous with the black family in a negative and derogatory context. Attention is largely devoted to descriptions of inner-city crime, drug abuse, teenage pregnancy, and unemployment. The picture of black families that the public is left with is one of unending weakness and hopelessness.

There is some truth in the matter. In fact, the numbers are alarming:

- *60% of African-American babies are born out of wedlock.*
- *54% of African-American children grow up in single-parent homes.*
- *31% of African-American families live below the poverty level*
- *1 out of every 4 African-American men aged 20-29 is either in jail, or on probation, or on parole.*
- *Homicide is the leading cause of death among African-American men aged 15-34.*

Does this mean the extinction of the black family?

That alarming possibility inspired Dr. Dorothy Height, President of the *National Council of Negro Women*, into action. She conceived of and produced a series of *"Black Family Reunion Celebrations"* across the nation—festivals "dedicated to the history, tradition and culture of the black family." Her goal: ending poverty and under-achievement through the restoration of the African-American family.

There are some facts that give her encouragement:

- *While 1 out of every 3 African-American families live **under** the poverty line, 2 out of every 3 live **above**.*
- *The African-American middle class has expanded by more than 30% since 1980.*
- *The number of African-American professionals has expanded by more than 63% between 1980 and 1985.*
- *The average income of middle class African-Americans has been rising steadily, 10% a year since 1985.*
- *Nearly 7 in 10 upper middle class African-American families are headed by both parents.*
- *Fewer than 1 in 10 African-American families is poor when both parents are present (while 3 out of every 4 of poor African-American families are headed by one parent, usually the mother).*

By making *family restoration* the core of its strategy to reverse African-American poverty and under-achievement, the *National Council of Negro Women* has taken on an issue that others have overlooked. By daring to be a "throwback" in a media-swamped nation addicted to fast living, by promoting marriage over single living and community over self-absorption, Dorothy Height has boldly dared to go against the grain once again in her life.

"The concept of self-help for the black family is contrary to public opinion. The image of dependency is always put forth in the media—but the reality is that we have always helped ourselves and provided for ourselves. In fact, we're taking the African concept of family—an ancient concept of extended family—and trying to revive it today."

Celebrities, church groups, marching bands, drill teams, fraternities, sororities, community organizations and families...all gather together for an opening march to kick off the celebrations.

This unique parade is designed to bring together all aspects of the African-American community.

It is a startling sight to behold: Reggae musicians with dreadlocks mixing with clergy from the church, inner-city teens hand in hand with city mayors, major league ballplayers wheeling handicapped children.

Activities

The weekend- long outdoor celebrations feature job fairs, cultural exhibits, health screenings, activities for children, give-aways, celebrity appearances and musical entertainment by some of today's top recording artists, like: singer *Melba Moore*, actor *Malcolm Jamal-Warner*, comedian *Dick Gregory*, actress *Jayne Kennedy-Overton* , athlete *Arthur Ashe*, 'Roots' author *Alex Haley*, and *Jesse Jackson*.

TENTED PAVILLIONS
host more than 100 educational workshops, covering a wide variety of themes, including:

- *Fitness and beauty*
- *Community networking*
- *Womens' issues*
- *Africa—the Diaspora*
- *Job opportunities*
- *Aids education*
- *Malnutrition*
- *Education in career advancement*

SPECIAL EVENTS
are held for young adults on subjects ranging from:

- *Being black on a white campus*
- *How to get and keep your first job*
- *Building scholar-athletes*
- *The impact of violence on the black family*
- *Drug abuse programs*
- *Teen pregnancy prevention programs.*

A family reunion is the oldest of black traditions. More than 3,000 African-American families hold reunions every year in the South alone.

The oldest consistently documented black family in the United States is the Quanter family. Recently, this family celebrated the 300th anniversary of Henry and Margaret Quanter's emancipation from slavery in 1864. On August 31, 1986 the old Summerset Place near Creswell, North Carolina was the scene of a truly unique family reunion. Over 2,000 people—direct descendants of the 21 slave families who worked the pre-Civil War plantation returned to the slave quarters that gave birth to their mothers and fathers.

They came from almost every state on the East Coast—in bus loads of aunts, uncles, and cousins from Baltimore, in car pools and trains from New England, and in planes from as far away as California, Washington and Nevada. They sat down and ate with each other in a scene eerily reminiscent of the vision set forth by Dr. Martin Luther King, Jr. in his 'I Have A Dream' speech:

"I have a dream...that one day, on the red hills of Georgia, the sons of former slaves and the sons of former slave owners will be able to sit down together at the table of brotherhood."
                                    —Dr. Martin Luther King Jr.

National Council of Negro Women

Founded: 1935 **Founder:** Mary McLeod-Bethune, the legendary human rights activist. In 1955, Mary gathered 28 women leaders and shared her dream of forming one organization that would harness the strength of all black women; a daring idea that resulted in the *National Council of Negro Women*.

Executive Director: Dr. Dorothy Height

Goal: To enhance the quality of life for black women and their families.

Membership: 232 chartered local sections across the United States. 32 affiliated national womens' organizations in 42 states.

Programs:
• Education and career advancement
• Economic opportunity
• Teen pregnancy prevention programs
• Drug abuse prevention programs
• Malnutrition and health care programs Aids education

Programs in Africa: The NCNW conducts development work throughout Africa dedicated to improving the economic status of women through agriculture, food production, and income generating projects.

"Sisters" a Monthly Magazine: The NCNW also publishes a magazine comparable to *Ebony* or *Time* called "Sisters," dealing with topical issues ranging from the plight of women on the African continent to profiles of celebrity black women in America.

For further information, please contact:

NATIONAL COUNCIL OF NEGRO WOMEN, INC.
1211 Connecticut Avenue, NW, Suite 702
Washington, D.C. 20036
Telephone: (202) 659-0006
FAX: (202) 785-8733

The Martin Luther King Jr. Center for Non-Violent Social Change

After 14 years of frustration and uncertainty over what seemed like insurmountable odds, Coretta Scott King has her dream—the construction of a monumental "living laboratory" for discussions and applications of her husband's ground-breaking ideas.

The King Center is a multi-faceted, non-profit community center that attracts people young and old from the world over. It is testimony to the life force generated from the programs that over 1 *million* people visit the King Center each year.

> "From time immemorial, men have lived by the principle that self-preservation is the first law of life . But this is a false assumption. All life is inter-related and all people are neighbors."
>
> —Martin Luther King Jr.

Founder: Coretta Scott King

Founded: 1968

Purpose: *To preserve and advance Dr. King's unfinished work through teaching, interpreting, advocating and promoting the non-violent elimination of poverty, racism and war.*

"We are here today because non-violence is still needed. We need it because we are losing a generation to crack cocaine, guns and gang violence. We need it in China and Palestine... we need it because nothing else has worked."

—Coretta Scott King

Facilities

Freedom Hall

An international conference center which has a conference hall, six meeting rooms, a 251-seat auditorium and a 90-seat film screening room, Freedom Hall is ideally suited for meetings and seminars. It is equipped with multi-lingual translation equipment and an unique library. Scholars from the world over come to do their research at the library's archives—home of the world's largest collection of primary source material on the Civil Rights Movement (as well as the most comprehensive collection of Dr. King's personal papers.)

Exhibition Hall

A display of photographs and memorabilia covering Dr. King's public and private life, a gift shop, the eternal flame, Dr. King's crypt, and the Chapel of All Faiths.

The Community Center

Located nearby, it houses a combination gymnasium and auditorium, an olympic-sized swimming pool, arts and crafts facilities, and outdoor sports facilities for basketball, football, baseball and tennis.

Rosa Parks Room

One of a kind photographs and displays featuring this woman's role in inspiring the Montgomery bus boycott.

Gandhi Room

Displays, photographs and writings of this remarkable man, leader of the world's largest non-violent revolution and an outspoken critic of South Africa's racism.

Note: Within a two-block area are Dr. King's birth home and the Ebenezer Baptist Church, both open for tours.

Programs

Cultural Affairs

Involves film festivals, original theater productions, childrens' theater, King Week, and Kingfest (a series of summer musical and cultural performances which provide Georgia with free entertainment). Often appearing are major artists such as *Stevie Wonder*, *Harry Belafonte*, *Tony Bennett*, and *Dick Gregory,* among others.

Summer Workshop on Non-Violence

Participants are accepted from all occupations to educate themselves in three and one-half days of intensive training dealing with today's most critical issues.

Youth Training

Designed for youngsters and teens to improve their status in society and develop a positive self-image.

Governmental

Work is undertaken with government agencies and private enterprise to develop strategies to reduce violence and conflict within the family, in schools, in the work place, in prisons, in the armed services and among nations.

Early Learning

Provides day care for pre-school children of low income families.

The King Birthday Observance

On November 2, 1983 Martin Luther King, Jr. became the first black and the second American to have a national holiday named in his honor. The King Center offers guidelines to schools, church groups, organizations and cities on how to successfully conduct their Dr. King birthday observance program and provides materials.

Other Programs
- Voter education
- Housing development
- Federal prisons projects
- Small city and rural economic development project

The Scholar's Internship Program

The scholar's internship program assists graduate and undergraduate students in developing leadership skills, while providing four major areas of support: (1) academic instruction; (2) work placement; (3) leadership development; and (4) housing.

Begun in 1974, the scholar's internship is one of the Center's oldest programs, attracting students of all races and economic status from across the United States and from nations abroad. Students live, study, and work together, enjoying seminars led by spokespeople like *Archbishop Desmond Tutu, Mayor Andrew Young* and *Congressman John Lewi*s .

It is an inspiring sight, 500 young people assembled energetically at the King Center for basic training. But this basic training is not one for military combat; it is one for applying the principles of non-violence to every aspect of life—from relationships within the family to relationships between nations. Coretta Scott King urges the generation:

"We are here today because non-violence is still needed. We need it because we are losing a generation to crack cocaine, guns, and gang violence. We need it in China and Palestine...we need it because nothing else has worked."

Two Palestinian students in the audience are anxious to see how the four day workshop will bear upon ruling out violence in their country as a means of bringing about social change.

"I think the whole idea is new to me," says Haitham Khalil, age twenty. *"In my country, Palestine, violence is met with violence."*

Another participant from Taiwan commits himself to translate all of Dr. King's work into Chinese. Reverend Jesse Jackson finishes the day by proclaiming the King Center to be "the Mecca" for non-violent social change in the world today. Harry Belafonte (entertainer, United Nations Ambassador for UNICEF, and civil rights activist who worked by Dr. King's side) adds that "there has never been a change in society when the youth were not pivotal for that change."

For other information on these programs or other activities, please contact:

THE MARTIN LUTHER KING, JR. CENTER for Non-Violent Social Change

449 Auburn Avenue, N.E.
Atlanta, GA 30312
Telephone: (404) 524-1956

The Schomburg Center for Research in Black Culture

The Schomburg Center for Research in Black Culture of The New York Public Library is not only one of the most widely used research facilities in the world devoted to the preservation of materials on black life, it is also a hub of black cultural life. The Center's collections first wins international acclaim in 1926 when the personal collection of black scholar, *Arthur A. Schomburg*, is added to The New York Public Library. Renamed in his honor in 1940, the collection grows steadily through the years. Today, the Schomburg Center stands as guardian over a collection of 5,000,000 items and remains firmly committed to its duel mission: (1) *to collect, preserve and provide access to materials documenting black life,* and (2) *to promote the study and interpretation of black culture.*

Reference Collections

This section hold more than 100,000 volumes; 80,000 microforms, 400 black newspapers and 1,000 periodicals from areas in the world with sizeable black populations.

Rare Books, Manuscripts

This section is built upon the rare finds in Arthur Schomburg's personal collection. It has grown to encompass over 3,000 rare books and pamphlets, 13,000 pieces of sheet music and other rare printed materials — including the original manuscript of Richard Wright's *Native Son.*

Art and Artifacts

One of the most comprehensive of its kinds. Its 6,000 items reflect three broad areas: (1) paintings and sculpture, (2) works on paper and textiles and (3) artifacts. The collection is particularly strong in Caribbean art, African art, and art produced during the Harlem Renaissance and WPA periods.

Photographs and Prints

Over 250,000 images document major historical events of black life. Stereographic views depict scenes from slavery through the Civil War. Portraits can be found of many 19th and 20th century black heros — artists, political figures, actors, musicians, and athletes.

Films and Recordings

Its resources include early radio broadcasts and recordings of speeches by heros such as *Marcus Garvey, Booker T. Washington* and *George Washington Carver.* Among its more than 2,000 motion pictures and videotapes can be found early "black film classics." Film footage exists of black artists, performers, political leaders and civil rights activists. Music ranges from African chants to American jazz.

Education Programs

The Schomburg Center sponsors year-round activities to participants ranging from school children to senior citizens — exhibitions, tours, seminars, forums, film screenings and performing arts. The Center also sponsors a Scholars-in-Residence Program.

For information call or write:

**THE SCHOMBURG CENTER
for Research in Black Culture**
515 Lenox Avenue
New York, NY 10037
(212) 862-4000

UNICEF *(United Nations Children's Fund)*

3 United Nations Plaza, N.Y., NY 10017, (212) 326-7000

PURPOSE: To provide for the well being of women and children in Africa and throughout the world.

ACTIVITIES: Special programs for: African urban street children (vocational and school training), AIDS education for African youth (locally produced), working with local youth organizations like the UNDUGU society based in Kenya, continent wide programs for health care, immunization and "baby-friendly" hospitals,

African-American Institute

833 United Nations Plaza, N.Y., NY 10017, (212) 350-2900

PURPOSE: The oldest non-profit organization working for African development has a two-fold mission (1) to develop Africa by developing its human resources, (2) to promote mutual understanding between Americans and Africans.

PROGRAMS: Specializing in obtaining fellowships to bring African students to the United States for graduate studies. Also provides educational opportunities for students in South Africa, holds conferences for African leaders and publishes the AFRICA REPORT.

Africare

440 R Street N.W., Washington, D.C. 20001, (202) 462-3614

PURPOSE: A non-profit organization dedicated to improving the quality of life in rural Africa.

ACTIVITIES: Africare helps Africans to (1) grow more food, (2) develop water resources, (3) improve health services and, (4) protect the environment. Africare also provides emergency assistance to refugees and drought victims.

Trans-Africa

1744 R St. N.W., Washington, D.C. 20009, (202) 547-2550

PURPOSE: To monitor United States policy towards Africa (and the Caribbean) in order to insure that it is in the interest of the African people.

ACTIVITIES: Range from testifying in Congress, to boycotting and organizing the "Free South Africa Movement." A quarterly journal, TRANS-AFRICA FORUM, deals with issues of concern to the African world.

IFESH: *(International Foundation for Education and Self-Help)*

5040 East Shea Blvd., Suite 260,, Phoenix, AZ 85254-4610, (602) 443-1800

PURPOSE: A non-profit foundation to help train and serve one million needy people throughout Africa and other developing countries.

ACTIVITIES: Recruits American graduate students, primarily from black colleges to work in Africa for nine months on self-help projects such as literacy, farming, health-care and vocational skills. The foundation pays for costs of travel, training and an over-seas allowance. Also holds an African-American Summit and a Teachers-to-Africa program.

Africa News

P.O. Box #3851, Durham, NC 27702, (919) 286-0747

PURPOSE: a non-profit educational news agency dedicated to replacing wide-spread myths about Africa with accurate up to date information.

ACTIVITIES: Publishes a bi-weekly newspaper dealing with issues ranging from a "behind the scenes" look at Somalia to bicycling across Africa (available to schools).

ILLUSTRATIONS

▰▰▰▰▰▰▰▰▰▰▰▰▰▰▰◤

PHOTO CREDITS

PAGE	REGION	SUBJECT	COURTESY OF	PHOTOGRAPHER

PART I: NORTH AFRICA

Chapter 1

PAGE	REGION	SUBJECT	COURTESY OF	PHOTOGRAPHER
	MOROCCO	Arab girl in alley in Fez	UNITED NATIONS	© JOHN ISAAC
	MOROCCO	Three Berber children	UNITED NATIONS	© JOHN ISAAC
2	MOROCCO	City of Casablanca	UNITED NATIONS	© JOHN ISAAC
2	NORTH AFRICA	Two teenagers at restaurant Mosaic	UNITED NATIONS	© JOHN ISAAC
3	MOROCCO	Street water vendor with pots and cups and "hat umbrella," in Fez	UNITED NATIONS	© JOHN ISAAC
3	NORTH AFRICA	Getting water from a streetside faucet	UNITED NATIONS	© JOHN ISAAC
0	MOROCCO	"Fantasia" traditional opening ceremony, horsemen firing muskets	UNITED NATIONS	© JOHN ISAAC
	NORTH AFRICA	Spectators at a concert		© MICHAEL WINN
		Photographer at concert	REGGAE CONCERT	© JOHN BALLARD
	MOROCCO	Boy on man's shoulders	UNITED NATIONS	© JOHN ISAAC
	NORTH AFRICA	Men beating drums		© MICHAEL WINN
2/23	MOROCCO	Women singers at reggae concert	REGGAE CONCERT	© JOHN BALLARD
		Woman reggae singer	REGGAE CONCERT	© JOHN BALLARD
		Reggae guitarist	REGGAE CONCERT	© JOHN BALLARD
/23		Berber singers on stage with tambourines	UNITED NATIONS	© JOHN ISAAC
		Reggae singer with microphone	REGGAE CONCERT	© JOHN BALLARD
		"MacBurnie King" at concert	WORLD CITIZENS	© JOHN BALLARD
		"Brock," "Neil" and "Ramona"	WORLD CITIZENS	© JOHN BALLARD
		Rasta man with dreadlocks	REGGAE CONCERT	© JOHN BALLARD
	NORTH AFRICA	Swimmers at the beach	UNITED NATIONS	© JOHN ISAAC
		Fisherman on pier in Casablanca	UNITED NATIONS	© JOHN ISAAC

Chapter 2

PAGE	REGION	SUBJECT	COURTESY OF	PHOTOGRAPHER
	MOROCCO	Man selling foods from sidewalk	© UNITED NATIONS #68533	
	MOROCCO	Two men selling hats in Fez	UNITED NATIONS	© JOHN ISAAC
	MOROCCO	Woman sewing and selling cloth	UNITED NATIONS	© JOHN ISAAC

Chapter 3

PAGE	REGION	SUBJECT	COURTESY OF	PHOTOGRAPHER
	FEZ, MOROCCO	Gateway to the Kasbah, in Fez		© MICHAEL WINN
	FEZ, MOROCCO	Sheepskins drying out on rooftops		© MICHAEL WINN
	FEZ, MOROCCO	Man and boy in the tanning vats	UNITED NATIONS	© JOHN ISAAC
	FEZ, MOROCCO	Several men in the tanning vats		© MICHAEL WINN
	FEZ, MOROCCO	Old man selling dishes	UNITED NATIONS	© JOHN ISAAC
51	FEZ, MOROCCO	The "Suk" or marketplace with donkey carrying sheepskins	UNITED NATIONS	© JOHN ISAAC
	MOROCCO	Seated Berber woman with her child	UNITED NATIONS	© JOHN ISAAC
	NORTH AFRICA	Laundry hangs on a line between stone archways inlaid with mosaics by a wood carved door	© LIBRARY OF CONGRESS #12314	
	MOROCCO	A traditional Berber family	UNITED NATIONS	© JOHN ISAAC
		Young woman	WORLD CITIZENS	© JOHN BALLARD

PART II: WEST AFRICA

Chapter 4

PAGE	REGION	SUBJECT	COURTESY OF	PHOTOGRAPHER
	WEST AFRICA	Woman with baby in sling on back	© LIBRARY OF CONGRESS I.D. 93583	

PHOTO CREDITS

PAGE	REGION	SUBJECT	COURTESY OF	PHOTOGRAPHER
64	WEST AFRICA	"The Motorcycle Kid" (Fulani)		© STACY SURLA
64	MALI	Hoe market in the town of Segou	© UNICEF #317/83	SEAN SPRAGUE
64		Two camels at the "Suk" market	© UNITED NATIONS #152,185	JOHN ISAAC
67	CHAD	A N'Djamena child drinks clean water from a UNICEF water pump	© UNICEF #018/82	MAGGIE MURRAY-LEE
67	CHAD	Boy and girl suffering from malnutrition	© UNICEF #008/82	MAGGIE MURRAY-LEE
68	KOLOKANI, MALI	Woman and teenagers in doorway to their home	© UNITED NATIONS #153378	KAY MULDOON
68		"MacBurnie" at outdoor market	AFRICAN MARKETPLACE	© JOHN BALLARD
69	MALI	Woman carrying tray of plantains (bananas) on her head		
69	WEST AFRICA	Black veiled Tuareg women at market		© MICHAEL WINN
70-71	WEST AFRICA	Two women walking ghost-like down alleyway		© MICHAEL WINN
70	MALI	Chamber of Commerce in Timbuktu		© MICHAEL WINN
71	MALI	Man repairing mud brick shrine		© MICHAEL WINN
71	MALI	Mud brick rooftops in town		© MICHAEL WINN
72		Camel market at the Souk El Gimmal	© UNITED NATIONS #152,184	JOHN ISAAC
77		Two Berber women chatting		© MICHAEL WINN
77		Berber men with tambourines and women singers circling		© MICHAEL WINN

Chapter 5

80		"Neil Silver" and "Brock James"	WORLD CITIZENS	© JOHN BALLARD

Chapter 6

90		A captured slave, hands bound and held captive in a net	© THE MUSEUM DE L'HOMME, PARIS	
94	DAKAR, SENEGAL	Goree Island slave station	UNITED NATIONS	© JOHN ISAAC
94	DAKAR, SENEGAL	Entryway to the Maison des Esclaves "the house of slaves" on Goree Island		© BILL KEPNER

Chapter 7

102	MALI	Women with bird patterned robes	UNITED NATIONS	© JOHN ISAAC
108	DAKAR, SENEGAL	Skyscrapers in the city of Dakar	UNITED NATIONS	© JOHN ISAAC
108	DAKAR, SENEGAL	Young school women in an Independence Day parade	© UNITED NATIONS #96753	
109	DAKAR, SENEGAL	The Grand Mosque of Dakar seen from the top of the Minaret	© UNITED NATIONS #96598	
109		Washing hands and feet in a fountain outside of a mosque in Fez	UNITED NATIONS	© JOHN ISAAC
109	DAKAR, SENEGAL	Women crossing street near the Sandaga market	UNITED NATIONS #101,792	
110		"MacBurnie" "Veronique" "Ramona" and "Ayoko" playing the oud	WORLD CITIZENS	© JOHN BALLARD
110	WEST AFRICA	Young boys and girls	PHOTOVAULT PLP V4 P8#1	© WERNHER KRUTEIN
111	WEST AFRICA	Young boy with hands on face	PHOTOVAULT PLP V4 P8#B	© WERNHER KRUTEIN
111		MacBurnie" playing an African thumb piano, "Veronique," "Brock" and "Neil"	WORLD CITIZENS	© JOHN BALLARD

PHOTO CREDITS

AGE	REGION	SUBJECT	COURTESY OF	PHOTOGRAPHER
1	DAKAR, SENEGAL	Woman dancing in the streets	© UNITED NATIONS #96714	
1		"Veronique," with her water colors, and "Ayoko" watching	WORLD CITIZENS	© JOHN BALLARD
2	MALI	Two women friends	UNITED NATIONS	© JOHN ISAAC
7	WEST AFRICA	Tuareg woman offering milk to boy	UNITED NATIONS	© JOHN ISAAC
7	ETHIOPIA	Women who have walked three hours to collect water selling it at the market	© UNICEF #1423/86	JOHN ISAAC

ART III: THE RIVER NIGER

hapter 8

	REGION	SUBJECT	COURTESY OF	PHOTOGRAPHER
⊃	MAURITANIA, WEST AFRICA	Tuareg woman with child facing starvation (1/3 of the 30 million people in the area suffer from malnutrition)	© UNITED NATIONS #136,970	
5	WEST AFRICA	Roadside BP gas station		© LIZ SMITH
5	WEST AFRICA	Traveling van loaded with equipment		© DR. ADAM KOONS
5	WEST AFRICA	Village homes made from dried mud and grass		© LIZ SMITH
4	OUGADOUGOU, BURKINA FASO	Man with his bicycle	© UNITED NATIONS #152,839	
6	SEGOU, MALI	Woman selling pottery	© UNITED NATIONS #106,731	
3/127	NIGER	Woman drawing water from a well (cement rings have reduced water contamination)	© UNICEF #1190/84	DANOIS
	WEST AFRICA	Little child outside grain storage vault raised off the ground to keep rats out		© LIZ SMITH
	SENEGAL	Women pounding and grinding grain for a meal (hard, time-consuming work)	© UNICEF #038/83	N. ENGEL
	WEST AFRICA	Nigerian driver in a locomotive	© UNITED NATIONS #78365	
	WEST AFRICA	Carcasses of dead cattle	© UNITED NATIONS #153,703	JOHN ISAAC
	WEST AFRICA	Examining a dead goat	© UNICEF #6918-109	DAVICO
	NIGER	Hausa fisherman floating on a calabash to free his fishing lines in Lake Madarounfa	© UNITED NATIONS #146,732	C.H.W. REDENIUS
	WEST AFRICA	Family of teenagers and children	PHOTOVAULT PLP V4 P9#14	© WERNHER KRUTEIN
	NIGER	Nomadic herdsmen water their cattle	© UNITED NATIONS #108,968	
		Two Fulani herdsmen with cattle	© LIBRARY OF CONGRESS #93581	
√137	WEST AFRICA	Black robed nomadic Tuareg family outside their desert tents	© UNITED NATIONS #153,728	
	NORTH CHAD	Refugee children of the Goram tribe	© UNICEF #681/83:12	MAGGIE MURRAY-LEE
	CHAD	Health care worker seated by van	© UNICEF #1677	CAROLYN WATSON
		Woman health care worker inoculating child	© UNICEF #1678	CAROLYN WATSON
		Young boy with flies on eyes	PATRICK'S WALK	© PATRICK GIANTONIO
	MAURITANIA	Tuareg woman feeding her dehydrated child	© UNICEF #298/83	MAGGIE MURRAY-LEE
		Boy walking with tray of food	PATRICK'S WALK	© PATRICK GIANTONIO
		Poste De Sante health care clinic	PATRICK'S WALK	© PATRICK GIANTONIO
	CHAD	Mother and child waiting at the Ati Hospital	© UNICEF #020/82	MAGGIE MURRAY-LEE

PHOTO CREDITS

PAGE	REGION	SUBJECT	COURTESY OF	PHOTOGRAPHER
142	WEST AFRICA	Tuareg men selling music cassettes		© MICHAEL WINN
142		"MacBurnie" taking photos of marketplace	AFRICAN MARKETPLACE	© JOHN BALLARD
143		Two bearded men talking to Muslim men		© DR. ADAM KOONS
143	BURKINA FASO	Movie posters in a village	© UNITED NATIONS #78150	
144	IBADAN, NIGERIA	"Shakespeare" and students of the forestry faculty at University College Clearway; Ficus Vogelli, a typeof fig which strangles oil palms	© UNITED NATIONS #101,387	
144		Children laughing	PATRICK'S WALK	© PATRICK GIANTONIC
145	WESTERN NIGERIA	"Shakespeare" with men packing coconuts for shipping	© UNITED NATIONS #101,85	
148/149	JUFFURE, GAMBIA	Author Alex Haley presenting photo from the cover of People Magazine to Binte Kinte (widow of Kunte Kinte)	© NATIONAL GEOGRAPHIC AUG.1985, PP 236-7	MICHAEL + AUBINE KIRTLEY
150	BURKINA FASO	Women of Zisgra village sing and dance to greet foreigners	© UNITED NATIONS #148,530	CAROLYN REDENIUS
150	SENEGAL	Man with cigarette from the Bassari tribe playing cowhide "violin"	© UNITED NATIONS #96726	
150/151	WEST AFRICA	Village women dance inside a circle of spectators	PHOTOVAULT PTD V7 P7#5	© WERNHER KRUTEIN
151	BURKINA FASO	Two village men beat drums from a welcoming ceremony	© UNITED NATIONS #136,418	RAY WITLIN
151		Rastafarian drummer	BLACK FAMILY REUNION	© JOHN BALLARD
152		Spectators seated in chairs		© STACY SURLA
152		Rastafarian drummers and their friends	BLACK FAMILY REUNION	© JOHN BALLARD
153		Woman dancing in Nefratiti T-shirt	AFRICAN MARKETPLACE	© JOHN BALLARD
153		Man dancing	AFRICAN MARKETPLACE	© JOHN BALLARD
153	BURKINA FASO	Two seated men playing drums	PHOTOVAULT PTD V7 P9#16	© WERNHER KRUTEIN
153		"Brock," "MacBurnie" and "Bad Boy"	WORLD CITIZENS	© JOHN BALLARD
153		Man playing wood xylophone	AFRICAN MARKETPLACE	© JOHN BALLARD

Chapter 9

PAGE	REGION	SUBJECT	COURTESY OF	PHOTOGRAPHER
160	MOPTI, MALI	Standing Muslims outside mosque in Mopti	© UNITED NATIONS #152,891	
160		Arabic writing on prayer board	UNITED NATIONS #153,652	© JOHN ISAAC
		Students studying the Koran	© UNESCO/ UNITED NATIONS #99934	ALMASY-VAUTHEY
161	MALI	Camel kneeling in front of two Tuareg men		© MICHAEL WINN
161	MALI	Market outside the Muslim mosque of Djenne		© MICHAEL WINN
162	MOPTI, MALI	Young woman with chickens traveling to the market		© MICHAEL WINN
162	NIGER RIVER	Slabs of salt being loaded onto river boats		© MICHAEL WINN
163	WEST AFRICA	Two Nigerian Muslims sit on sandbags by the Gongola River	© UNITED NATIONS #78387	
163	MOPTI, MALI	Woman carrying fish in basket to marketplace	© UNITED NATIONS	
164/165	NIGER RIVER	Man in "slipper shaped" long boat	#106,676	© MICHAEL WINN
166	BURKINA FASO	A farmer wearing a pointed straw hat (probably inspired by Chinese laborers brought to the region)	© UNITED NATIONS #152,891	KAY MULDOON
168	NIGER RIVER	Fisherman on the Niger River under a modern bridge	UNITED NATIONS	© JOHN ISAAC

PHOTO CREDITS

AGE	REGION	SUBJECT	COURTESY OF	PHOTOGRAPHER

PART IV: NIGERIA

Chapter 10

AGE	REGION	SUBJECT	COURTESY OF	PHOTOGRAPHER
)	NIGERIA	Nigerian singing star "Fela" Anikulapo-Kuti on stage with his back-up singers		© MICHAEL WINN
4	NIGERIA	The City of Lagos		© MICHAEL WINN
3	NIGERIA	"Go-slow" traffic jam in the island city of Lagos, capital of Nigeria	© UNITED NATIONS #88224	
3	NIGERIA	Broken down car lot in Lagos		© MICHAEL WINN
	NIGERIA	Car on the streets of Lagos	© UNITED NATIONS #88228	
	NIGERIA	Construction workers in Lagos		© MICHAEL WINN
	NIGERIA	"Fela" with saxophone on stage		© MICHAEL WINN
		Two West African musicians with guitars	WORLD CITIZENS	© JOHN BALLARD
	NIGERIA	"Fela" with microphone		© MICHAEL WINN
	NIGERIA	Woman dancer in Fela's group		© MICHAEL WINN
	NIGERIA	Dancers and singers with arms uplifted		© MICHAEL WINN

Chapter 11

AGE	REGION	SUBJECT	COURTESY OF	PHOTOGRAPHER
		Drums	© AMERICAN MUSEUM OF NATURAL HISTORY #33051	THOMAS LUNT
		Wood xylophone, horn, and guitars	© AMERICAN MUSEUM OF NATURAL HISTORY #322,450	
		Trumpet made by the TUNG people from the horn of a Kudu "antelope" 24 inches long	© AMERICAN MUSEUM OF NATURAL HISTORY #330,070	
		Twins	BLACK FAMILY REUNION	© JOHN BALLARD
		Man with shaker rattle gourd	AFRICAN MARKETPLACE	© JOHN BALLARD
		Yoruba man with "talking drum"	BLACK FAMILY REUNION	© JOHN BALLARD
	IBADAN, NIGERIA	Bare-chested worker at a sawmill	© UNITED NATIONS #101406	
	IBADAN, NIGERIA	Four young men working at a sawmill	© UNITED NATIONS #101367	
191	NIGERIA	A line of students at the Federal Advanced Teachers College of Nigeria in Lagos	© UNITED NATIONS #101,616	
	NIGERIA	Young woman student with schoolbooks at Teachers College of Nigeria	© UNITED NATIONS #101,617	
191	NIGERIA	Students in qualitative analysis in the laboratory of the Teachers College in Lagos	© UNITED NATIONS #101,625	
	NIGERIA	Two male students studying French at the Teachers Training College in Lagos	© UNESCO/ © UNITED NATIONS	ALMASY-VAUTHEY
	NIGER	First year nursing student at a desk in pediatrics class a the Nursing Training School in Niamey, Niger	© UNITED NATIONS #108,869	
		"Brock James" on his saxophone	WORLD CITIZENS	© JOHN BALLARD

Chapter 13

AGE	REGION	SUBJECT	COURTESY OF	PHOTOGRAPHER
	NIGERIA	Young men in Lagos ride their bicycles to work	© UNITED NATIONS #88226	
	NIGERIA	Horseback riders in Kano raise their 8-foot long trumpets in Sallah celebration		© LIZ SMITH

PHOTO CREDITS

PAGE	SUBJECT		COURTESY OF	PHOTOGRAPHE
205	NIGERIA	Dignitaries from Kano on camelback		© LIZ SMITH
206	NIGERIA	Horn and drum corps on parade in Kano		© LIZ SMITH
206	WEST AFRICA	Rifle corps of men		© STACY KOONS
207		Press photographers	BLACK FAMILY REUNION	© JOHN BALLARD
207	WEST AFRICA	Spectator with cameras		© DR. ADAM KOONS
208		"Chicken" sign	BLACK FAMILY REUNION	© JOHN BALLARD
208		Singer with microphone	AFRICAN MARKETPLACE	© JOHN BALLARD
208	WEST AFRICA	Spectator with sunglasses		© DR. ADAM KOONS
208		"MacBurnie" at marketplace	REGGAE CONCERT	© JOHN BALLARD
209		Woman selling musicians' portraits	REGGAE CONCERT	© JOHN BALLARD
209		Bass and xylophone players	AFRICAN MARKETPLACE	© JOHN BALLARD
209		Rastafarian woman selling fruit	REGGAE CONCERT	© JOHN BALLARD
210		Man with dreadlocks tipping hat	REGGAE CONCERT	© JOHN BALLARD
210	WEST AFRICA	Seated man with 4-pointed cap		© STACY SURLA
210		Woman with hat and scarf	REGGAE CONCERT	© JOHN BALLARD
210/211		African-American drummers	AFRICAN MARKETPLACE	© JOHN BALLARD
211		Man with "One Love" cap	AFRICAN MARKETPLACE	© JOHN BALLARD
211		Nigerian man selling "MacBurnie" a hat	AFRICAN MARKETPLACE	© JOHN BALLARD
212/213		Four photos of African and African-American dancers	AFRICAN MARKETPLACE	© JOHN BALLARD
214		"MacBurnie" with two friends	REGGAE CONCERT	© JOHN BALLARD
214		Three young women	BLACK FAMILY REUNION	© JOHN BALLARD
219		Half figure of an ONI (an Oba king) cast in bronze by the ancient people of Ife and placed on alters	© AMERICAN MUSEUM OF NATURAL HISTORY #325,536	ROTA
220		Head of a "court dignitary" cast in bronze by the people of Ife, using a wax method now lost	© AMERICAN MUSEUM OF NATURAL HISTORY #325,541	ROTA
221		Lovers drinking cups, coil process black pottery incised and stamped, from the Congo	© AMERICAN MUSEUM OF NATURAL HISTORY #123187	ROTA
221		Two Janus heads, a wood carving of the Yoruba people (from the Shango cult)	© AMERICAN MUSEUM OF NATURAL HISTORY #330,268	ROTA
221		Old man with pipe and cane, cast bronze from Dahomey	© AMERICAN MUSEUM OF NATURAL HISTORY #125,808	ROTA
222		An Akua'ba, a fertility doll used by Ashanti women to give sanctuary to the spirit of a baby not yet born	© INDIANA UNIVERSITY ART MUSEUM #72.106.1	MICHAEL CAVANAGI KEVIN MONTAGUE
222		Wooden masks	AFRICAN MARKETPLACE	© JOHN BALLARD
222		Three terra cotta figures from the Ibo people of Nigeria	© AMERICAN MUSEUM OF NATURAL HISTORY #331,003	ROTA

PART IV: MOZAMBIQUE

Chapter 15

PAGE	SUBJECT		COURTESY OF	PHOTOGRAPHE
230	MOZAMBIQUE	A woman freedom fighter in Mozambique's FRELIMO army	© UNITED NATIONS #123,817	VAN LIEROT
235	MOZAMBIQUE	Wall painting of Lenin		© MICHAEL WINN
235		Armored tank on a city street	PHOTOVAULT MYA V1 P5#5	© WERNHER KRUTE

PHOTO CREDITS

GE	REGION	SUBJECT	COURTESY OF	PHOTOGRAPHER
	MOZAMBIQUE	Anti-imperialism graffiti on a wall in Maputo		© MICHAEL WINN
	MOZAMBIQUE	Father and son on alley sidewalk		© MICHAEL WINN
	MOZAMBIQUE	Two boys on wall with graffiti in Maputo		© MICHAEL WINN
		Soldiers on the streets	PHOTOVAULT MYA V1 05#19	© WERNHER KRUTEIN
		Overview of the city of Maputo, capital of Mozambique	© MICHAEL WINN	
		Street of Maputo showing Portuguese design on sidewalks	© MICHAEL WINN	
	SOUTH AFRICA	Youth with "uhuru" (freedom) T-shirt, from the Langa Township, South Africa	© UNITED NATIONS #155,568	
	SOUTH AFRICA	Woman forced to stand by "whites only" bench at Johannesburg railway station	© UNITED NATIONS #151,613	
	SOUTH AFRICA	South African security guards arresting a demonstrator in Johannesburg	© UNITED NATIONS #134,830	
	SOUTH AFRICA	Children of Soweto, a black township 10 miles outside of Johannesburg. The Zulu word "Amandla" scrawled on the wall means "power"	© UNITED NATIONS #151,670	
	SOUTH AFRICA	Families in tin shack slum near Johannesburg	© UNITED NATIONS #134,816	
	SOUTH AFRICA	Tin shacks sweltering in the sun at Crossroads	© UNITED NATIONS #143,359	P. MUGABANE
	SOUTH AFRICA	Family behind barbed wire in a "resettlement" village in KwaZulu "homeland," Natal.	© UNITED NATIONS #151,707	

apter 16

GE	REGION	SUBJECT	COURTESY OF	PHOTOGRAPHER
	SOUTH AFRICA	The homestead of a Ndebele family, painted in the traditional bold geometrical designs		© MARGARET COURTNEY-CLARKE
	SOUTH AFRICA	A Ndebele woman, wearing brass neck rings		© MARGARET COURTNEY-CLARKE
	SOUTH AFRICA	A wounded boy being carried by his friends in Langa Township, Cape Province	© UNITED NATIONS #155,581	
	SOUTH AFRICA	Friends examining the back of a boy wounded by South African police	© UNITED NATIONS #155,582	

VER PHOTO CREDITS

SUBJECT	COURTESY OF	PHOTOGRAPHER
Composite photo inside map of Africa: MacBurnie King with young woman of Kikuyu descent	WORLD CITIZENS	© JOHN BALLARD
Musicians from Kassala, Sudan playing guitar-like instruments	WORLD CITIZENS	© JOHN BALLARD
"MacBurnie", "Veronique" and three young women with a Moroccan "oud" guitar and tambourine	WORLD CITIZENS	© JOHN BALLARD
"Neil Silver" and "Brock James"	WORLD CITIZENS	© JOHN BALLARD
Women of Ethiopia performing a traditional song and dance during the construction of a hut		© MICHAEL WINN
Photo behind title: Demonstrations in South Africa	© UNITED NATIONS #155586	

WORLD CITIZENS
━━━━━━━━━ HOW TO ORDER! ━━━━━━

SPECIAL *2 books in 1* EDITIONS

1) By **PHONE** (orders only) 1-800-247-6553 (toll free)
2) By **FAX** (orders only) 1(419) 281-6883
3) By **MAIL** make your check or money order payable to:
BookMasters, Inc., and send to:

BookMasters Distribution Center
P.O. Box #2039
Mansfield, Ohio 44903

Quan.	Title	1-4 copies	5-25 copies	box of 26	TOTAL
	Book One: SOUL to SOUL	$14.95 ea.	$11.95 ea.	$9.95 ea.	
	Book Two: BROTHERS & SISTERS	$14.95 ea.	$11.95 ea.	$9.95 ea.	
	*SET of SOUL to SOUL & BROTHERS and SISTERS	$24.95 per set	$17.95 per set	$14.95 per set	
	AF-AM GUIDE (256 pages)	$14.95 ea.	$11.95 ea.	$9.95 ea.	
	MONSOON (Hard Cover)	$14.95 ea.	$11.95 ea.	$9.95 ea.	
	MONSOON (Soft Cover)	$ 9.95 ea.	$7.95 ea.	$6.95 ea.	

* Save 16.5 % when you order *Soul to Soul* and *Brothers and Sisters* together.

All editions of *Soul to Soul* and *Brothers and Sisters* include 128 pages of the *African-American Guide.*

Total number of books ordered _____ **SUBTOTAL $_____**

Please include $1.00 per book for shipping/handling **$_____**

TOTAL $_____

☐ Payment Enclosed (Check/Money Order) ☐ Purchase Order # _____

☐ VISA ☐ Mastercard   card # _____ Exp. _____

Signature, address & phone # of card holder_____

PLEASE *SHIP* MY BOOKS TO:

PLEASE *BILL* MY BOOKS TO:

NAME: _____

NAME: _____

ORGANIZATION: _____

ORGANIZATION: _____

ADDRESS: _____

ADDRESS: _____

CITY   STATE   ZIP

CITY   STATE   ZIP

For information other than book orders write:
MacBurnie King c/o World Citizens
Post Office Box 10904
Marina Del Rey, CA 90295

PHOTO CREDITS

PAGE	SUBJECT	COURTESY OF	PHOTOGRAPHE

PARTIAL BIBLIOGRAPHY

No book is the product of one person — especially an historical work of this nature. This work is the result of innumerable scholars both ancient and contemporary who have devoted their lives to the preservation and illumunation of African culture. While space does not permit a complete biography to be listed in this limited edition, a comprehensive listing of over two hundred entries can be found in **The Soul to Soul Guide to African-American Consciousness,** *Volume I.*

Mazrui, Ali A. *The Africans* (Little Brown and Company, 1986)

Davidson, Basil. *Great Ages of Man: African Kingdoms* (Time Life Books, 1966)

Crowther, Geoff. *Africa on a Shoestring* (Lonely Planet, 1977)

Gerster Ph.D, Georg. *"The Niger: River of Sorrow. River of Hope"* from *National Geographic*
Vol. 148, No. 2, August 1975 (National Geographic Society, 1975) pp. 152-189

Diop, Cheikh Anta. *The African Origin of Civilization* (Lawrence Hill Books, 1974)

Sertima, Ivan Van. *They Came Before Columbus* (Random House, 1976)

Balandier, Georges and Maquet, Jacques. *Dictionary of Black African Civilization* (Leon Amiel, 1974)

The Horizon History of Africa (American Heritage / McGraw - Hill, 1971)

National Geographic (National Geographic Society, various volumes)

Moorehead, Alan. *The White Nile* (Penguin Books, 1973) *The Blue Nile* (Penguin Books, 1983)

Barbey, Bruno. *"Morocco's Ancient City of Fez"* from *National Geographic* Vol. 169. No. 3. March
1986 (National Geographic Society. 1986) pp. 330-353

Sieber, Roy. *"Traditional Arts of Black Africa"* in *Africa* ed. by Phyllis M. Martin and Patrick O'Meara
(Indiana University Press, 1986) pp . 212 - 232

Stone, Ruth M. *"African Music Performed"* in *Africa* ed. by Phyllis M. Martin and Patrick O'Meara
(Indiana University Press, 1986) pp. 233-248

Karp, Ivan. *"African Systems of Thought"* in *Africa* ed. by Phyllis M. Martin and Patrick O'Meara
(Indiana University Press, 1986) pp. 199-211

Martin, B.G. *"The Spread of Islam"* in *Africa* ed. by Phyllis M. Martin and Patrick O'Meara (Indiana
University Press, 1986) pp. 87-103

Barrett, Sr., Leonard E. *The Rastafarians* (Beacon Press, 1977)

Jacobs, Virginia Lee. *Roots of Rastafari* (Avant Books, 1985)

Davis, Stephen and Simon, Peter. *Reggae Bloodlines: In Search of The Music and Culture of
Jamaica* (Anchor Doubleday Press.1979)

Earth Book (Graphic Learning International Publishing Corporation, 1987)

PHOTO CREDITS

E	SUBJECT	COURTESY OF	PHOTOGRAPHER
	Tutankhamun and his wife	EGYPTIAN KINGDOMS p. 59	© HOLLE VERLAG GMB, H, BADEN-BADEN
	2nd "coffin" of Tutankhamun, guilded wood	EGYPTIAN KINGDOMS p. 60	© HOLLE VERLAG GMB, H, BADEN-BADEN
	The temple of Ramses II, at Luxor	© MAGNUM	ELLIOTT ERWITT
	Ruins of a Roman aqueduct in Tunisia	UNITED NATIONS	© JOHN ISAAC

APTER 6: ETHIOPIA

	St. George church in Lalibela, Ethiopia		© MICHAEL WINN
	The ancient pyramids at Meroe, Ethiopia	© UNESCO	KEATING
	The Sphinx (side view)		© MICHAEL WINN
	Ethiopian painting of Emperor Theodore	© AMERICAN MUSEUM OF NATURAL HISTORY #322894	
	Ethiopian Coptic priest		© MICHAEL WINN
	Aerial view of St. George church in Lalibela, Ethiopia	© COMSTOCK	GEORG GERSTER
	Two photos of side view of St. George church		© MICHAEL WINN
	Coptic priest		© MICHAEL WINN

APTER 7: COLONIALISM

	Wooden carving of a horse with a colonial rider and rifle	© AMERICAN MUSEUM OF N.H.#327027	ROTA
	Explorers and humanitarians Mr. and Mrs. Johnson with tribes people on a lion hunt in East Africa	© AMERICAN MUSEUM OF N.H. #314008	MARTIN JOHNSON
	A San ("bushman") being measured by Mr. Vernay	© AMERICAN MUSEUM OF N.H. #116942	
	An Afrikaaner boer girl with a pet monkey on an umbrella	© AMERICAN MUSEUM OF NATURAL HISTORY #211943	CARL E. AKELEY

APTER 8: SLAVERY

	A captured slave, hands bound and held captive in a net	© MUSEE DE L'HOMME, PARIS	
	Portrait of Joseph Cinque, an African prince who led the mutiny aboard the Amistad slave ship	NEW HAVEN COLONIAL HISTORICAL SOCIETY	
	Singer Joan Baez hand-in-hand with novelist James Baldwin and civil rights leader James Forman marching in Alabama	SCHOMBURG	© LAURENCE G.HENRY
	South African youth with "uhuru" T-shirt	© U.N. #155,568	
	South African woman by "whites only" bench	© U.N. #151,613	
	South African guards arresting demonstrator	© U.N. #134,830	
	Children of Soweto,"Amandela" means "power"	© U.N. #151,670	

OVER PHOTO CREDITS

	Composite photo inside map of Africa: West African woman in bandana	© LIBRARY OF CONGRESS I.D. 93,583	
	Composite photo inside map of Africa: Bare chested Nigerian man with stick	© U.N. #101,406	
	Four young Nigerian men working at a sawmill	© U.N. #101,367	
	Muslims praying outside mosque in Mopti, Mali	© U.N. #152,891	
	A Ndebele woman smokes her pipe	© U.N. # 151,661	

PHOTO CREDITS

PHOTO CREDITS

PHOTO CREDITS

PAGE	SUBJECT	COURTESY OF	PHOTOGRAPH
54	St. George church in Lalibela, Ethiopia		© MICHAEL WINN
55	Side view of St. George church		© MICHAEL WINN
55	Coptic Christian priest outside St. George church		© MICHAEL WINN
57	Coptic priest displaying Ethiopian bible		© MICHAEL WINN
58	Muslim worshippers bowing in front of a Mosque	© UNITED NATIONS/ UNICEF #106724	
60	Arabic writing on prayer board	UNITED NATIONS #153,652	© JOHN ISAAC
61	Students studying the Koran	© UNESCO/ UNITED NATIONS #99934	ALMASY-VAUTHEY
63	Man and woman picking crops	© UNITED NATIONS…	
63	Two school children under blackboard, in Tanzania	© UNICEF #395	BERNARD WOLFF
63	Classroom of students, in Tanzania	© UNICEF #401	BERNARD WOLFF
64	Rock paintings from Tassili n'Ajjer, Algeria. Two men drawing water from a well using a similar leather bucket as is still used today, from the Period of the Horse, 1,000 B.C.	© MUSEE DE L'HOMME, PARIS	original renderings of paintings by mission Lhote
65	Women, highly respected, wearing elaborate hairdos, ride atop beautifully tattooed oxen; from the Period of the Herder, 4000-1500 B.C.	© MUSEE DE L'HOMME, PARIS	original renderings of paintings by mission Lhote
69	A wrestler from the Nuba tribe in Sudan	© MAGNUM	GEORGE RODGERS
70	4 men from the Masaai tribe in East Africa with Roman-like spears and beautiful scar designs	© AMERICAN MUSEUM OF NATURAL HISTORY #281669	R. BOULTON
70	A long-limbed Nilotic teenager from Sudan	© UNICEF #1253/85	MARIA ANTONIETTA PERU
70	4 young Nigerian men working at a sawmill in the city of Ibidan	© UNITED NATIONS #101367	
71	2 Berber women with coin headdresses		© MICHAEL WINN
71	2 women from Mali chatting	UNITED NATIONS	© JOHN ISAAC

CHAPTER 3: ROOTS (ANCIENT KINGDOMS)

PAGE	SUBJECT	COURTESY OF	PHOTOGRAPH
72	A tribal chief from Ghana with his attendant. The umbrella symbolizes his authority. A chief can only be addressed through an intermediary, never by direct conversation. The two men seated in front of the chief are his intermediaries and hold the linguist sticks to symbolize their roles	© UNITED NATIONS #86842	
75	Mansa Musa, King of Mali, holding up a huge nugget of gold to an Arab trader on camelback. From facsimile of a 1375 catalin map by Abraham Cresques, colored ink on parchment	BRITISH MUSEUM, LONDON	R. B. FLEMING
77	The Muslim mosque at Djenne, Mali and the marketplace outside		© MICHAEL WINN
78	Cast of two heads by the Ife people of Nigeria, in bronze	© AMERICAN MUSEUM OF NATURAL HISTORY #325345	© ROTA
79	Men squatting on the river bank		© MICHAEL WINN
83	Camel market at the souk el gimmal	© UNITED NATIONS #152184	JOHN ISAAC
83	Slabs of salt being loaded onto boats on the Niger River		© MICHAEL WINN

PHOTO CREDITS

SUBJECT	COURTESY OF	PHOTOGRAPHER
A San ("bushman") from the Kalahari Desert carrying two hands full of stork chicks	© AMERICAN MUSEUM OF NATURAL HISTORY #116945	
Young Berber girl from Morocco	UNITED NATIONS	© JOHN ISAAC
3 Berber children	UNITED NATIONS	© JOHN ISAAC
A bare-chested Nigerian worker at a sawmill in the city of Ibadan	UNITED NATIONS #101406	
A woman from Mali		© MICHAEL WINN
3 teenagers from Khartoum, Sudan	WORLD CITIZENS	© JOHN BALLARD
A long veiled woman from Somalia	UNITED NATIONS #6867	
3 young girls at irrigation project in Sudan	WORLD CITIZENS	© JOHN BALLARD
A Ndebele woman from South African smokes her pipe	UNITED NATIONS #151661	
A black veiled woman of the Nomadic Beja people in Sudan	© UNICEF #1176/85	MARIA ANTONIETTA PERU
Young men wearing caps in South Africa	© UNITED NATIONS #133245	P. DAVIS
3 San ("bushmen") women walking with child, Kalahari Desert	AMERICAN MUSEUM OF NATURAL HISTORY #116944	
A Nilotic man from southern Ethiopia over 6'4" tall		© MICHAEL WINN
White woman from South Africa	© UNITED NATIONS	
Arab woman	UNITED NATIONS	© JOHN ISAAC…
Hindu woman from India	© PHOTOVAULT	WERNHER KRUTEIN
2 Nigerian students studying French at the Teachers Training College in Lagos	© UNESCO/ UNITED NATIONS	ALMASY-VAUTHEY
A Jewish synagogue of the Falasha people in Ethiopia		
A Jewish Falasha teenage girl with her goat in Ethiopia		
A priest carrying the Coptic cross in Lalibela, Ethiopia		© MICHAEL WINN
A Muslim young woman wearing an Islamic star and crescent scarf	PHOTOVAULT	© WERNHER KRUTEIN
A priest of the Matabele people	© AMERICAN MUSEUM OF NATURAL HISTORY #14076	
Men from the Kikuyu tribe of East Africa perform a "Ngoma" (dance) with leopard skin skirts	© AMERICAN MUSEUM OF NATURAL HISTORY #281, 639	R. BOULTON
Two San ("bushmen")	© AMERICAN MUSEUM OF NATURAL HISTORY #116940	
Two Fulani herdsmen with cattle	© LIBRARY OF CONGRESS #93581	
A tribal chief in Ghana. The umbrella is a symbol of authority, the two men holding the linquist sticks in front of him are his intermediaries.	© UNITED NATIONS #86842	
Cast of an Oni (king) of the Ife people of Nigeria, in bronze	© AMERICAN MUSEUM OF NATURAL HISTORY #325342	ROTA
Camel caravan crossing the desert		© MICHAEL WINN
Star of David atop Jewish synagogue in Ethiopia		© MICHAEL WINN
Jewish Ethiopian boy		© JOHN ISAAC

PHOTO CREDITS

PAGE	SUBJECT	COURTESY OF	PHOTOGRAPHE

INTRODUCTION

PAGE	SUBJECT	COURTESY OF	PHOTOGRAPHER
5	Woman with Nefertiti shirt	AFRICAN MARKETPLACE	© JOHN BALLARD
5	African-American dancers	AFRICAN MARKETPLACE	© JOHN BALLARD
5	Photographer with African shirt	REGGAE CONCERT	© JOHN BALLARD
5	"Brock", "Veronique" and "Ayoka", African-American youth	WORLD CITIZENS	© JOHN BALLARD

PART ONE: IDENTITY

CHAPTER 1: THE LAND

PAGE	SUBJECT	COURTESY OF	PHOTOGRAPHER
16	Backpackers through African rainforest	PATRICK'S WALK	© PATRICK GIANTON
23	Two Kikuyu women in Nairobi, Kenya	WORLD CITIZENS	© JOHN BALLARD
23	Man with his bicycle, Burkina Faso	© UNITED NATIONS #152, 839	
23	People praying in Kassala, Sudan	WORLD CITIZENS	© JOHN BALLARD
23	Three women in Khartoum, Sudan	WORLD CITIZENS	© JOHN BALLARD
25	Man selling shoes in Mali	© UNITED NATIONS #154734	JOHN ISAAC
25	Women pounding millet into flour, Burkina Faso	© UNITED NATIONS #104569	
25	Women drawing water from a well	© UNICEF #1190/84	DANOIS
25	Man Carrying a Blade at a Sawmill in Nigeria	©UNITED NATIONS #101369	
26/27	Sand dunes in the Sahara Desert		© MICHAEL WINN
26	Rock desert. Two camels with portable huts		
28	Man watering plants to hold back "desertification" in Senegal	© UNITED NATIONS #133250	CARL PURCELL
28/29	The "Sahel" where grasslands fight to survive the encroaching desert sands	© UNITED NATIONS/ UNICEF #153722	
30/31	Grassland savannah with Mt. Kilimanjaro in clouds, Tanzania		
30	Two giraffes	© AMERICAN MUSEUM OF NATURAL HISTORY #334383	R. VAN GELDER
32/33	Great Rift Valley, a Masaai tribesman crossing road with his cattle	WORLD CITIZENS	© JOHN BALLARD
34/35	Victoria Falls known as "moisi-oa -tunga" (the "smoke that thunders") in Zambia	PHOTOVAULT NFS V1 P4 #9	© WERNHER KRUTEIN
36	The Atlas Mountains, home to some of the Berber peoples of Morocco		© MICHAEL WINN
36/37	Aerial view of Mount Kilimanjaro	© NATIONAL GEOGRAPHIC APRIL 1975, P.476-7	EMORY KRISTOF, SR.

CHAPTER 2: PEOPLES

PAGE	SUBJECT	COURTESY OF	PHOTOGRAPHER
38	Woman from West Africa with baby in sling on her back	© LIBRARY OF CONGRESS I.D. #93583	
38	A Berber woman seated with her child	UNITED NATIONS	© JOHN ISAAC
38	White Afrikaaner woman with her child at "whites only" rally in South Africa	© UNITED NATIONS	
38	Veiled young girl from Chad with her baby brother at a hospital in Ati	© UNICEF	MAGGIE MURRAY-LEE

Africans in the Old World and Africans in the New World strive for freedom!

The
oul to Soul ™
Guide to

African-American
Consciousness

Reclaiming
Your
History!

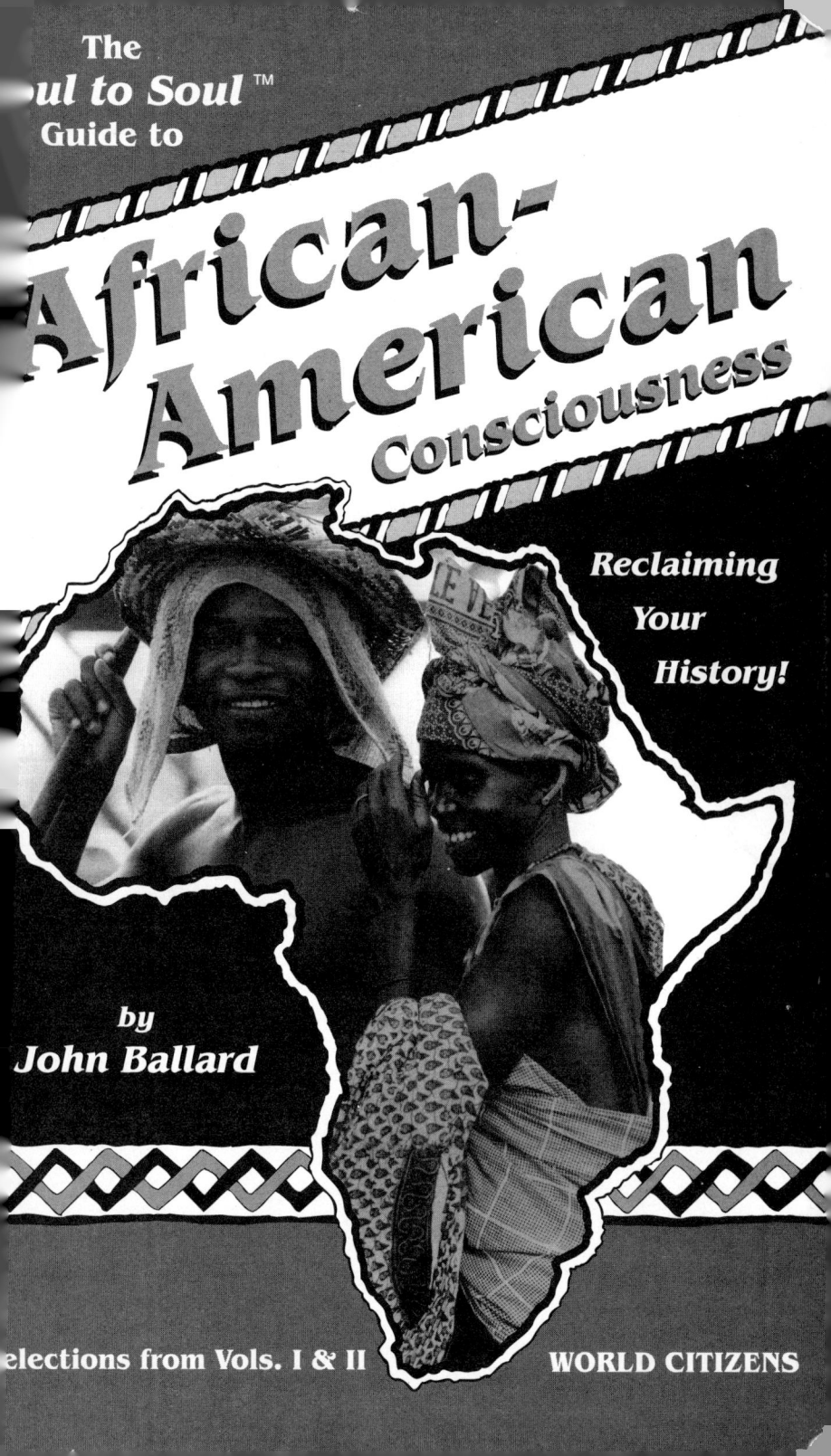

by
John Ballard

WORLD CITIZENS

Author's Note

The Soul to Soul Series is committed to bringing the peoples of the world closer together so that world problems, such as prejudice and hunger, can be solved.

No book is the product of one person — especially an historical work of this nature. This work is the result of innumerable scholars both ancient and contemporary who have devoted their lives to the preservation and illumination of African culture. Among the many, some of the primary sources have been: Ali A. Mazrui, Checkh Anta Diop, Phyllis Martin, Patrick O'Meara, Alan Moorehead, Basil Davidson, Leonard Barrett, Sr., and the many contributors to National Geographic and the Horizon History of Africa.

In attempting to provide a "counterbalance" to the sometimes Eurocentric histories of Africa, chapters emphasize themes such as the Nubian contribution to Egyptian culture and the beauty of "primitive art." I have used phrases such as "those of us" (who are of African descent), and "us", "we" or "our people" in order to give this historical work a more familiar tone to the African-American reader. It is my intent that with more familiarity and respect for each other's cultures, such distinctions will become less and less needed.

Selections from Volume I

PLEASE NOTE: As these pages have been *individually* selected from the actual pages of a larger two volume edition of this work, page numbers herein will not always follow in exact sequence. The individual selections for this special edition have been made by the author, personally, to ensure you the most accurate chapter-by-chapter representation of his work.

"To take part in the African revolution, it is not enough to write a revolutionary song; you must fashion the revolution with the people. And if you fashion it with the people, the songs will come by themselves and of themselves.

"In order to achieve real action you must yourself be a living part of Africa and of her thoughts; you must be an element of that popular energy which is entirely called forth for the freeing, the progress and the happiness of Africa. There is no place outside that fight for the artist or for the intellectual who is not himself concerned with, and completely at one with the people in the great battle of Africa and of suffering humanity."

— *Sékou Touré*
President and Prime Minister of Guinea

INTRODUCTION...

From university campuses to sidewalk street fairs, from playground courts to kindergarten classes, African-Americans are learning a radically new version of history — a version that has shaken to the core the Western point of view from which American students have historically been taught to evaluate their world — a new version of history that has lit a fire of controversy over just *what should* and *what should not* be included in a school's core curriculum. Its name...*Afrocentrism.*

Recording stars glorify Afrocentric myths on MTV. Rastafari slogans flash from black power T-shirts. The outline of the African continent has been shaped into a fashion statement of earrings, pendants and rings. In cities across America, community groups commemorate their heritage at African markets, festivals, tribal dances and the celebration of *Kwanzaa.*

All speak of a dynamic trend, begun as the first slave set foot on American soil, nurtured by Marcus Garvey in the 1920's and 30's and brought into a new focus by Malcolm X in the 60's — a trend that resonates in the hearts and minds of black Americans...to "return to Africa!"

Is this a mere form of what *Newsweek* magazine calls "intellectual apartheid?" Or is it a much needed attempt to rectify real and cruel divisions? Can Afrocentrism fulfil the wish of a people to reunite with their past...to bridge the gap between a family divided by 2,000 miles of ocean and 300 years of racial oppression?

...the AFROCENTRIC point of view

As the Eurocentric world view is being dismantled, what does the Afrocentric world view have to offer in its place? What does this "new vision" offer for the future of America — an America entering a new millennia, an America that must add to the "melting pot" of its European ancestry its "new immigrants," an America that will soon find in its many cities European whites as the minority and Latin-Americans and non-whites as the majority?

Can we, by dismantaling the Eurocentric point of view, secure for ourselves a healthy enjoyment of each others' differences and, at the same time, uncover our commonality?

Can Afrocentrism help to forge a society that reaches *beneath* "intellectual apartheid?"

Can Afrocentrism dismiss this need
to glorify the accomplishments of one race
by diminishing the accomplishments of another race?
Can Afrocentrism cause us, instead,
to take pride in each other's accomplishments
as if they were our own?

What is Afrocentrism?

Before analyzing the arguments for and against Afrocentrism, it is essential first to understand just what Afrocentrism is — not only the effects of its teachings; but also the purpose for its existence.

The purpose of Afrocentrism is to transform our point of view of the world to allow for the true achievements and contributions of African civilizations. Afrocentrism uses scholarship to reconstruct for African-Americans a cultural heritage that we were deprived of. It provides us with a sense of history and roots that other peoples have enjoyed the security of as their birthright.

It is an attempt to recover our past, to restore to us a *sense of identity* violated by an abrupt discontinuity when we were torn from our homelands during slavery. Much like a patient suffering from amnesia who must rediscover his or her true identity in order to be healthy; we too must recover our past.

In doing so, Afrocentrism, at times, seeks to overturn the world view and heritage previously taught in American schools — and replace it with a world view in which white people of European ancestry no longer automatically stand at center stage and black peoples of African ancestry take their rightful role in the unfolding of our interrelated human drama.

Integrating African-Americans
A question of race - or class?

In my thesis "Heroes, Villains and Fools" (Harvard, 1967), I attacked the leading remedies advanced by social workers of the day — that the "negative" identities of lower class blacks could be overcome by instilling "positive" middle class values. White society had redefined a centuries-old problem of *race* as a problem of *class*.

What was needed was *not* an infusion of white middle class values which would further alienate us as African-Americans from our identity by denying our "blackness." What was needed was what followed, an acceptance of our "blackness," a decade-long "black pride" movement followed by what is now developing into what Ali Mazrui calls a *"re-Africanization of the African-American."*

Why is it that so many well off blacks who have moved out of the lower class inner city ghettoes and have become so-called "buppies" (Black Urban Professionals) *still feel alienated from white America?* Why is it that white Americans, however, even though they may occupy the same social clas, lower class blacks,(the "poor white trash" Appalachia, etc.) *still feel connected to American identity*. The problem is not clas it is racism — racism based on a societal e cation of our young that *excludes the con butions of blacks to the American identit*

Although efforts have been made to e cate whites and blacks, we still live in a so ety where the eyes of the media are blin by bigotry. Where black boys hear J Wayne and Spencer Tracey defined as "typical American." Where black girls h a 42% lower chance to be economically in pendent as their white sisters. Where the of "racism" like the cry of "wolf" is in d ger of losing its credibility when used by de agogues seeking to exploit the emotions c people denied an equal opportunity.

How can Afrocentrism correct the ali ation and civil strife resulting from Eurocentric educational system? What pr is there for the Afrocentric point of view?

uncovering your

roots

Proving th...

To the Afrocentric scholar, the contributions of European civilization came not from an isolated breakthrough originating in ancient *Greece* but from a long heritage of innovations *African* in origin. In order to prove this point of view, Afrocentrists first attempt to reclaim Egypt as a largely "black culture." The seeds of the world's first sophisticated civilization, they claim, w... uprooted by prejudiced 19th-Cent... European scholars who replanted Egypt i... melting pot of white Mid-Eastern herita... Afrocentrists find the roots of ancient Eg... planted firmly in black African soil.

Egyptian civilization (although a cro... roads of white mid-eastern and wh...

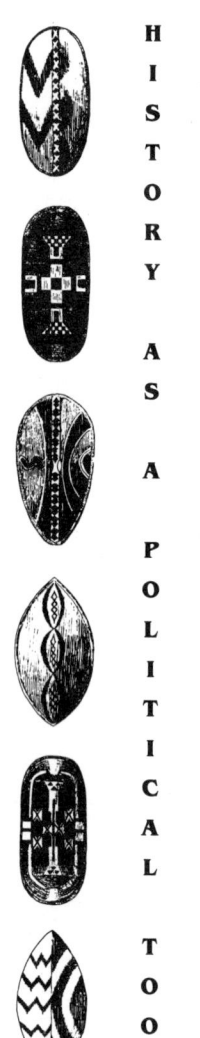

H I S T O R Y   A S   A   P O L I T I C A L   T O O L

The Arguments For And

FOR

- Afrocentrism exposes how some whites have manipulated history, both unconsciously and consciously to their own selfish advantage.

- In Europe, some scholars erased the contributions of entire African civilizations.

- American scholars invented arguments to alter history in order to justify the practice of slavery.

- An African spiritual leader is called a "witch doctor," a European spiritual leader, a "priest." Academics need to be cleansed of biased words like "witch doctor," "wild indian," "bushmen," etc.

- African-Americans have, in effect, been raised to believe they share the same history and culture as whites. In truth much of African culture survived the wrenching dislocation of slavery, was maintained on the plantations, and has been passed down through the family into the cities of the North.

- African-American children sit in classes, alienated and sensing no connection to the issues being discussed.

- Afrocentrism seeks to portray African people as *actors* and *creators* rather than people who are *acted upon.*

- Education is meant to build students' self-confidence and Afrocentrism does just that.

- Afrocentrism will give pride to poor blacks, allowing them to make greater contributions to American culture.

- The current curriculum is a white self-esteem curriculum. Afrocentrism, instead, provides a *multi-cultural* esteem that, ideologically, is more truly American.

- Multi-cultural classrooms are needed to honor the contributions of ethnic groups whose histories have too long been absent from Western education. Its benefits are for all ethnic groups, black and white, Indian and Latino, Asian and Semetic.

source: Newsweek Magazine, 1991

frocentric Theory

editerranean civilizations) did, in fact, orig-
ate in the black civilizations of the Sahara
fore it was a desert. As the "green Sahara"
gan to dry up, these black peoples migrat-
d east and created the ancient kingdoms of
ush and Nubia. From these black kingdoms
me the first pharaoh of Egypt — a black
naraoh – named Menes.

Having demonstrated the black origins of
Egyptian civilization, Afrocentric scholars
then attempt to prove that the roots of
"Western" philosophy and technology did not
originate in ancient Greece but are actually
"black Egyptian" in origin, transplanted to
Greece through trade and colonial settlements.

Against Afrocentrism

AGAINST

In exposing the myths of Eurocentric domination, overzealous
Afrocentric scholars seem to make everything that came out
of Europe evil and everything that came out of Africa good.

It is ironic (as Henry Gates, Jr. points out) that Afrocentrists
go to such great lengths to downplay the contributions of
Western culture while, at the same time, they go to such great
lengths to claim authorship of it.

When Europeans force their culture on conquered Africans,
the Afrocentrist calls it "imperialism." But when Egyptians
force their culture on Greece, the Afrocentrist considers it to
be a "cultural contribution."

When Afrocentrists point out the "primitive" witch hunts and
barbaric atrocities committed during Europe's Dark Ages,
they neglect to point out barbaric atrocities black tribes have
historically imposed not only on their rivals *but also on their
own people.* (No "civilization," black or white, seems to have
a monopoly on violence.)

"Black" people — raised in an American culture, not an
African culture — are Americans. They possess the same values of individuality, free enterprise, human rights, self-expres-
sion and privacy that are American cultural traits — not the
values that are typically African.

At the heart of Afrocentrism is a belief that race or blood can
determine destiny. Afrocentrism demonstrates, at its core, the
very racism it allegedly seeks to destroy.

Afrocentrism will further alienate the poor who are already
alienated from the American mainstream.

There is too often an "anti-white" edge to arguments
advanced by Afrocentric scholars.

History becomes a political tool — attempting to remedy in
one's mind what has not been gained through economic
progress or social mobility.

Are we now reclaiming our history through Afrocentrism — or are we now reinventing one to suit our political and psychological purposes?

"...too many people still regard African-American studies as a way to rediscover a lost cultural identity — or invent one that never quite existed. We are scholars first, not polemicists. For our field to survive [we cannot] seek ideological conformity. Afrocentric studies should be the home of free inquiry into the very complexity of being from African descent in the world — rather than a place where critical inquiry is drowned out by ethnic fundamentalism. [We cannot] reduce the astonishing diversity of African cultures to a few simple-minded shibboleths.

"We do nothing to help our discipline by attempting to make of it a closed shop, where only blacks need apply. What would we say to a person who said to teach Milton, you had to be Anglo Saxon, Protestant, male...and blind!

"Nobody comes into the world as a "black" person or a "white" person; these identities are conferred on us by a complex history...and are never as rigid as we like to pretend.

"Afrocentrism should be more than wearing tinted glasses and celebrating kwanzaa instead of Christmas. Scapegoating other ethnic groups only resurrects the worst of 19th Century racist pseudo-science. We must not succumb to the temptation to resurrect our own version of the thought police, to determine who, and what, is "black." "Mirror, mirror on the wall, who is the blackest one of all" is a question best left behind in the 60's."

Henry Lewis Gates, Jr.,
Chair of Afro-American Studies, *Harvard University*,
author of *"Loose Cannons".*

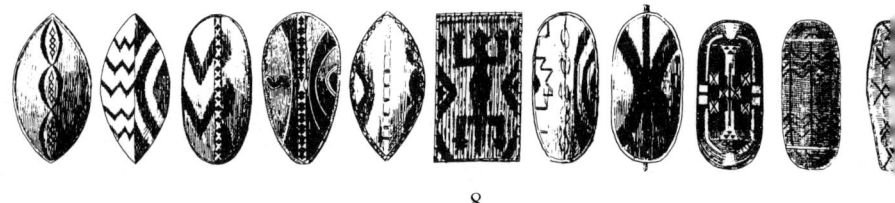

ow can we reach beyond the divisive argument over whether or not the crowning accomplishments of humanity came from "whites" or "blacks?" Can't we see that they are, by definition, human accomplishments and, in doing so, take pride in our shared humanity?

Conclusion

The movement for Afrocentrism is not only a movement to restore to our people the sense of cultural pride of which we have been robbed, it is also a way for those of us who are parents to voice our dissatisfaction with the politics of a society that turns its back on the education of its young.

There is undeniably a great need, particularly, to bolster the opportunities for black young men — young men who confront a fate where 1 out of every 4 will be imprisoned before they are age 25. Afrocentrism is but one step in raising American society's need for a *multi-cultural curriculum* — a curriculum that must also include the growing numbers of Latinos and Asians as they, too, become more political and culturally prominent.

This is not a question of "Afrocentrism — whether or not," but of "multi-culturism — how soon and how much." If we *are* the products of our history, then our future is dependent upon the history we make today. And, today, the students who are making history have a choice of what will be written in the history books their children will read tomorrow — did we at this time weave together a society in which all can participate? ...or did our society come apart at the seams?...Today's students are tomorrow's historians.

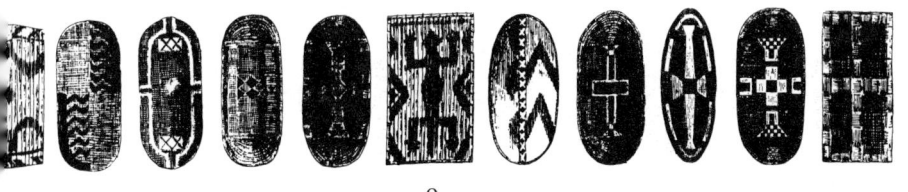

LISBONA
ITALIA
MARE
MEDI
TERANEV
MADERIA
CANARIE
C. DEBUGA
C. BIANCHO
C. VERDO
AFRICA
ARA
GID
MECHA
SINVS
ARABI CVS
MELIDO
MONTE NEGRO
PRASV PMON

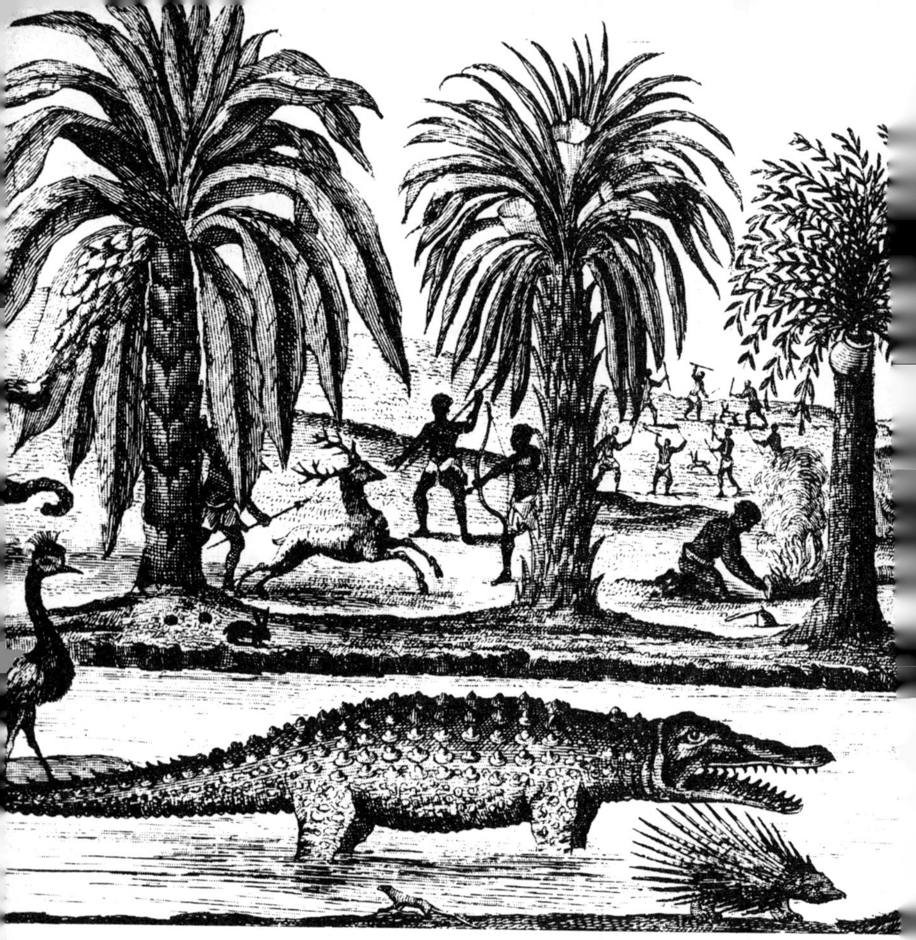

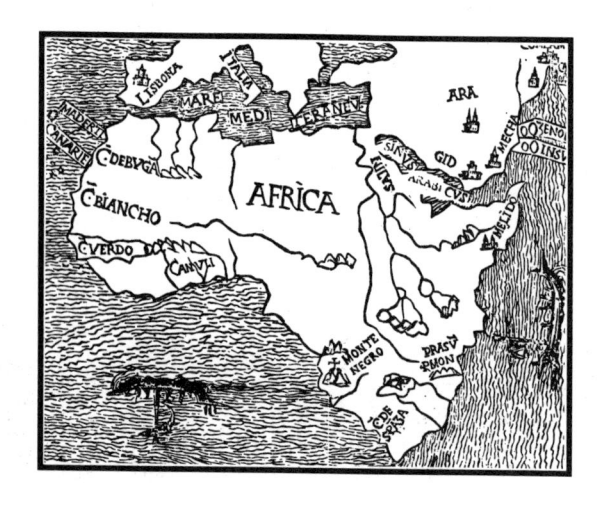

Where Is Africa?

For centuries Africa was known only to Europeans as the "dark continent," a mysterious world filled with bizarre animals and savage people. Through this point of view, Africa was "discovered" and its people were given an identity.

In truth, Africa was unknown only to the Europeans and the foreigner — *not* to the people living there.

What you and I do is see is all of life through a particular *point of view* inherited from the culture we live in. We see other people and societies through a pair of eyeglasses—one lens colored with the prejudgements of our culture, the other lens colored with our interpretation of our prejudgements. I challenge you to strip away these biases, take off your glasses and see each other soul to soul.

The first step: *be aware that you are seeing others through a point of view.*

The second step: *discover just what your point of view is.*

11

The Eurocentric Point Of View

In his provocative book *The Africans,* Ali A. Mazrui shows us how Africa is at war with both itself and the world, fighting to keep or erase its own "ancient world views" while at the same time being thrust into a world culture which is, at its heart, "Eurocentric."

In reality, it was *Europeans* who invented the identity of Africa. And it was *Europeans* who shaped our concepts of the world.

Today what African people know about each other *still* comes through a mass media inherited from the Western world. African politicians rule their people with laws generated by Europeans. Schools teach in European languages (English, French and Portuguese) which shape the possibilities of young peoples' minds. Morality is shaped, in part, by the Christian religions of Europe. Even time, as Mazrui points out, is distorted. The world sets its clocks based on an imaginary line drawn through a city in England — *Greenwich Time.*

"*Africa is a peninsula so large that it comprises the thrid part, and this the most southerly, of our (european) continent.*"
— **The Geographer Royal of France,** 1659

Looking at life from the Eurocentric point of view of the 19th Century, Africa (in fact, the whole world) was seen to be an *extension* of Europe. Historically, however, Europe was *not* the center of this "civilized world." Early "Western" civilization was centered *around* the Mediterranean Sea, and — as Mazrui claims — it is just as logical to think of Europe as an extension of North Africa as it is to think of North Africa as an extension of Europe.

In fact, it wasn't until the 19th Century that the concept of "a Europe" was invented. In earlier times there was no "Europe." The Roman Empire was, truthfully, a *Mediterranean* world and "the West" included North Africa along with what's now called Europe.

GREENWICH TIME

The infamous Mercator projection map distorted the size of the world's continents to favor the North. North America is *not* 1½ times bigger than Africa. In fact, Africa is:

- 3½ times as big as the United States.
- Larger than China and India put together.
- And large enough to include all of the colonial nations that conquered it!

"DISTORTED" PROPORTION OF
AFRICA'S SIZE IN RELATION
TO OTHER COUNTRIES

The Afrocentric Point Of View

What is a "Cultural Point of View?"

Like a child, the world revolves around you. People are put there by God to serve your interests, and the resources of the world become your toys and playthings. Maps are designed in such a way that your country is the center of the world, much as your world becomes the center of the universe, with all the planets, the sun and the moon, revolving around you.

All peoples fall into this understandable misinterpretation of their world. All create myths about the creation of the Earth from their own cultural standpoint. When the map makers of England drew their maps, they drew England in the center with the countries in the farthest corners of the earth vanishing into obscurity. On the old Soviet Union map, it was Russia that stood out; and in Japan, maps once showed this tiny island as the birthplace of man.

This is how "western" school children learn about our world and come to see the world as an extension of their own country. This is how you and I as school children living in another culture, but taught with a Eurocentric point of view, come to see ourselves as second class or inferior citizens.

Even the actual location of the world's continents on our maps reflects the bias of the European. Why is Europe on top and Africa at the bottom? If you were an astronaut circling our Earth and looked down, you would see no signs saying "North Pole" or "South Pole." The "Far East" and the "West," are also concepts based from a European point of view. Why is Africa not seen "on top" and "Europe" at the bottom?

Why not make Africa, the birthplace of man, the center of our maps?

Why Not Turn the World Upside Down?

"CORRECT" PROPORTION OF
AFRICA'S SIZE IN RELATION
TO OTHER COUNTRIES

What is Africa?

The RACIAL definition: *Africa is based on race—the "real Africa is south of the Sahara Desert." Here Africans are black.*

The CONTINENTAL definition: *Africa is based on geography — "Africa is not a race, but a continent. The northern boundary is not the Sahara Desert, but the Mediterranean Sea." Therefore, the light-skinned Arabs and Berbers of the north are also Africans.*

This controversy, as Mazrui demonstrates, has caused centuries of schizophrenia and bitterness. Scholars have gone to great lengths trying to prove that Egypt (located in Africa) was, in fact, an "African" (black) civilization. Skulls have been dug up and scrutinized for "Negroid" features. Egyptian murals and statues like the Sphinx have been argued over to prove that peoples' noses were flat. "Is nothing African unless its black?" asks Mazrui.

Should Africans think of themselves as a race of black people? Or should Africans think of themselves as people who came from a continent that includes both the Negroid peoples south of the Sahara Desert and the Caucasian peoples of North Africa? Should Africans think of themselves as a "multi-colored people?"

Then Who is African?

Someone who is born on the continent of Africa? Or someone who has "black" skin? Black-skinned people exist in India and other parts of the world, but they are not racially Negroid. Peoples existed in most of Africa for thousands of years also who are not Negroid nor even have black skin. Is the light-skinned Muslim of the north not an African? What about the Jews who settled in Africa over 2,000 years ago, centuries before Islam was even created — or the Dutch who settled in South Africa 400 years ago and call themselves Afrikaans? Can a white person be an African?

THE ARABIAN PENINSULA
Part Of Africa?

Why should the Arab peninsula, asks Mazrui, which is united in culture and history to north Africa, be divided from the African continent? Why is the Red Sea, not the Persian Gulf, considered to be the border where the continent ends?

Geographically, the Arabian peninsula *was* part of the African continent, split apart by the Great Rift Valley that cuts through the Red Sea. But why should islands like Madagascar, over 200 miles (400 km.) offshore from the mainland be part of Africa and not the Arab peninsula once connected to it by land?

By chopping off the border of Africa at the shores of the Red Sea, the map makers of Europe cut an Islamic world in two. Would the hatreds some of the "Arabs of Asia" have for us "blacks of Africa" change if they realized that they, in fact, may be the "Arabs of Africa?"

QUESTION: Are the white Arabs living on the north shore of Africa by the Mediterranean Sea:
(1) a northern arm of black civilization south of the Sahara Desert?
(2) a western arm of Muslim civilizations on the Arab peninsula?

Creating an African Identity

"Africans, all over the continent, without a word being spoken either from one individual to another or from one African country to another, looked at the European, looked at one another, and knew that in relation to the Europeans they were one."

— **Julius Nyerere**

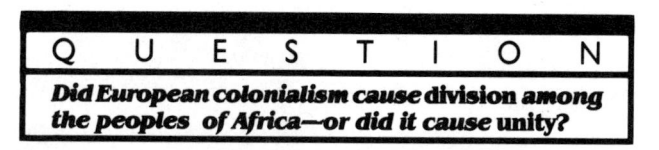

Q U E S T I O N

Did European colonialism cause division among the peoples of Africa—or did it cause unity?

Mazrui argues that, ironically, it may be the white man who created the African identity inside of the continent of Africa. Racism and colonialism forced the many different peoples of Africa to look upon themselves for the first time as *one people* — giving birth to not only the movement *"Pan-Africanism"* but also to the identity of *"Negritude."*

It is wrong to think that all black people were "Africans" until the colonialists split them into Kenyans, Tanzanians, Ugandans, etc. In fact, they were *rival* tribes (Kikuyu vs. Maasai, Ibo vs. Hausa, etc.) that united to overthrow the foreign rulers. Africans did not put their continent back together *after* colonialism. There was never an united Pan-African identity *until* colonialism.

Creating a New Identity
The "African-American"

Much of the way you and I think about ourselves is based on the country and nationality our families came from. But black people in America were systematically and purposely cut off from this sense of identity.

When African slaves were brought to America, our heritage was forever erased along with our names from the slave books. Alex Haley in his book *Roots* tells how Kunte Kinta was forced to surrender his tribal name for the name "Toby." Slavers purposefully set out to destroy any reminders of our African heritage. We were taught to be ashamed of the rich traditions of the Mandinka and Yoruba peoples and to look down at the very place where we were born. Slavery was a "deliverance" from the "primitiveness" and "savagery" of our homes. Whereas the names of most people in America provide a clue about their cultural heritage, most African-Americans can never know their own home culture.

Even "African-American," while more accurate than "black-American," still does not carry the cultural roots of knowing the tribe of your ancestors.

What Mazrui calls the "re-Africanization of Black America" has really just begun. Maybe these "soul to soul" stirrings will become a real attempt for people of both continents to reach out their hands to each other across the vast expanse of ocean and rejoin the links of this chain broken by history.

---

[1]African Americans were the only group in the U.S. to be named by a physical characteristic (the color of our skin) rather than by a nationality. While other groups are Greek-Americans, Italian-Americans, Japanese-Americans . . . people from Africa were called "coloured," "darkies," "niggers," "Negroes," or "Black Americans."

Snow, Desert, Grasslands, Beaches

Africa has some of the most varied landscapes in the world! From snowcapped mountains to arid deserts, from thundering waterfalls to tropical rain forests. Most of Africa is built on a vast rigid block of ancient rocks. These form huge plateau regions that drop down steep "escarpments" to narrow plains along the coast.

- *40% of Africa is desert*
- *8% of Africa is savannah grassland*
- *The rest is rugged mountain ranges, rain forests, sparkling lakes, river swampland, jungle and sandy beaches*

A RAIN FOREST

- *Towering trees grow close to each other, lacing together at the top to form a "canopy" that blocks out all sun from reaching the soil on the forest floor.*
- *This soil lacks minerals. When a rain forest is cut down for lumber or homes, the soil is useless for growing crops.*
- *Rain falls almost every day.*
- *Temperatures stay around 80 degrees year round.*

THE CANOPY
Drenched by sunlight, the canopy is home to huge populations of birds, monkeys, insects and yet-to-be discovered species.

EPIPHYSES
Climbing plants like orchids and lianas use the larger trees as a ladder to the sunlight. Some are parasites; others are "stranglers" which choke the host plant.

PALMS
Grow from the forest floor in spots where sunlight filters down through the canopy.

THE SOIL
Because the canopy blocks out almost all sunlight, the forest floor is in constant shade and its soil, reddened from iron oxides, is almost infertile. Fallen leaves decompose, leaving a thin layer of *humus*.

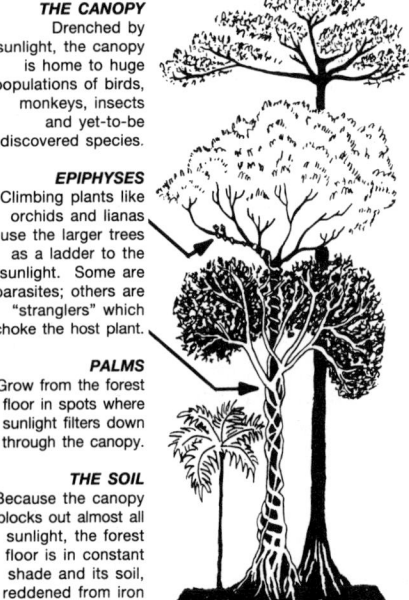

The Sahara DESERT

Larger than the continental U.S. and stretching clear across the northern third of Africa, the Sahara Desert has been a major barrier between the Mediterranean civilizations of the Muslim North and the Bantu civilizations of the Christian South.

The Sahara (Arabic for *"wasteland"*) is not a total wasteland. Once green with forests, rivers and lakes, at times it is still alive with creatures big and small. Nor is it all unending dunes of sand. Towering dry mountains rise from the desert over 10,000 feet. Depressions are sunk into the desert floor like those sighted on the moon. Underground rivers burst into trickling springs of water. And green oasis pools are fringed by settlements of peoples.

The Kalahari DESERT

Less dry than the Sahara, the Kalahari Desert is located in the southwestern tip of Africa. Scattered brush provides refuge for game and the few "Bushmen" who, forced from their original homelands, now live there.

SAVANNAH GRASSLANDS

Sweeping grasslands dotted with trees cover most of what we think of as "traditional Africa." These great savannahs have both a dry and a wet season. It is here that the great herds of antelope, zebra, giraffe, and elephants roam. And it is here that the tribes of East Africa raise their cattle.

JUNGLES

Thick jungles are found along riverbanks. The trees here grow so far apart that the sun *does* reach the ground and vegetation grows so thick you need a machete to cut a path.

TROPICAL RAIN FORESTS

A tropical rain forest is not a jungle. The fictional Tarzan did not swing from vines through towering trees in a jungle—he lived in a tropical rain forest. Most are located in either West Africa near the Ivory Coast, or from Nigeria south to Zaire and east to the highlands of East Africa.

desert

Not all desert is shifting sand dunes. There are three types of desert: *sand* ("Erg" in Arabic), *stone* ("Sarir") and *rock* ("Hammamet").

Sand Desert
Shifting dunes of sand which can bury farmland and, sometimes, an entire village.

Stony Desert
Desert littered with stones, some big as boulders, some small as gravel. Densely packed, these stones can create a "desert pavement."

Rock Desert
Here, the wind has stripped off all the soil, leaving just "bedrock" often criss-crossed by "wadis" (river beds usually dried out).

savanna grasslands

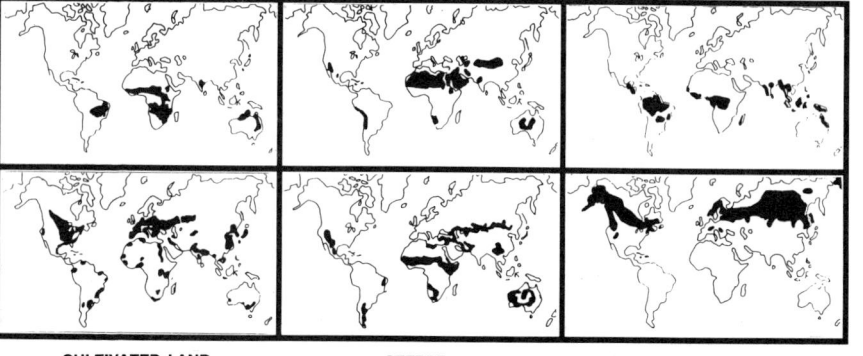

Farming the green pastures

In North America, prairie grasslands have mostly vanished. In Africa, the population explosion has resulted in a "burning off" of the savanna grasslands in order to replace them with farmland (which has proved to be of doubtful vitality in these drying areas). This has caused, in turn, an ever-shrinking homeland for animal life.

SAVANNA	DESERT	RAINFOREST
CULTIVATED LAND	STEPPE	CONIFEROUS FOREST

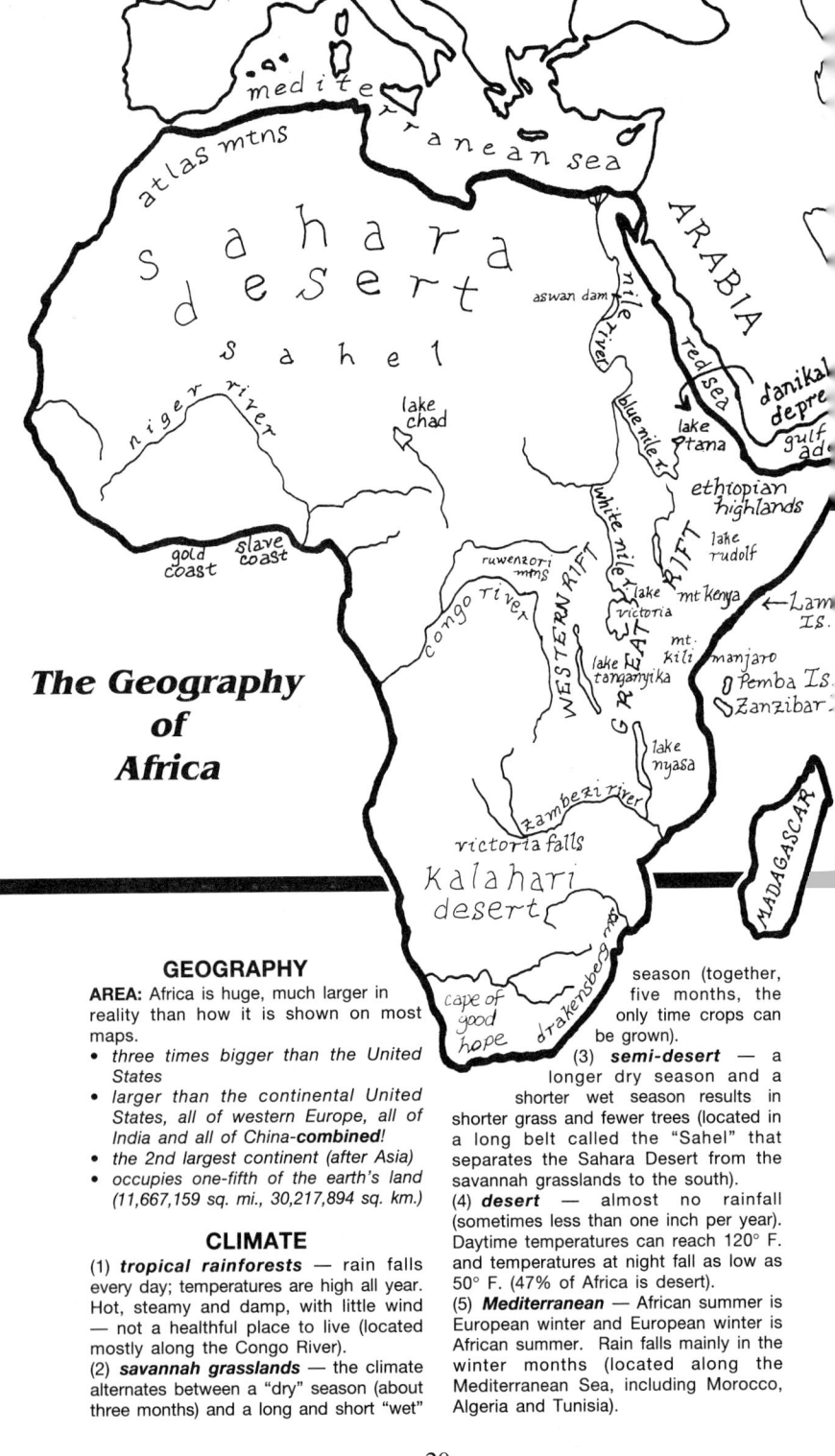

The map shows:

med it e rranean sea
atlas mtns
s a h a r a
d e s e r t
s a h e l
ARABIA
aswan dam
nile river
red sea
danikal depre
gulf ad
niger river
lake chad
blue nile
lake tana
ethiopian highlands
white nile
lake rudolf
ruwenzori mtns
WESTERN RIFT
mt kenya
Lam IS.
gold coast
slave coast
congo river
lake victoria
mt. kili manjaro
Pemba Is.
Zanzibar
lake tanganyika
GREAT RIFT
lake nyasa
zambezi river
victoria falls
kalahari desert
drakensberg mts
cape of good hope
MADAGASCAR

The Geography of Africa

GEOGRAPHY

AREA: Africa is huge, much larger in reality than how it is shown on most maps.

- *three times bigger than the United States*
- *larger than the continental United States, all of western Europe, all of India and all of China-**combined**!*
- *the 2nd largest continent (after Asia)*
- *occupies one-fifth of the earth's land (11,667,159 sq. mi., 30,217,894 sq. km.)*

CLIMATE

(1) **tropical rainforests** — rain falls every day; temperatures are high all year. Hot, steamy and damp, with little wind — not a healthful place to live (located mostly along the Congo River).

(2) **savannah grasslands** — the climate alternates between a "dry" season (about three months) and a long and short "wet" season (together, five months, the only time crops can be grown).

(3) **semi-desert** — a longer dry season and a shorter wet season results in shorter grass and fewer trees (located in a long belt called the "Sahel" that separates the Sahara Desert from the savannah grasslands to the south).

(4) **desert** — almost no rainfall (sometimes less than one inch per year). Daytime temperatures can reach 120° F. and temperatures at night fall as low as 50° F. (47% of Africa is desert).

(5) **Mediterranean** — African summer is European winter and European winter is African summer. Rain falls mainly in the winter months (located along the Mediterranean Sea, including Morocco, Algeria and Tunisia).

20

MOUNTAINS

East Africa (Africa's highest)

- **Mt. Kilimanjaro** — the highest in all of Africa at 19,340 feet (5,895 meters) above sea level.

- **Mt. Kenya** — rising nearly to 17,058 feet (5,199 meters) above sea level.

- **The Ethiopian Highlands** — rising to 15,000 feet are Africa's most massive mountain area.

- **The Ruwenzori Mountains** — "Mountains of the Moon" rise in East central Africa over 16,000 feet. Here can be found the long sought for source of the Nile.

Northwest Africa

- **The Atlas Mountains** on the West Coast rise up to 13,600 feet to wall off this tiny corner of Africa, keeping the fertile plains of Morocco safe from invaders for centuries.

South Africa

- **The Drakensberg Mountains** in South Africa rise to over 11,000 feet.

The Great Rift Valley

Millions of years ago, volcanic eruptions and shifting crusts of the earth caused the land in Africa to rise in some places and sink in others. Where the land sank, it formed a canyon thousands of miles long. Its walls sometimes are like cliffs, 15 to 100 miles apart, forming the sides of a deep fault or "rift" that splits East Africa in two.

This "Great Rift Valley" begins at the mouth of the Zambezi River in Mozambique and runs north to Tanzania where it divides into *two* branches — the *Western Rift* and the *Eastern Rift*.

- The walls of the *Western Rift* hold the great lakes of Tanganyka, Edward and Albert. It is through these "walled-in" valleys that the nomadic tribes herd their cattle.

- The walls of the *Eastern Rift* stretch into *Ethiopia*, then form the bed of the *Red Sea*, then exit into the Jordan Valley in Syria — 4,000 miles away from their start.

The Danikal Depression

Here, on the coast of Ethiopia and Djibouti where the Danikal people live, the rift bottom drops nearly 400 feet below sea level and temperatures reach a scalding 120 degrees. The Red Sea vanished as a volcanic ridge rose to wall the sea water out. The evaporation left salt deposits more than 15,000 feet (3 miles) deep.

RIVERS

Because of erratic rainfall, Africa's rivers can bring life or take life away. In the dry season, crops dry up and exposed rocks make some rivers unnavigable. In the rainy season, rivers can overflow their banks, flooding roads needed for transport and drowning crops.

Africa has 4 major rivers:

- **The Nile** — The world's longest river (4,160 miles) is actually two rivers (the White Nile and the Blue Nile) that join together at the city of Khartoum to form one.

  Down through the centuries, the mighty Nile has been the only real link through the Sahara Desert (other than camel caravans) to connect the peoples of the north to the peoples of the south. Yearly floods deposited fresh topsoil on its river banks, allowing food to grow. And on these banks were cradled some of the world's earliest civilizations.

- **The Niger** — flows in a broad arc through some of the driest areas of West Africa. Without the River Niger, the ancient kingdoms of Ghana, Mali and Songhia could not have developed. Navigation can be hard as the Niger can change 20 feet in depth between wet and dry seasons.

- **The Congo** — 3,000 miles long, drains the huge river basin area of Central Africa. It was along this river that the Bantu peoples migrated to take over most of southern Africa.

- **The Zambezi** — flows through Zambia, tumbling down over towering cliffs to form Victoria Falls. Then runs through Zimbabwe to empty into the Indian Ocean.

LAKES

Most are in East Africa and are formed by the Great Rift Valley.

- **Lake Victoria** — largest in all Africa, 3rd largest in all the world.

- **Lake Tanganyika** — the world's 7th largest.

- **Lake Chad** — not part of the Great Rift system, but the remains of an ancient inland ocean, it became the center for a kingdom controlling trade across the desert. Very shallow, it grows five times wider (from 4,000-10,000 sq. miles) in the wet season than it is in the dry.

WATERFALLS

- **Victoria Falls** — in Zambia was named after Queen Victoria of England by explorer Dr. David Livingston, (believed to be the first European to "discover" it). It is two times as high and 1½ times as wide as Niagara Falls. A cloud of mist, visible from 20 miles away, gives the falls its African name: "Mosi-O-Tunya" ("smoke that thunders").

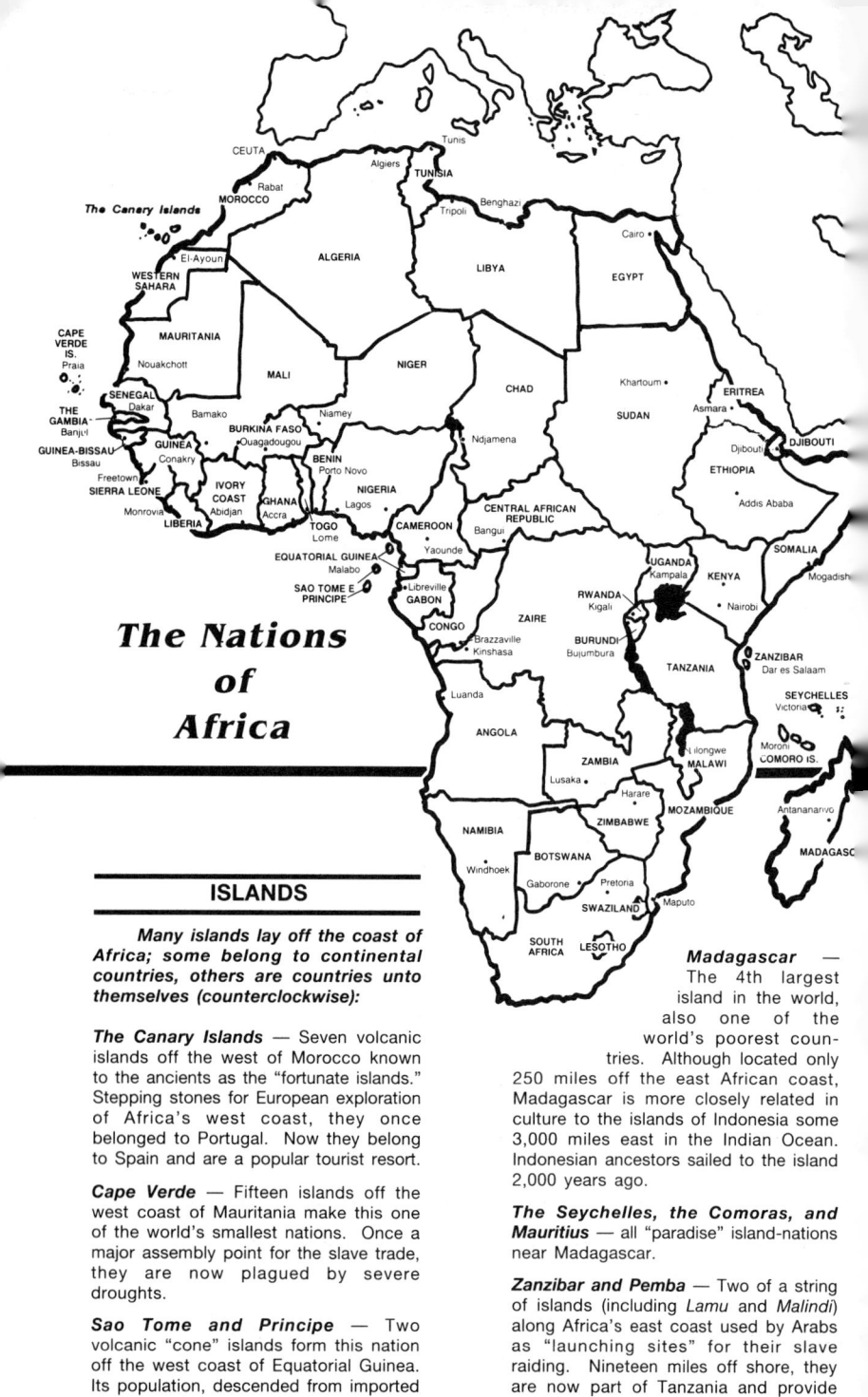

The Nations
of
Africa

ISLANDS

Many islands lay off the coast of Africa; some belong to continental countries, others are countries unto themselves (counterclockwise):

The Canary Islands — Seven volcanic islands off the west of Morocco known to the ancients as the "fortunate islands." Stepping stones for European exploration of Africa's west coast, they once belonged to Portugal. Now they belong to Spain and are a popular tourist resort.

Cape Verde — Fifteen islands off the west coast of Mauritania make this one of the world's smallest nations. Once a major assembly point for the slave trade, they are now plagued by severe droughts.

Sao Tome and Principe — Two volcanic "cone" islands form this nation off the west coast of Equatorial Guinea. Its population, descended from imported slaves, produces cocoa as its main crop.

Madagascar — The 4th largest island in the world, also one of the world's poorest countries. Although located only 250 miles off the east African coast, Madagascar is more closely related in culture to the islands of Indonesia some 3,000 miles east in the Indian Ocean. Indonesian ancestors sailed to the island 2,000 years ago.

The Seychelles, the Comoras, and Mauritius — all "paradise" island-nations near Madagascar.

Zanzibar and Pemba — Two of a string of islands (including *Lamu* and *Malindi*) along Africa's east coast used by Arabs as "launching sites" for their slave raiding. Nineteen miles off shore, they are now part of Tanzania and provide over 90% of the world's cloves.

Country	Capital
Algeria (1962)	Algiers
Angola (1975)	Luanda
Benin (1960)	Porto-Novo and Cotonou
Botswana (1966)	Gaborone
Burkina Faso (1960)	Ouagadougou
Burundi (1962)	Bujumbura
Cameroon (1960)	Yaoundé
Cape Verde (1975)	Praia
Central African Republic (1960)	Bangui
Chad (1960)	Ndjamena (Fort-Lamy)
The Comoros (1975)	Moroni
Congo (1960)	Brazzaville
Djibouti (1977)	Djibouti
Egypt (1922)	Cairo
Equatorial Guinea (1968)	Malabo (Santa Isabel)
Eritrea (1993)	Asmara
Ethiopia	Addis Ababa
Gabon (1960)	Libreville
The Gambia (1965)	Banjul (Bathurst)
Ghana (1957)	Accra
Guinea (1958)	Conakry
Guinea-Bissau (1974)	Bissau
Ivory Coast (1960)	Abidjan
Kenya (1963)	Nairobi
Lesotho (1966)	Maseru
Liberia (1847)	Monrovia
Libya (1951)	Tripoli
Madagascar (1960)	Tananarive
Malawi (1964)	Lilongwe
Mali (1960)	Bamako
Mauritania (1960)	Nouakchott
Mauritius (1968)	Port Louis
Morocco (1956)	Rabat
Mozambique (1975)	Maputo (Lourenço Marques)
Namibia	Windhoek
Niger (1960)	Niamey
Nigeria (1960)	Lagos
Réunion	Saint-Denis
Rwanda (1962)	Kigali
São Tomé and Príncipe (1975)	São Tomé
Senegal (1960)	Dakar
Seychelles (1976)	Victoria
Sierra Leone (1961)	Freetown
Somalia (1960)	Mogadishu
South Africa (1910)	Pretoria and Cape Town
Sudan (1956)	Khartoum
Swaziland (1968)	Mbabane
Tanzania (1961 and 1963, with Unification in 1964)	Dar-es-Salaam
Togo (1960)	Lomé
Tunisia (1956)	Tunis
Uganda (1962)	Kampala
Western Sahara (1976) (Saharan Arab Democratic Republic)	El Aaiún
Zaire (1960)	Kinshasa (Léopoldville)
Zambia (1964)	Lusaka
Zimbabwe (1980)	Harare (Salisbury)

When the Europeans carve up Africa, they draw their borders with little concern for the tribes living within them.

Some tribes find their own people divided, straddling the border of two nations that are now enemies!

Other tribes find themselves locked inside the same nation as a another tribe, traditionally their enemy.

africa-at-a-glance

ECONOMY

Yearly GNP Per Person: Ranging from a high of $8,510 in Libya to a low of $67 in Chad. Most countries average $200-400 per person per year.

Yearly GNP per Country: Ranging from highs of $87 billion in South Africa, $44 billion in Algeria and $77 billion in Nigeria to lows of $.34 billion in Chad, $.22 billion in the Gambia and $.14 billion in Guinea Bissau.

Produce:
- the world's largest producer of - yams, cashews and cocoa beans
- a major world source of - peanuts, coffee, bananas and cotton

Forestry: From Africa's vast forests come products such as timber, rubber, palm oil and palm oil products.

Livestock: the savannah and grasslands are ideal for grazing.
- 1/3 of the world's goats are raised by African herders
- 1/7 of the world's cattle and sheep are raised by African herders
- camels are also raised and marketed

Minerals: The mineral resources of Africa are immense but unevenly distributed. A handful of countries control most of the wealth while most countries have little or no mineral resources.
- 90% of the world's diamonds (mostly from South Africa)
- 90% of the world's cobalt
- 50% of the world's gold (outside of the Soviet nation block) comes from South Africa
- 30% of the world's chromite (needed for chromium used in steel)
- 30% of the world's uranium (fuel for nuclear energy)
- 27% of the world's bauxite (aluminum)
- large deposits of copper (used in wire and metal work) produced mostly in Zaire and Zambia, and nickel (used in stainless steel)
- much of the world's zinc, manganese and coal
- much of the world's phosphate (used in fertilizer)

Water Power:
- 40% of the world's potential hydroelectric power (created by dams such as the *Kariba Dam* on the Zambezi River and the *High Aswan Dam* on the Nile River. These dams control flooding and provide water for irrigation. Most waterfalls still remain untapped.

Agriculture:
- 75% of Africa's people are farmers
- agriculture is the leading economy on the continent. during colonialism, farmers were forced to shift from raising their own "subsistence crops" to raising one or two "cash crops," for sale to outside markets, thereby becoming dependent upon outside market prices to earn enough money to buy imported food instead of raising their own food.

GOVERNMENT

There is no such thing as a political entity called Africa. Africa is divided into 54 countries, many of which are not united by historical tribal ties. The colonialists created the borders arbitrarily without consideration for the peoples who lived within them — so, what were once politically cohesive tribes now find themselves either straddling the border of two countries opposed to each other or occupying a country with a rival tribe historically their enemy. Old forms of *kingship, matriarchal rule* and *democratic councils of elders* gave way under colonialism to *parliamentary rule* and, after independence, *military tyranny* or *one party rule*. A unique form of *"African socialism"* has been experimented with, notably in Tanzania, with mixed results. Marxist countries, once Soviet-supported, have altered their views with the decrease of aid coming from what was formerly the Soviet Union.

above left: A tall, dark-skinned mother from Senegal with her baby bundled on her back.
above right: A young Berber mother from Morocco.
below right: A veiled young girl from Chad with her baby brother at the hospital in Ati.
below left: A white Afrikaaner mother with her child at a "white's only" rally in South Africa.
opposite page: A San ("Bushman") from the Kalahari Desert, carrying two hands full of stork chicks.

Who Is African?

Someone who is born on the continent of Africa? Or someone who has "black" skin? Black-skinned people exist in India and other parts of the world but they are not racially Negroid. Peoples have existed in most of Africa for thousands of years who also are not Negroid nor even have black skin. Is the light-skinned Muslim of the north *not* an African? What about the Dutch who settled in Africa 400 years ago and call themselves *Afrikaans*? Can a white person be an African?

Africa has a wider variety of people living inside its borders than any other continent in the world. Aside from having major populations of white and Asian peoples, the tallest (over 7 ft) and the shortest (under 4 1/2 ft) people in the world live in Africa. Certainly all black people do not "look the same;" in fact, the black peoples of Africa are as different and varied as Greeks are from Swedes.

Endangered Peoples

The SAN ("Bushmen")

Probably the earliest of people in Africa, these gentle yellowish brown-skinned people, forced out by neighboring Bantu tribes, are now confined to the Kalahari Desert. Famous for their ancient art work and rock paintings, they survived by hunting animals and gathering birds' eggs, fruit and nuts. The "Bushmen" (also known as *San* for Khoisan, the *"click"* language they speak) are about 5 ft 5 in tall. Many scholars consider the Khoi, the San, and the Pygmy *not* to be Negroid.

Today, there are fewer than 44,000 "Bushmen" left.

The KHOI ("Hottentots")

Also confined to a small part of Southern Africa (mostly Namibia), the "Hottentots" became herders of cattle and sheep. Those who were not hunted down and killed by the whites, intermarried and became part of the Cape's "colored" peoples.

Today, less than 30,000 "Hottentots" exist.

The PYGMIES — Forest People

Believed to be the oldest people of Africa, these spiritually-minded people have lived in the lush tropical rain forests of the Congo River Basin for thousands of years. They, too, are in great danger of becoming extinct. Some have been enslaved by, or married into, larger tribes. Others have fallen victim to diseases they had no defenses for.

About 4 feet, 6 inches, the Pygmy today make their home the rainforests of Rwanda, Burundi, Cameroon, Gabon, The Congo and Zaire. Today, there are fewer than 100,000 "Pygmies" left.

"NON-NEGROID" NATIVES OF AFRICA ARE BECOMING EXTINCT

Who Started

- **Central and Southern Africa** — before the migration of the Bantu peoples, were originally settled by the *Khoisan* ("click")-speaking peoples (the *Khoi* or "Hottentots" and the *San* or "Bushmen").

- **West Central Africa** — was originally settled by the *Pygmies* in the *tropical rain forests.*

- **North of the Sahara Desert** — was settled by people called *Hamites,* related to Arabians.

- **South of the Sahara Desert** — was settled mostly by either *Bantu-speaking* people from the West or *Nilo-Saharan-speaking* people from the East and Upper Nile.

Negro Peoples of Africa

Africa's largest percent of "black" people live *south* of the Sahara Desert. Here you will find hundreds of tribes and lifestyles. But most come from 4 groups of peoples:

(1) Bantu-speaking

(Ba means "many," *ntu* means "human being." Therefore, *Bantu* means "many human beings, many people"). Originally, their homelands were the rivers of Eastern Nigeria and Cameroon. Eventually, they migrated along the Congo River to take over most of Southern Africa, pushing out the smaller "Bushmen" into the desert. Today, there are over 70 million Bantu-speaking people, including the *Ibo* and *Yoruba* of Nigeria, the *Kikuyu* of Kenya and the *Zulu* of South Africa.

(2) Nilo-Saharan-speaking

These are people who live near the Sahara Desert Basin of Lake Chad, the upper Niger River, or the Blue Nile River Basin. In the *"Nilotic"* tribes who live along the upper Nile, men commonly are over 7 feet tall. Today there are over 35 million Nilo-Saharan people, including the *Maasai* of Kenya and the *Dinka* and *Nuer* of Sudan.

(3) Chari-Nile-speaking

These are people who live along the middle Nile River, the White Nile, or the lakes of East Africa (including the *Nuba* of Sudan).

(4) Afro-Asian-speaking

These are people who live mostly north of the Sahara desert (including the *Berber*); some live south (the *Hausa* of Nigeria), or east (the *Somali* of Somalia and the *Amhara* of Ethiopia).

Out Where?

HAMITES
NILO-SAHARAN
CHARI-NILE
BANTU
PYGMIES
PYGMIES
PYGMIES
KHOI SAN

opposite: *San women, under 5 ft*
this page: *Long-limbed Nilotic man, over 7 ft.*

43

European Whites

Whites have lived in North Africa since ancient times, crossing the Mediterranean Sea to settle and trade. Beginning in the 17th Century, Europeans built trading cities, sailing down the West Coast until they reached the Cape of Good Hope, then working their way up the East Coast where colonies were set up in Kenya and Tanzania.

- **Portuguese** *settled mostly in Angola and Mozambique.*
- **Dutch** *(Boers) arrived in the mid-17th Century to settle in South Africa.*
- **English** *arrived in the 19th Century to settle in what is now Zambia, Zimbabwe and East Africa.*
- **French** *arrived to settle in West and North Africa.*
- **Germans** *settled in southwest Africa and Namibia.*

Today, 2 million European whites live as welcomed citizens in Africa's newly independent nations. Another 4 million whites live in the aftermath of the revolution in South Africa.

Arab Whites

Arab whites swept across North Africa from the Arab Peninsula during the 7th Century. Today, 80 million make their homes in Egypt, northern Sudan, and along the Mediterranean coast.

Asian People

Shipped in by colonial whites from Pakistan and India to build Africa's great railways, Asians settled in South Africa and along the coast of East Africa, Kenya and Tanzania. Becoming merchants and shopkeepers, some of this moneyed middle class were evicted and discriminated against by blacks during the fight for independence.

Today, there are over 900,000 Asian people on the continent of Africa, many in South Africa; and over 5 million Asian peoples on the Island of Madagascar, most of whom are descendents from Malayans and Polynesians who sailed to the island 2,000 years ago.

Languages

The words you and I speak, our phrasing and the dialect we use, provide a clue to our "roots," our homeland. Scholars trace the source of over 1,000 languages used in Africa today to the roots of 4 major language groups:

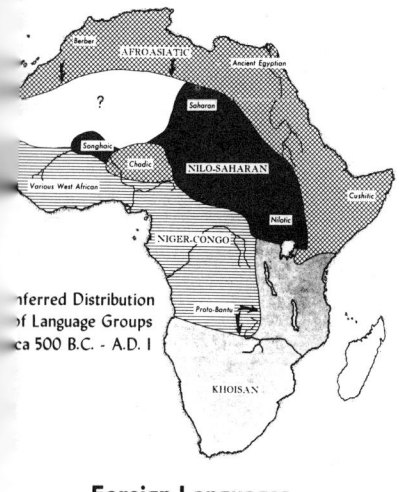

Inferred Distribution of Language Groups ca 500 B.C. - A.D. I

**Foreign Languages
Allow Africans To
Talk To One Another**

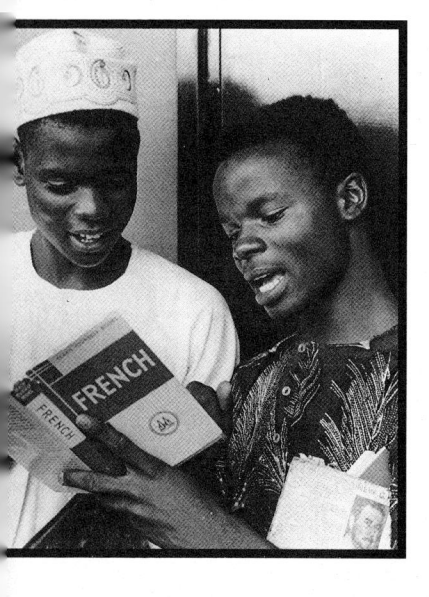

NATIVE Languages

1. Niger-Congo — These include the 300 Bantu languages spoken by the peoples of eastern, central and southern Africa (like the *Ibo* and *Yoruba* of Nigeria, the *Kikuyu* of Kenya and the *Zulu* of South Africa.

2. Nilo-Saharan (Nilotic) — Spoken by 35 million people from eastern and central Sudan (like the *Maasai* of Kenya and the *Dinka* and *Nuer* of Sudan).

3. Afro-Asian — Spoken by peoples in North Africa. Afro-Asian includes languages such as: Hebrew, Arabic, Amharic (spoken in Ethiopia), ancient Egyptian, Somali and other semitic Cushitic or Chadic languages (like the *Berber* of North Africa and *Hausa* of Nigeria).

4. Khoisan — Called "click" language because of the clicking sounds made by the tongue while speaking. Spoken by the *San "Bushmen"* and the *Khoi "Hottentots."*

FOREIGN Languages

There are over 1,000 languages spoken today in Africa. In Nigeria alone, people speak over 100 languages. Because of difficulties in communication, many newly independent nations adopted the colonial language as their own official language. *French* is now taught in former French colonies, *English* in former English colonies, and sometimes *Portuguese, Italian* and *German* are taught in their former colonies. *Malagasy* is spoken by 5 million people on Madagascar.

AFRIKAANS

Africaans is a Dutch dialect used by the *Boers* (Dutch farmers who settled in South Africa). The forced teaching of this language to blacks in the schools of South Africa fueled demonstrations in townships like Soweto and, in turn, led to the "black consciousness" movement.

SWAHILI

Swahili is a mix of the languages of black Bantu people on the East Coast and white Arab traders. Once used for commercial purposes along the east coast, Swahili now is the official language of Kenya and Tanzania and is spoken by 100 million people.

Religion

Africa has three basic religions:

(1) traditional religions

(2) Islam

(3) Christianity

NOTE: *Judaism* and *Hinduism* are also practiced in Africa.

Judaism

"mother of Christianity and Islam"

Judaism's roots in Africa begin ancient times — over 2,000 years a (while Islam enters Africa just 500 yea ago).

Traditional Religions

Long before foreign Christian and Muslim missionaries convert much of Africa to their faiths, religions native to Africa hold tribes together with common beliefs. Today, more than 100,000,000 Africans practice traditional religions. There are as many different religions as there are tribes. But they do have traits in common:

- *Ancestor Worship*
- *Animism*
- *Fetishes*
- *Priests or Doctors*

Christianity

- *1 out of every 4 people in Africa is Christie*
- *Of the 100 million who are Christian, million belong to the Roman Cathol church.*

After Jesus Christ is crucifie Christianity spreads from the Holy Lan around the Mediterranean Sea and int Africa. Taking root in the City *Alexandria* in Egypt, Coptic churche spread the new religion *(1)* east across th North African coast and *(2)* south dow along the Nile River. A string of Christia churches run south down along the Nil Valley. By the 4th Century, Copti Christianity takes hold in Ethiopia an

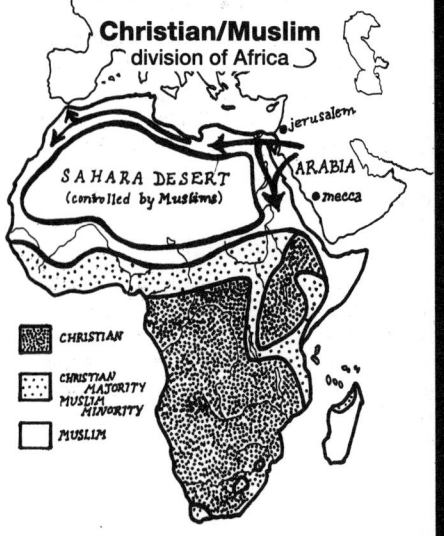

Christian/Muslim division of Africa

jerusalem

SAHARA DESERT
(controlled by Muslims)

ARABIA

mecca

CHRISTIAN

CHRISTIAN MAJORITY MUSLIM MINORITY

MUSLIM

Islam

- *Africa's most recent and fastest growin religion*
- *1 out of every 4 people in Africa (over 3 million people) are Muslims; most all them live north of the Sahara Desert*

Founded by the Prophet Muham mad, 700 years after the death of Chris Islam honors many of the Jewish an Christian prophets, including Noah Abraham, Moses and Jesus. There is onl one God, revealed to Mohammed by th Christian angel, Gabriel, in a series o revelations he set down into a holy boo — the *Koran*.

46

The impact of Judaism on African culture is more profound than most historians report, arriving in three ways: *1)* directly through Jews living in Africa (mostly Morocco, Egypt, Algeria and South Africa), *(2)* directly through the religious faith of Judaism (as practiced by the "Falasha" of Ethiopia), and *(3)* indirectly through the impact of Judaism on Christianity and Islam (to this day, the ancient Semite symbol of a crescent moon with a star appears on all Muslim flags).

thrives from 500 to 1500 A.D. However, in the 7th Century, Christians are overwhelmed by Arabs invading the coast, bringing with them a new religion: *Islam.* Christianity disappears from the north, leaving behind an Ethiopian church cut off and isolated up in the rugged highlands.

To be "civilized" the African is asked to cast out his traditional spirituality. During the fight for independence, Political freedom follows religious freedom. Africans decide to create *their own* Christian churches and African Christians begin to reinterpret their faith within an African context.

From the deserts of the Arabian peninsula, Islam spreads like lightening into Egypt, across all of North Africa. By 750 A.D. Islam has taken hold, forever altering the course of North African history.

How does Islam spread so quickly? Not only a religion, Islam is also a culture, a nation — and an enormous business and trading market. Spread by local traders, the message of Islam is carried into black Africa along with the trader's goods. It unites the Mediterranean world for the first time in centuries, bringing stability to a Muslim empire even larger than the empires of the Greeks or the Romans.

47

The Origin of Mankind

From what we know, you and I are Africans. Every human being on earth — red, yellow, black, white — can trace their ancestry back to Africa. In fact, for the greatest amount of time homo sapiens' homeland has been Africa.

THE GREEN SAHARA
Birthplace of Early Man?

Where today desert sands eclipse almost all living things and rain falls barely every few years . . . eight thousand years ago, the great Sahara Desert was lush and green. Grasses teemed with herds of antelope, elephant and giraffe. Rivers and lakes filled with fish. And all were hunted by bands of two-legged beings who roamed through what is now a desert almost the size of the entire United States.

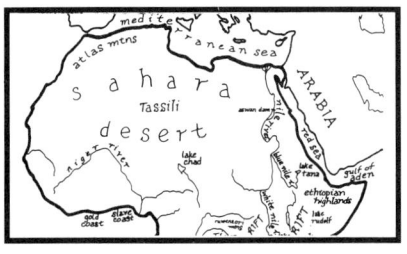

The Rock Paintings of Tassily

In the western Sahara Desert, on a high plateau called Tassily n-Ahaggar, today you can find rocks and cave walls painted over with beautiful hunting scenes of rhinoceros and elephant — painted six thousand years ago.

The Splitting Apart of Mankind

It is six thousand years ago . . . Lakes and rivers in the great Sahara begin to dry up. Vegetation burns out. People scatter in all directions, dividing Africa into two worlds — those who live *north* of the great desert and those who live *south* of it.

Some go north to the Mediterranean coast then cross over the narrow straight of Gibraltar into Europe. Others go east to the Nile River, then travel far south. Still others cross the Arabian peninsula, migrating east into India and China, then across the Bering Straits into what is now Alaska and down the North American west coast.

This may explain why some customs in the farthest reaches of the earth have some similarities. But one of the world's great mysteries remains:

Q U E S T I O N
Why did people become so isolated and lose contact with one another?

How did you and I evolve and adapt physically in different environments — changing our skin color in response to the demands of the sun, creating languages and customs that could not be understood by our distant relatives — before our great rediscovery of each other within the last few centuries?

Two Negroid Peoples Dominate Africa

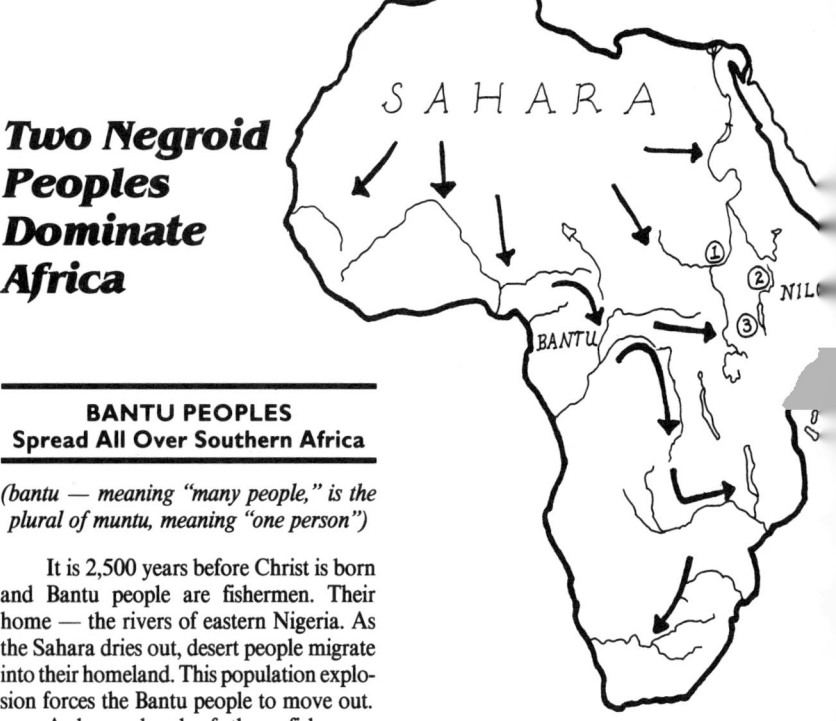

BANTU PEOPLES
Spread All Over Southern Africa

(bantu — meaning "many people," is the plural of muntu, meaning "one person")

It is 2,500 years before Christ is born and Bantu people are fishermen. Their home — the rivers of eastern Nigeria. As the Sahara dries out, desert people migrate into their homeland. This population explosion forces the Bantu people to move out.

A brave band of these fishermen packs up all their belongings and sets out in dugout canoes. The river takes them south, deep into the fearsome rain forests of the Congo. Over time, this 2,900 mile long river becomes a highway for an enormous migration of Bantu-speaking people. Gradually, they begin to fan out in every direction, some east to Somalia, others south to the Zambezi River Valley — creating the greatest upheaval of peoples in all of African history. Ultimately they overtake most all of Africa south of the Sahara.

In their wake, local tribes are either overcome or absorbed through intermarriages, mixing their languages and customs, calling themselves Kongo, Kikuyu, Nguni, Ndebele or Shona. Along the way, the Bantu develop a totally new way of life. From the Nilotic cattle people of East Africa, they learn how to be herdsmen. From the peoples along the Zambezi River they learn to grow crops (like the banana, introduced from Asia), and some now become farmers. Most importantly, they spread the use of smelting iron.

By the 5th Century, they have moved down from the Zambezi Valley into the *Transvaal* (the north part of the Republic of South Africa). By the 13th Century, they have already reached South Africa's Cape — forcing out the smaller *"Bushmen"* and *"Hottentots."* Here, some Bantu people settle in *kraals* (a cluster of huts circled around a cattle corral) and call themselves Zulus.

NILOTIC (Nile River) PEOPLE
Spread All Over East Africa

On the opposite end of the desert, over 2,000 years ago, another great people arises. Originally, their homeland lies between the White Nile and the highlands of Ethiopia. But by the time Christ is born, they split into three groups:

(1) *Western Nilotic* peoples who migrate along the White Nile River into Sudan (today's Nuer, Nuba, Shilluck, and Dinka tribes)

(2) *Eastern Nilotic* peoples who stay near their Ethiopian highlands.

(3) *Southern Nilotic* peoples who migrate down along the Great Rift Valley into East Africa (today's Maasai, Turkana, Pokot, Somburu, and Nandi tribes)

While the broad-shouldered **BANTU PEOPLES** spread from West Africa to conquer all of southern Africa, the towering, long-limbed **NILOTIC PEOPLES** make the Nile River Valley of East Africa their homeland.

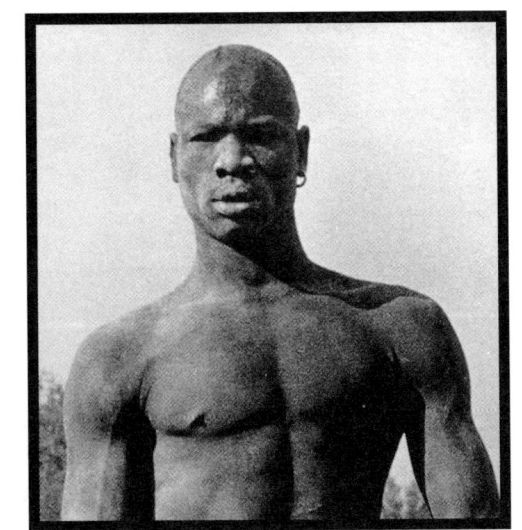

These differences can still be found in Africa's youth today. What do they reveal about our roots?. . . .

above left: A long-limbed teenager from Sudan
below left: Four sawmill workers from Nigeria

above right: Two young Berber women chatting in Morocco
below right: Two young Bantu women chatting in Mali

"The whole of this country has had the names of Aetheria, Atlantia, and Aethiopia . . . towards the end of this region, men and animals assume a monstrous form . . . Indeed, in the interior, there is a people that have no noses . . . others again are missing the upper lip and others are without tongue. Others again have the mouth grown together and still others missing nostrils, breathe through their mouth only..."
— **Pliny, the Elder,** *from his "Natural History"
based on a Roman expedition by Nero
to discover the source of the Nile*

The "Dark Continent"

Africa was long known only as the "dark Continent," shrouded by mystery and tall tales of monstrous animals and strange people. This point of view was the European point of view. Africa was "unknown" only to the foreigners who found it difficult to explore — not to the people who were living there. To the African, it was the foreign traders who, with their funny clothes and bizarre customs, seemed strange.

Many people are not aware that:

- *Until just 120 years ago almost all of interior Africa was completely unknown to the European*
- *Colonial rule didn't begin until 100 years ago*
- *Lasting only 80 years, it had a wrenching impact, overturning centuries-old means of living and shattering the lives of people over the entire continent.*

What was life like . . . *before* the Europeans?

73

GHANA gives rise to	MALI which gives rise to	SONGHAI

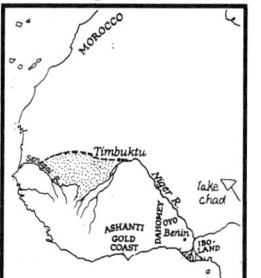 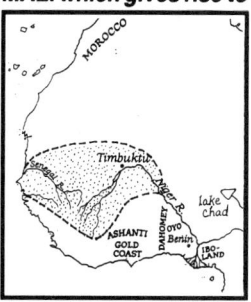 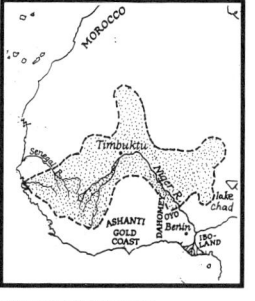

GHANA (700-1200 A.D.)   MALI (1300-1500)   SONGHAI (1350-1600)

Kingdoms of West Africa

Long before the European colonists arrive, a series of great Bantu kingdoms rise and fall in West Africa. Each possesses a richness and sophistication that will astonish the foreigner upon his "discovery" of their ruins.

THE EMPIRE OF GHANA (700-1,200 A.D.)

Here, at the trade crossroads between the Arab lands of the North and the rich forests and gold mines of the South, Ghana grows into a powerful empire which will last almost 1,000 years. Iron weapons allow Ghana (which means "war chief") to fight successfully. Gold is plentiful and is traded for salt which is scarce in the forests (salt, needed for health, is literally "worth its weight in gold"). Caravans, some with 10,000 camels, cross through their empire, and the kings of Ghana charge taxes for every load.

Kumbi is their capital — two cities six miles apart. Inside one city, walled inside a fortress, lives the king. Inside the other city are the marketplaces and homes of teachers, craftspeople and merchants. In 1076, Muslims overrun the Kingdom, converting the people to Islam.

THE EMPIRE OF MALI (1230-1433)

In the ruins of Ghana, a new kingdom is built by a new tribe who call themselves Mandingos, one that will become much larger than Ghana ever was — the Empire of Mali.

Islam becomes their chief religion (this encourages trade with the Arabs). The *Mandingo* capture their black neighbors and sell them to the Arabs as slaves. But there are differences between the Arab and the people of Mali, particularly, as one Arab traveler noted, in the way the men of Mali honor their women:

> *"The women [of Mali] are of surprising beauty . . . their men show no sign of jealousy whatsoever. No one claims descent from his father; but, on the contrary, from his mother's brother. A person's heirs are his sister's sons, not his own sons."*
>
> **— Stanlake Samkange,**
> *"African Saga," pp. 127-128*

Gold For Salt

A nomad tribe, the *Taureg,* living in the oases of the desert, mine the salt in great blocks. Taxes are charged by the cities through which their camel caravans pass, and soon great trading centers arise in Mali.

Timbuktu becomes the desert crossroads for trade along the Niger River, and the location for a great Muslim university, *Qarawiyin.*

74

The Richest King in Africa

This 1375 map shows Mansa Musa holding up a huge nugget of gold as an Arab trader rides in to barter for it

P R O F I L E

Mansa Musa — Mali's Greatest King

"Mansa" (meaning "Emperor") Kankan Musa, the most powerful leader of Mali, leads his empire literally into a Golden Age (1307 to 1322) turning it into one of the most civilized countries in the world.

"They have a greater abhorrence of injustice than any other people. A traveler has nothing to fear from robbers or men of violence. They do not confiscate the property of any white man who dies in their country...."
Roland Oliver *"The Dawn of African History"* p. 41

At this time China is equally safe — but not Europe. Europe is a continent divided. Petty kingdoms wage war on each other. Witches are horribly tortured. Heretics are boiled in oil, and any traveler risks his life and property.

But Musa is a religious man, a devout Muslim. In 1324, he begins one of the most incredible journeys in all of history — a pilgrimage, 3,000 miles across the burning desert, all the way to Mecca.

He sets out with a caravan of ten thousand camels, carrying several tons of gold. Sixty thousand people, as well as all his wives and children, will join him along the way. When he reaches Cairo, he showers its rulers with gifts of gold nuggets the size of coconuts. So much gold floods Cairo's marketplaces that its price falls radically (it will take more than 12 years for gold to regain its value in Egypt). Legends of his enormous wealth spread throughout Europe and he is called "Lord of the Negroes."

Returning to Mali, he brings Muslim scholars to his kingdom and builds a great school for theology and law in Timbuktu.

THE EMPIRE OF THE SONGHAI
(1375-1591)

Suni Ali

In 1375 the city of Gao breaks from the Kingdom of Mali and soon becomes its rival. Crowned emperor in 1464, Suni Ali sets out on a fierce campaign to make his kingdom the largest of West Africa. His city of *Djenne* soon becomes a trading city to rival Timbuktu. Through warfare, he overruns Mali. When he dies in 1492 (same year Columbus lands in America) he has never lost a battle. Today, nearly 500 years later, people still talk of him as a hero.

Askia Muhammad

One of Suni Ali's officers, Askia, seizes leadership upon his death. Under Muhammad's rule, the kingdom is solidified. So wealthy now is Songhai, that the ruler of nearby Morocco, Al Mansur, attacks. In 1589, Askia Muhammad leads an army of 44,000 men and 9,000 transport animals across the desert to fight him. It takes him six months and only 1,000 men survive. Two years later, the Songhai King again meets the enemy — this time with 18,000 calvary and 9,000 infantry —but still he cannot overpower the Moroccan forces. Weapons are the key. The Berbers from Morocco are armed with a new primitive gun, a musket they call the *"Acubus."* The swords and spears of the Songhai are no match.

Morocco invades West Africa

The great trading cities of the Songhai Empire are looted and destroyed. Intellectuals are imprisoned. *Ahmad Babba* (a world renown scholar and author of 40 books on subjects like astronomy and Arabic grammar) is exiled to Morocco. Philosophers and businessmen are driven out. Moroccan soldiers go from home to home, robbing maps and historical writings.

Timbuktu is raped

The Royal Pasha from Morocco orders the holy men of Songhai to swear obedience to the sultan of Morocco. When they come to the mosque, the governor tricks them, murdering some without warning and sending the others with their wives and children in chains across the deserts to be sold as slaves.

The great university in Timbuktu lies now in a pile of broken bricks and mud. The light of knowledge is snuffed out . . . No one alive can remember the great scholar Ahmad Babba.

below: A reconstruction of the old mosque in Djenne, a rival intellectual center to the University at Timbuktu. Perhaps of equal architectural glory to Mecca, the Djenne mosque was destroyed in 1830 by the Muslims in a Fulani jihad (holy war) as punishment for the moral corruption that they believed was being taught.

Made from sun-baked mud brick this mosque echoes an earlier mosque which matched Mecca in architectural beauty. Protruding boards of wood serve not only as an architectural decoration but also as a built-in step ladder for repairs. The great mosque dates from the 14th Century and Is located on the Niger River.

The Djenne mosque

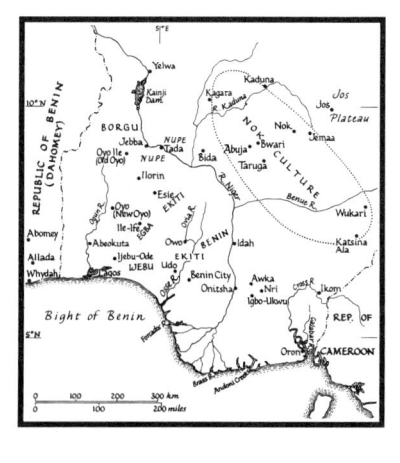

Kingdoms of West Central Africa

THE FOREST KINGDOMS
of IFE and BENIN

On the delta of the Niger River (in what is today Nigeria), the Yoruba people build a great walled city, grand homes, wide streets and a luxurious palace for their king. Oyo-Ife becomes the center for gifted sculptors for centuries.

While the Yoruba pass on their expertise to the nearby kingdom of Benin, slave raiding decimates the population and by 1400, the glorious city of Oyo-Ife is left in ruins.

The rest of the world will not learn about this ancient kingdom — until just 100 years ago. Gorgeous heads of bronze and brass will be uncovered by a British exploration, and proclaimed to be among the greatest art works of the world *[see: ART]*.

Kanem-Bornu rises separately around Lake Chad

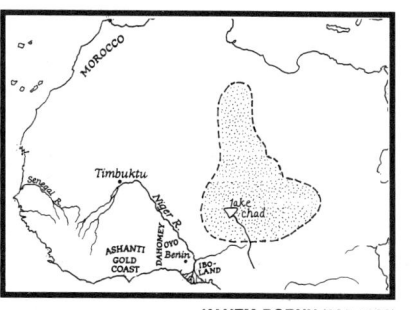

Kanem-Bornu (800-1800)

Around the marsh-trimmed waters of Lake Chad another great kingdom arises, that of *Kanem-Bornu*. This ancient kingdom stretches along the edge of the Sahara from the Tibesti Mountains to the shores of Lake Chad and covers much of what is today known as the Republic of Chad.

The *Kanuri* people remain the "core people" in this area for a thousand years, mixing with and battling other nomadic peoples in a series of wars — the *Hausa-speaking people* to the west, the *Nupe people* in the Benue Valley to the south, *Berbers* raiding from the north and the *Fulve (Fulani)* from the west. Largely free of the menace of tsetse flies, these people of Kanem-Bornu are able to take advantage of the grasslands, raising cattle or becoming farmers.

Q U E S T I O N

How much early contact is there between those peoples along the NIGER River and those peoples along the NILE River?

The answer is not fully known; but if this area had once in ancient times been a trading crossroads, by the 9th Century these trade routes had fallen into disuse. No longer are the great camel caravans crossing the desert over this "Nile to Niger" trade route, having found alternate routes to the north.

Now the people of Kanem-Bornu are left to evolve their own unique culture, undisturbed from outside traders.

The remains of an ancient inland ocean, this lake becomes the center for a kingdom controlling trade across the desert. Lake Chad grows five times wider (from 4,000-10,000 square miles) in the wet season than it is in the dry season.

trade routes

The Berber camel caravans begin to lay out a spider web of trade routes criss-crossing the Sahara Desert. Great trading crossroad cities rise from the desert like Timbuktu, Djenne, and Kano, laying down support lines for the growth of West Africa's many kingdoms.

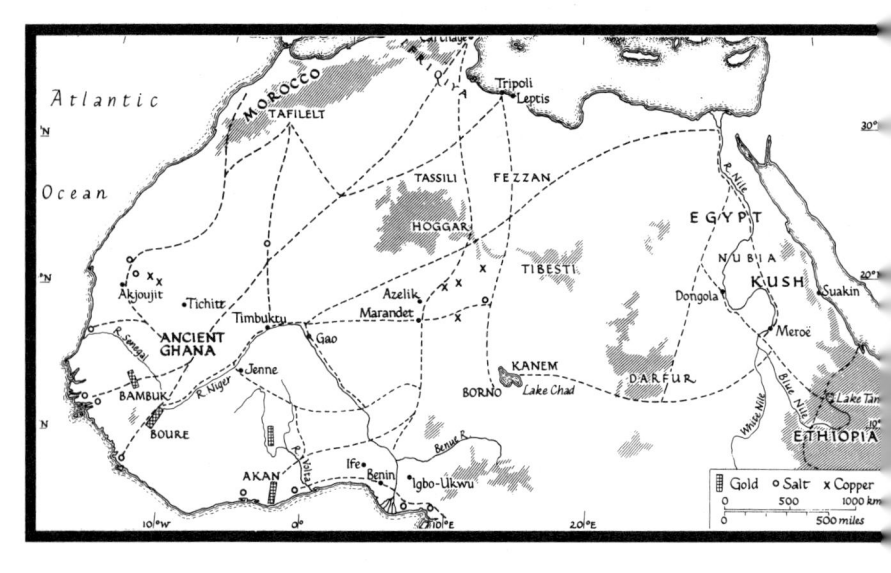

money

Before paper is invented by the Chinese and before metals are minted into coins, almost any object considered valuable by a people serves as money. Ivory, tea, tobacco, feathers, shells...all at one time or another are used as money. In Rome, soldiers are paid with a prize possession — salt. Hence, the phrase, "worth one's salt." In West Africa, it is the *cowrie* shell that becomes most popular, weaved into clothing much in the same way that silver coins will later be worn by people who literally will "wear their wealth" sewn into their clothes.

The first use of a symbolic object made for trade comes from China during the Shang Dynasty. Here traditional farmers trade spades and knives for other goods; so the first money is shaped in the form of a spade. Soon gold, silver and other rare metals are shaped into circles. These "coins" can be carried and recognized easily. Governments carefully guard their rights both to produce them and to set their value.

It is gold from West Africa that literally finances the growth of empires of the imperialist European nations. Made into coins for the kings and queens of Spain, France and England (the small relief of an elephant at the coin's bottom betrays its source), West Africa's gold will finance Europe's successes until the supplies become exhausted and new sources in a "New World" (in Mexico, the Americas and Brazil) are discovered.

About a thousand years after the death of Christ, the Chinese invent movable type and become the first to use paper for money, thereby "lightening" the load that the heavy weight of metal coins brought to long distance trade.

82

Gold for salt...

Camels are "ships of the desert," traveling in caravans of thousands across the blistering sands. "Longboats" thread through the Niger River and down the Nile.

Gold is traded for salt, at times in equal weights (salt is in great demand in the saltless forests of West Africa). Where the water has evaporated, salt is left — at times hundreds of feet deep. This salt is cut out of the dried waterbeds in huge blocks and transported like sheets of lumber on camelback or by boat.

Inner and Southern African Kingdoms

- BUGANDA
- BURUNDI
- KONGO
- RWANDA
- ZIMBABWE
- ZULU

The Bantu Migration

It is over 1,500 years ago ...The Bantu peoples of west central Africa migrate south and east along the Congo River, eventually mixing with the Hamites and overtaking all of southern Africa.

Some settle between Lake Victoria and the smaller lakes nestled in the western arm of the Great Rift Valley. These are people who are ruled by kings for four centuries (until kingship is rejected with the coming of independence from Colonial rule).

These people are the *Rwanda* and *Burundi* people south of Ankole and the *Bunyoro, Toro* and *Ankole* in southwestern Uganda.

Historical Overview

The Bantu migration gradually takes over peoples of central and southern Africa. Over 500 years ago, one group calling themselves the "(*Ba)chwezi* settle the area now known as Uganda. It is the Chwezi that first introduce the idea of one government under one king. Other groups in the area follow their example and several competing royal bloodlines of kings are formed (the last will remain unbroken until 1966).

In the 1300s the large state of *Kitara* is developed by the Bantu-speaking Chwezi people; but by 1450 it is overrun by the tall Nilotic-speaking people who have moved down into the area from the White Nile. The Bantu-speaking Chwezi rulers of Kitara are defeated. Some *Chwezi* migrate south and create a series of smaller kingdoms on the southwestern shores of Lake Victoria (*Ankole* and *Karagwe* become the largest).

On the northwestern shores of the great Lake Victoria, the Chwezi rulers have been replaced by the invaders, the *Bunyoro*, who create two tiny states, one of which will become *Buganda*. The (Bu)ganda people become the most powerful and populous group, but Buganda and Bunyoro remain rival neighbors. From 1500 to 1800, *Buganda* and *Bunyoro* struggle against each other for leadership while *Rwanda* emerges as the leading kingdom in the south.

Southern African Kingdoms

The Bantu migration that begins from the forests of western Africa is not a single mass movement but a gradual one over centuries, following the Congo River south and east to ultimately occupy all of southern Africa.

The Empire of ZIMBABWE
(600 - 1500)

It is 600 years after the death of Christ...people speaking the Bantu language arrive in southeast Africa, meeting and mixing with the people between the Zambezi and Limpopo Rivers. In the high, rocky grounds between these rivers they find flashes of gold. Within a few hundred years they begin to dig deep holes straight into the rock by hammering iron stakes, following the veins of gold down underground. The only bodies small enough to slip down these narrow mine shafts are those of girls and women. It is they who become the first miners of Zambezi gold. Many women fall to their death; others are crushed when a mine shaft caves in. Today, archaeologists still find the skeletons of these early women miners.

From 600s to the 1500s a group of buildings are constructed from stone (Zimbabwe means "stone houses") which will someday become the great center for another branch of the Bantu people, the *Shona*. It is the Bantu-speaking people known as the *Karangas* that construct this city of Zimbabwe as a temple for their king. The city walls are awesome, rising as high as three-story buildings. At their base some walls are as wide as three cars parked side-by-side. Here, the gold is stored before being traded by boat to the Arabs who, in return, bring goods from as far away as China.

NOTE: *Today scholars believe some of these Arab traders were, in fact, Bantu people — among the first ocean voyagers to "discover" lands as far away as India and China.*

In about 1440, one ambitious Karanga king, *Mutoto*, decides to take over the gold trade and establishes his authority over the Karanga people. It is he that creates an empire he calls Monomotapa (today's Zimbabwe and Mozambique). In 1485 one of the many chiefs, *Changa*, rebels against Mutoto's successor and builds a new empire using the city of great Zimbabwe as a center and building its walls even higher.

But Changa's revolt has weakened the empire and, when the Portuguese finally attack in 1650, they are able not only to invade Monomotapa but also to occupy its territories. Jungle fever slows the Portuguese occupation. The Changi are able to continue to mine gold and iron until the 1800s — then black armies rising from South Africa defeat the Changi rulers.

Amongst the ruins of these ancient mines, archaeologists will later find Chinese coins and Indian pottery — proof positive that an advanced civilization once existed here — a civilization built by black people who went into the area over 1,500 years ago, a civilization of black people who carried on a far-flung trade reaching all the way across the Indian Ocean to the shores of India and China.

The Great Empire of Zimbabwe

Ghana and other empires will leave behind them some written history (when they converted to Islam, they adopted Arabic letters). But the Zimbabwe Empire will leave no writing—just a maze of spectacular rock wall towers and a legend telling of Nutotoca, a great Bantu king, who ruled this empire using Great Zimbabwe as his home base.

Not until 1868 do Europeans discover these colossal structures built entirely of stone. They are shocked by their sophistication and believe they could only have been built by Europeans who somehow "got lost down there."

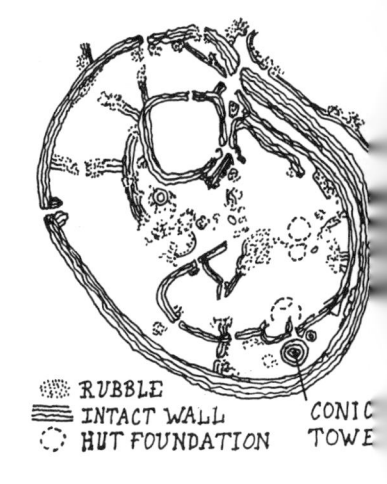

RUBBLE
INTACT WALL — CONIC
HUT FOUNDATION — TOWE

The walls of Great Zimbabwe are in places feet thick and over 30 feet high. The stones cut and placed in such a way that no morta needed to hold them in place.

In "discovering" Great Zimbabwe, Europeans reveal their prejudices by refusing to believe that blacks could have had the ability to build them.

Between one hundred and five hundred years after the death of Christ some of these Bantu-speaking people make their way south from the valley of the Zambezi River down into the Transvaal (the northeast of what is now South Africa). By the 13th Century, they find their way all the way down to South Africa's southernmost cape.[1]

Here, the Bantu people meet and overcome two groups of Africans some believe to be "non-negroid" and in fact the earliest inhabitants of the area; the *San* ("Bushmen") and the *Khoi* ("Hottentots"). The "Bushmen" are gradually pushed out into the Kalahari Desert and the "Hottentots" intermarry with the newly arrived Bantu-speaking people.

Now the Bantu-speaking Nguni peoples break into several main tribes: the *Swazi*, the *Xhosa* and the *Zulu*.

[1] *There is some evidence they may have arrived even earlier.*

The Zulu People

NAME: At first, Zulu is the name of only one of many clans of the Isibongo peoples, but when Chaka, a leader of this small Zulu clan, conquers the surrounding tribes, *all* the tribes come to be called "the Zulu nation."

LANGUAGE: Zulu, a form of Bantu.

POPULATION: 5 million.

HOMELAND: After losing fierce and bloody battles with the British and Dutch, the Zulu people loose most of their wealth by the end of the 1900s. Today, they live mostly in Natal, a province of South Africa. Half live in *KwaZulu* ("Land of the Zulu") carved out as a homeland by the white South African government.

ORIGIN: The Zulu are a group of Nguni Bantu-speaking people who migrate into southern Africa many centuries before the first Europeans come.

RELIGION/BELIEFS: Ancestor worship is the core of a religion that flows from one Creator. A special college of magicians hunts out sorcerers. Uncovered, the sorcerers are impaled with stakes; their entire family is massacred; and all their possessions are confiscated. So great becomes the authority of these magicians that Chaka has to "purify" their ranks by slaughtering them.

LIVELIHOOD: Men alone raise the tribe's prized cattle. Royal power is equal to the size of the royal herd. Cattle are divided according to the colors of their coats (there are 300 words in the Zulu language for different shades of cattle).

NOTE: Once cattle raisers and farmers, today most Zulu work as laborers in cities, mines or farms owned by South African whites.

FAMILY LIFE: Zulu men may take many wives.

HISTORY: By the end of the 1800s, two great clans arise - the *Mtetwa* led by chief Dingiswayo, and the *Ndwandwe* led by chief Zwide. Each tries to dominate the other. Finally, after Chief Zwide kills Dingiswayo, Chaka (a friend of Dingiswayo) beats Zwide and units all the clans under one Zulu nation.

NOTE: Chaka will be killed by his half brother, Dingaan, who ultimately, in 1938, will be beaten by the Boers in "The Battle of Blood River." Zululand is taken over by these Dutch Boers, then by the British.

Zulu Proverbs

"A man is not stabbed to death by one spear."
"A mouth is the shield to protect oneself."
"He cries with one eye only."
"One does not follow a snake into its hole."
"A king is a king because of his people."

The heart of the village is the cattle enclosure or "kraal."

Around this "kraal," homes are built which women are not allowed to enter.

A Traditional Zulu Family

The Zulu, at first, are only one of many small clans of farmers and cattle owners who swear allegiance to the king of the Mtetwa people. In 1786, a son is born to the Zulu chief — he is named "Chaka."

One day he will fight to unite his people under one Zulu nation. One day he will fight to save his people from becoming slaves to the whites. One day he will reshape the course of history for all of South Africa.

P R O F I L E

Chaka — Zulu King
(1787 - 1828)

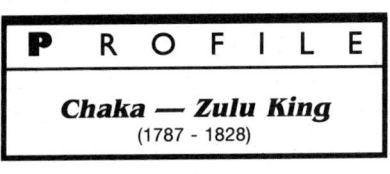

As a boy, Chaka's life is not easy. He doesn't get along with anyone well, except his mother, Nandi, who protects him against his father (Chaka refuses to wear the lion skin his father has given him; and all Zulu boys must wear this skin before becoming warriors).

He finally finds a friend in Dingiswayo, who also has had a hard time getting along with his father (King Jobe). In fact, Dingiswayo's father has driven him into exile (Dingiswayo means "the wanderer"). So Chaka accepts from his new friend what he has turned down from his father—a lion's skin. He joins Dingiswayo's warriors and helps him become King of the Mtetwa. Dingiswayo, in turn, helps Chaka become King of the Zulu. The two best friends — (one now King of the Mtetwa, the other now King of the Zulu) lead their clans into battle together. When Dingiswayo is murdered by one of his enemies, the Mtetwa people turn to Chaka as their leader and take the Zulu tribe's name as their own.

Now Chaka is the ruler of a powerful war machine. He begins conquering the smaller kingdoms nearby, bringing them under his domination into one enormous Zulu nation.

Chaka reforms Zulu life, structuring it around his central authority and his strong-arm military tactics. As a priest-king he is responsible for the fertility of his women, the health of his cattle, and the strength of his army. Although, as a judge and a legislator, he cannot act against the wishes of his *induna* (counselors of local chiefs) he often does.

His army of over 100,000 warriors are trained with rigid routines and forged into the fiercest fighters in the world. Based on age groups, new regiments are formed every six or seven years. His main military tactic he

Military Genius or Strong-Armed Tyrant?

Chaka wearing his crane feather and carrying his *assagai* (spear), soon to be shortened for bloody hand-to-hand combat.

calls *Mfekene* ("the crushing"). It is a *crescent* formation. At the "center" of the crescent, he keeps his royal guard — they engage the enemy while the "wings" circle around and close in. Any warrior who does not have sex with a woman after killing an enemy has not fulfilled his duty.

Chaka becomes invincible. Within four years, Chaka is ruler over a land bigger than France. There are no enemies left to conquer.

NOTE: *In 1828, at the age of 41, still mourning his mother's death, Chaka will be stabbed to death in his sleep by his half-brother who has crept into his hut. With Chaka gone, his half-brother, Dingane, will keep up the fight against the whites; but ultimately, in the month of December, 1939, he will lose to the Boers in the "Battle of Blood River.*

94

a meeting with Chaka

Henry Flynn, one of the few white men who will ever intimately know Chaka, is an Englishman and governor of Capetown. Exploring north to Natal, he finds the area controlled by a powerful Zulu warrior king—Chaka. He request a meeting with this mysterious man—and Chaka uses the opportunity to demonstrate his power by providing an awesome reception. Here is Flynn's journal...

"...about a mile before us, we saw the residence of Chaka — a native Kraal nearly two miles in circumference...

"...on entering the great cattle Kraal, we found joined up within it about 80,000 natives in their war attire. I galloped into the circle...one general shout broke out from the whole mass, all pointing at me with their sticks..."UJojo wohalo!"

"One king raised his stick in his hand...and the whole mass broke from their position and formed up into regiments...it was...surprising to us, who could not have imaged that a nation termed "savages" could be so disciplined...

"Elephant tusks were then brought forward. Regiments of girls entered the center of the arena, 10,000, decorated in beads and brass...carrying on their heads large pitchers of native beer, milk, and cooked food...They joined in a dance which continued for about two hours, dancing and receding as one sees the surf do on a seashore. The king came up to us and told us not to be afraid of his people...The Hlambamanzie assured us that Chaka was 'the greatest king in existence,' that his people were 'as numerous as the stars,' and that his cattle were 'likewise innumerable'...

"We found him sitting under a tree, decorating himself and surrounded by 200 people. A servant was kneeling by his side holding a shield above him to keep off the glare of the sun. Around his forehead, he wore a turban of otter skin with a crane feather erect in front, fully two feet long...From shoulder to shoulder, he wore bunches of the skins of monkeys...by his side stood a white shield with a single black spot.

Chaka: "I hear you have come from umGeorge, is it so? Is he as great a king as I am?"

Flynn: "Yes, King George is one of the greatest kings in the world."

Chaka: "Have you medicine by you?"

Flynn: "Yes."

Chaka: "Then cure me or I will have you sent to umGeorge to have you killed."

Flynn: "What is the matter with you?"

Chaka: "That is your business to find out."

"Chaka went on to speak of the gifts of nature...he asked how could the Europeans (give) us all the knowledge of arts if they had kept from us the greatest of all gifts, such as a good black skin. This does not necessitate the wearing of clothes to hide the white skin, which is not pleasant to the eye."

— **Henry Flynn**
English explorer and businessman,
from his diary

Boy Soldiers

"When a boy reached the age of 14 or 15, he would be drafted with other boys to the nearest military Kraal where he would have to herd and milk cattle, fetch firewood, etc. At the same time he was being taught how to fence with sticks and perform military drills.

"This was very rough training...Zulu discipline was very strict. Disobedience was punished by death...Death was the only penalty served. The guilty one would not only bring death to himself, but to all his family and friends...The Zulu soldier showed no mercy and he expected none."
— **Colonel Hamilton-Browne**
from "A Lost Legionary in South Africa" (1879)

opposite page: the Temple of Abu-Simbel in Nubia

5

BLACK EGYPT

Ancient kingdom of the pharaohs . . . land of pyramids and the mysterious sphinx . . . birthplace of Cleopatra, Nefertiti and King "Tut" — all make Egypt, with a recorded history of over 6,000 years, the site of one of the world's oldest civilizations.

Until recently, most scholars viewed the origins of ancient Egypt as arising out of a "white" *Middle Eastern* culture rather than arising out of a "black" *African* culture. Today this view is rapidly changing. It is now known that early Egyptian kingdoms had far more contact with the peoples on the rest of the African continent than was previously believed.

Egypt's early culture was, at its core, *African* — inseparably linked to the Stone Age people who populated what is now the Sahara Desert during its long period of its "greenness."

- *The spiritual power or "godship" of the pharaoh has parallels to the "divine kingship" of the black rulers south of the swamps which separate Egypt from the interior of Africa.*

- *Women in the Congo (thousands of miles from the Nile) rested their heads on wooden "pillows" whose style was practically identical to those thought to be invented by the Egyptians.*

But questions remain:

Was the influence upon the black civilizations of Africa a *FLOW FROM EGYPT INTO BLACK AFRICA?* Or was it a flow *FROM BLACK AFRICA INTO EGYPT?* . . .

| the "living king" Horus | reddish-skinned from Egypt | brown-skinned from Canaan |

Were The Egyptians Black? . . .

No one knows the answer. Many different races made Egypt a mighty civilization and blacks were often, clearly, the rulers. The infamous dark red pigment used to portray Egyptian men is proof to some scholars of a black ancestry, to others of an artistic tradition that dictated that men be painted red and women yellow.

Black Pharaohs ruled Egypt

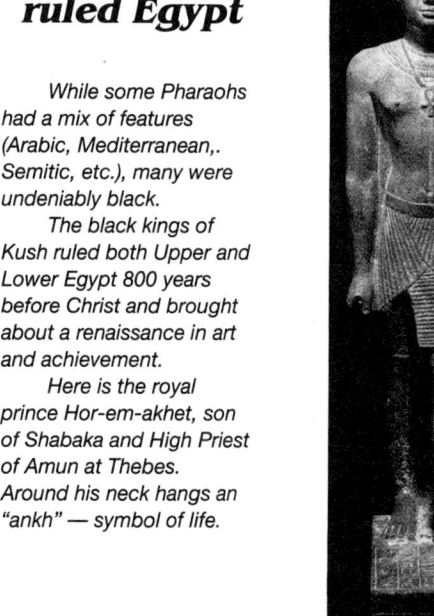

While some Pharaohs had a mix of features (Arabic, Mediterranean,. Semitic, etc.), many were undeniably black.

The black kings of Kush ruled both Upper and Lower Egypt 800 years before Christ and brought about a renaissance in art and achievement.

Here is the royal prince Hor-em-akhet, son of Shabaka and High Priest of Amun at Thebes. Around his neck hangs an "ankh" — symbol of life.

black-skinned from Kush (Nubia)

white-skinned from Libya

The answers lay buried somewhere back in the "nursery" cultures of the old Sahara before it was turned into a wasteland. As so much Egyptian culture rose out of this mysterious area it is just as likely that the influences flowed the other way — that our Saharan African brothers carried their culture into Egypt and that "black Africa's echoes of Egypt" could very well be "Egyptian echoes of black Africa."

If this is the case — if it can be said that "black Africa is at the root of Egyptian civilization" and "Egyptian civilization is at the root of Greek civilization" — can it also be said that "black African culture is at the root (through Egypt and Greece) of all Western Civilization?"

The glory of ancient Egypt, in fact, did dazzle all who beheld it, even the Greeks who claimed it to be the mother of their own civilization.

> *"The names of all our gods have been known in Egypt from the beginning of time...."*
>
> — **Herodotus,**
> *the Greek Historian, 5th Century B.C.*

hair or wigs?

The braiding and tight curls on some Egyptian figures seem similar to the styles worn at the time by black Nubians

What is the truth to these counter claims? What can we discover by uncovering the "black roots of ancient Egypt?"

117

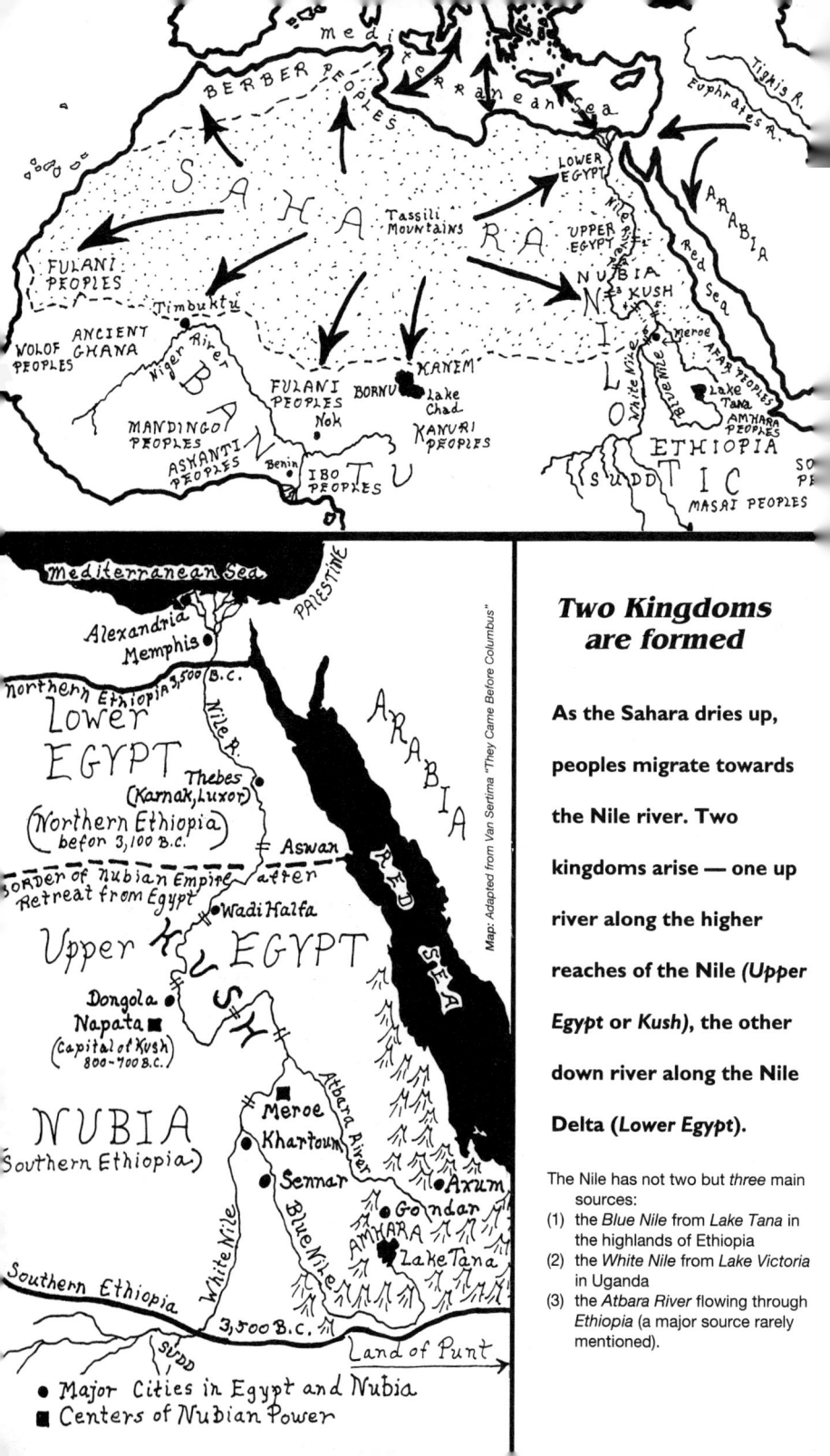

Map: Adapted from Van Sertima "They Came Before Columbus"

Two Kingdoms are formed

As the Sahara dries up, peoples migrate towards the Nile river. Two kingdoms arise — one up river along the higher reaches of the Nile (*Upper Egypt or Kush*), the other down river along the Nile Delta (*Lower Egypt*).

The Nile has not two but *three* main sources:
(1) the *Blue Nile* from *Lake Tana* in the highlands of Ethiopia
(2) the *White Nile* from *Lake Victoria* in Uganda
(3) the *Atbara River* flowing through *Ethiopia* (a major source rarely mentioned).

● Major Cities in Egypt and Nubia
■ Centers of Nubian Power

As the desert dries up — peoples split up

It is nearly 12,000 years ago . . . the so-called *Paleolithic* Age. Hunters roam the northern lands of Africa. The area that is now the burning sands of the Sahara Desert is broad rolling grasslands threaded with many rivers. Wild animals roam through these savannahs.

Gradually, over centuries, the climate becomes drier and drier. The Earth is warming after the last Ice Age and this green land now begins to turn into desert. People are forced to move out to the edges of the growing desert to search for water supplies. Some move to the banks of the Nile Delta. Others to the swamps of the upper Nile Valley. Still others move far away into West Africa and form independent kingdoms while retaining similar traditions.

Now, people of the *Neolithic* age begin to farm these fertile lands. The first crops are planted around 7,000 years ago and wild animals are domesticated. Tools are made from wood and stone. Pottery is made on rotating potters' wheels. Clothing is made by weaving fibers and copper is worked. . .

Before 10,000 years ago the Nile delta was inhabitable — the river was very wide and bordered by impassible marshlands and swamps. But as the desert dries up, the swamps shrink and *two* small kingdoms emerge. One along the upper reaches of the Nile (*Upper Egypt* or *Kush*) and the other along the silted meadows of the Nile delta (*Lower Egypt*).

Nubian Egypt
"Gift of the Nile"

The Greek historian *Herodotus*, writing over 2,500 years ago, sees the truth about Egypt: that the country is "the gift of the Nile," the world's longest river (6695 km or 4160 miles).

Its rich riverbank soils have supported a series of ancient civilizations since history began. Year after year for thousands of years, rain and melting snow from the mountains at the source of the Nile causes the river to overflow. The waters spread out over the flat lands of the Nile valley, reaching their highest level in September. As the flood recedes, the water drains off gradually, leaving behind a nutritious layer of *silt* (fertile soil).

From the beginning of recorded time, farmers plan their work according to these floods. As there is almost *no rainfall at all* in Egypt, the moisture left over from the flood is good for one planting only.

- *Papyrus reeds that grow along the bank are used for baskets, sandals, mats and even boats.*
- *Mud from the river is used for clay pots, jars and building bricks.*
- *Limestone, cut into blocks from the river's rock walls, is used to build the great pyramids.*

121

The two Kingdoms are United by a Black King, the first Pharaoh of Egypt

It is this black Pharaoh, Menes, who begins the first *dynasty* (a family of rulers). In the following 2,500 years there will be about 30 Egyptian dynasties, divided into....

FOUR PERIODS

The Old Kingdom
(2850-2181 B.C.)

The Middle Kingdom
(2050-1797 B.C.)

The New Kingdom
(1570-1085 B.C.)

The Decline
(1379-945 B.C.)

It is about 3100 B.C. . . . These early people have settled into *two* separate kingdoms called *Upper Egypt* and *Lower Egypt.* (Upper Egypt is up near the source of the Nile and Lower Egypt is down where the river enters the Mediterranean Sea.)

The king of Upper Egypt, *Menes*, clearly a black king, conquers Lower Egypt and is the first to unite the two Egypts into one kingdom. It is he who builds a glorious capital city (near modern *Cairo*) and calls it *Memphis*. This unification of the two Egypts marks the beginning of the *Old Kingdom* — a period during which Egypt will remain united politically and its civilization will reach its most glorious heights.

The rulers are religious leaders as well as political leaders and are looked upon as gods. Soon they take the title *pharaoh* (meaning "great house") after the palace in which they live. The pharaoh is above all other ordinary people. He is both judge and priest. As general of the army, he has absolute unlimited power (but it is also his duty to care for and protect his people).

Pharaoh Menkaure, builder of pyramids, with his wife

THE OLD KINGDOM
(2850-2181 B.C.)

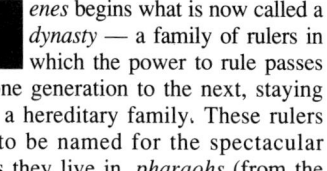he Old Kingdom is probably the most glorious period in all of Egyptian history — for it is during this period that the pharaohs build their greatest pyramids.

Egyptian society is sharply divided between *two* main classes of people: (1) *the upper class* (the pharaohs, the royal family, the priests and officials) and (2) *the lower class* (everyone else).

The Pharaohs

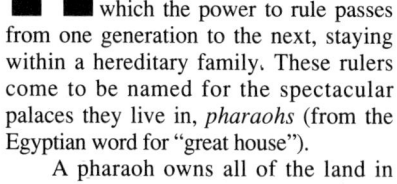*enes* begins what is now called a *dynasty* — a family of rulers in which the power to rule passes from one generation to the next, staying within a hereditary family. These rulers come to be named for the spectacular palaces they live in, *pharaohs* (from the Egyptian word for "great house").

A pharaoh owns all of the land in Egypt. He or she will allow people to use the land but will collect taxes and services and always will maintain the right to take the land away. The pharaoh controls not only his or her own people but also the natural world (this is why in Egyptian art you will always see the pharaoh drawn larger than any other human or animal). Pharaohs are the descendants of the gods, the supreme rulers of all of Egypt and the judges of all its people. But they are also expected to provide for the public welfare.

Upper class officials begin to develop their own hereditary line of nobles that grows stronger at the end of the Old Kingdom. With the nobles' growing strength, civil wars begin to rage. From 2200 to 2050 B.C., the power of the pharaoh weakens. Police and local nobles now fight among themselves for control — and Egypt becomes a divided country. . .

THE MIDDLE KINGDOM
(2050-1797 B.C.)

A prince from the City of Thebes restores the power the pharaohs once had and begins what is now known as *The Middle Kingdom*. The work of reuniting Egypt is completed by the powerful pharaoh, *Amenemhet I*.

The role of the pharaoh, however, changes. Before, pharaohs were gods. Now they no longer have absolute power. They share their wealth with the nobles and priests. People no longer fear them but consider them to be their "protectors." In turn, the pharaohs themselves are more concerned with the welfare and justice of their own people.

It is a time of peace and prosperity. Now, since all classes of people have equal access to the next world, even the poor receive fine funerals. The role of the priests rises again.

Egypt Invaded!
The Hyksos Take Over

T he "Hyksos" people from Asia invade ancient Egypt by crossing the Suez isthmus into the Nile delta around 1730 B.C. Riding lightweight chariots pulled by fleet-footed horses, the Hyksos strike swiftly, overpowering the Egyptian people. They will rule Egypt for the next 100 years — until the Egyptian princes learn how to use the Hyksos' weapons and drive them out in 1570 B.C. Egypt now builds a new kingdom . . .

THE NEW KINGDOM
(1570-1085 B.C.)

A series of strong pharaohs reunite Egypt from their capital city of *Thebes*. Now, like the pharaohs of the Old Kingdom, they become absolute rulers again, stripping the priests and the nobles of most of their power. They form a professional army modeled after the Hyksos, using horses, chariots and weapons of bronze. With their military might, they begin to forge *the Egyptian Empire* — conquering an enormous stretch of land up the east coast of the Mediterranean Sea (including Jerusalem and Damascus) reaching far north into the Taurus Mountains. Driving south up the treacherous river cataracts, they also penetrate deep into the region of the *Sudan*, home of the *Nubian* peoples.

But, as with most empires, the pharaohs, too, soon find out that it is sometimes easier to *conquer* a land than to *rule* it! Only the strongest of pharaohs is capable of putting down far-flung revolts to hold the empire together. By the 12th Century B.C. most all of these newly conquered lands are lost.

Social Class

S ociety in Egypt is still divided into *two* classes — an *upper class* (the pharaoh's royal family, the nobles and the priests), and a *lower class* (everyone else) and there remains an enormous gulf between the two.

The riches reaped from one military victory after another do not filter down to the common people. Most all of Egypt's people live in poverty while their rulers grow rich and corrupt. They have no rights whatsoever politically and their very lives depend entirely upon the whims of the pharaoh.

above: An Egyptian driving a chariot modeled after the Hyksos chariots

124

Slavery

Slavery is the rule, not the exception in ancient Egypt. As prisoners of war are captured during the New Kingdom, they take their place at the bottom rung of an already disenfranchised Egyptian society. Most slaves live a short, brutal life — rowing boats for the pharaohs, laboring in the king's mines, or doing back-breaking work building the Pyramids. Many of these slaves are captured farmers from Nubia — like these shown held prisoner on the tomb of Pharaoh Horemheb.

Women, however, are the equals of their husbands. A woman in Egypt can own her own property and leave it for her daughter.

forty armed Nubian soldiers, recruited for battle
(wood carving, from a Middle Kingdom tomb)

Measuring Time

At first the ancient Egyptians invent a *lunar calendar* (one based on the moon's movements), but it does not precisely fill out the entire year. Noticing a bright star that seems to rise into the dark night sky above the horizon yearly, just before the Nile floods, they base their revised calendar on the rising of this star — now called by us *Sirius*, the "Dog Star."

The time between one rising of *Sirius* to the next is, in fact, 365 days and the ancient Egyptians divide this time into 12 months, each month made of 30 days. Five days are left over — they use them for feasting and holidays.

Mathematics

To achieve their extraordinary works, the ancient Egyptians need not only exact measurements but also a system of mathematics:

- They invent *a number system based on 10* (similar to the decimal system we use today, but using signs for 1's, 10's, 100's and 1,000's . . . up to 1 million). They invent *fractions* in addition to whole numbers.
- They invent a measuring unit they call the *royal cubit* (equal to the length of your arm from fingertip to elbow, about 21 inches).
- *Geometry* is developed to lay out a complicated system of dikes and canals.

Hieroglyphics

Over 3,000 years before Christ is born, even before the Old Kingdom begins, Egyptians have already worked out a system of writing now called *hieroglyphics.*

When upper and lower Egypt are united in 3,000 B.C., ancient Egyptians have an alphabet of 25 single pictorial letters. But the temple priests confound the literature by adding almost 700 signs and symbols only *they* can understand!

At first the Egyptian priests carve their hieroglyphics on rocks. But soon they find a better material — they dig up a plant that grows throughout the marshes of the Nile River, cutting it into long, thin slices. Placing each slice together side-by-side, they moisten and pound them to form a mat with a smooth surface. They call this new material *papyrus* (from which we now get the word "paper").

Over time, a *hand writing* is developed called *hieratic*. The difference is this: *hieroglyphics* are carved into stone — *hieratic writing* is drawn on papyrus with a brush dipped in ink.

The use of these *hieroglyphic symbols* dies out by the 4th Century — but the Egyptian language itself continues to be spoken by the Coptic priests. Hieroglyphics remain inscrutable, a mystery for centuries — until Napoleon's soldiers in 1799 find a unique stone written in three languages side-by-side — *the Rosetta Stone.*

The Life of a Scribe

Papyrus allows for 50 times more writing room than the old cuneiform clay tablets. Lighter in weight, rolls of papyrus can be carried easily and help spread Egyptian writing to Phoenicia where it is developed into the Phoenician alphabet.

Scribes (official writers) assume an important place in ancient Egyptian life. They have to attend a special school for 12 years and master mathematics, bookkeeping and the law as well as surveying and mechanical techniques.

The Rosetta Stone

Today most of what we know about Egypt comes from our ability to decipher these hieroglyphics. But we have not always been able to do so. Late in the 18th Century a stone is discovered by Napoleon's soldiers in the mouth of the Nile River. It is named for a nearby city, *Rosetta,* and contains *three* different types of writing: (1) *Greek*, which was known, (2) *hieroglyphics*, which were not known, and (3) *Demotic*, a later form of Egyptian writing, which also was not known. Seeing the Greek side-by-side with the other two unknown writings allowed a French scholar to decipher them. Finding "Ptolemy" in two scripts, he "cracks the code" and discovers that hieroglyphics can be written right to left, left to right, or up and down! How can you tell? . . . because the animals always stare in the direction of the beginning of a sentence.

Deciphering the Ancient World

Cartouches
("royal mongrams")

Kings and queens encircle their names in "cartouches" or monograms. Here are two famous royal monograms you will see on temples and tombs:

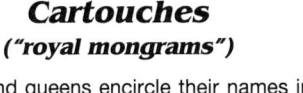

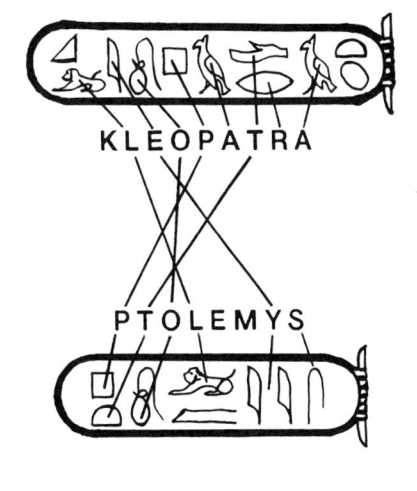

Hieroglyphics
("sacred carvings")

Hieroglyphics (from the Greek *Hieras* "sacred" and *glyphe* "carving") — the use of over 700 Egyptian pictures or symbols to indicate words or sounds:

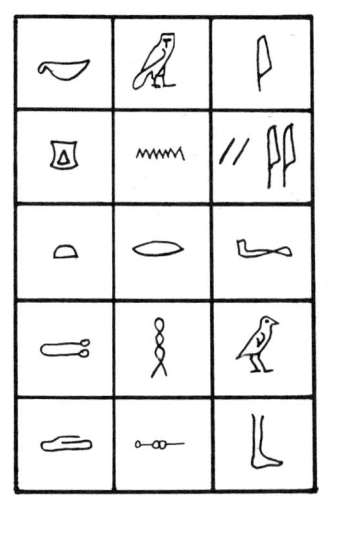

ankh

symbol of life for the Egyptians

Art

akua'ba

fertility doll for the Ashanti of West Africa

In no other published books have these two life-giving figures been compared -- but, to me, the similarity is unmistakable, perhaps further evidence of a past where ancestors of Egyptians and ancestors of West Africans, now separated by thousands of miles and thousands of years, once shared a common culture.

OVER TIME, EGYPTIAN ART BECOMES DISTINCT

- *The head and feet are always shown in profile — but the shoulders face forward.*
- *There is a stiffness and formality to the characters.*
- *The larger the character is in life — the larger the character is shown in the drawing (thus, you can always tell the relative social status of a figure by its size in relation to the others; the pharaoh being the largest).*

Here sits *Akenaton* (who worshped the sun god, Aton) with his beautiful wife, *Queen Nefertiti* and their children. Notice the new, flowing "free-style" of art work — so unlike the stiff, stylized royal families depicted earlier. Here, the pharaoh and his wife are shown in intimate, everyday activities. This new art style is called *amarna*.

136

"King Tut"

"King Tut," as he has come to be called, would have been a mere footnote in history books — had it not been for the discovery of his tomb — the first ever from the ancient royal tombs to be found almost intact. All others found in the *Valley of Kings* had been looted over the centuries by robbers; the entrance to King Tut's tomb became covered over by rubble left by these robbers as they plundered the larger tombs nearby. It isn't until 1922 that this, one of the most important archeological discoveries of the 20th Century, is made.

Tutankhamun
(1361-1352 B.C.)

Treasures of a Teenage King

He is only 8 years old when he becomes pharaoh. And he dies at the age of 19, buried hurriedly in a tiny 4 room tomb — but this tomb reveals over 5,000 treasures, including the life-size death mask made of solid gold, inlaid with jewels and colored glass. On "King Tut's" headdress are the *vulture* and *cobra* — symbols of the duel crown over *Upper* and *Lower* Egypt.

one of three coffins nested inside of each other, one is 24-carat gold

Tutankhamun and his young wife (Amarna style)

Bishari men
trading in "gum-Arabic"
on the shores of Lake Tana

Women of Nubia
with traditional "Dreadlocks"

Foreign Empires in North Africa

THE ROMAN EMPIRE

It is 146 years before Christ is born ... Roman soldiers destroy a trading colony built by the Phoenicians on the North Coast of Africa and end the last of three Punic Wars. Their prize — Carthage, Rome's first territory in Africa.

The colony grows under Julius Caesar's rule. Emperor Augustus Caesar expands on his African holdings, building 19 colonies, including a "new Carthage" which, second only to Rome, becomes the mightiest city in the West. For four centuries, North African farms provide olives, cereals and fruit for the Roman Empire. Two thirds of Rome's grain is produced here in Africa! Buildings and sports coliseums are built and many people (living in what today is Libya) become Roman citizens.

As the 4th Century draws to a close, German vandals conquer Carthage and Roman life in Africa disappears. Berber tribes, forced by the Romans to become farmers, now can resume their nomadic life.

ROMAN RUINS

Traces of Roman ruins can still be found toda, in stone roads, bridges, and this crumbling aquaduct in Tunisia.

hadrian's wall

BRITAIN

atlantic ocean

GERMANIC TRIBES

rhine

danube

GAUL

SPAIN

sea of galilee

Nazareth

Jerusalem

Bethlehem

dead sea

Christ's Birth

PALESTINE

ITALY

Rome

SARDINIA

mediterranean sea

SICILY

BERBER TRIBES

Carthage

Tunis

black sea

Constantinople

GREECE

Athens

CRETE

CYPRUS

SYRIA

ASIA MINOR

euphrates r.

tigris r.

Babyl

caspian

ROMAN EMPIRE
(Christian World)
---- 400 A.D. ----

[LIBYA]

s a h a r a

Alexandria

Cairo

EGYPT

nile

PALESTINE

syrian desert

red sea

ARABIA

N U B I A

[Mecca]

EGYPT UNDER FOREIGN CONTROL

I n 525 B.C., a Persian warrior leads an invasion force that dethrones the pharaoh of the 26th dynasty. Egypt will now remain a Persian province — until its conquest by the Greek emperor, *Alexander the Great* in 332 B.C. This legendary figure builds *Alexandria* — the port city that will soon become one of the greatest trading centers in the entire Mediterranean world.

It is now 323 B.C. . . . Alexander has died and commander *Ptolemy* gains personal control over Egypt and takes the title pharaoh for himself. His Ptolemaic blood line will end 30 years before Christ is born — with the suicide of *Queen Cleopatra. Emperor Augustus* then seizes direct Roman control over Egypt — initiating almost seven centuries of foreign rule by either Romans or Byzantines.

Christianity is brought into Egypt soon after Christ's death by St. Mark (A.D. 37). The new religion spreads quickly under Roman rule. However, in A.D. 642 Egypt is invaded! Warriors on horseback from the Arab peninsula sweep across the country, killing and converting people to a new religion, *Islam.*

After being conquered by the Romans, Egypt had fallen into relative obscurity on the world stage and stayed that way — until these armies of *Islam* sweep over the Egyptian countryside shortly after the death of their prophet, *Mohammed.* Now *Cairo* rises again to become a great city and the foremost center for scholarship in this new Islamic world.

A few isolated pockets of *Coptic (Egyptian) Christianity* remain in the rugged highlands of Ethiopia and some isolated monasteries long the Nile — but now centuries-old Egyptian ways left over from the times of the pharaohs are gradually replaced by the Islamic customs of Muslims from the Arab peninsula.

It will not be until the arrival in 1798 of the Emperor of France, *Napoleon Bonaparte*, that Egypt will again fall under the influence of Europe.

As the Arabs overtake Northeast Africa, they cut off the black Christian kingdoms of the south from contact with the capitals of Christianity in Rome and Constantinople. Now left isolated high in the rocky mountains of the upper Blue Nile, there evolves a unique Christian civilization destined to become a legendary kingdom — ETHIOPIA . . .

ETHIOPIA
. . . a
Christian
Kingdom
in a
Muslim
Sea

The Ethiopian Connection

Ethiopia . . . the first nation mentioned in the Bible . . . the mythic "land of Punt" Herotus spoke about to the Greeks . . . the lost kingdom of Prester John medieval Europeans dreamt about . . .

Down through the centuries, Ethiopia has held a magnetic pull on the minds of the world's peoples — particularly African slaves who were forcibly exiled from their homeland.

The Bible was the only book most slaves were allowed to see. References were found in its pages of an "ancient black race" — and a mythology about Ethiopia began to grow. When slavery tore at our own sense of humanity, our black ministers pointed to the creation of humanity in Ethiopia. When white slavers falsified our history (claiming blacks were "uncivilized" and "inferior" so they could justify their brutality), we found in the Bible proof of glorious civilizations in Ethiopia.

Ethiopia came to symbolize not only our glorious past, but also one African nation powerful enough to resist both white Arab and white European domination — an empire respected by all the world's nations.

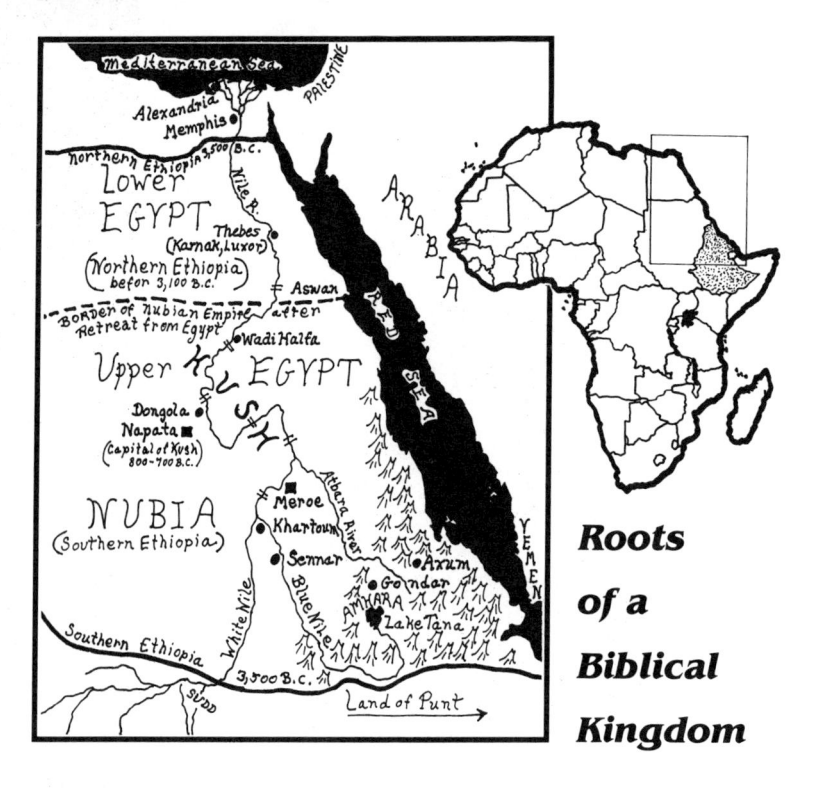

Roots

of a

Biblical

Kingdom

THE KINGDOM OF KUSH

2,000 years before the birth of Christ, an empire rises south of Egypt that will one day become strong enough to conquer its northern masters. Five kings of Kush will eventually serve as Pharaohs of upper Egypt.

At first the Egyptians build forts along the Nile River, trying to stop the people of Kush (Egyptian for *"nubia"*) from coming north. Time and again they send expeditions south to conquer the wealthy land, fighting their way up the treacherous water of the cataracts.

"I passed through Kush, sailing south, and reached the borders of the earth . . . His Majesty returned in safety, having overthrown his enemies in Kush, the Vile."

- inscription from an unknown Governor of Middle Egypt

Kush now becomes a part of Egypt. Its people serve in the Egyptian armies and in the Egyptian government. The great dynasties of Egypt are built on the backs of

Nubian slaves and gold taken from the south. Kush, gateway to the south, grows in power and wealthy Egypt falls apart in a wave of lawlessness.

MEROE

The year is now 591 B.C. . . . the capital city of Kush, Napata, is looted and burned by Greek mercenaries hired by an Egyptian Pharaoh. It is these Greeks that first call the people of Kush *"Aethiopians"* (ancient Greek for *"burnt faces"*). The Aethiopians of Kush move their capital from Napata to Meroe, a choice "island" between the Nile and Atbara Rivers. Here, they create an alphabet based on hieroglyphics, and build irrigation systems and elaborate palaces.

Lost to the outside world for centuries, only recently have archaeologists uncovered the spectacular glory of this ancient kingdom of Kush. On the "island" of Meroe can be found the ruins of great royal pyramids, spectacular temples to rival those of Egypt.

144

AXUM
Rises To Challenge Meroe

In the remote highlands of northern Ethiopia, a rival empire is slowly being built that will one day overthrow Meroe. 700 years before Christ is born, a band of people flee from Yemen across the Red Sea and settle up in the plateau, mixing and marrying with its people. They bring with them an ancient semitic tongue used in Saba (Sheba) that evolves into a new language, *Ge'ez*. A group of these people, the Habashada, build a capital for their new kingdom and call it *Axum*.

Now it is 300 years after the death of Christ. Axum becomes a Christian state protected by the Roman empire. They destroy Meroe and their powers grow —until traders from Arabia seize control of the surrounding lowlands and Muslim coastal seaports.

Now, completely cut off from Rome's churches, the people of Axum become absorbed into the kingdom of Ethiopia and, here high in the mountains, a unique Christian civilization evolves — using the now ancient language of Ge'ez.

ETHIOPIA

Of all the nations in Northeast Africa, only one does not become Muslim. Axum, the heart of present day Ethiopia, remains Christian. Once closely tied to Egypt, it adopts a "Coptic" Christianity (*"Coptic"* in Arabic means *"Egyptian"*).

Cut off for centuries from the outside world, they develop and maintain their Christianity alone. Massive churches are carved out of solid rock high on the cliffs of Lalibela. The church service is performed in the ancient language of Ge'ez.

Ethiopia becomes one of the oldest Christian nations in the world — and the first mentioned in the Bible. The kingdom continues unbroken through the centuries, until Emperor Haile Selassie is overthrown in 1974 by his Marxist generals and a communist government under Hiriam Mengitsu seizes power.

Even during the European colonial takeover of Africa, Ethiopia remains independent (except for 4 years during World War II) — one of only two black nations in Africa to do so.

145

Coptic Christianity

Coptic (Egyptian) Christianity originated close to Christ's birthplace shortly after his death. It became a formal religion as a result of a split in the Christian religion over an argument about *what is God* and *what is man*.

t is just 38 years after Christ is born . . . The Byzantine Empire declares the capital of the Christian church to be Constantinople, not Rome. Christians in Egypt protest, insisting that their city of Alexandria should be the capital. They use a religious controversy to test their control over the Byzantine Church. The Christians in Constantinople believe in the *duality* of nature — God and man are separate. The Christian Copts in Egypt, however, believe that God and man can be *one*.

A council is called in the City of Chalcedon to clarify the issue of the "two natures" (one *divine,* the other *human).* The entire council, except one group, overrules the Copts and declares that the two natures are united in Jesus Christ to form one person, who is both at the same time God *and* man. *Only Jesus Christ is capable of being this.* And only through Jesus Christ can man know God.

The Copts, however, believe that instead of there being *two separate natures* (one divine and one human) that join to form one being, there is but *one nature* (in which what is divine and what is human can't be told apart). Furthermore, they believe that *any* human being is capable of being divine. Being divinely of God is not exclusive only to Jesus, but is possible for all.

Because of this belief in the "oneness" of our nature the Coptics are called *"monophysites."* They compete with the Orthodox Christians for converts in Egypt and one Coptic group breaks off south into the highlands of Ethiopia. There, living as monks, they labor to translate the holy scriptures of the Bible into the ancient Ethiopian language of *Ge'ez.*

Some scholars say that this Ethiopian Bible (which has not suffered through further translations) is one of the purest versions of early Christianity still existing on Earth.

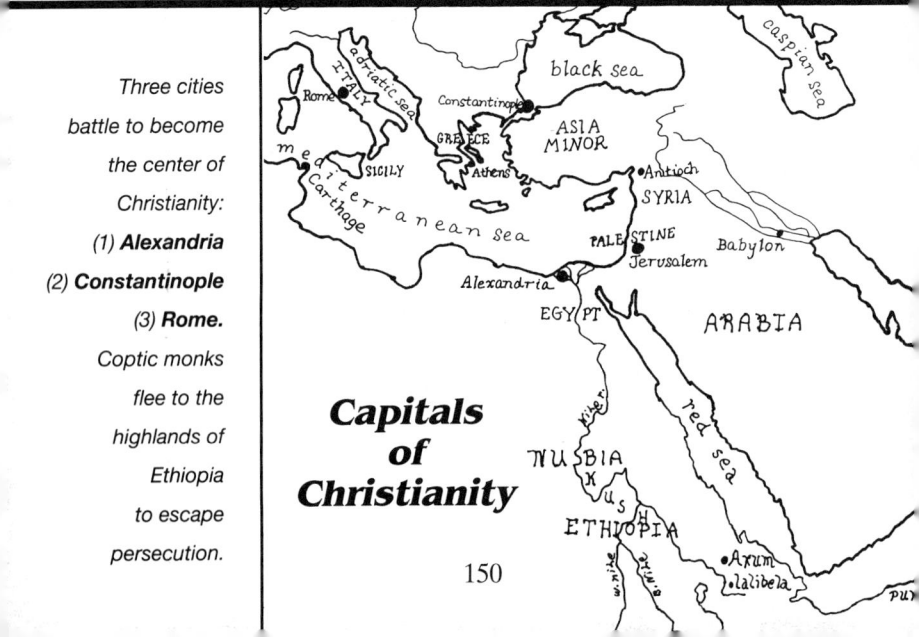

Three cities battle to become the center of Christianity: (1) **Alexandria** (2) **Constantinople** (3) **Rome.** Coptic monks flee to the highlands of Ethiopia to escape persecution.

Capitals of Christianity

150

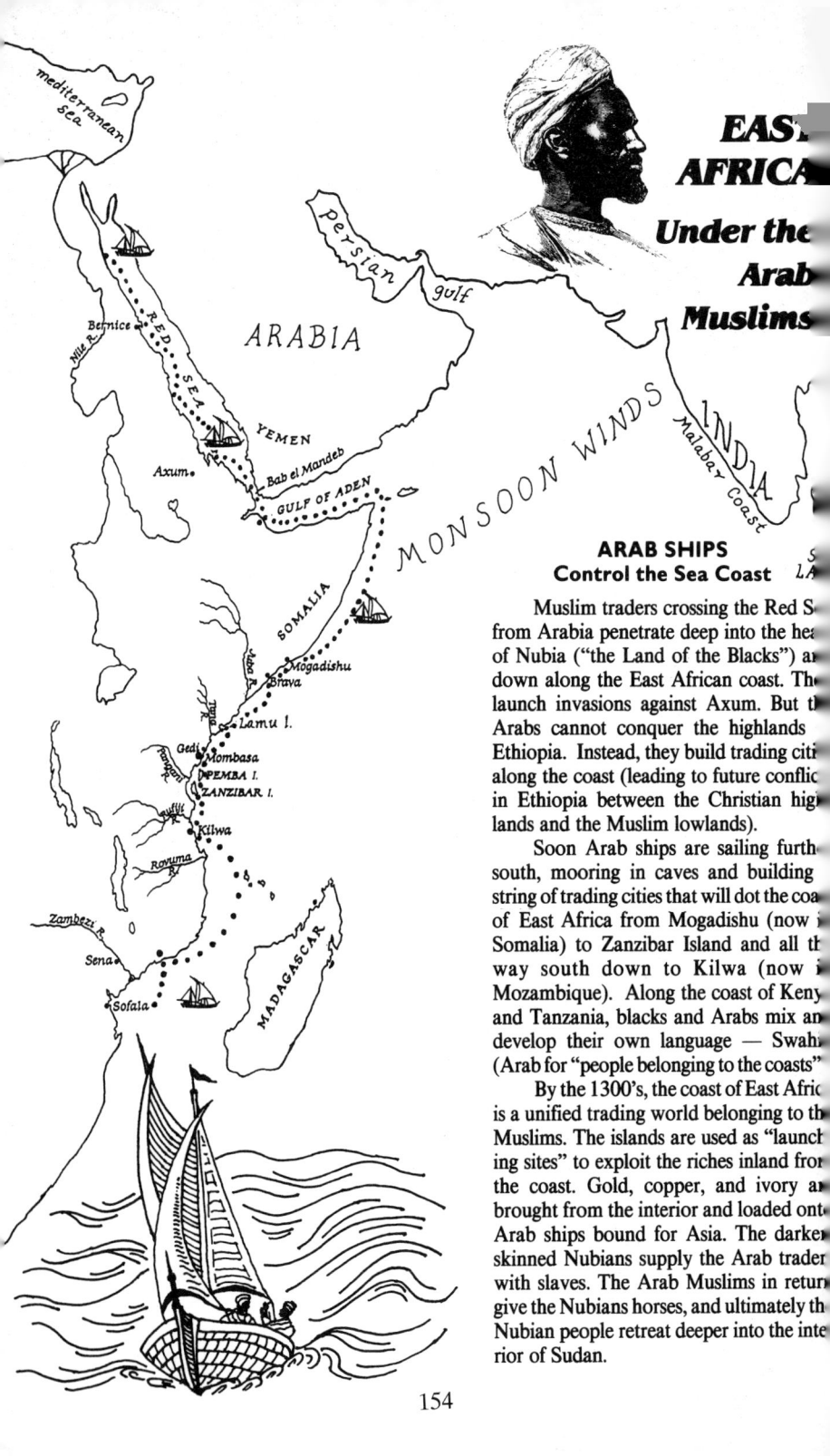

EAST AFRICA
Under the Arab Muslims

ARAB SHIPS
Control the Sea Coast

Muslim traders crossing the Red S[ea] from Arabia penetrate deep into the he[art] of Nubia ("the Land of the Blacks") a[nd] down along the East African coast. The[y] launch invasions against Axum. But t[he] Arabs cannot conquer the highlands [of] Ethiopia. Instead, they build trading citi[es] along the coast (leading to future confli[ct] in Ethiopia between the Christian hig[h] lands and the Muslim lowlands).

Soon Arab ships are sailing furth[er] south, mooring in caves and building [a] string of trading cities that will dot the coa[st] of East Africa from Mogadishu (now [in] Somalia) to Zanzibar Island and all t[he] way south down to Kilwa (now [in] Mozambique). Along the coast of Keny[a] and Tanzania, blacks and Arabs mix an[d] develop their own language — Swah[ili] (Arab for "people belonging to the coasts"[).]

By the 1300's, the coast of East Afri[ca] is a unified trading world belonging to th[e] Muslims. The islands are used as "launch[-] ing sites" to exploit the riches inland fro[m] the coast. Gold, copper, and ivory a[re] brought from the interior and loaded ont[o] Arab ships bound for Asia. The darke[r] skinned Nubians supply the Arab trader[s] with slaves. The Arab Muslims in retur[n] give the Nubians horses, and ultimately th[e] Nubian people retreat deeper into the inte[-] rior of Sudan.

154

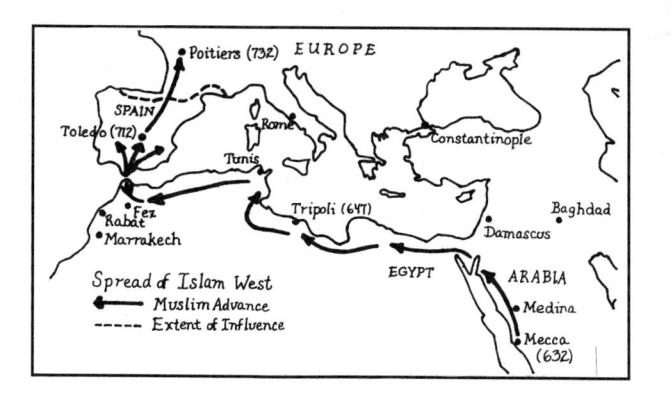

NORTH AFRICA
The Moors Spread Islam

Map labels: Poitiers (732), EUROPE, SPAIN, Toledo (712), Rome, Constantinople, Tunis, Fez, Rabat, Marrakech, Tripoli (641), Baghdad, Damascus, EGYPT, ARABIA, Medina, Mecca (632)

Spread of Islam West
← Muslim Advance
----- Extent of Influence

BLACK MOORS
Help Build A Muslim Empire — And Help Give Birth to A Renaissance In Europe

Black Africans played a major role often neglected by historians in the rise of Islam.

Bilal (an Ethiopian), after the Prophet Mohammed himself, is named the first high priest of Islam's empire. Tarik ibn Zayyad (the great Moor general) leads the Arab and Moor army in 711 A.D. to conquer most of Spain's peninsula (Gibraltar, in fact, is named after Tarik; *Gibel Tarik* means *"Hill of Tarik"*).

More than a military conquest of Spain, it is an intellectual conquest. The Moors (a mix of Berbers, black Africans, and Arabs) will shape Spain's art and literature—and question the moral foundations of Western civilization.

After the fall of the Roman empire, the Moors find a Europe of weak, divided people who have lost their moral strength. The brilliant scientific and philosophical discoveries of the Greeks and Romans are lost to most Europeans during these "Dark Ages." Princes live in their castles, peasants in their huts, petty kingdoms wage war on each other.

The Muslims rediscover the Greek "classics", translate them and add their own thoughts, creating a body of scholarly work that will give birth to Europe's Renaissance. In Spain, they build Cordova, a modern city with paved streets, sidewalks, and street lamps; and, in Morocco, they build a great university, *Qarawiyin.*

Muslims and Christians battle over Europe

711	Tariq ibn Ziyad leads an Arab-Berber Muslim army into Christian Spain, capturing most of the country.
732	France, led by Charles Martel, stops the Arab-Berber invasion of Europe in a battle at Poitiers, France.
778	France's Charlemagne now invades Spain, but fails.
800	In an attempt to unite Christian Europe against the Muslim Arab-Berber advance, Charlemagne is crowned Holy Roman Emperor by Pope Leo III.
900	The height of the black Moors' rule of Spain. The city of Cordoba becomes the center of Arab Muslim teachings.
1094	El Cid captures Valencia. Eight years later the Arab-Berber black Moors recapture it.
1095	The first Christian Crusade against the Muslims begins.
1172	Moorish Spain and Morocco are, at last, united by the Almohad faction of Berbers who set up capitals at Seville and Marrakech.
1236	The city of Cordoba is recaptured by the Christians.
1248	Seville is recaptured by the Christians. The black Moors and Arabs are pushed back further into southern Spain.
1275	A new group of Berbers from Fez invade Spain and defeat the Christians at Castile.
1340	The Moroccan invasions of the Spanish peninsula come to an end as the Christians defeat them at Salado in Spain.
1347-1352	25 million people in Europe are killed by the plague of Black Death.
1415	In Portugal, Prince Henry (the Navigator) begins a school for navigation.
1428	The French army is led by Joan of Arc against the British.
1453	The hundred years war between France and England comes to an end.
1469	Isabella of Castille marries Ferdinand of Aragon.
1492	Isabella and Ferdinand defeat the last stronghold of the Moors in Granada. Later the same year they finance Christopher Columbus's visionary voyage to find a "New World."

Arab men
in the city of Cairo, North Africa

The Crusades

Europe Unites to Fight Off The Muslim Invasion

The Turks have conquered the Arab Muslims and have won control over Palestine. When they attack the Byzantine Empire the Pope in Constantinople appeals to the Pope in Rome for help. Kings, knights and commoners set out by land or by sea to fight the "infedels" back.

A religious and military failure, the Crusades nevertheless open new worlds and discoveries to a Europe still shrinking in the shadows of the Dark Ages. The Crusaders are astounded to find wealthy kingdoms and centers of learning and art in Africa. They return to Europe with gunpowder (first invented by the Chinese), crossbows, catapults, rice, sugar and cotton and encourage their kings to launch a new age of exploration.

DEFINITION: "Crusade"

(from the Latin "cruciata" meaning "marked with the cross")

A series of 4 major military expeditions launched by European Christians in the Middle Ages (from 1096-1204 A.D.). Their purpose was to regain the Holy Land which had been overrun by Seljuk Turks*.

***Seljuk Turks** were Sunni Muslims who invaded Eastern Europe in a "jihad" or "Holy War" against the Christian Byzantine Empire.

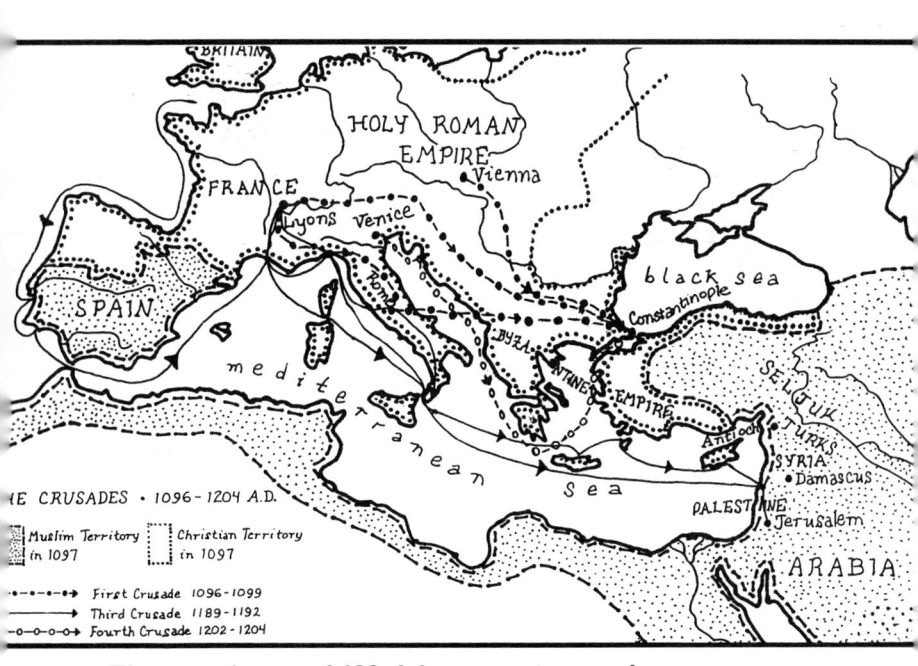

THE CRUSADES · 1096 - 1204 A.D.

Muslim Territory in 1097 | Christian Territory in 1097

·—·—·—·→ First Crusade 1096 - 1099
————→ Third Crusade 1189 - 1192
-0—0—0—0→ Fourth Crusade 1202 - 1204

The year is now 1492. Islam, torn apart by internal fighting, loses its hold over Spain and Portugal. Europe again now rises to dominate North Africa — and a new era of *Colonialism* begins . . .

157

The year is 1880 . . . European nations control just a few coastal ports of Africa. In less than thirty years —they carve up the entire African continent. How do they do it? . . .

Europe's contact with *North* Africa began in ancient times. Facing each other from opposite sides of the same Mediterranean Sea, sailors 2,000 years ago crossed over, building up trading cities on the coast that would become the foundation for Greek and Roman empires.

But contact with Africa *south* of the Sahara Desert didn't begin until just 500 years ago. Most people don't realize that until *just 120 years ago,* almost all of the interior African continent was not seen by white people. *Why? . . .*

Barriers to Exploration

- *The Sahara Desert cannot easily be crossed from the north.*

- *There are almost no roads, even pack animals and human bearers collapse under the strain of the heat.*

- *Disease (malaria, yellow fever, sleeping sickness) kills off expeditions.*

- *Moving inward along the rivers is impossible. Towering waterfalls and rocky cataracts block the way (later, boats are built that can be carried above the cliffs where the rivers become passable again).*

159

Portuguese Ships Lead The Way

By the 1400's, tiny Portugal is able to build large enough ships that can work their way down Africa's West Coast. Along the way, they build forts and settlements. In their wake, follow the Spanish, English, and French . . .

- *1488 — **Bartholomew Dias** sails around the southern cape of Africa*

- *1497 — **Vasco da Gama** sails clear around the African continent — all the way to India, establishing a sea rout that will ultimately replace land routes for trade to the "East Indies."*

Still by the 1870's, little of Africa south of the Sahara is known to the Europeans — mainly trading posts along the coast. But within 35 years — *every square foot* of Africa (except for Ethiopia, Liberia, and the Republic of South Africa) will be under foreign control.

King Leopold II of Belgium starts the rush. Pretending to launch a "scientific" expedition to guard against the slave trade, in fact he seizes control of the entire Congo River basin. He does this through his business partner — Henry Stanley.

Henry Stanley, a vulgar English showman after wealth and fame, launches his expedition from the East Coast. From the island of *Zanzibar,* he crosses into mainland Africa near Lake Victoria, then works his way down the Congo River.

In 1870, Stanley finds the "missing" *Dr. Livingston* and captures the front pages of newspapers all across Europe. He offers his "discoveries" to King Leopold II. Together they conspire to set up a business corporation to selfishly exploit the Congolese people. Stanley kills off many of the Congo's trees for their rubber and returns home with a wealth of copper.

The race is on . . .

Doctor David Livingston, a Scottish missionary, may have been the first European to see Victoria Falls.

Early Explorers

The Vikings *(1)*
The Polynesians *(2)*
The Chinese *(3)*
The Arabs *(4)*
The Africans *(5)*

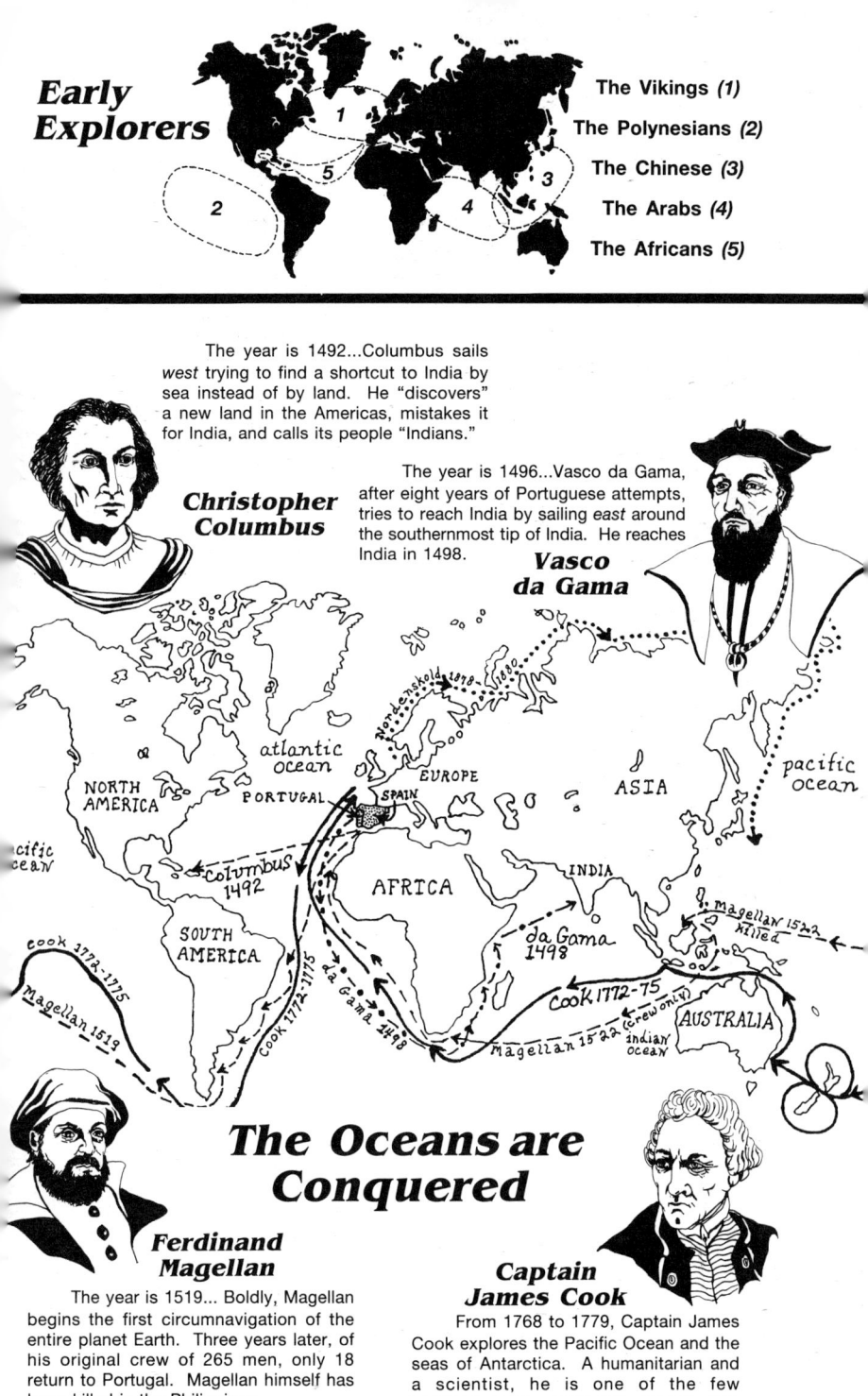

The year is 1492...Columbus sails *west* trying to find a shortcut to India by sea instead of by land. He "discovers" a new land in the Americas, mistakes it for India, and calls its people "Indians."

Christopher Columbus

The year is 1496...Vasco da Gama, after eight years of Portuguese attempts, tries to reach India by sailing *east* around the southernmost tip of India. He reaches India in 1498.

Vasco da Gama

The Oceans are Conquered

Ferdinand Magellan

The year is 1519... Boldly, Magellan begins the first circumnavigation of the entire planet Earth. Three years later, of his original crew of 265 men, only 18 return to Portugal. Magellan himself has been killed in the Philippines.

Captain James Cook

From 1768 to 1779, Captain James Cook explores the Pacific Ocean and the seas of Antarctica. A humanitarian and a scientist, he is one of the few "enlightened" explorers during this ruthless time.

John Speake leads an expedition to discover the source of the Nile

"Some evil spirit appears to rule in this horrible region of everlasting swamp. The fabulous Styx must be a sweet rippling brook, compared to this horrible creation."
— Baker

"We passed on to an enormous hut, where sat Chitapanga, an enormous tusk was brought for me. The chief saluted courteously. He has a fat, jolly face, and legs loaded with brass and copper leglets."
— Livingston

Here (below) is a captured Speake escaping in disgrace from the spears of the Somali people.

After an initial curiosity wears off, some Europeans become settlers and make lifelong friendships with the African people, sharing childhood adventures and adult accomplishments.

170

LAISSEZ-FAIRE

Definition: *(French for "Let them do as they please.")* A theory, advanced by economists like Adam Smith, that government should interfere as little as possible in business and trade.

In Europe some poeple begin to feel that the new colonies should be left on their own. More can be gained by trading with African empires than by dominating and exploiting them. Africa's colonies are meant to pay for themselves. They are just not worth what it costs to rule and defend them.

IMPERIALISM

Definition: The control of the foreign trade and raw materials of a poor country by a wealthy one (usually including the conquest and colonization of an empire by military means).

Imperialism replaces Laissez-Faire as the policy of the European nations. And the imperialists justify their brutal actions in three ways:

(1) It is "the right" and "sovereign duty" of a more advanced industrialized nation to control its colonies.

(2) Colonialism "makes sense." Factories in the homeland need cheap raw materials like cotton and rubber. And the homeland also needs new markets where they can sell their extra goods and make even more money.

(3) It is the "White Man's Burden" to look after our "uncivilized, poor black brothers and sisters."

Imperialist nations hide behind a cloak of nobility and achieve their ends using "the front" of business. It is never their *government* that is taking over Africa, they claim, but *businesses* and syndicates with charters. In this way, governments hide their responsibility behind private corporations that do the dirty work of negotiating treaties, buying and selling human beings, and taking over the land.

The competition becomes cut-throat. Agents write fraudulent treaties and cheat each other. Soon, soldiers are shipped over by the Europeans to "protect their interests."

Europe Scrambles for Africa

At first the European "mother countries" are content to let their African colonies do as they please (*"Laissez-faire"*). Later, they decide to control and exploit them through military conquest (*imperialism*).

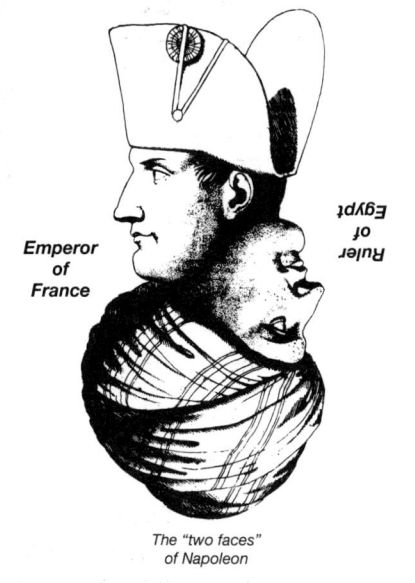

Emperor of France

Ruler of Egypt

The "two faces" of Napoleon

Soon, the nations of Europe fight each other to "carve up" the continent.

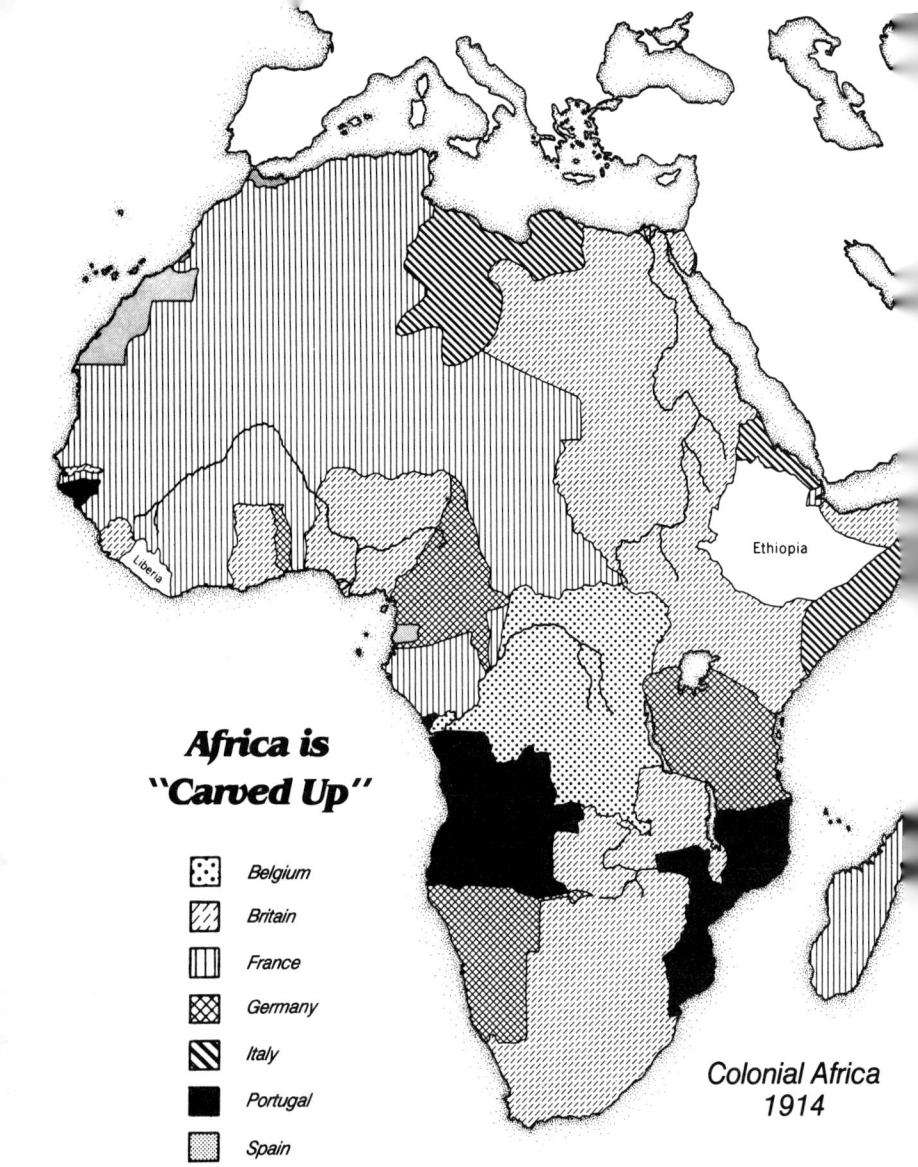

Africa is "Carved Up"

Belgium

Britain

France

Germany

Italy

Portugal

Spain

Colonial Africa
1914

Ethiopia

Liberia

The Berlin West African Conference

A conference is held in Germany in 1885 to set down some "ground rules" for the competing countries staking a claim to land in Africa: (1) any foreign country seeking to stake a claim now needs to notify other countries who sign this agreement —they also need to demonstrate their control over the area, (2) the Niger and Congo Rivers are to be left free for navigation.

Consequences

The consequences of this agreement will wreck havoc with Africa for a century to come, creating civil wars and rebellion:

- *The European nations agree to draw lines through the entire continent, carving up Africa into "French West Africa," "British Sudan," etc., while most Africans have no idea their homes now are the territory of foreigners.*

- *Only Ethiopia and Liberia remain independent (the Republic of South Africa, while not under foreign control is under the control of a white minority).*

- *Conflicts are created on paper that will last a century, leading to civil wars and costing millions of lives.*

- *Territories are divided up arbitrarily — with no care or regard for the people who are living in them.*

- *Tribes are left straddling the borders of two nations — with more loyalty to their own tribe than to their foreign occupiers.*
  Rival tribes now find themselves citizens within the borders of one nation they didn't create.

- *Vast plantations are set up. African farmers are pulled away from their traditional ways of farming and enslaved on plantations to produce "cash crops" for foreign use.*

The conquest of Africa is not easy. The Africans fight bloody wars of resistance, and the French and English battle each other to stake a foothold on the continent. In Algeria, the Arabs fight off the French for many years, losing over 90 thousand men in just one battle. The Arabs massacre French prisoners; and in retaliation the French Foreign Legion burns whole villages of people.

The colonialists bring new technologies, housing, schooling, hospitals, communications, and put to use raw materials and minerals. But with this "progress" comes the problems of city life — slums, overcrowding, disease, and lack of jobs. Workers are most horribly exploited in the Congo and South Africa — forced to work on railways or mines and live in makeshift workhouses far from their families.

Blacks become second-class citizens in their own home . . .

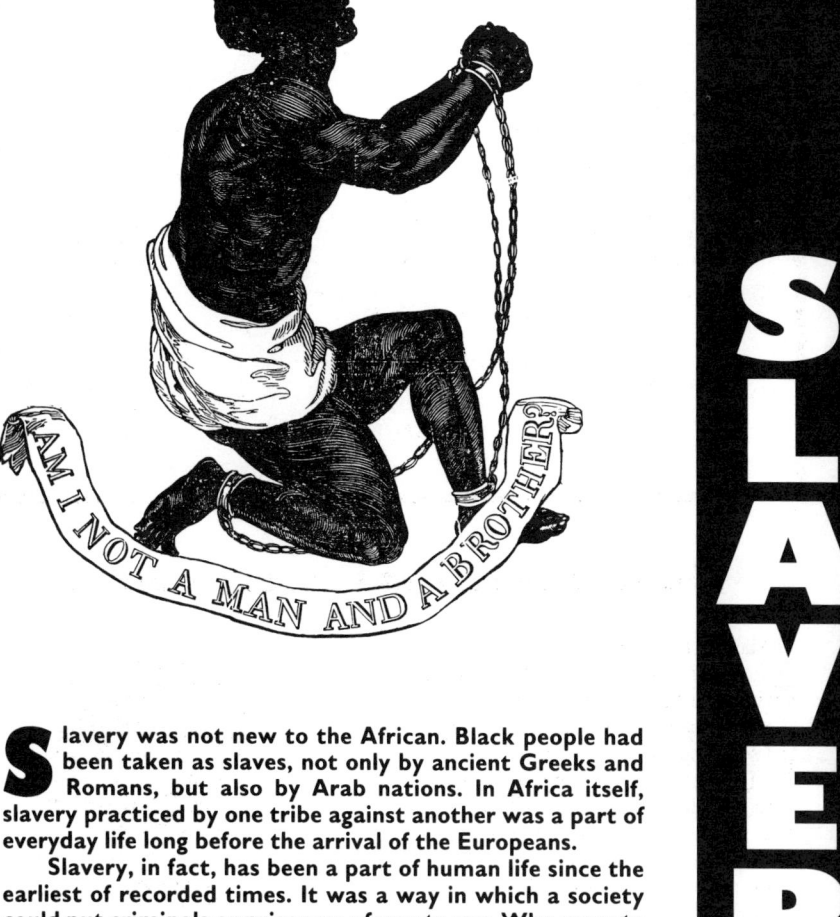

I AM I NOT A MAN AND A BROTHER?

SLAVERY

Slavery was not new to the African. Black people had been taken as slaves, not only by ancient Greeks and Romans, but also by Arab nations. In Africa itself, slavery practiced by one tribe against another was a part of everyday life long before the arrival of the Europeans.

Slavery, in fact, has been a part of human life since the earliest of recorded times. It was a way in which a society could put criminals or prisoners of war to use. Why execute the captured enemy when they could become a source of income?

What was new to the African was the brutality and inhumanity of slaving as institutionalized by the European. Slavery in traditional Africa was humane by comparison:

- *Slaves could become members of a family, even gain the same social status.*
- *Children born from a free man and a woman slave could become members of their father's clan and live free.*
- *Slave owners and slaves often worked side by side in the fields.*

Three Routes Of The Slave Trade

(1) By boat from East Africa

Slaves are purchased by Arab traders from black Africans on the East Coast, shipped across the Indian Ocean and sold in Arabia, Persia, and India.

(2) By land across the desert

Blacks are led by Arab caravans across the desert sands to be sold in the Mediterranean world.

(3) By boat from West Africa

Slaves are bought by Europeans or American traders, then shipped across the Atlantic Ocean to the West Indies, the United States and Brazil.

GREAT BRITAIN
EUROPE
PORTUGAL SPAIN
ARABIA
③ ② ②
③ ①
atlantic ocean
indian ocean

The Arab Desert and Coastal Routes

Islam forbade making slaves out of fellow Muslims but it did not forbid using non-Muslims as slaves. History books often overlook the fact that Arabs bought and sold human cargo from Africa since the 12th century. Slaving stations on Zanzibar island were filled with captive Africans *a hundred years* before Portugal and Europe even entered the seas! Thousands died being transported across the burning desert sands. In all, several *million* African men, women and children were bought and sold by Arab Muslims over the coastal route, and untold millions more sold over the gruelling Sahara desert route.

Tippu Tib, a trader born on Zanzibar Island, drives deep into the heart of the Congo. With his guns, he captures slaves for Sayyid Said, Sultan of the Persian Gulf.

The European and American Sea Routes

THE PORTUGUESE —
First To Exploit The Slave Trade

A tiny nation dependent on fishing and overseas trade, the Portuguese become expert shipbuilders. Soon their ships are venturing down the unexplored West Coast of Africa.

Their *Prince Henry "the navigator,"* has two goals: (1) to find the legendary Prester John, (leader of a lost Christian kingdom in Africa) and unite with him in a mighty crusade against Islam, and (2) to discover a route by sea to the wealth of India and Asia. At first, Portuguese sailors are in awe of the rich kingdoms in West Africa. Then, their lust for power turns the friendships they make into a new relationship — one of master and slave.

THE CONGO
Welcomes The Colonialists

The Bantu people of Congo receive the first Portuguese with open arms. In fact, they convert to Catholicism, and their leader, *King Affonso,* wants to make his kingdom into a Christian kingdom. He appeals to Portugal to stop the slave trade and help him "Westernize." But the Portuguese are too greedy. They are getting too wealthy by exploiting the slave trade.

- **By 1492, some Portuguese provinces have more black slaves living in them than white people.**

- **By 1530, five thousand slaves are being forcibly removed from the Congo yearly, draining the advanced region of all of it's youth.**

THE AMERICANS —
Looking For Cheap Labor

When the Americas are discovered, the "motherlands" of Portugal, Spain, and England can't find enough cheap labor to work the plantations in their new overseas colonies. One source of labor is servants who are in debt. Another source is trading passage to America for several years' work in the New World. Soon, this is not enough; and the colonists turn their eyes to Africa.

The Largest Forced Migration In The History Of The World

In 1518, a Spanish ship carries the first boatload of slaves directly from West Africa to the American West Indies. In 1619, the first black slaves, twenty of them, are carried to the mainland of the United States (landing in Jamestown, Virginia).

What begins as a minor trade in a few slaves, by 1650 becomes big business. More than gold or ivory, *human beings* now become the main cargo being taken out of Africa. Ultimately, 15 *million* African men, women and children are brought to America to slave on white owned plantations of sugar, cotton and tobacco, and to dig out riches of silver and copper from the white-owned mines.

Guns, Slaves And Rum — The Unholy Triangle

(1) Colonialists set sail from New England to Africa with guns and rum they trade for slaves.

(2) They then set sail back to the islands of the West Indies and trade their human cargo for sugar and molasses.

(3) These they carry back home to New England and make into rum.

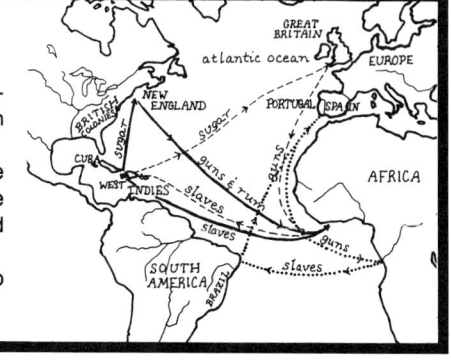

The Cost Of Slavery —
Three Centuries Of Human Devastation

- Between the 1500's and 1800's, Africa loses 15-30 million people to slavery in the Americas, and millions more to the Arab slave trade.
- Countless others die in tribal warfare.
- Still others die on the long trek to the coast, or in slaving stations on islands like Goree.
- Still others die from diseases brought by the Europeans.
- And still others die in the slave ships.
- In all, roughly 60 *million* African women, men and children will lose their lives as a result of the slave trade.

How many people were captured and sold as slaves can never exactly be known. How many died in battle, or died along the long treks to the coast, or in the diseased slaves ships can also never be known.

But the human effects of slavery have *always* been known. They can still be seen today in the crushing poverty and broken families suffered by blacks in America and in the ravaged economies and decimated kingdoms left to blacks in Africa.

The After Shocks Of Slavery

- Wars are encouraged between tribes. Mutual trust among neighbors is destroyed.
- Thriving civilizations are drained of their youth and devastated by foreign diseases. Africa's major resource, human labor, is stolen.
- The production of local goods is disrupted. Crafts people cannot compete with Europe's goods. Market towns completely vanish.
- The great art and sculpture vanish and become forgotten. Great centers of learning crumble. Whole kingdoms are destroyed.
- The economy is violently altered. Farmers are forced to give up farming their own local crops to work for whites farming one or two "cash crops" for foreign use — thereby making Africa dependent on foreign control for a century to come.
- Families are uprooted; centuries old traditions are assaulted.
- Forced nationhood creates tribal rivalries that will lead to a century of civil wars.
- Millions of African-Americans are stripped of their humanity and degraded. Their identities and heritage are erased forever — laying the foundation for a bloody civil war in the United States and a century of racist oppression.

Why go inland when the blacks themselves brought slaves to the coast? Many times it was *black* Africans who captured blacks in tribal warfare and delivered them as slaves to the European traders.

Why? Why would some African kings cooperate with this brutal business?

In West Africa, some kings fight to save themselves by cooperating and extending their power over their neighbors (who are regarded as enemies anyway). They want European goods — especially guns.

Blacks Enslave Blacks

With enough guns, an African king can wage war on his neighboring tribe, massacre and capture it's people, sell them off as slaves and gain more power.

Some kings even falsely accuse members of their own tribe of crimes so they can be taken prisoner and sold. Often, the king believes these slaves will be treated humanely and is ignorant of the brutality they will suffer.

Here's How It Worked

A slave ship anchors at harbor and sends word inland to the African slavers who then raid a village and capture hundreds of prisoners of war...

Those who are too weak may have their heads split open

at the coast, those still alive are kept in slave stations until they are sold off at the slave markets...

Those sold are loaded aboard ships then re-sold in slave markets overseas.

Chained and Brutalized —

"As the present writer can testify from what he has himself seen, a slave gang on it's march to the coast was loaded with heavy collars with chains and irons that cut into the flesh and caused virulent ulcers. Arab, Negro and white slavers alike developed a deliberate love of cruelty . . .

"The slaves are half starved, over driven, and recklessly exposed to death from sunstroke. If they threw themselves down for a brief rest or collapsed from extreme exhaustion, they are shot, or speared, or had their throats cut with fiendish brutality . . .

The March To The Sea

"Children whom their mothers could not carry had their
brains dashed out. Many slaves I
saw committed suicide because
they could not bear to be separated from their homes and children . . ."

Sir Harry H. Johnston
"A History of Colonization of Africa
by Alien Racists," pp. 8, 182

The Slave Market

"On the eighth day of August, 1444, very early in the morning . . . captives are gathered together in a field . . . some of a rosy whiteness, fair and well made; others less white, others again as black as moles . . . And what heart was so hard as not to be moved to pity by the sight of this multitude?

Some stood groaning with eyes uplifted toward heaven, as if to implore help from the Father, and the love of all mankind . . . others flung themselves down upon the ground, and gave in to their sorrow in a dirge . . .

. . . Men came to parcel them out into five distinct lots . . . they tore the son from his father, the wife from her husband, the brother from his brethren. No tie of blood or comrade-ship was respected . . .

Parents and children, finding themselves in different groups would run back to each other. Mothers clutched up their children and ran away with them, caring not about the blows they received so long as their little ones should not be torn from them . . ."

— Gomez Eannes de Azurara, "Chronicle of Guinea," Henry "The Navigator"

Trading in Flesh

Heavy forked tree trunks are used to keep an African slave in place.

"... When we treat to buy them, they are all brought out together ... and thoroughly examined ... Those which are approved as goods are set on one side; and the lame or faulty are thrown out ... The remainder are numbered ... a burning Iron with the arms of the companies lies in the fire ... Ours are marked on the breast ... but we take all possible care that they are not burned too hard, especially the Women who are more tender than the Men."

William Bosman,
agent for the Dutch West Indian Company 1705

TO BE SOLD on board the Ship *Bance-Island*, on tuesday the 6th of *May* next, at *Asbley-Ferry*; a choice cargo of about 250 fine healthy NEGROES, just arrived from the Windward & Rice Coast. —The utmost care has already been taken, and shall be continued, to keep them free from the least danger of being infected with the SMALL-POX, no boat having been on board, and all other communication with people from *Charles-Town* prevented.

Austin, Laurens, & Appleby.

N. B. Full one Half of the above Negroes have had the SMALL-POX in their own Country.

Black Cargo —

"A common type of slaving vessel . . . was called a snow . . . On leaving the coast of Africa she carried, in addition to her crew of forty-five, 609 slaves. (351 men, 127 women, 90 boys, 41 girls). Overcrowding was almost essential . . . Captain Tallers had them three months aboard. They are almost suffocated and starved . . . fed with little else than musty corn.

"Between decks where . . . a tall man could not stand upright, the human cargo was stowed, . . . the men are generally kept throughout the voyage chained in pairs, wrist to wrist, ankle to ankle. Those who are left unchained are packed in couples, side by side, like sardines, or spoon-fashion. The head of one against the feet of another. They are about as comfortable . . . as a man might be in his coffin.

The Slave Ship

"Wet weather occasioned the port-holes to be shut . . . fevers among the Negroes resulted . . . I frequently went down among them . . . and often found dead and living chained together . . . The deck floor was so covered with their blood and mucus . . . that it resembled the slaughter house."

Edmund B. D'Auvergne,
reporting first hand accounts in
"Human Livestock, The Maintenance and
Abolition of Slavery"

Mutiny Aboard A Slave Ship —

JOSEPH CINQUE
an African Prince
(early 1800's)

Kidnapped and sold into slavery, Joseph Cinque, an African prince, leads a daring mutiny.

As a slave in Havana, Cuba, Joseph is loaded into a boat, the Amistad, with fifty-two other African slaves for transport to a plantation in the West Indies. Two days out in the raging ocean, he and his friends seize some cane knives and kill the captain. They order the boat to head back to Africa; but the navigator, unknown to them, steers them east. After seven weeks they are forced to land in America.

The American courts rule the mutineers were originally taken to Cuba illegally. Joseph Cinque is free to return home to Africa.

190

The Resistance

Throughout all of Africa, people fight fiercely to rid themselves of the Europeans.

In Angola, the *ngola* (ruler) rallies his warriors and forces 60,000 Congolese troops led by 50 European officers to a standstill that halts the explorer Bartholomew Dias from advancing up the river. In the Congo, King Affonso (Nzinga Mvenba) protests the slave trade time and time again to Portugal's deaf ears.

July 1839 . . . Joseph Cinque, sold into slavery, kills the captain of the Amistad.

P O R T R A I T

QUEEN NZINGA
a woman of fierce courage
(about 1581-1663)

As queen of Ndongo, she will not allow herself to be called "queen." Leading her warriors into battle, she wears a man's clothes and demands to be called "king."

Refusing to submit to the Portuguese, she brilliantly plays off the Europeans against each other. She persuades the Dutch to give her a militia of their soldiers to fight off the Portuguese. In the back of her mind, she knows she can then turn around and defeat the Dutch. Her dream — her *own* empire in the west.

A brilliant speaker, she gathers huge audiences to hear her. She appeals to their pride as Africans and persuades slaves who are forced to be soldiers for the enemy to desert and join her.

For thirty-five years she fights fearlessly to force the Portuguese out of Angola. But when her sister is captured and drowned in a river, even she begins to wonder if this Catholic god might be, in fact, stronger than her own. Now, more than 75 years old and overwhelmed by superior weaponry, she is forced to sign a treaty with the Portuguese. On December 17, 1663, Queen Nzinga dies.

With the death of this powerful African woman, the Christian cross is planted in West African soil . . . and the Portuguese slave trade is free to begin its savagery.

Whites Fight to End Slavery

"If I ever get the chance to hit that thing [slavery], I will hit it hard."

- Abraham Lincoln
at New Orleans, 1828

In Europe, white people (disgusted by the brutality of the slave trade) organize themselves into a movement to abolish slavery and call themselves *abolitionists.*

As early as 1607, the government of France declares that any slave shall be set free as soon as he or she sets foot on French soil and becomes baptized a Christian. In England, Christians begin a crusade to pressure the government to outlaw slavery both at home and in the entire empire.

In the United States, white men and women risk their lives to create a daring *"underground railroad."* Slaves who escape from their masters' plantations down south are hidden in *"safe homes,"* then transported at night from home to home over hundreds of miles to be set free in the north.

BACK TO AFRICA

In England, 15,000 of the "black poor" are set free. They unite with free blacks from Canada and a black tribe from Jamaica, the *Maroons.* Together, they go back to Africa and begin a new country, *Sierra Leone,* they call their capital *Freetown.*

In the United States, a movement led by *Marcus Garvey* grows into reality with the founding in 1822 of a new nation, *Liberia,* for the sole purpose of creating a homeland for freed slaves who wish to go "back to Africa."

White members of the "underground railroad" risk their lives to hide runaway slaves on their road to freedom

THE ROAD TO LIBERTY; A STATION ON THE UNDERGROUND RAILROAD.

INJURED HUMANITY;

A *Representation of what the unhappy Children of Africa endure from those who call themselves* CHRISTIANS.

The husband and wife, after being sold to different purchasers, violently separated; probably never to see each other more.

When slaves are purchased by the planters, they are generally marked on the breast with a red hot iron.

A representation of a slave at work cruelly accoutred, with a Head-frame and Mouth-piece to prevent his eating—with Boots and Spurs round his legs, and half a hundred weight chained to his body to prevent his absconding.

The manner of fixing the slaves on a ladder to be flogged, which is also occasionally laid flat on the ground for severer punishment.

The respectable and increasing numbers of those, who, from motives of humanity, have concurred in rejecting the produce of West-India slavery, cannot but afford a subject of the sincerest joy to every friend of mankind. Even those who, from motives of interest, still favour or engage in the trade, have been obliged to be silent upon the injustice of first procuring the Negroes, and have not had the hardiness to excuse or palliate the horrors of the *middle passage:* but still they assert, that the treatment the slaves meet with in the West-Indies amply counterbalances their previous sufferings; nay, they have not scrupled to extol a state of servitude as a happy asylum from African despotism; and calmly maintain, that the condition of the labouring poor in England is much harder than that of the Negroes in the West-India islands. Upon this ground, the opposers of slavery are willing to meet its advocates, and the design of the following extracts is to enable the public to form an impartial and decisive judgment on the subject.

WHEN a ship arrives at the port in the West-Indies, the slaves are exposed to sale, (except those who are very ill, they being left in the yard to perish by disease or hunger.) The healthy are disposed of by public auction, the sickly by scramble. The sale by scramble is thus described; the ship being darkened by sails, the purchasers are admitted, who, rushing forward with the ferocity of brutes, seize as many slaves as they have occasion for. In none of the sales, is any care taken to prevent the separation of relatives or friends; but husbands and wives, parents and children, are parted with as little concern as sheep and lambs by the butcher. Abstract of the evidence, as laid before a committee of the British parliament, page 46 and 47.

With respect to the *general* treatment of the slaves, Mr. Woolrich says, that he never knew the *best* master in the West-Indies use his slaves so well, as the *worst* master his servants in England. Abstract of the evidence, see page 53.

To come to a more *particular* description of their treatment, it will be proper to divide them into different classes: the first consisting of those bought for the use of the *plantations:* the second of the *in* and *out-door* slaves.

The field slaves are called out by daylight to their work: if they are not out in time, they are flogged. When put to their work, they perform it in rows, and, without exception, under the whip of drivers, a certain number of whom are allotted to each gang. Such is the *made* of their labour: as to the time of it, they begin at daylight, and continue with two intermissions (one for half an hour in the morning, the other for two hours at noon) till sunset. Besides this, they are expected to range about and pick grass for the cattle, either during their two hours *rest* at noon, or after the fatigues of the day.

Sir G. Young adds, that women were, in general, considered to miscarry, from the cruel treatment they met with; and Captain Hall says, that he has seen a woman seated to give suck to her child, roused from that situation by a severe blow from the cart-whip. Abstract of the evidence, see page 53, 54, 55.

The above account of their labour is confined to that season of the year which is termed *out of crop*.

In the crop season, the labour is of much longer duration. Mr. Dalrymple says, they are obliged to work as long as they can, that is, as long as they can keep awake or stand. Sometimes, through excess of fatigue, they fall asleep, when it has happened to those who feed the mills, that their arms have been caught therein and torn off. Mr. Cook, on the same subject, states, that they work, in general, eighteen hours out of the twenty-four: he knew a girl lose her hand by the mill while feeding it, being overcome with sleep, she dropped against the rollers. Abstract of the evidence, page 35, 56.

To this account of their labour, it should be added, that it appears, that on some estates, the slaves have Sunday and Saturday afternoon to themselves; on others, Sunday only, and on others, only Sunday in part. It appears again, that *in crop,* on no estate have they more than Sunday for the cultivation of their own lands. Abstract of the evidence, page 56.

The point next to be considered is the *food* of the slaves, which appears to be subject to no rule; on some estates, they are allowed land; on others, provisions; and some are allowed provisions and land jointly. The best allowance is at Barbadoes, of which the following is the account. The slaves, in general, says Gen. Tottenham, appeared to be ill fed: each slave had one pint of grain for 24 hours, and sometimes, half a rotten herring. When the herrings were *unfit for the whites,* they were bought up *for the slaves.* Nine pints of corn, and one pound of salt-fish a week, are, in general, the utmost allowance. As a proof that some have not food enough, Mr. Cook says, that he has known both Africans and Creoles eat the putrid carcasses of animals *through want.* Abstract of the evidence, page 57 and 58.

As to the accusation of their being *thieves,* all the evidences maintain, that it was on account of their being *half starved.* Abstract of the evidence, p. 58.

Concerning the *property* of the field-slaves, all the evidences agree in asserting, that they never heard of a field-slave amassing such a sum as enabled him to

---

The manner of yoking the slaves by the Mandingoes, or African slave merchants, who usually march annually in eight or ten parties, from the river Gambia to Bambarra; each party having from one hundred to one hundred and fifty slaves.

The Log-Yokes are made of the roots of trees, so heavy as to make it difficult for the persons who wear them to walk, much more to escape or run away.

A front and profile view of an African's head, with the mouth-piece and necklace, the hooks round which are placed to prevent an escape when pursued in the woods, and to hinder them from laying down the head to procure rest.—At A is a flat iron which goes into the mouth, and so effectually keeps down the tongue, that nothing can be swallowed, not even the saliva, a passage for which is made through holes in the mouth-plate.

An enlarged view of the mouth-piece, which, when long worn, becomes so heated, as frequently to bring off the skin along with it.

A view of the leg-bolts or shackles, as put upon the legs of the slaves on shipboard, in the middle passage.

An enlarged view of the boots and spurs, as used at some plantations in Antigua.

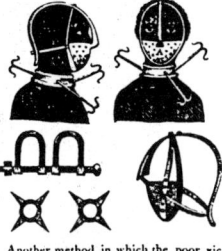

Another method in which the poor victims are placed to be flogged.

Black and White Together . . .
the next generation

Even after the slave trade ends, legal slavery persists for many years in the United States (and longer still in Brazil). White supremacist groups like the Ku Klux Klan fight to preserve the "Southern Way of Life" by lynching, dismembering, or burning thousands of blacks. Eventually America is ripped apart and a civil war is fought to end slavery and free black people once and for all.

But the hopes of black people for equality in America are soon dashed and the legacy of segregation is to continue on into still another century.

Impoverished and locked out of mainstream America, black people unite in a largely nonviolent civil rights protest led by a Christian preacher, Rev. Martin Luther King; and, in 1964, a white southern president, Lyndon Baines Johnson, joins him to pass a landmark Voting Rights Act.

Again the hopes of black Americans are betrayed by the American government. The promises of equality and the war on poverty are never met, and the effects of slavery on African-Americans is still felt today in a legacy of unequal opportunity, broken families, poor educational facilities, restricted housing, a lack of self respect, and racial tension.

above: Singer-activist Joan Baez marches hand-in-hand with writer James Baldwin and civil rights activist James Farmer in Alabama.

As a new century begins, young white Americans are beginning to discover the richness of African-American friendships and culture; and blacks are trying to recover from 300 years of brutality, humiliation and disenfranchisement. Soul sisters and soul brothers from two continents are rediscovering their common bonds, broken for so long by being forced to live in two worlds an ocean apart.

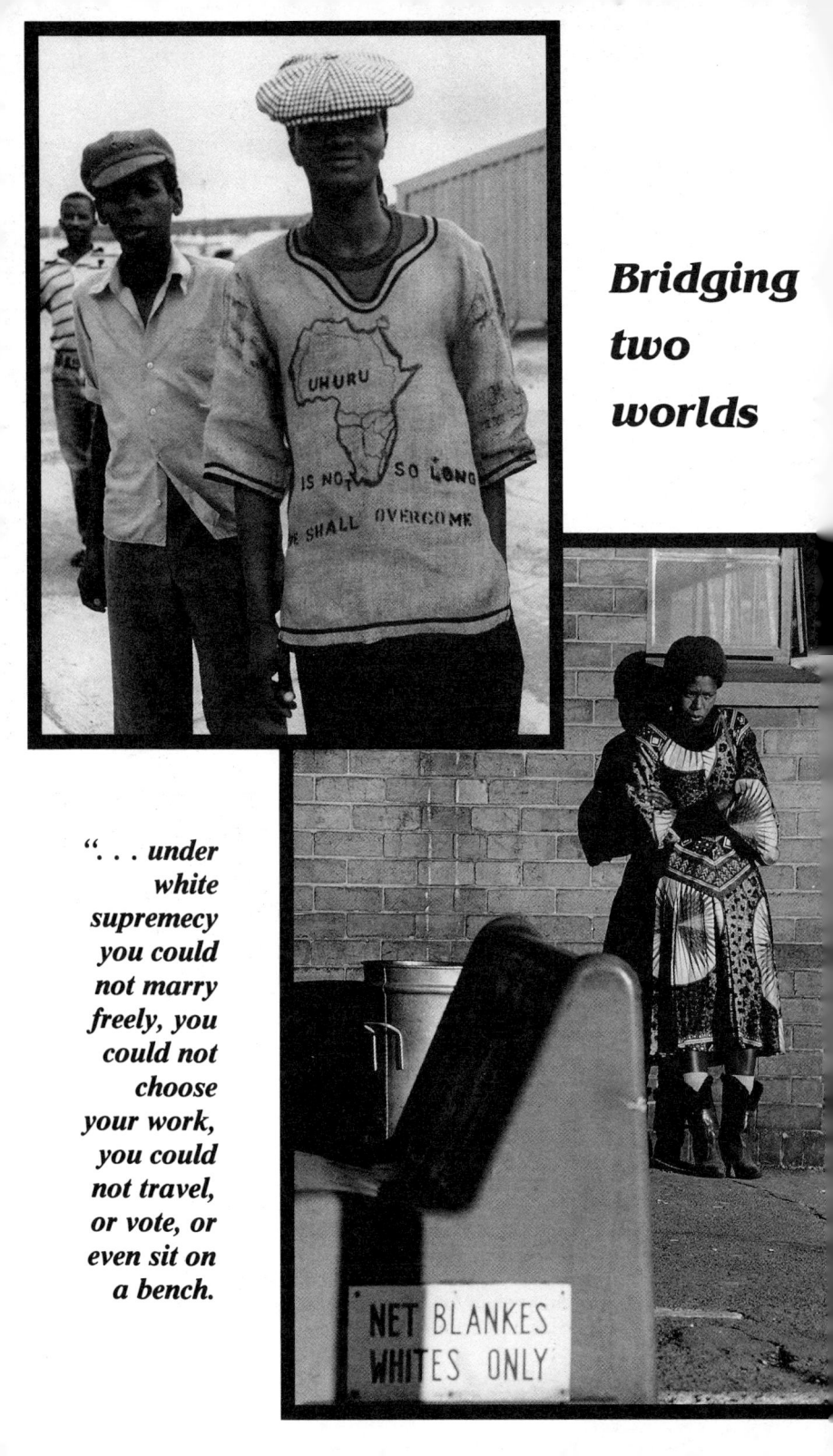

Bridging two worlds

UHURU IS NOT SO LONG WE SHALL OVERCOME

"... under white supremecy you could not marry freely, you could not choose your work, you could not travel, or vote, or even sit on a bench.

NET BLANKES
WHITES ONLY